HOME TO WHISKEY CREEK

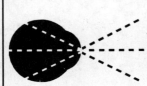

HOME TO WHISKEY CREEK

BRENDA NOVAK

THORNDIKE PRESS
A part of Gale, Cengage Learning

GALE
CENGAGE Learning®

Detroit • New York • San Francisco • New Haven, Conn • Waterville, Maine • London

Copyright © 2013 by Brenda Novak, Inc.
Whiskey Creek Series #4.
Thorndike Press, a part of Gale, Cengage Learning.

Thorndike Press® Large Print Romance.
The text of this Large Print edition is unabridged.
Other aspects of the book may vary from the original edition.
Set in 16 pt. Plantin.

LIBRARY OF CONGRESS CATALOGING-IN-PUBLICATION DATA

Novak, Brenda.
    Home to Whiskey Creek / By Brenda Novak. — Large Print edition.
        pages cm. — (Whiskey Creek Series ; #4.) (Thorndike Press Large Print Romance.)
    ISBN 978-1-4104-6309-8 (hardcover) — ISBN 1-4104-6309-5 (hardcover)
    1. Homecoming—Fiction. 2. Life change events—Fiction. 3. Family secrets—Fiction. 4. Large type books. I. Title.
PS3614.O926H66 2013
813'.6—dc23   2013030039

Published in 2013 by arrangement with Harlequin Books S.A.

Printed in the United States of America
1 2 3 4 5 6 7 17 16 15 14 13

To Anna . . .

I really enjoy working with you.
Thank you for being so dependable,
responsible and supportive. You've
helped make my annual online auction
for diabetes research a fabulous event.
I consider you a good friend and
a great blessing.

Dear Reader,

The concept for this story has been percolating in the back of my mind for some time. I was interested in the heroine's journey — how she might overcome the terrible incident she endured at a high-school graduation party — but I was just as interested in exploring how the boys who impacted her life might feel as adults. Where might they be? What might they be doing? And how would they cope with their past mistakes, especially if the past came boomeranging back? I strongly believe that there are very few people who are all good or all bad, and I think that can be said for the characters in this story, which is what made them so fascinating to work with.

This is the fourth book in the Whiskey Creek series (following *When Lightning Strikes, When Snow Falls,* which was nominated for the *RT Book Reviews* 2012 Book of the Year Award, and *When Summer Comes*). In addition to these full-length books, you might want to look for the prequel novella called *When We Touch,* where you will meet Brandon and Olivia (who also appear in this story). Next up, we have the fifth book, *Take Me Home for Christmas,* which will be available in November.

For more information on these books and my other novels, please visit brendanovak .com, where you can enter monthly drawings, order cookies from Just Like Mom's, get autographed cover cards or drop me an email. I love hearing from my readers. I'd also like to invite you to get involved in my annual online auction for diabetes research (my youngest son has this disease, and so do million of others — someday I fear it will affect everyone in one way or another). The auction runs May 1–May 31 at my website, so please register right away at brendanovak.auctionanything.com so you'll get the updates. So far we've raised nearly $2 million and hope to raise much more!

Here's to making a difference!

Brenda Novak

1

The past is never dead. It's not even past.
— William Faulkner

No way would he be able to reach her, not with his bare hands. And Noah Rackham didn't have anything else — just his mountain bike, which lay on its side a few feet away. In the pouch beneath the seat he kept a spare tube, the small plastic tool that made it easier to change a tire and some oil for his chain but no rope, no flashlight. He wouldn't have packed that stuff even if he'd had room. For one, he'd come out for a quick, hit-it-hard ride before sunset and wasn't planning to be gone longer than a couple of hours. For another, no one messed around with the old mine anymore. Not since his twin brother had been killed in a cave-in a decade and a half ago, just after high school graduation.

"Hello?" Kneeling at the mouth of the

shaft where someone had torn away the boards intended to seal off this ancillary opening, he called into the void below.

His voice bounced back at him, and he could hear the steady drip of water, but that was all. Why wasn't the woman responding? A few seconds earlier, she'd cried out for help. That was the reason he'd stopped and come to investigate.

"Hey, you still there? You with me?"

"Yes. I'm here!"

Thank God she'd answered. "Tell me your name."

"It . . . it's Adelaide. But my friends call me Addy. Why?"

"I want to know who I'm talking to. Can you tell me what happened?"

"Just get me out. Please! And hurry!"

"I will. Relax, okay, Addy? I'll think of something."

Cursing under his breath, he rocked back on his haunches. Ahead of him, the dirt road that temporarily converged with the single track he'd been riding disappeared around a sharp bend. To his left was the mountain, and to his right, the river, rushing a hundred feet below. He saw more of the same scenery behind him. Trees. Thick undergrowth, including an abundance of poison oak. Moist earth. Rocks. Fifty-year-

10

old tailings from the mine. And the darkening sky. There were no other people, which wasn't unusual. Plenty of bikers and hikers used this trail, but mostly in the warmer months, and certainly not after dusk. The Sierra Nevada foothills, and the gold rush-era town where he'd grown up, were often wet and chilly by mid-October.

Should he backtrack to the main entrance of the mine? Try to get in the way they used to?

He'd already passed that spot. Someone had fixed the rusty chain-link fence to keep kids from slipping through. Noah couldn't get beyond it, not without wire cutters or at least the claw part of a hammer. That entrance and this shaft might not even connect. It was likely they didn't, or whoever was stranded down there would've made her way over — provided she was capable of moving.

Scooping up his bike, he hopped on and went to check. Sure enough, the fence, with its danger keep out sign, was riveted to the rocky outcropping surrounding the entrance. He couldn't get through; he didn't have the proper tools, and there was nothing close by he could substitute. The only foreign object in the whole area was a bouquet of flowers that lay wilting in the mud. Noah guessed Shania Carpenter, Cody's old girlfriend, had placed them there. She'd probably come up here to commemorate the anniversary of when she and Cody had started dating, or become an item, or first made love or . . . whatever. She'd married, divorced and had a kid, in that order, but she'd never gotten over Cody's death.

Neither had Noah. It felt as if a part of him had died that night.

And now someone else's life could end the same way.

Certain that this entrance wasn't the answer to his problem, he returned to the shaft. He never would've noticed this other opening if not for that cry for help. The boards that'd been pried loose were so covered by moss they blended in with the rest of the scenery.

"I'm not going to be able to reach you," he called down. "Is there some other way out? A tunnel that might not be sealed off?"

Considering what had happened to his brother, was it safe for her to move?

"No. I — I've tried everything!"

The hysteria in those words concerned him. "Okay. Listen, I know you're . . . frightened, but try to stay calm. How badly are you hurt?"

"I'm not sure." It sounded as though she couldn't suck in enough air to speak normally, but he couldn't tell if that came from fright, exhaustion or injury. "Help me, please."

He *wanted* to help; he just didn't know how. The shaft was too deep to reach her without rope. But if he hurried off to notify rescue personnel, he wasn't sure she'd be alive when he got back. Trying to bring others would take too much time. There was no place for a helicopter to land. And it wouldn't be easy to get an ambulance in here. A Jeep or truck could make it, but even that would be a challenge in the dark. Flooding several years ago had washed away parts of the old road.

But if he stayed, he'd soon lose all daylight and he had no flashlight. Even if he managed to get the woman out, how would he transport her in the pitch-black?

"Can you walk?" he called.

There was a slight delay. "How far?"

"I'm wondering if you're mobile, so I can assess the situation."

"I — I'm mobile."

That made a difference. It meant she wasn't so badly off that he couldn't sit her on his bike and run alongside. If he could get to her.

He was pretty sure he had a flashlight and a length of rope in his truck. He might even have food or something else that would come in handy. A sweatshirt would keep her warm, at least. *He* could use it if she didn't need it. It'd been a nice day, hence his lightweight bike shorts and T-shirt, but it was growing colder by the minute.

"Sit tight," he called down. "I have to go to my truck but I'll be back. I promise."

"Don't leave me!"

Panic fueled those words. "I'll be back," he repeated.

Tension tied his stomach into knots as he ignored her protests and clipped his feet into the pedals of his bike. The uneven ground and rocks and roots that offered the challenges he so enjoyed suddenly became unwelcome obstacles, jarring him despite the expensive shock absorbers on his bike. He was moving faster than ever before, especially through this stretch, where the riding was so technical, but he had no choice. If he didn't . . .

He couldn't even think about what might happen if he didn't. He'd seen his brother's crushed head. They'd made the decision as a family not to have an open casket.

Small pebbles scattered, churned up by his tires as he charged through patches of

14

gravel. Hoping to shave off a few minutes, he climbed a steep embankment he typically tried only when he wanted maximum difficulty.

He made it up and over the ridge, and down the other side without mishap, but it felt as if it were taking forever to reach the highway.

By the time the trail leveled out, his lungs burned and his quads shook, but he knew that had more to do with fear than physical exertion. He owned Crank It Up, a bike shop in Whiskey Creek, and raced mountain bikes professionally. Thanks to endless hours of training, his body could handle twenty minutes of balls-to-the-wall riding. It was the memories of the day he'd learned his brother was dead and the frightened sound of Addy's voice that made what he was doing so difficult.

In case her life depended on his performance, he forced himself to redline it, but daylight was waning much faster than he expected. What if he couldn't see well enough to return? Considering how narrow the trail was in places, and the sharp dropoff on one side, his tire could hit a rock or a groove in the hard-packed dirt, causing him to veer off and plummet into the freezing-cold river — an accident he wasn't likely to survive. The road, though wider, would take twice as long.

You won't fall. He knew this trail far too well. This was where he felt closest to his brother — and not because Cody had died here. They'd started mountain biking when they were only thirteen, used to explore these mountains all the time. That was how they'd found the mine in the first place. It was Cody who'd turned it into a popular hangout during the final weeks of high school. Kids could bring booze or weed up there without being noticed or interrupted by the police, so a core group from the baseball team had thrown parties that had occasionally gotten out of hand. Toward the end, Noah had stopped going. He hadn't liked watching his brother snort coke, didn't appreciate the way Cody behaved when he was stoned. Noah had also been afraid Cody would get Shania pregnant before they had the chance to leave for college and he didn't want to attend San Diego State without him. They'd done almost everything together since birth.

He'd mentioned the risks to Cody many times, but no amount of warning seemed to faze him. Although Shania hadn't been at the party — her parents had whisked her away to Europe as soon as she had her diploma in hand — his brother had gone a little crazy that night with all the drinking and drugs, and he paid the ultimate price. From what Noah had heard, the party Cody had thrown graduation night had been as wild as they came.

Maybe if his brother had been thinking straight, he would've made it home safely, like everyone else. . . .

After navigating a few final twists and turns, Noah spotted the gravel lot next to the two-lane highway where he'd parked, and raced down the straightaway.

Sweat rolled off him the second he stopped, despite the cold, but he barely noticed as he searched his truck. He found the towrope in his toolbox, a sweatshirt shoved under his seat not far from the flashlight and a stash of energy bars. He already carried all the water he had in a bladderlike contraption on his back. Unfortunately, he'd drunk most of it, but he found a first-aid kit in his jockey box, which was some consolation.

He had what he needed, but in case things didn't go as smoothly as he hoped, he wanted to call for help so there'd be a rescue team waiting.

He'd put his cell phone under his floor mat to keep it out of sight. There'd been a rash of car burglaries several months ago, courtesy of a group of teenagers who smoked pot and hung out at the river all summer — "river rats" they were called.

He fished his phone out to check for service. Coverage was spotty in these mountains. But obtaining a signal didn't turn out to be the problem. His battery was dead.

"Shit!" He wasn't one of those people who kept his phone attached to his ear 24/7. It was more of an afterthought — obviously, since he didn't carry a charger.

He gazed up and down the road, hoping a vehicle would come by, but after a few seconds, he realized he couldn't keep standing there. He had to make a decision. Should he drive to Jackson, which was closer than Whiskey Creek, or go back for the woman as he'd originally intended?

Jackson would take too much time. He'd promised he wouldn't be long and for some reason it was important to him to make good on that.

Draping the rope around his neck, he tied the sweatshirt to his waist and tossed out the extra tube and tire-changing equipment he had in his seat pack without even caring where it fell. He needed room to squeeze in the energy bars and the contents of the first-aid kit. Then he held the flashlight against

18

the handlebars and took off.

He had to get back to the mine before full dark. Otherwise, he'd be forced to take the road or travel even more slowly on the trail, and he feared that whoever was stranded in the shaft couldn't survive the delay.

2

Adelaide Davies stared at the hole above her, the only thing she could see in this dark space. Would the person who'd called to her really come back?

It didn't look hopeful. She had no way of keeping track of the passing minutes, but it seemed as if an hour had gone by since he'd promised to help.

Maybe he was the same person who'd put her down here and he'd just returned to make sure she didn't survive. Maybe he knew she was guilty of something even worse than what *he'd* done, and felt that this would be a fitting end. . . .

No! No one knows the truth. Except me. She had to quell the fear charging through her, or she wouldn't survive this emotionally, even if she survived it physically. It was fifteen years since she'd last been inside the mine, since she'd been anywhere close. As a matter of fact, she'd been here only once before — to attend a high school graduation party when she was a sophomore.

It'd all seemed so exciting, so hopeful when she was invited. But that party had changed her forever. Never again would she be the same shy but happy girl she'd been before. And, unlike so many other victims, she knew exactly who to blame. There'd been five of them, five of the most popular jocks, all upperclassmen.

The memories of that night made her sick. She would've gone to the police, would've seen to it that they were prosecuted as they deserved. But she couldn't, for a lot of reasons.

It was getting too cold. She had to do something or she'd freeze to death in this damp, dark hole. After myriad attempts to climb or dig her way out, she could hardly move. Her wrists burned from the welts she'd caused by straining against the rope that had bound her hands. One whole side of her body was bruised from when she'd landed. But she had to scream, at the very least. She couldn't let the discouragement, the heartbreak, the memories, win.

"Hello? Can someone help me? *Please?* I'm in the mine!"

There was no answer; calling out seemed futile. The guy who'd stopped before was gone.

Her throat too raw to continue, she got to her feet and made another attempt to climb. She had to save herself before it grew any darker. But she slipped and slid down on her aching bottom. Nothing worked. The walls were irregular and too steep, and the pile of broken and fallen beams, jutting out in all directions, gave her slivers when she tried to use it for support.

What now? she asked herself. The person who'd thrown her down here had only beaten her enough to get her to comply with his demands. He hadn't raped her. But the moment she dropped her guard or became too distraught, the memories of what it'd been like that other time — the night of the party — washed over her, lapping higher and higher, like the incoming tide, until her mind was saturated with the past and she felt no different than the terrified girl she'd been at sixteen.

It was the smell, she decided. The smell conjured up that night as vividly as though she'd just lived it.

Sweet sixteen and never been kissed, one of them had breathed in her ear.

Hugging herself, she began to rock. She was shaking so hard she could hear her teeth chattering but couldn't stop. Was she in shock?

Would she even think of shock if she were?

Either way, she had a black eye. There was little doubt about that. Her face throbbed where she'd been struck, full-on, by a man's fist. She'd broken a couple of fingernails trying to fend him off. She could tell those fingers were bleeding. All the digging to create handholds or footholds or find crevices that might lead out hadn't helped. She guessed the scratches on her arms and legs from the many tumbles she'd taken were bleeding, too, but she couldn't see whether that was really the case. Not anymore. The light filtering through the opening was almost gone.

Would she have to spend another night in this place?

The prospect of that, of the cold and the rats and the fear of flooding, made her rock faster, back and forth, back and forth. It hurt to move, but she had to concentrate on *something* or she'd go crazy.

"You — you are powerful. You are . . . c-capable. You can overcome." This kind of self-talk had fostered the determination that had carried her through the long hours so far, close to seventeen if her guess was accurate. It was at least 3:00 a.m. when she'd been dragged from her bed, wasn't it?

She wasn't sure exactly. She only knew that, after two and a half days of being "home" to take care of Gran, she'd been awakened by a man who whispered that he'd "stab the old lady" if she screamed or tried to escape; and that was all he had to say. She'd do anything to protect her grandmother Milly, even relive the nightmare of fifteen years ago. But he'd simply issued a terse warning telling her he'd kill her if she ever talked about that graduation party and then threw her down the mine shaft.

It was a miracle she hadn't been more badly hurt. The demolition they'd done after Cody's death had felled most of the support beams, sealing off some of the deeper crevices, or she might have fallen much farther.

"Hey, you still down there?"

Her heart lifted with hope. The man she'd heard before was back!

"I'm here!" she called. "C-can you help me? You have t-to help me. I don't want to spend another night in here."

"*Another* night? God, what happened to you?" he said, but she could tell he was busy and not waiting for an answer. He'd probably ask again once the pressure was off. For now, he seemed focused on the task at hand.

Closing her eyes, Adelaide tilted her head back and let the tears she'd refused to shed roll down her cheeks. She'd made it through another traumatic experience. The boys from Whiskey Creek hadn't broken her yet. She'd survived. Again.

"I have a rope. Do you have the strength to hang on to it long enough for me to haul you up?"

If she tried, she'd fall. Not only was she battered and bruised, she'd had barely three hours of sleep before being abducted. Dressed in the shirt and panties she'd worn to bed, she was shivering violently. And she hadn't had anything to eat or drink in over a day.

She wanted to be brave, to say she could do whatever getting out required, but she felt as helpless as a baby. It'd taken everything she had just to stave off the panic and despair. Now that someone had arrived, now that she had support, the adrenaline that'd kept her going left her drained.

"I . . . don't think so," she admitted.

"Don't cry," he said. "I won't leave you again. I'll stay here all night if necessary, okay, Addy?"

She hadn't realized her emotions were that apparent. She wished she could maintain a stiff upper lip, at least until she got home and could fall apart in private. But she had no more reserves of any kind.

Fortunately, the gentleness in his voice and the commitment behind those words made her feel as if he'd wrapped a warm blanket around her shoulders. "I — I appreciate that," she stammered, and meant it.

"I'm going to make a loop. All you have to do is slip it over your head and down under your butt. Can you do that?"

She was still conscious. She had to be capable of doing that much. "I'll try."

It was now completely dark. She couldn't see her hand in front of her face, let alone the end of a rope coming toward her, but he had a flashlight that illuminated the area above her head. "Do you see it?"

"Yes," she responded when it nearly hit her in the face.

"Great. That's the first step. Put it on. I'll wrap this end around a tree so I can keep from falling in with you if I lose my footing. Then I'll start bringing you up."

He hadn't asked how much she weighed, how her size compared to his. He was a guy; he expected to be bigger. But not all guys were. At six feet, she was taller than most women and a good number of men, too. Although she'd always been thin, she wasn't convinced he'd have the strength to raise her.

Should she tell him the job might be more difficult than he expected and risk having him decide to go for help instead?

No. She couldn't wait another second. Maybe he'd drop her on the ascent, but if this was her only hope of getting out *now,* she was taking that chance.

After wiping her tears, she did as he instructed. "Ready."

"That's what I want to hear. See? Everything will be fine. All I need you to do is keep the rope under your bottom. Can you do that?"

She didn't have any choice, not if she wanted out. "Yes."

"Perfect. Here we go."

The rope drew so taut it cut into her thighs, but nothing happened.

Terror ripped through her. The task was too much for him, just as she'd feared! She stifled a whimper, preparing for the moment when he'd admit defeat. But then he began to reel her toward him, inch by painstaking inch.

Dangling in midair, completely dependent on a stranger she couldn't even see, was frightening. But he was trying to help, and that was better than being alone in the mine. Anything was better than being alone.

When at last she reached the opening, she couldn't see a lot more than she could in the shaft, but the fresh air sweeping over her confirmed that she was no longer inside the mine.

I'm free. She choked on a sob. She didn't have the strength to crawl over the lip, but he grabbed her arms and hauled her out before sinking down next to her.

"There . . . you . . . go," he said, as if her problems were over. But, in some ways, the mine still held her captive, and she was afraid that would always be true.

Heedless of the gravel and dirt, she rolled onto her back so she could stare up at the starry sky. "Thank you."

He propped himself up beside her. She could hear his movements but couldn't make out more than a dark figure. "I'm glad I heard you. How badly are you hurt?" he asked.

It was cold, colder than inside the mine, thanks to the wind, but she didn't care. "I'm n-not sure."

"Anything broken?"

Relieved that he was giving her a chance to recover before waving that flashlight in her face, she put her arm over her eyes in case he angled it at her before she was ready.

"I don't think so. I'm just . . . rattled and b-banged up."

"What happened?" He seemed to have caught his breath. "How'd you wind up in the mine?"

You tell anyone about graduation and I'll kill you. I'll stab the old lady, too. Do you understand? No one wants to hear it. It's old news. And in case you've been gone so long you haven't heard, Cody's dad is mayor now. Going to the police won't get you anywhere. Consider this a little . . . FYI.

How much did she dare tell before she was asking for more trouble? She couldn't say she'd *fallen* into the mine and expect to be believed. Once he could see her clearly, he'd notice that she was in her underwear and her eye was swollen almost shut. The marks from the rope would be another giveaway.

But she couldn't be honest, or the man who'd done this might think she was blabbing, exactly as he feared.

"I, uh, s-sleepwalk sometimes." It was an obvious lie, one that would most likely be interpreted as a refusal to answer, but that seemed her only option.

"You . . . *sleepwalk*?" When he raised the flashlight, she tried to cover herself. Her pink Victoria's Secret tee fit tight and short, and her panties were barely a scrap of fabric, but there wasn't much she could do about her nightwear at this point.

Fortunately, he didn't seem to focus on her state of undress. He was too surprised by the condition of her face. She knew it was her injuries that had caught his attention when he turned her chin toward him so he could have a better look. "Sleepwalking, my ass."

"I, uh, hit my face when I fell."

"Right." The sarcasm that dripped from that word screamed *bullshit*. "Why are you lying, Addy? Do you know the person who did this to you? Is that it?"

Not quite the way he thought. . . .

"Was it your husband or boyfriend or . . . lover?"

"No. I'm not m-married." Thank God! She had been once, but for such a brief period it wasn't even worth counting. Saying "I do" to Clyde Kingsdale had been a bad fit from the beginning. Fortunately, she'd realized her mistake almost immediately.

"You have to be protecting someone," he said. "You don't need to tell *me*. But I hope you'll tell the police."

Unable to tolerate the brightness of his flashlight, she jerked her chin away. "There's no reason to include the police. I — It was my own stupid mistake."

He didn't shine the light in her face again. He set it aside so he could help her pull on his sweatshirt. The soft fleece warmed her but not enough to stop the shivering. "Where do you live?"

"Whiskey Creek. At the moment," she added because she hadn't yet come to terms with the fact that, depending on what she convinced Gran to do, she might need to stay longer than the few months she was planning.

"Hey! I'm from Whiskey Creek, too," he said with obvious surprise. "What's your last name?"

"Davies."

"Have we met?"

How could she tell? What she'd seen of him so far had been dark and indistinct. He was tall and muscular; she'd gathered that much from his general shape. He was strong, too, or he couldn't have lifted her out. But that was all she knew. She couldn't even see the color of his hair.

"Maybe," she said. "Who are you?" Chances were good she'd recognize the name. Gran owned Just Like Mom's, one of the more popular restaurants in the area, and she used to help out there.

She'd anticipated *some* degree of familiarity, but the name came as a shock.

"Noah Rackham."

She said nothing, *could* say nothing. It felt as if he'd just punched her in the stomach.

"My father used to own the tractor sales and rental place a few miles out of town," he explained to provide her with a frame of reference.

Fresh adrenaline made it possible for her to scramble to her feet, despite the pain the movement caused her scraped and bruised body. "*Cody's* brother?" She had the urge to rip off the sweatshirt he'd given her.

Noah stood, too. "That's right. You knew him?"

He sounded pleased, excited. She might have laughed, except she was afraid that if she ever got started she'd end up in a padded cell. Of all the people who could've come by and offered her aid, it had to be Cody's fraternal *twin.* There wasn't a greater irony than that.

"You and Cody were friends?" he prompted, trying to interpret her reaction.

She was glad she couldn't see his face. That would be like meeting a ghost, especially here, at the mine. "Not really," she said. "I was behind the t-two of you in sch-school, but . . . I remember him."

She'd never be able to forget him, but it wasn't because they'd been friends. Not only had Cody raped her, he'd talked some of his baseball buddies into joining the fun. And, when he came back after the others were gone, she'd done what she had to in order to get away.

3

Noah didn't know what to make of Addy. Although she claimed they'd gone to the same high school, he didn't remember her. He didn't recognize her from around town, either. Of course, that could be due to the condition of her face. Someone had done quite a number on it.

While he drove to the accompaniment of a classic rock station, she curled up, as much as a tall woman could curl up while wearing a seat belt, against the passenger door. He'd told her three times she could lie in the seat, knew she'd be more comfortable if she would. But she acted as if she didn't want to get too close to him. She went stiff whenever he touched her, which hadn't made it any easier to wheel her out to the road or help her into the truck. The whole process had taken a couple of hours.

"Which hospital?" he asked.

She lifted her head. "Excuse me?"

He pulled his gaze away from the head-lights flowing toward them on the other side of the road. "Which hospital should I take you to? I have a first-aid kit, but that won't be enough."

"I'm not going to the hospital."

He felt his eyebrows notch up. "But . . . you're hurt, and you're still shaking even though it has to be a hundred degrees in here." He'd been slightly chilled when he got in, too, but thanks to the heat blasting through his vents, he was sweltering now. "I really think you should be checked out."

"Great idea. And what will I tell them?"

Her tone indicated it was a rhetorical question, but he answered, anyway. "How about the truth?"

Her head bumped against the door. "No, thanks. I'll be fine."

"You're not doing yourself any favors, you know. If you go back to the bastard who did this, he could do it again. And maybe next time there won't be anyone around to help you." She was lucky he'd heard her. What if he hadn't gone riding today? Or chosen a different location? It was only when he was feeling particularly nostalgic or really miss-ing Cody that he took their favorite trail.

"A repeat performance is precisely what I'm hoping to avoid."

He turned down the volume on "We Will Rock You" by Queen. "Meaning what? You think he'll come after you if you go to the authorities?"

She raised one hand. "Look, I'm grateful for your help but . . . will you let it go?"

Shouldn't he insist she seek medical assistance? "You need to document your injuries. Then, if you change your mind, you can file a report later and have proof to go with it."

"I'll pass, but thanks," she muttered.

"If you decide to press charges, you'll need pictures."

"I won't be pressing charges."

Obviously, she was covering for someone. No woman wound up stranded at the bottom of a mine shaft in her underwear, in the middle of the night without a little help getting there. "I wish you'd see a doctor."

"I'll do it later if I have to."

"Why not now, when you need it?"

"If you drive me to a hospital I'll walk out. Please, take me home. Or if that's too much trouble, drop me at a pay phone so I can call someone else."

"I'm happy to drive you. It's just . . ." Did he have any right to keep pushing? No. He didn't even know this woman. "Never mind. We'll do whatever you want." She wasn't his problem. But telling himself that didn't make it any easier. He hated to see whoever had attacked her get away with it.

"Thank you."

She'd spoken so low he could barely hear her response, but she'd softened, or seemed to have softened, and that tempted him to dive back into the same argument. "So . . . where's home?" he asked, fighting the impulse.

Her eyes had drifted shut. He could see her profile in the light of his instrument panel, thought she might be pretty without the swelling and abrasions. Lord knew she had nice legs. . . .

"Mildred's place on Mulberry Street."

"You're staying with *Milly*?"

The widow who owned Just Like Mom's was one of his favorite people; he'd had no idea this woman might be associated with her. She'd said her name was Davies, but that was a common enough name, and Milly had lived alone for so long he hadn't connected them.

"For the time being."

He gave the truck enough gas to pass the car ahead. "Are you related to Milly, or —"

"I'm her granddaughter."

The vision of a tall, gangly, flat-chested blonde with more hair on her head than any two people popped into his mind. She'd come to all the varsity baseball games. She'd even walked up to him once, after he'd hit a home run, and stammered her congratulations.

Could this woman be that shy girl?

She wasn't flat-chested anymore. That was for sure. But she still had thick hair. Although matted and snarled at the moment, it was one of her best assets because it was such a rich blond color and so full of body.

He steered back into the right lane before glancing over at her again. "How long have you been in town?"

Her eyelids rested against her cheeks. If he had his guess, her head was pounding like a jackhammer, but she didn't complain. "Since Saturday."

"I mean . . . before that."

"I was born in Whiskey Creek."

"Then we'd be more familiar with each other, wouldn't we?"

"Not necessarily."

"I know most people in town pretty well, especially those close to my age."

"You were caught up in your own life."

There was a slight undercurrent as she spoke, but it was subtle enough that he couldn't call her on it. In any case, he wasn't convinced he'd been any more self-absorbed

38

than other teenagers. "In what way?"

"Never mind."

"Are we talking about when I was ten or fifteen or . . . twenty? 'Caught up' at twenty being the least flattering, of course," he added with a chuckle.

A muscle jumped in her cheek. Then she sighed and opened her eyes, as if she was about to give him all the facts about her background at once so he'd leave her alone. "I spent my summers with Milly until eighth grade," she recited in clipped syllables. "Then, when my mother left for Germany to be with her — what was it then, third? — husband I stayed with Gran."

He skipped over the number of marriages, figured it wouldn't be wise to comment on that, not when he was trying to put her at ease. "She married a German? How'd that happen? I'm guessing this was before online dating."

At this, she actually smiled. "It was. They met via a dating service. He's American. After dating here, they married. Then he accepted a contract with the military for some consulting work and that required him to live in Frankfurt. She wanted to tour Europe."

"What about your father?"

"He died in a motorcycle accident before

I was born."

"I'm sorry."

"He was racing when he died. He and my mother weren't married. I don't get the impression he would've been a big part of my life if he'd lived."

He veered away from that subject, too. "So we were teenagers during the period you were referring to?" He grinned at her. "At least that's younger than twenty."

She didn't hurry to reassure him that she hadn't meant anything negative by her earlier statement. And he noticed the slight, couldn't help wondering if it was intentional.

"Yes," she said. "I lived with her until I graduated from high school."

He found it odd that a mother would give up her child to tour Europe, but he didn't want to probe what could be a sensitive subject. He was more interested in figuring out why he didn't remember her, and why she was so . . . prickly. He'd never encountered anyone determined to dislike him right from the get-go. He might've thought he'd slept with her and never called, but he hadn't done anything like that until college. In trying to cope with the pain of losing Cody, he'd done what he could to distract himself, and sex had been a more effective distraction than any of his other options. "Which would mean we went to Eureka High together for what . . . two years?"

"You were a junior when I first noticed you."

She seemed to remember him distinctly, which made him slightly uncomfortable. Was it possible that she'd had a crush on him? Was that what she held against him — some unrequited love thing? Unlike his brother, he hadn't been interested in girls until he'd started at San Diego State. "Was it on the baseball diamond?"

"It was in the halls, but I saw you on the diamond, too. I watched you play every game."

So that *was* her who'd congratulated him so awkwardly. And . . . she'd watched *him* play? Specifically? Maybe he'd guessed correctly about the crush, too. The girl who'd approached him after that home run had turned beet-red the moment he'd looked at her, had seemed to regret being impetuous enough to draw his attention.

"Then you're a baseball fan." He was about to explain that he could now recall having seen her, but she cut him off.

"Not anymore."

Why did it feel as if there was a personal element in that response, as well? As if she

41

was saying she was no longer *his* fan? "What's wrong with baseball?" *Or me, for that matter?*

"It's become a bit of a symbol to me."

"That's cryptic."

She'd gone cold again, remote. "I'm a cryptic person."

"So you won't tell me."

"There's no point."

But he was curious. He'd always loved baseball, still played slow-pitch softball in a co-ed league. For him, sports didn't symbolize anything except a challenge. "Listen, if I said or did something that hurt your feelings back in the day, I'm sorry. I honestly don't remember it."

She attempted another smile, but this one fell short of the more sincere grin she'd flashed him after his online dating comment. "You didn't do anything wrong," she said. "Don't mind me. I'm not at my best."

He could understand why. She had to feel like shit. So he cut her some slack. "No problem."

He drove farther before breaking the silence again. "Where'd you go after high school?"

She stared straight ahead, through the windshield, instead of turning like most people would during a conversation. Her

42

resistance gave him the impression that she didn't like looking at him. He almost checked the mirror to see what the sweat and mud from his ride had done to his face.

"The California Culinary Academy in San Francisco," she said.

"You're a chef?"

Her eyes still wouldn't meet his. "I was. I quit my job a week ago."

"In the Bay Area?"

"No, Davis."

"Why'd you quit? Were you planning to move back to Whiskey Creek? Or are you in town for a visit?"

Sliding lower in her seat, she pulled her legs up under his sweatshirt. "I'm not sure exactly how long I'll stay. I quit because Gran needs my help. She's getting old and can't move around like she used to. She shouldn't be driving, for one thing, yet she visits me once a month."

"You can't come here?"

"I haven't been back since I graduated."

"Because . . ."

"I don't enjoy returning. But I don't want to put her in assisted living. That's never been what I envisioned for her. And some decisions have to be made about the restaurant."

"Darlene Bigelow basically runs it for her,

43

and she seems to do a good job. Won't she continue?"

"I plan to keep Darlene on as long as possible, but I'm hoping Gran will agree to sell the restaurant and come back to Davis with me."

He didn't like the sound of that. "I'd hate to see the restaurant go to anyone else," he said. "Just Like Mom's is an institution in Whiskey Creek."

She cleared her throat. "As much as I wish otherwise, Gran won't live forever."

"But you have restaurant experience. And you need a job." He grinned, hoping to tempt her into taking his suggestion seriously, but she shook her head.

"I'm a good chef. I'll find something elsewhere."

"Then, considering how you feel about coming home, it's nice of you to give up your job."

"Actually, quitting wasn't completely altruistic," she admitted. "My ex-husband was coming on as manager, so both things sort of cropped up at once."

Noah *had* to adjust the heat. He could hardly breathe. "Your ex, huh? That's bad luck."

She shrugged. "Luck didn't have much to do with it. His family owns the restaurant.

That's how we met. But after our divorce, he lost his business — a pest control company — and hasn't been able to get anything else going. They feel obligated to help, of course. And if I'd forced them to choose between us . . . well, you know who'd they'd pick."

"Blood's thicker than water and all that."

"Exactly."

"So . . . you're divorced?"

"The marriage was so short it doesn't really feel that way."

She was quite an enigma. He leaned forward, hoping to get her to look at him, but . . . nothing doing. It was almost as if he *repelled* her. Maybe he stank. After such a difficult ride, that was possible. "Any chance you said 'I do' following a hard night of drinking in Vegas?"

He was teasing and he could tell she understood that. "Sadly, we were both sober, just . . . misguided."

"How?"

"I thought he'd be true. And he thought I'd put up with him seeing other women."

Noah knew better than to ask, but he couldn't resist. "He's not the one who did this to you. . . ."

"No."

"Then I don't understand why you won't

45

let me take you to the —"

"Who'd you end up marrying?"

She'd interrupted because she didn't want to deal with the pressure he was putting on her. This was the first personal question she'd asked; he knew it was merely an attempt to distract him.

"No one."

"What do you do for a living?"

"I'm a professional biker. Mostly I race in Europe — during the spring and summer. This is the off-season, so I get to stay home and run my bike store, which is a nice change. Traveling so much can get old."

"You own Crank It Up?"

"You've been there?"

"No, I saw it when I drove through town on Saturday. You took over the building where the old thrift shop used to be."

"That's right."

"So . . . business is good?"

"Fortunately, mountain biking has become a popular sport. For the most part business *is* good."

"Do you ever see Kevin Colbert?"

There was an odd, husky quality to her voice with this question that hadn't been there before, but he didn't know what to attribute it to. "Occasionally."

"Who'd he marry?"

"Audrey Calhoun. They were an item back in school, remember? Got together junior year."

"I remember. So they're still in Whiskey Creek?"

"Yeah. They live in that new development not too far from the Pullman Mansion — the place where they have weddings and stuff? He's a P.E. teacher at Eureka High these days. He's also the football coach."

"Somehow that doesn't surprise me."

"He was always a decent player."

"Any kids?"

"Three."

"What about Tom Gibby?"

She seemed to know all his old teammates. "He's around. He's a postal clerk. Figures that the nicest guy in school turns out to be the steadiest, most devoted family man. You're never going to believe this, though. He married Selena."

"Parley Mechem's little sister?"

He couldn't tell if she was surprised. He couldn't even tell if she liked the people they were talking about. She gave no indication one way or the other. "Yeah. She was about *twelve* when we were in high school."

She rested her chin on her knees. "Are Cheyenne Christensen and Eve Harmon still friends?"

47

"Definitely."

A faint smile curved her lips. "I'd be shocked if they weren't. They were always close."

"Except for Gail, who moved to Los Angeles, that whole clique still hangs out together."

"You mean *your* clique?" she said dryly.

Minus the baseball players. He wasn't quite as close to the guys who used to be on the team with him, but they had a drink every now and then. "Yeah. I see Eve and Cheyenne and the others at the coffee shop on Fridays. But . . . those people were all in *my* graduating class. Did you hang out with seniors?" He couldn't recall seeing her at any of the parties, dances or other get-togethers. That one moment on the ball field was his only memory of the girl she used to be.

"By the end of the year, I had quite a few senior friends because those were the people in my classes."

"What classes did you have?"

"AP Econ. AP World History. Honors Chem. The usual. I had calculus with Cheyenne and Eve."

He whistled. "That isn't usual. You were in calculus *as a sophomore*? And advanced placement classes? You must've been a brainiac. A shy brainiac," he added, combining the two images he now held of her.

"I was naive," she stated flatly.

They'd reached Jackson, so he pulled into the first fast-food restaurant he could find. She'd downed two energy bars and finished his water, but she needed a full meal. "What would you like?"

Her eyes widened as if his actions surprised her. "Nothing. I thought maybe *you* wanted dinner. I can wait."

"There's no reason to. We're already here, and it's only getting later. Nothing will be open in Whiskey Creek."

Her eyes were riveted to the clock, which read eleven-thirty. "Gran will have food. I really don't want to be seen like this."

"You're in a dark truck. No one will notice you. Let me buy you a bite to eat."

She hesitated.

"Come on. It'll help your headache."

"How do you know I have a headache?"

He waited for her to finally look at him, and made a face that suggested anyone would have a headache.

"Okay," she relented. "I'll have a burger. Thank you."

"Anything else?"

"No, that's enough. I'll mail you a check since I don't have any money with me."

Assuming she must be joking, he laughed. "It'll be all of a couple bucks. And even if I wanted it back, why would you mail it? We live in the same town, remember?"

"True, but our paths won't cross."

She didn't know that. She'd only been back a few days, and one of those had been spent in the mine. Their paths *could* cross. For whatever reason, she didn't want them to. "I think I can afford to buy you a burger."

After ordering two double cheeseburgers, two fries and two shakes, he idled forward to wait for the food. "Have you been in touch with anyone from Whiskey Creek since you left?"

"Besides Gran and Darlene? No."

That didn't sound as though she'd been particularly close to the people she'd mentioned. "Do your friends know you're back?"

"Not yet. I'm not here to socialize. I'm here to help."

So she'd said, but wouldn't most people automatically do both?

He slung his arm over the steering wheel. "I could go to my father for you. He's the mayor these days. Once he retired, he decided, out of the blue, to go into politics. Shocked us all. But the point is, he now has some pull with the police. If I tell him what

50

happened, I know he'd have Chief Stacy look into the situation . . . discreetly. Would that make a difference?"

She shook her head, a resolute no.

"He'll see to it," he pressed. "And no one will be the wiser. Trust me."

"No! Please. I don't want your father to know anything about this."

"Why not?"

"I'd rather go on about my business. Why does it matter to you whether I report what happened?"

"Okay, I get it." And yet he hated feeling so . . . out of control when there was something he *wanted* to control. "It's just . . . beyond me to let this go," he explained. "Whoever did it deserves to be punished."

"That's not up to you."

She had a point there.

The girl working the drive-through pushed open the window to collect his money — and gave him a thousand-watt smile the moment she recognized him. "Hey, Noah!"

He was tempted to roll his eyes at her enthusiasm. She was *maybe* seventeen. "Hi, Cindy."

"What are you up to tonight?" A calculated dimple appeared in her cheek. She didn't live in Whiskey Creek, but he saw her when she came to visit her married sister, who happened to be his closest neighbor.

"Just got back from a ride. How's school going?" He hoped that would remind her of her age.

"Fine. Can I get you anything else?"

As he'd promised, she hadn't realized he had company. The way Adelaide hugged her door kept her completely in shadow. He wasn't sure he'd ever had a woman sit so far away from him in his truck. He could only assume that, after what she'd been through, she was afraid of men. "No, thanks."

Cindy counted out his change and passed him his receipt with the sack. "Well, if you'd like something later, you know where to find me."

Embarrassed by the innuendo in her voice, he pretended not to notice. "Thanks."

He handed the food to Adelaide as he drove off. Had she picked up on the offer he'd just received? He hoped not. He knew it wouldn't reflect well on him.

Why he cared, he couldn't say.

Addy stretched her legs as she sat up, and he cranked the heat again so she'd be comfortable.

"If you won't go to the police, what will you tell Milly?" he asked.

"I haven't figured that out yet."

"I *really* think you should come forward."

"That changes everything."

The sarcasm in her response took him by surprise. "Pardon me?"

She lifted her chin, revealing her unwillingness to bend on this issue. "I *can't,* okay? If I come forward, whoever did this will hurt Gran. He told me so."

"Why would anyone want to hurt either of you?"

She didn't answer.

"Are you not going to respond?"

"It's just a freak thing that happened. If I put it behind me and forget, it won't happen again."

"You hope."

She didn't answer.

"What if Milly already filed a missing-person report?"

Obviously not enchanted by that idea, she caught her bottom lip between her teeth. "Would Chief Stacy allow her to? It's only been one day. Doesn't it take, like . . . three days for the police to consider a missing adult as a criminal case?"

"Depends on the circumstances."

"Right." She slumped over, as if her chances of having the ordeal go unnoticed weren't as good as she'd hoped. "I was taken from my bed."

"How'd that happen?"

"There's a door to the outside in my bedroom, where the porch wraps around the house. I left it open to get some air, and he cut through the screen door."

"Then it's not like you drove off with him. I'm guessing the police are already involved."

She stuck a French fry in her mouth. "So . . . I'll just tell everyone the same thing I told you."

"That you must've been sleepwalking."

She had to roll back the sleeves of his sweatshirt; they were too big to stay pushed up on her long, thin arms. "Why not?"

The marks on her wrists suggested she'd been bound, which upset him more than any of it.

"Because no one will believe you." Especially once they saw what he did.

"That part doesn't matter."

"It only matters that they not learn the truth. Is that it?"

She'd been shoveling the food down pretty fast, but at this she slowed. "Basically."

He stopped at the light where he needed to turn to go to Whiskey Creek. "You're not making sense," he said in frustration. But then something occurred to him that he should've thought of before. "Wait a second. He didn't . . . rape you, did he?"

She'd had her panties on, and they'd been intact. Her shirt hadn't been torn off, either. But those marks on her wrists . . .

"No, he didn't," she said, but she'd spoken too quickly and the tears that welled up called her a liar.

Shit! He was an idiot for not catching on sooner. She'd been beaten but his sweatshirt had covered her wrists until she started eating. And the way she'd responded when he questioned her led him to believe she knew the person who'd hurt her and was even trying to protect him. That screamed domestic violence, not rape — at least, not stranger rape.

If she'd been sexually assaulted, maybe she was refusing to go to the hospital because she didn't want anyone to find out, didn't want to go through the humiliation.

Or she had no confidence it would make any difference.

"Adelaide, please," he said, "let me take you to the hospital. I know it'll be degrading and . . . terrible but . . . I don't think you should make this decision in your current, uh, condition."

A tear crested her lashes and ran down her cheek as she shoved the rest of the food away. "You don't know anything."

A car honked behind them. The light had turned green, and he hadn't noticed.

"I know this is . . . a hard situation," he said as he accelerated. "But . . . they have what's called a rape kit. You need to try and get a sample of his DNA while you can." He grappled for other reasons that might convince her. "You don't want anyone else to be hurt, do you?"

She covered her ears. "Stop it! He won't hurt anyone else. That's not an issue."

Could he believe her? Or was it wishful thinking?

Either way, her expression broke his heart. She'd reached her limit. One more push and she might shatter. "Okay," he said. "I'll back off."

After that they drove in silence. When they reached the house, he thought she'd get out and go in without saying goodbye. Although they couldn't see Milly through the windows, every light seemed to be on. He could sense Adelaide's eagerness to get behind that closed door. But she turned back with her hand on the latch. "So . . . is this our little secret?"

He studied her. "Is *what* our little secret?"

She hesitated, obviously trying to define what she was asking. "Just . . . don't make a big deal out of what happened. That's all. Let me do the talking."

"*I'm* not going to make a big deal of it. But if your grandmother's called the cops, others will know about it. Even if it doesn't reach the major news outlets, it'll be reported in the weekly paper. You won't be able to avoid the *Gold Country Gazette.*"

Her shoulders drooped as she recognized the truth in what he said. "Yeah, I guess you're right." She started taking off his sweatshirt.

He stopped her. "Keep it. I get free T-shirts and sweatshirts all the time, and it's cold out."

She seemed tempted to return it, anyway, but probably realized that would reveal more of her than she wanted him to see. "Thanks for the help."

"No problem," he murmured, but she'd already climbed out and was limping across the lawn.

4

The house was quiet. But the lights in the kitchen and living room would've told anyone who really knew Milly that all was not as it should be. She never stayed up past ten o'clock and, other than on the porch, she never left a light burning when she went to bed.

Adelaide had hoped to slip into her room and put on some clothes before she disturbed Gran. She didn't want Milly to see her looking so battered. But she heard her grandmother call out the second she returned the hide-a-key container to its place under the porch. Gran had probably been lying in bed with her hearing aids in and turned up high, praying for her safe return and listening for the door.

"Addy? That you?"

The worry in her voice upset Adelaide, made her even angrier with the man who'd thrown her down the mine shaft. She'd always live in the shadow of the past, but Gran had nothing to do with graduation night fifteen years ago. Stephen, Derek, Tom or Kevin — whichever one of them had abducted her — had no right to put Milly through the panic of finding her missing.

"Yeah, Gran, it's me. Sorry to wake you." Intent on getting into a pair of sweatpants, she started toward her bedroom, but her grandmother wasn't in bed. Gran intercepted her at the hallway entrance, fully clothed, walker and all.

"*Wake* me?" She definitely had her hearing aids in. Addy could tell without having to look because Milly was speaking at a normal volume. "I've been absolutely frantic. Where've you been?"

She was carrying her eyeglasses, hadn't put them on yet. Adelaide was grateful for that small reprieve, even though she knew it wouldn't last long.

"I didn't mean to give you a scare. I had a little . . ." God, Noah was right. No way could she keep this quiet. Not in Whiskey Creek. Her injuries, not to mention the timeline, refuted every excuse she could devise. "Mishap," she finished weakly.

"What kind of mishap? What happened?" Her grandmother's hands shook worse than Adelaide had ever noticed but, steadying herself with the walker, she managed to slip her glasses on her nose. Then she covered her mouth. "Good Lord!" she breathed through her fingers. "Who did this to you?"

Thanks to shock and righteous anger, Gran's voice rang truer and stronger than it had in months. For a moment, Adelaide felt like the little girl who'd been so well cared for by this woman. Part of her wished she was still young enough to crawl into Gran's lap for the love and solace she used to find there.

But Gran was almost eighty. It was Adelaide's turn to take care of her. And she wanted to do that. Her mother certainly never would help out. She always had an excuse to be off doing whatever she pleased. "I don't know," she said. "Someone cut the screen on the outside door to my room and dragged me from my bed."

Gran's fingers, gnarled with arthritis, gripped Adelaide's arm. "I saw that. Scared me so much I called Chief Stacy right away."

There went Adelaide's hopes for not involving the authorities. But, deep down, she'd known she wouldn't be able to avoid it. "You've called the police?"

"Of course! Chief Stacy's been as worried about you as I have. He started searching the minute he left here, him and the other officers."

"All three of them?" It wasn't a large force; it never had been.

"All three of them," she confirmed, oblivious to Adelaide's sarcasm. "But . . . how'd someone get past the door? Wasn't it locked?"

Adelaide was embarrassed to admit she'd not only unlocked it, she'd left it open. Gran kept the house so hot she couldn't sleep. "I needed some air," she explained.

The skin below Gran's throat wagged as she shook her head. "In this day and age, you can't go to bed with your doors unlocked. Even in Whiskey Creek. I haven't done it in twenty-three years, ever since your Grandpa passed."

The house had no air-conditioning. During the summer, they had to open their windows — essentially the same thing, but Adelaide didn't argue.

Gran's gaze lowered to Adelaide's bare legs. "The man who took you . . . he didn't —"

"No." She understood where her grandmother's thoughts were going. Noah's had just traveled down the same path. Anyone would think of sexual assault, especially since she wasn't fully clothed.

"Then why'd he do it?" Gran persisted.

61

She needed to downplay what had occurred. Tell only as much as she had to so it
would go away as soon as possible. And
whatever she said had to be believable, first
and foremost. "I think he *intended* to rape
me but . . . I fought him off."

"What took you so long to get home? You
haven't been with him this whole time, have
you?"

Adelaide wished she didn't have to mention the mine. She didn't want it connected
to her, didn't want anyone to be reminded
of Cody and his graduation party. But even
if she lied about that part, Noah would give
away the truth when he said where he'd
found her. She hadn't been able to offer
him a single compelling reason not to share
that information. She couldn't, not without
raising his suspicion as to why she wanted it
kept quiet. And, other than Chief Stacy and
maybe his father, he was the last person
whose curiosity she wanted to arouse.

Left with no choice, she told Gran what'd
happened, and who'd saved her.

"Noah's such a nice boy," she said.

Not if he was anything like his brother.
Adelaide owed him for what he'd done
tonight, but she didn't have a positive
impression of him from high school. He'd
been one of those senior "gods" she'd

worshipped, one who'd acted as if he owned the school. Never had she known him to be aware of the plight of those around them or to care. She told herself it was a miracle he'd bothered to come to her rescue.

"Thank goodness he was in the right place at the right time," Gran was saying. "That's one of the Lord's tender mercies. But why didn't he take you to the hospital?"

"I wouldn't let him."

"Then we need to go now." She moved her walker forward as if intent on getting her purse, but Addy caught her arm.

"There's no need."

"Of course there is. You're bleeding!"

"I'm fine, Gran. This looks much worse than it is. Trust me, it'd be a waste of time and money. Nothing's broken."

"We should still —"

"I wasn't raped," she insisted. "What can they do other than clean my wounds? We can do that here."

Gran's concern warred with the practicality of Adelaide's argument. She'd always been frugal. "You're certain?"

Adelaide mustered a reassuring smile. "Positive."

"Okay, but I should at least let Chief Stacy know you're home. He'll be anxious to talk to you —"

"Not tonight," she interrupted. "There's no need to wake him. I'm too exhausted to answer any questions at the moment."

"But you'll want to give him a statement as soon as possible, while you can remember the details."

"I don't know anything that will help figure out who did this, Gran. I can't even provide a description. The man was wearing a ski mask." She actually had four men to choose from, but she couldn't make a determination by body type alone, not when they'd all probably filled out and changed so much. Chances were she'd recognize their faces if she happened across them, but the person who'd dragged her from her bed last night had been careful to hide his identity.

"There's his height, his weight —"

"Both a blur to me. Can't it wait until tomorrow? Please? I'm not up to being grilled." She managed a pleading expression. "Even by you."

Empathy etched deeper grooves in Gran's wrinkled face. "Okay, we'll wait, if that's what you want. Maybe you'll remember something important once you've had a chance to recover."

Or not. "Thanks."

"I'm so glad you're back, honey. I don't

know what I would've done if . . . if this had ended differently. You've always been my Addy, my pride and joy."

Hearing the tears in her voice, Adelaide gave her another hug. "Don't worry. Everything's going to be fine."

Milly was a proud woman, not one to cry easily. With a sniff, she straightened her spine and motioned for Adelaide to follow her to the kitchen. "Come in here so we can get you cleaned up."

"Shouldn't we do that in the bathroom?"

"There's more room in the kitchen. More light, too."

That was true. Gran's house was one of a handful of local homes listed on the National Register of Historic Places. As was the style a hundred years ago, it had tall ceilings, thick molding, elaborate cut-glass windows and — the one downside besides the old plumbing and wiring they'd had to replace — small bathrooms. "I've got to shower first."

Reluctantly, Gran let her disappear into the bathroom, and Adelaide took her time stripping off Noah's sweatshirt and her filthy clothes before standing beneath the hot spray.

Blood and dirt ran off her body, circling the drain and taking the last of her energy with it. When she'd finished scrubbing, she could only stand there and stare as the last of the soap bubbles disappeared.

"Addy, you coming?"

Gran's voice brought her out of her stupor.

"Be right there," she called, and turned off the water. She'd hoped her grandmother would give up and go to bed, allow her to recover on her own. But she should've known better. Gran would never leave her like this.

"Can you grab the bandages from under the bathroom sink before you come?"

"Sure." Her body complained at the movement but — even injured — it was easier for her to crouch than Gran. Tossing her towel aside, she sorted through the laxatives, extra soap, Listerine and bath salts.

She found a small box of Band-Aids, but she wasn't sure what good they were going to be. Abrasions covered most of her arms and legs.

"We need gauze," she muttered, but she wasn't about to go to the store — or let Gran attempt to drive there. The only drugstore open this late would be halfway to Sacramento.

Gran had a cup of tea waiting for her when she entered the kitchen. Adelaide could smell the mint. She normally liked tea, but tonight she didn't have enough strength to hold the cup. And she had another problem. While pulling on a pair of cutoffs and a tank top she'd figured out why her legs hurt worse in back. Thanks to the fact that she'd slid down the wooden supports of that mine shaft when whoever it was had shoved her in, she had as many slivers in her butt and thighs as she did on her hands.

They had to come out and she couldn't do it on her own, so she'd brought the magnifying glass Gran used for reading and a pair of tweezers, along with the Band-Aids. She hoped her grandmother would be able to help because Adelaide couldn't wait to crawl into bed and block the past twenty or so hours from her mind. Everything from that first terrifying image of a man looming over her bed to the shocking realization that it was Cody's brother who'd pulled her out of the deep, dark hole. The hole that might otherwise have become her grave.

The lights were still on at Milly's house, only now the blind in the kitchen was down.

Conscious of the late hour and that he'd be intruding, Noah hesitated on the stoop with the bag of supplies he'd brought from his place. He knew that Adelaide, who'd tried to avoid even incidental contact with him in his truck, wouldn't be happy to see him. She'd disliked him instantly. But most people didn't have the kind of first-aid supplies he kept on hand for mountain bike spills. And Adelaide had refused to go to the hospital, so . . . he figured she might need them.

Telling himself he was going the extra mile largely for Milly's sake, because he knew how much her granddaughter's injuries would upset her, he took a deep breath and knocked.

The curtain moved; someone was peering out at him. After what'd happened, he was relieved to see they were taking precautions.

He raised the bag to show he'd brought something. Then he heard the bolt slide back.

"Noah!" Milly exclaimed as soon as she got her walker out of the way so she could open the door. "How nice of you to come back."

Surprised by the intensity of her relief, he looked over her gray head to find the living room empty. Was Adelaide in bed? "She okay?"

Milly lowered her voice. "Who knows? She refuses to see a doctor. Do you think I should make her?"

He'd already tried and was sure it wouldn't work. In his estimation, they were better off going with the "do-it-yourself" method he held in his hand, unless her injuries were worse than she'd let on. "Have you found anything serious?"

"Not really. She says nothing's broken. And I'm doing all I can to get her cleaned up, but . . . it's not easy when your hand shakes like mine." She motioned to the sack. "What do you have in there?"

"Iodine, painkiller, large bandages." He didn't mention that the painkiller was prescription-strength, a couple of pills he had left over from when he'd broken his jaw in a free-ride bike race six months ago.

"That'll come in handy." She glanced over her shoulder. "But what I need right now is another pair of eyes and a steadier hand."

"For what?"

He'd expected her to take the bag and say goodnight. Instead, she drew him inside. "Come see what you can do."

"With?"

She didn't clarify because Adelaide called out. "Gran, who is it?"

Milly used her walker like a cattle prod, herding him into the kitchen. "It's Noah. He's here to help. Isn't that nice of him?"

"Noah!" Adelaide was at the sink, rinsing out a cup. But she whirled to face him, and he immediately jerked his gaze up to her face. She was dressed in a tank top and cutoffs that weren't even fastened. She wasn't wearing a bra, and the cutoffs were very short, the sort a girl might wear around the house but not out in public. Obviously, she wasn't prepared for company.

"We'll be up all night without him," Milly said, oblivious to everything except her worry. "I'm not much help. And you can't keep standing there. You're about to collapse."

Adelaide glared at her grandmother as if she was trying to convey a deeper message — something closer to "Hell, no!" than the words that came out of her mouth. "Gran, I'm fine. And if you're not, we can take a break. Or finish in the morning."

Milly shook her head in defeat. "I don't think I'll be much more use to you in the morning. I'm too old for this, honey. So unless you'd rather go to the hospital — and Noah will carry you to the car if need be — you'll hold still and let him finish up so we can all get some sleep." With that, she managed a smile for Noah. "Can I make you some coffee?"

"No, thanks." She could barely get

70

around; he didn't want to put her to the trouble. He was too distracted to think about eating or drinking, anyway. He saw a dish towel on the counter, speckled with blood. But it wasn't until he noticed the magnifying glass and tweezers beside it that he began to understand. "You're extracting . . . slivers?"

Milly frowned. "I removed the ones in her hands. Problem is she's got them all up and down her backside, too."

"But we wouldn't want to inconvenience you," Adelaide interjected. "It's late and . . . I'm sure you have better things to do."

He did. Like going to bed. But he couldn't leave such a tedious job to poor Milly.

"I'm happy to help," he said. "Just not in here. Come lie on the couch before you drop."

"You don't need the light?" Milly asked.

"One lamp will be fine. I'll pull it close."

What were the chances? Adelaide wondered. It wasn't bad enough that she'd been beaten and thrown down a mine shaft? Now she had to suffer the embarrassment and indignity of having Cody's brother remove myriad small splinters from the backs of her thighs?

Maybe it wouldn't have been so bad in

the middle of the day. But with the late hour, the quiet of the house and Gran sleeping so deeply in the chair across the room, it all felt very . . . intimate.

"You okay?" he asked when she shifted.

She'd taken the two Percocets he'd given her. Gran hadn't caught on to the fact that they weren't aspirin, but Noah had made sure she was aware of it. She'd been in so much pain she'd tossed them back almost immediately, and she was glad she had. He'd done all he could with the tweezers. Now he was using a sterilized needle to dig out the deeper slivers. "Yes. You?"

He cleared his throat. "I'm not the one who's hurt. But . . . what am I supposed to do about the ones that are . . . a bit higher?"

He'd studiously avoided touching her anywhere that could be considered inappropriate, but her butt had as many slivers as her legs. That was part of the reason she'd agreed to self-medicate. She'd needed something to get her through the embarrassment as much as the pain.

"Maybe I should've gone to the hospital." The fewer people who saw her beaten up, the better. But she'd never dreamed that her plan to avoid medical care could be thwarted by *slivers.* When she was in Noah's truck insisting he bring her home, she'd been hurting but hurting everywhere. She'd assumed all the injuries would heal with time, had no clue she'd need *this* kind of help.

Relaxing into his chair, he sighed. " 'Bout time you said that. Come on, I'll take you."

Somewhat dazed by the drugs, she rose up on her elbows. Did they *really* have to go to the hospital? They'd made it this far. . . . "How much longer do you think it'll take to get the rest?"

"I haven't seen what I'm up against, of course. But I'm guessing . . . twenty minutes?"

Did it really matter that they were on her butt cheeks? Gran was sitting right there. She was asleep, but Noah wasn't hoping to touch anything he shouldn't. Chances were the E.R. doctor would be a man, if they did go to the hospital.

"That's not long." Twenty minutes would certainly be shorter than going to the emergency room. She didn't think she had the strength to get up. She definitely knew she couldn't walk, not without staggering. And how would they explain that she was doped up?

That could get Noah in trouble.

"No . . . but you'd have to take off your shorts," he pointed out.

She didn't plan on ever seeing Noah again, anyway. They might pass each other once or twice over the next few months while she was in town, but she could muster a wave and move on, couldn't she? Forget that this ever happened?

Gathering her nerve, she reached beneath her to undo her cutoffs. Then she wiggled them, along with her panties, down over her hips.

"Hurry," she said. As innocuous as her actions were, she didn't want to add to her humiliation by having Gran wake up to such a sight.

She'd taken him by surprise. His sudden silence and stillness told her that.

"You don't have a problem with finishing, do you?" Was the painkiller she'd taken affecting her decision-making ability? Maybe. She felt sort of . . . distant and relaxed, despite what was going on.

He cleared his throat again. "I'm thinking . . . maybe we should wake Milly and let her do this part."

"Except she couldn't see well enough to do the other part."

Tension hung thick and heavy in the room — awkwardness, embarrassment, hesitation. She'd already bared her ass and he wasn't quite sure what to do about it.

"It's just a butt, no big deal." She kept her face turned into the couch because she didn't want to look at him. He'd changed since high school, but not enough that she couldn't recognize him — or see the resemblance to Cody. There was also the hero worship she'd once felt. This was worse than walking up and congratulating him on a good baseball game. . . .

But finishing what they'd begun seemed the most direct route to accomplishing their goal. She'd get through it and then she'd forget about it. Noah wasn't part of the life she'd built since leaving Whiskey Creek. He didn't matter. No doubt he'd forget this by tomorrow, too. He hadn't even remembered her, and she'd watched him for two years with such longing. . . .

"I know you can't be shy," she prodded when he didn't move.

"I'm definitely *not* shy, but I've never touched a woman who . . . who's been —"

"Noah, I wasn't raped last night." She wondered what he'd think if she told him the only rape she'd ever suffered had been instigated by his *brother* and carried out by his teammates, that the man who'd thrown her down the mine shaft was one of those teammates. "Just get the job done, okay? I understand the difference between removing a few slivers and . . . and other activities."

"Maybe it would be easier if you didn't cringe every time I touch you."

After everything he'd been in high school, and she saw no reason his status in Whiskey Creek would've changed, it probably came as a shock that she didn't want his hands on her. As far as she was concerned, a dose of indifference now and then would be good for his ego. "This isn't exactly a pleasurable process."

"I'm not talking about now. I'm talking about earlier when I was trying to get you out of the mountains."

Because of who he was. He was the twin brother of the man who'd caused her so much pain. They weren't identical, but there was a strong family resemblance and that was a hurdle she had to clear whenever she looked at him, even if it was merely a glance.

But he didn't understand that, of course, and she couldn't tell him. So she cut to what mattered at this particular moment.

"Don't worry. I'm not that fragile." Not anymore, anyway. It'd been fifteen years since she was raped by a handful of Whiskey Creek's most popular athletes. She'd slept with two men since, men she'd cared about and hoped to have a deeper relationship with. The last one she'd married. With three years' therapy in her early twenties, she'd gotten past the trauma.

Anyway, having Noah help her out with a medical problem had nothing to do with sex or rape, even if it dealt with the same general region of her body. "Can you please, er, hurry? You've already gotten an eyeful, and you're holding the needle. It doesn't make sense to stop."

"Right." Despite his reluctance, his hand, when he touched her, was warm and firm. She jerked as he went after one of the deeper slivers, and he cupped her bottom. She wasn't sure if he was trying to soothe her or hold her still, but he immediately re-alized what he was doing and let go.

"You hangin' in?" he murmured after several minutes.

For the most part, Adelaide couldn't feel pain anymore. She seemed to be floating somewhere up near the ceiling, looking down on the scene. "Yeah."

She wasn't sure how much longer it took. She didn't care. She was too tired to care about anything except drifting off to sleep. . . .

She woke because something had changed. He was rubbing antibiotic oint-ment on her, which felt good despite all the reasons it shouldn't. Somehow she'd lost her anxiety. Pure exhaustion, and painkiller, had carried her beyond that.

"You ready for bed?" He helped get her shorts up. Then he woke Gran and walked her into her room. When he returned to find Adelaide unable to drag herself off the couch, he offered to help her, too. She said no, that she'd be fine right where she was, but when he lifted her in his arms and brought her to bed, she didn't argue.

"Thanks," she mumbled as he laid her on the soft mattress and covered her. "Your sweatshirt's on the bedroom floor. I — I'll repay you for what you've done. The burger, too. I won't forget the burger."

She could tell she was slurring her words, but her unwieldy tongue couldn't do any better. It didn't matter. Nothing mattered, except that she was home, out of the damn mine and even the slivers were gone.

"I don't want your money, Adelaide." He checked to make sure the door leading to the porch was locked.

"Then I'll give you something else." What? A homemade pie? A meal? She felt she had to compensate him, if only to keep from thinking of him too kindly. She definitely didn't want to feel she was in his debt.

"What exactly did you have in mind?" he

drawled.

She heard the teasing note in his voice and covered a yawn. "How about my first-born child?"

He hesitated at the foot of her bed. "Your future husband might have a problem with that."

"Don't worry. I won't ever have another husband." She frowned as she followed that thought to its obvious conclusion. "Oh! And that means I probably won't have a baby, either." Somehow that seemed sad, but she was flying so high she refused to worry about it.

"So . . . what would you like?" Her eyelids drooped and she felt herself slipping away. "I've got to . . . have *something* . . . you want." That hadn't come out right. It sounded suggestive even though she didn't mean it that way. Surely he'd interpret it correctly.

"After the past half hour, that's not a fair question to ask me," he said, and then he was gone.

5

Chief Stacy banged on the door first thing the next morning. Gran, always an early riser, was up, despite having gone to bed in the wee hours. Regardless of the challenges she faced, she clung rigidly to her routine.

When Adelaide heard her greet the police chief and invite him in, she buried her head beneath the pillow. Her whole body ached, and she was *so* tired. She wanted to sleep for a week, not drag herself out of bed to answer a million questions. Now that she was safe and had some perspective on the past thirty hours, she could plainly see that whoever had dropped her into that mine shaft meant to give her a warning, nothing more. He'd hit her, but only when she fought him. He'd probably assumed she could climb out and make her way home. It was even possible, had she not returned to town, that he would've come to make sure she didn't die. If he'd really been planning

80

to kill her, he could just as easily have tossed her in the river.

You tell anyone about graduation and I'll kill you. I'll stab the old lady, too. Do you understand me?

What would be the point of those words if he believed she wouldn't be around to talk?

Too bad he didn't know he'd gone to the effort of abducting her for nothing. She wasn't going to say a word about what happened when she was sixteen — with or without the possibility of imminent danger. He'd only succeeded in creating a mystery for everyone else to solve. Thanks to him, she had Chief Stacy to contend with.

Way to cause more *problems. . . .*

"I would've called you when she got home, but I didn't want to wake you in the middle of the night," she heard Gran explain.

"Like I told you this morning, I'm available whenever you need me," he responded. "Goes with the job."

Adelaide could almost see him puffing out his chest as he spoke and would've rolled her eyes if her head wasn't already under her pillow.

"You're so devoted," Gran gushed. "Whiskey Creek is lucky to have you."

Which was, no doubt, the compliment

he'd been fishing for.

Or maybe he was being sincere. Maybe Adelaide was just in a terrible mood.

"Can I get you a cup of coffee?"

"You bet. Your coffee's the best in town."

"Better than Black Gold down the street?" she asked in surprise.

"As good," he hedged.

Now Adelaide knew he was full of shit. Gran's coffee wasn't one of her better offerings; it was basic and cheap because she couldn't tell the difference.

"Then I'd like to speak with Adelaide, if possible," Stacy was saying.

"Of course. I'll tell her so she can get dressed."

Her grandmother's walker thumped as she moved down the wooden hallway and stopped at her door. She didn't bother to knock. She didn't see the point in giving Adelaide any privacy. Adelaide would always be her little girl; it didn't matter if she was three or thirty.

"Addy?" she said, poking her head in. "Chief Stacy's here. He'd like a word with you."

Static electricity made strands of her hair stand up when she set her pillow aside. "I heard. I'm coming."

"You have a few minutes while I get him

82

some coffee."

A few minutes? She'd barely be able to dress and comb her hair. Knowing she must look like she'd been dragged behind a horse, she swallowed a sigh. "Be right there."

Clomp. Shuffle. Clomp. Shuffle. The noise from Gran and her walker receded as Adelaide kicked off the covers and sat up. She expected a headache. She'd had a whopper of one last night. But her head seemed to be the only part of her body that *didn't* hurt.

Thank God for small favors.

She dressed in a pair of jeans and an orange tee, gingerly avoiding all the bandages Noah had applied, as well as the memory of his sure, gentle hands applying them. Then she went into the bathroom, brushed her teeth and pulled her hair back before making her way into the living room.

Chief Stacy was sitting in her grandmother's antique rocker, looking quite comfortable with a steaming cup of coffee and a slice of cinnamon-walnut cake. Maybe Gran's coffee wasn't anything special, but her baked goods were out of this world. Of course, her recipes were also "old school," meaning there was enough fat, sugar and cholesterol in each serving to bring on a heart attack. Adelaide had long wanted to introduce a few new, interesting and organic options, at least on the meal side of the menu.

She thought she still might try to do that.

If they hung on to the restaurant long enough . . .

"Well, hello, Addy." Setting his plate and cup on the side table, Chief Stacy got up to greet her, but it was awkward. She couldn't tell if he intended to hug her or shake her hand. He'd been a regular officer when she lived in town, a position slightly less prominent than the one he held now, but she'd known him. He'd eaten at Just Like Mom's once a week or so; she'd often served him.

She offered her hand to let him know what she preferred, and he acted as if that was the most he'd expected.

"I'm glad you're okay," he said.

She conjured up a pleasant expression as they shook. "So am I."

Once she sat down, he sobered in apparent concern. "Can you tell me what happened?"

"Sure. Although there isn't a lot to tell."

He returned to his seat but didn't pick up his cake or coffee. He took out a pad and pen. Whiskey Creek was pretty uneventful. A true abduction would be the case of a lifetime for a backwoods cop like Stacy — could make or break his career.

Too bad she wasn't about to give him anything that might help him solve the crime. Even if, as a victim, she could be completely honest about what she knew and remembered, Adelaide wouldn't pit him against a very wily kidnapper. He seemed long on confidence but short on experience. As far as she could remember, the most he'd ever had to find was a runaway horse or dog. A big day for a cop in Whiskey Creek was handling security for the annual Fourth of July parade or the Victorian Days festival every Christmas.

"Just start from the beginning," he said.

Lacing her fingers together, she stared down at the fingernails she'd broken. "Before I went to bed, I opened the door in my bedroom —"

"The one that leads out to the street?"

"To the porch. Yes."

"Because . . ."

"I needed some fresh air."

He raised his eyebrows. "It's fall," he said.

Not wanting to blame Gran for her heavy hand with the thermostat, she glossed over that. "My room hasn't been used much since I left. It was sort of . . . stuffy."

"So you opened the door to air it out."

"Yes. There was the screen door, of course, which was locked."

"A screen provides little protection. . . ."

As if she didn't feel foolish enough. "I wasn't too worried about protection. Not here at home." It wasn't until she'd disobeyed her grandmother, back in high school, and ventured to the mine that she'd gotten into trouble. And pointing out that she should feel secure in a town *he* was supposed to keep safe shifted the blame back on to him.

"Nothing like this has ever happened before," he told her, backpedaling.

"Which is why I didn't worry about it. But someone, a — a man, cut the screen, dragged me from my bed and drove me up to the old mine."

"The Jepson mine, where Cody Rackham was killed?"

The fear that, at long last, she'd be implicated in Cody's death, tied her stomach in knots. But she'd expected the immediate association. They'd had their tragedies in Whiskey Creek — when Dylan Amos's father got into a bar fight and stabbed his opponent and when Phoenix Fuller used her mother's Buick to run down her rival, to name two — but the popular, wealthy and handsome Rackham family had always generated a great deal of interest. "Where Cody . . . died. Yes," she said.

"Did your abductor . . ." The way Stacy lowered his voice and shot a warning glance at Gran told Adelaide what he was about to ask.

She jumped in to save him the effort of formulating the rest of the question. "He didn't rape me, no."

His chest rose as if her answer allowed him to draw a deep breath for the first time since he'd arrived. He even left his pad and pen in his lap and reclaimed his coffee and cake. "I'm happy to hear that." He took a big bite, then paused to give her a searching look. "You'd tell me if he did," he said while chewing. "I realize there's a certain . . . stigma that goes with that word, with the act itself, but I can't help you if you're not honest with me."

Her mouth was so dry she could hardly speak. "He *didn't* rape me." But she could clearly remember the time before, when he had. . . .

"So you were awakened in your bed and then what? Let's go over it detail by detail."

She cleared her throat. "He whispered that he'd hurt me and Gran if I screamed. Then he tied my hands, blindfolded me and forced me to walk out to his truck or SUV."

"You're sure it was a truck or SUV."

"By the sound of the engine and how high

87

off the ground it was . . . yes." That was true, but she hardly saw it as revealing. Practically everyone in these parts owned a truck.

"Did you get the color, or the make and model?"

"No. The blindfold was too tight." And when she'd tried to remove it, he'd panicked and struck her. That was the first time he'd hit her, but it wasn't the most painful, just a glancing blow on the cheek.

"What about *before* the blindfold? Were you able to see him or any part of him?"

She wished she could tell the police chief to forget about the incident, but she knew that would only make him wonder at her reaction. She had to act as if she wanted her kidnapper caught. "Just that first glimpse."

"And . . ."

She swallowed. "I'm afraid I can't give you a description. It was so dark, and he was wearing a ski mask."

Stacy frowned as he formulated another question. "Did he have any exposed skin? Any tattoos or birthmarks?"

"He was completely covered."

"What was he wearing?"

"Black pants and a black sweatshirt." That much was true, but the sweatshirt had a strange logo on it, a bright yellow logo with a website URL that was easy to remember. Thanks to the light of a full moon streaming through that screen door, she'd spotted www.SkintightEntertainment.com before he'd managed to blindfold her. But she was giving Stacy only generic information, information she felt safe providing. As far as she knew, that URL could be connected to where the culprit worked, could lead police right to him.

"Were his clothes particularly expensive or cheap?" Stacy asked. "I mean —" he leaned forward, beseeching her with his body language "— did you notice anything that might help identify him? *What kind of guy was this?*"

A guy who wore a brand of cologne she normally would've liked. She remembered that, too — but it was another detail she planned to keep to herself. "They were just your basic cargo pants and a plain sweatshirt. They could've come from any department store."

He put his coffee down again so he could make a few notes. "Can you tell me how tall he was?"

She'd known instantly what the encounter was about, which had evoked immediate terror. And the abduction happened so fast.

She doubted she could answer all of Chief Stacy's questions even if she really *wanted* the man apprehended.

"About my height." She had no idea if that was true. He could've been an inch or two taller, or an inch or two shorter, but six feet sounded average. She was embellishing, changing this or that, describing a person who didn't exist, so what did it matter?

"And his build?"

This time she didn't have to make anything up. The truth described a large proportion of the male population, so she could speak honestly. "He was . . . fairly muscular, I guess. But not overly so."

"Can you guess at his weight?"

She went for what would be likely, given the height and body build she'd stated. "About two hundred. I can't recall, to be honest."

Stacy took another bite of cake. "What about age?"

"Middle-aged?" She certainly didn't want to say close to *her* age, which was what she believed. Anyway, age wasn't easy to determine in a situation like that.

"Did he speak with a lisp or an accent or . . . use foul language? Was there anything distinctive about his voice?"

Her kidnapper had spoken in a hoarse

whisper. That hadn't evoked the memory of any particular boy, but it had brought back what she'd experienced fifteen years ago, deluging her with the kinds of images that plagued her worst nightmares. *Hold her still, damn it!*

In retrospect, however, when she examined the details of this most recent attack, she felt he hadn't been taking any pleasure in what he was doing. Especially once she started shaking and crying and pleading with him not to rape her again. He'd muttered — and she'd only now remembered this — "Stop it! I — that's not who I am!"

"Adelaide?" Chief Stacy's voice intruded on her thoughts.

She glanced up. "Yes?"

"I asked if there was anything distinctive about his voice."

"Oh." She wiped her palms on her thighs. "No."

His cup clinked on the china saucer. "Do you know any reason someone would want to harm you? If he didn't . . . rape you, what did he want? Did he ask for anything? Demand money?"

"No." She shrugged. "At first, I — I thought he was intent on rape, but . . ."

"Looks like you fought tooth and nail. I'm sorry about your injuries."

91

His sympathy made her feel guilty for shading the truth, but she had to do what she could to make this go away. "I'm fine now, thank you. It's all . . . minor stuff, really. I'll recover."

"You forced him to reconsider. I'm proud of you for that."

Her kidnapper was the one who'd made it possible for her to fight by tying her hands in front of her instead of behind her back. She couldn't get them loose until she was alone in the mine, but she could use them — like when she'd attempted to remove her blindfold. Such a tactical error gave her the impression that he wasn't used to abducting people. He'd gone for what was quick and convenient because he was in a hurry and was afraid of getting caught, possibly by Gran. Maybe he figured his threats and the knife he'd brought would keep her cowed.

Anyway, she felt even more uncomfortable at Stacy's compliment than she'd already been. She wasn't out to elicit praise. She was hoping to present a degree of believability, to put together a coherent story, so that his curiosity would be satisfied and she could get out of the spotlight as soon as possible. "At one point, he mumbled that he couldn't go through with it and just . . . tossed me into the mine."

She'd fabricated his change of heart. He hadn't even attempted to rape her. She'd been fighting because she'd been afraid he might. She was so convinced that she was in for more of what she'd endured at sixteen that, once she was away from the house and he couldn't hurt Gran, she'd let loose with everything she had and nearly caused them to crash. The sound of scraping metal told her his vehicle had sustained some damage. That was when he'd slugged her — hard. Other than that, and when she'd nearly managed to remove her blindfold, he hadn't hit her.

"Doesn't mean he won't try to rape someone else," Stacy said. "I'll find this guy, I promise."

She hoped not. That was all she needed — a string that would unravel the past. Even an overzealous search could spook the man who'd appeared in her bedroom. Then there was no telling what he might do. Fear could push him into taking risks he wouldn't otherwise take. That was what it had done to her when she'd tried to crash his car.

"Is there anything else you remember?"

She shook her head, but she could probably describe Tom Gibby, Kevin Colbert or any of the others in great detail and Stacy would never suspect them. They'd been athletic, popular, good students — and were apparently successful adults. Tom Gibby was a postal clerk, *a steady, devoted family man.* And *Coach* Colbert was married to his high school sweetheart and had three kids. She hadn't asked about Derek Rodriguez or Stephen Selby. She hadn't wanted to string those four names together. But she doubted Derek and Stephen would be at the top of Chief Stacy's suspect list, any more than Kevin or Tom. They certainly hadn't acted out since high school. Or, if they had, no one knew about it. Gran had visited her regularly all the years she'd been gone, and they talked on the phone every few days when they weren't together. She would've heard if any of the people she'd known had been charged with a crime. She also received the *Gold Country Gazette,* Whiskey Creek's weekly paper, at her apartment in Davis. So even if Gran didn't mention an arrest, the newspaper would. She'd subscribed for that very reason.

For the thirteen years she'd been gone, all had been quiet.

"That's okay," Stacy said. "I'll still get him."

"I'm praying you will." This came from Gran, who'd been listening silently but intently.

Chief Stacy scooted forward in his seat. He'd been handed the worst crime to be perpetrated in Whiskey Creek in at least a decade and had just promised her he'd find the man responsible, but he had nothing to go on. "So why you?"

Wishing this could be over, Addy threaded her fingers more tightly together and searched for an explanation he'd find plausible. "I've heard . . . on various forensic shows that most crimes are crimes of opportunity. I guess . . . I guess I made it too easy when I left my door open." Essentially, she was taking the blame. She deserved some of it — not for leaving her door open, but for sneaking out and attending that stupid party in the first place. Gran had told her she couldn't go.

If only she'd listened . . .

"There's got to be a detail, some evidence we're missing," Stacy said.

"Nothing I can think of right now," Adelaide told him. "But . . . if I remember anything, I'll give you a call."

He put his notepad and pen in his pocket. "I did find an interesting object that might help."

Adelaide's chest constricted. "What did you say?"

"The man who attacked you must've

95

dropped his knife when he was wrestling you out to his truck, because I found this —" he straightened one leg so he could take something from his pocket "— in the flower bed outside the door to your bedroom."

If it had been a plain pocketknife, Adelaide wouldn't have paid it much heed. But it had a wolf carved into the handle, which wasn't something one saw every day.

Her mind raced. "Couldn't that have been dropped by someone else?"

"I doubt it. With all the watering in the summer and the rain we get in the winter —" he flipped out the blade "— there'd be some rust if it'd been exposed to the elements for any length of time." He pointed to the shiny steel. "Look at that. It's perfect. Someone loved this knife."

Palms sweaty, heart pounding, she sat in silence.

"So you didn't see him with it?" he asked.

"He — he said he had a knife. But . . . I didn't see it, no. And . . . I — I assumed he had it with him the whole time."

Stacy studied the carving. "Okay, I'll keep asking around. See if anyone can identify its owner."

"He must've used that to cut the screen," Gran said. "Were there any fingerprints on it?"

Adelaide held her breath. *Please, no.*

"Unfortunately not. I'm guessing he wiped it clean before he came here."

"He — he was wearing gloves," Adelaide said. "I remember that from when . . . from when he was tying my hands. The gloves made it difficult."

"Gloves." Chief Stacy sighed in a way that indicated he found this expected but disappointing. Then he lifted the knife. "But . . . this is *very* hopeful. We'll see what turns up."

The police chief and Gran moved on to other subjects while he finished his coffee and cake. Adelaide learned that he was recently divorced, that he was suing his wife for custody of their two kids, that his ex was "crazy" if she thought she was going to tell their son he couldn't play football.

At last Stacy got up to leave — with a final promise to see that her attacker was apprehended.

Closing her eyes, Adelaide stayed where she was while Gran showed him out. She was embracing the silence, wishing her return to Whiskey Creek could've gone smoothly and wondering what she should do now.

"I sure hope he can catch the man who did this to you," Gran said as she returned.

"So do I." Adelaide twisted around to smile up at her, but the prospect of a police capture scared her more than anything — because she knew where it would lead if Kevin, Tom, Derek or Stephen decided to point a finger in her direction.

6

Baxter stood at Noah's door, looking at him with that *odd* sort of expression Noah had noticed before, the one that made him so uncomfortable. He wanted to say something about it — had wanted to address the issue for some time because whatever was going on seemed to be getting worse instead of better. But he didn't know how to broach such a taboo subject without busting up a friendship that had lasted almost since birth. What could he say: "*Dude,* sometimes you look at me like you're dying to get in my pants"?

If Baxter wasn't gay, Noah knew how much that would offend him. *He'd* be offended if a buddy accused *him* of sexual interest. That kind of talk was out of bounds between two guys. But Baxter's look . . . It was *so* damn hungry.

"Why are you staring at me like that?" he snapped.

Baxter seemed taken aback. "Like what?"

Shit. Maybe he'd imagined it. That was another thing Noah hated — how he'd begun to second-guess his best friend's thoughts and reactions. It seemed as if he was always reading more into what Baxter said and did. Suspicion affected people that way; it messed with their minds. "Forget it."

Baxter seemed more than willing to let the subject go. "Do you know it's almost noon?"

With a yawn, he scratched his head. "Haven't looked at a clock. Just rolled out of bed."

"So Amy opened the shop for you?"

"She was supposed to. She's there now, isn't she?" For a moment, he was afraid that his employee hadn't shown up.

"She's there. But . . . I thought she had school."

When Baxter's gaze once again strayed to Noah's bare chest, Noah grabbed the football jersey he'd left on the couch sometime in the past few days and put it on. It wasn't as if he'd answered the door nude. He'd donned a pair of basketball shorts, but his state of undress seemed to be a distraction, which added to the creeping sensation that all was not as he'd believed with the kid who'd grown up next door. "She graduated

100

in June, remember?"

"I forgot. Does that mean you're off to-day?"

"No, but this time of year weekday mornings can be slow. There's no rush. I'll walk over in a bit, spell her for lunch."

"I can spell her if you're sick."

"I'm not sick. Just tired." He yawned again. "I got in late."

Baxter glanced beyond him, into his small bungalow. "Do you have company?"

"You mean a woman? No."

"Then where were you last night? I came by a couple of times."

Noah ignored the apparent subtext of that sentence — the possessive "where were you?" — because he wasn't even sure it existed. "Believe it or not, I was rescuing someone."

"You always wanted to be a superhero," Baxter joked.

"Now I just need the cape." Relaxing slightly, Noah held the door. What was wrong with him? This was *Bax*! They'd been on lots of double dates together. Noah knew for a fact that Baxter had slept with a number of women — at least when they were younger.

His friend grinned as he came in. "Who'd you rescue this time? Yet another chick from

101

the confinement of her clothes?"

See? When Baxter said stuff like that, as if he was just another one of the guys, Noah wondered if he was simply being conceited or . . . or paranoid to think Baxter was attracted to him.

But there was always that indefinable *something,* like the feeling that had triggered his desire to pull on a shirt.

Whatever was going on was so damn contradictory and confusing. . . .

"Is that the kind of rescue mission *you'd* like?" he said with a laugh.

Baxter didn't rush to convince him. "Now and then. There are too many risks and complications that go with sleeping around to do it very often."

"Yeah, well, I didn't get naked with anyone last night." He had seen — and touched — Adelaide's bare ass. That was memorable. But, in deference to what she'd been through, he wasn't going to mention it. Maybe the rest of the circumstances surrounding her ordeal would go public. The incident was too sensational for word not to spread. But nobody had to know about the private hour he'd spent in Milly's home, removing slivers. "Do you remember Adelaide Davies?"

Baxter's gaze lighted on everything that

was out of place. He'd been a neat freak since he was a little kid. "Adelaide *who*?"

"Went to high school with us. Would've been a sophomore when we were seniors."

"I don't recall anyone by that name."

"Doesn't surprise me. We were at San Diego State by the time she graduated, and she left town right after." Noah dropped onto the couch and dangled one leg over the arm.

Baxter sat in the opposite chair, but he did so with his usual decorum. He wasn't wearing one of his hand-tailored suits. He worked at a brokerage house in San Francisco Monday through Thursday, but his hours were flexible. Maybe he was taking two days off this week instead of one. Anyway, even his casual jeans and shirts came with expensive labels. He was stylish, well groomed, always had a perfect haircut and smelled like the men's department at Macy's.

But Noah tried not to file any of that under the "gay or not gay" headings going on in the back of his mind. He refused to define Bax — someone he was supposed to know better than anyone else — according to stereotypes. He was still hoping his so-called gaydar was wrong. . . .

Actually, he didn't care if his best friend

preferred men. He'd deck anyone who had anything to say about it. He just didn't want Baxter's preferences to include *him.* Any admission along those lines would be far too *weird.*

"She's back?"

"Just returned."

"And you didn't sleep with her? You're falling off your game, bro."

Noah scowled. He wasn't *that* big a player. Living in a small town made it impossible to screw around very much — and maintain any respectability. It wasn't as if he went out looking to get laid. Not very often, anyway. Women had always sort of . . . come to him. "Why do you keep bringing everything back to sex?"

"Isn't that what you usually want to talk about? How hot your latest conquest was?"

Maybe he *did* talk too much about the women in his life. But he was trying to convince himself that the loneliness that had begun to plague him in recent years wasn't going to taint his whole existence, that the life he led was fulfilling and would continue to be fulfilling even if nothing changed.

Besides, he couldn't think of a better way to put Baxter on notice that he wasn't about to get intimate with another man.

"She was beaten up! Of course I didn't

sleep with her. If you'll *listen,* I'll tell you what happened."

"Fine." Baxter spread out his hands. "Let's hear it, then."

"Forget it." Flipping him off for being so damn facetious, Noah got up and headed to the kitchen.

Baxter chuckled as he followed. "Now you're clamming up?"

"You don't really want to hear."

"That's not true. I'm dying to learn every sordid — or not so sordid — detail. Did you punish the guy who was giving her trouble, or what?"

Noah turned to face him. "She was in the mine."

At this, Baxter sobered. "What do you mean 'in the mine'? What mine?"

"The one we used to party in at the end of our senior year."

"The Jepson mine? She couldn't have been. They closed it off after —" his voice softened "— after Cody."

Noah didn't want to think about his brother. Ignoring the reference, he once again shoved away the memories of the June morning he heard his brother had been found. "That's what I thought, too," he said. "But . . ."

He pulled a carton of orange juice from

the fridge and shook it before offering some to Baxter.

"No, thanks." Baxter's lip curled in disdain. "I wouldn't drink from one of your glasses to save my life."

"Because you're OCD."

"Because you barely rinse them before you use them again."

Just to bug him, Noah drank from the container. "Wasn't enough for you, anyway," he said, and tossed the empty carton across the kitchen and into the trash can.

"Nice shot." Baxter transferred a stack of dirty dishes to the sink before leaning against the counter. "Back to Adelaide Davies. How'd she get into the mine? And how did you find her?"

"I was riding past the entrance when I heard a woman call for help."

"That must've freaked you out."

"Yeah. It was twilight and cooling off, so it's an odd time to run into someone up there. I certainly wasn't expecting to perform a rescue mission."

"That entrance is no longer sealed off?"

"It is. This was an ancillary opening. Someone had torn away the boards and, after beating her up, threw her down into the hole."

Baxter blinked several times. "You're kidding."

Noah could understand his surprise. Nothing like that ever happened in Whiskey Creek. There'd been rumors that Sophia DeBussi's husband, the wealthy world-traveler Skip, knocked her around once in a while, but that was the only hint of violence that had occurred in recent years. "No. And get this . . . she'd been taken *from her bed.*"

"Kidnapped? That's what she said?"

"She didn't have to say. It was obvious. She had rope burns. And she was in her underwear."

Baxter whistled. "That's serious. How badly had she been beaten up?"

"One eye was swollen shut, and she was all scraped and bruised."

"Who did it?"

Noah shrugged. "Who knows?"

Baxter pushed away from the counter. "Wait a second! When I stopped at the Gas-N-Go last night, I heard that Chief Stacy was asking about a woman who'd gone missing. It's Milly Davies's granddaughter, right?"

"That's right."

"*You* found her?"

"*I* found her."

"Milly must be relieved. But —" he hesitated briefly "— had she been raped?"

"Claims she wasn't, and I'm inclined to believe her."

"Because . . ."

"Her panties were . . . you know . . . on and intact."

Baxter looked baffled. "So . . . what was the point of taking her?"

Noah sighed. "No idea. Maybe he intended to rape her, but she fought too hard and he gave up."

"Wow. After *that* welcome home, I bet she's ready to leave town again."

"She can't."

"Why not? She left before, didn't she?" Baxter started cleaning up the kitchen, which he'd probably been itching to do from the second he got there.

"Milly's getting too old to run her restaurant. That's the reason Addy came back."

"It's a good thing you were there and that you heard her. The Jepson mine's not stable. She could have . . ."

He let his words trail off, but Noah knew what he'd been about to say.

Instead of following up with a comment about Cody, Noah focused on the mundane. Avoidance was always easier than trying to cope with the loss he still felt. As far as he was concerned, that was private. "Stop doing my damn dishes!"

"Why?"

"Because it makes me feel like a slob."

"You *are* a slob," Baxter joked, but there was no real energy or accusation in the statement. Noah could tell he was thinking about Cody. The three of them had been inseparable as children. Baxter wasn't a stellar athlete, but he'd joined all the same teams Noah and Cody had been on, even if he didn't get to play on game day.

"Compared to *you*," he said. "You iron your sheets and underwear."

"Makes them feel great. You should try it sometime."

Noah rolled his eyes. "No, thanks. I have better things to do with my time." He rinsed off a plate, but Baxter took it and put it in the dishwasher as if Noah would only put it in the wrong slot.

"Do you think Chief Stacy will catch the guy who kidnapped Milly's granddaughter?" Baxter asked, returning to their conversation.

"Not if she doesn't give him some sort of description."

"Maybe it was someone who followed her here from wherever she lived before."

Noah remembered how reticent Addy had been after he'd pulled her out of the mine.

Wouldn't most women be shaking and crying and begging to go to the police?

She'd wanted to pretend the whole thing had never happened.

"It *has* to be someone she knows." He couldn't get around that. She'd said it wasn't her ex, but . . . was she lying?

"Why?" Baxter spoke above the sound of the kitchen faucet.

"Because she acted strange, wouldn't give me any details. She wouldn't even let me take her to the hospital or the police."

"There could be other reasons."

"Like . . ."

"Maybe she hit her head, wasn't in her right mind. Or . . . it's possible that she *was* raped and she's too embarrassed and humiliated to talk about it."

Noah doubted she would've allowed him to remove those slivers if she'd just been violated. "That's not what happened. I believe she'll try to play it off as if it was a stranger. But . . ."

"What?"

He rinsed off another plate. "I got the impression it wasn't."

Baxter kept loading the dishwasher. "I'm not sure that makes sense. If she knew him, why not point the finger?"

"My guess? She's afraid." Actually, it

wasn't a guess. She'd said as much, hadn't she?

"That he might get to her before the police can get to him?"

"Absolutely."

"If she wasn't raped, what could her abductor have wanted? Was it a robbery?"

"No." Noah felt certain she would've said so if that were the case.

His cell phone vibrated on the counter, but when he saw the incoming number, he ignored it. It was a woman — a tourist he'd met when he'd stopped for a drink at Sexy Sadie's during the summer. She'd come through town with her sister, they'd spent one night together and she'd been calling him ever since.

The noise caught Baxter's attention. "You're not going to get that? Why not? Don't tell me Shania's been calling you again."

Noah wrung out the dishrag so he could wipe down the counters. "No, I think she's finally accepted that I'm not going to take Cody's place in her life. It's Lisa. *Again.*"

"I thought you liked her."

"As a friend."

"She wants more?"

"She hasn't asked for a commitment, but she sure wants to see me a lot."

"She's the one who took off your clothes in the car."

Noah could easily remember that night. Few women had come on as strongly as Lisa. And yet she'd seemed almost strait-laced when they were talking in the bar. "That's the one. She's been hounding me ever since."

Baxter's smile shifted to one side. "I guess you're just that good in bed."

Was there an undercurrent to that statement, too? It felt as if maybe there was, but Noah couldn't figure out why there would be. What was Baxter feeling? Jealousy? Envy? Or was there some criticism in those words? "Very funny."

The buzzing of his phone stopped but started up again a second later.

"You're right," Baxter said. "She *is* persistent. Maybe you should answer it and tell her you're not interested."

"I don't want to hurt her feelings. I don't mind seeing her now and then." As long as they were in the company of others. He was growing bored with the kind of sexual encounters that didn't mean anything, and had begun to think he was missing out on a whole other dimension. Actually, after seeing how happy and in love Gail and Cheyenne and Callie were, he *knew* he was missing *something.*

"Of course not. You're always up for a good time."

Noah studied his friend, searching for clues as to the correct interpretation of *that* line. But Baxter's benign expression suggested he should take it at face value and Noah felt it was in the best interest of their friendship to let it go. "You like a good time, too, don't you?"

"Sure," he said.

Noah grabbed a bowl from him. "Good. I'll tell her to come this weekend, and bring a friend."

Baxter met his gaze. They were only a few inches apart and Noah got that odd feeling again, but he refused to step away. He shouldn't have to. This was his best friend, damn it.

"Why would you have her bring someone?" he asked. "Now you're into threesomes?"

"No. The friend is for *you.*" Noah clapped him on the back and smiled, waiting for him to beg off. These days, that was what he normally did. He'd say he had to work, he was in the middle of a project at home or he'd be out of town. Noah had started hanging out more with Riley and Ted, especially if there were going to be women present.

But Bax didn't offer up the typical excuse. Although he didn't seem as pleased as Noah thought he should be, he accepted. "Why not?"

"So, if she can do it, we're on?" he asked in surprise.

"As long as it's not tomorrow night. Tomorrow's the big game, remember?"

It was Homecoming at the high school, but that didn't mean what it used to. They didn't attend the Friday-night games anymore; they were too old to hang with the high school crowd. But he had to go to *this* game. He, Cody and a lot of the friends they'd grown up with, including Baxter, had been part of the football team that won state during their senior year. Those who lived in the area had been asked to return and help present a memorial plaque to Coach Nobis, who was retiring and would be moving to Arizona in a few months. They were also going to retire Cody's number. Noah's father would be on hand to speak, in his capacity as mayor *and* as Cody's father and, because he was his brother's best receiver, Noah was expected to say a few words, too. But he wasn't looking forward to it. Cody was too emotional a subject for him. He hated speaking about the loss of his brother, especially in public.

"Right. The big game. Trust me, I'm not likely to forget."

Obviously picking up on his sarcasm, Baxter studied him. "You're spending too much time dreading it. It won't be that bad."

"I don't want to talk about it."

"You never do."

Noah rounded on him. "Why should I have to? Why does everyone want to hear about Cody?"

"It's been fifteen *years,* Noah. How much longer can you put off dealing with it?"

"*Dealing with it?* You're kidding, right? I have to deal with it every day of my life! I just don't want to *dwell* on it."

"So you'd rather talk about people who mean nothing to you. Lisa, for instance."

"Sure, why not?" Lisa was an uncomplicated subject. He'd been honest with her about his level of interest and owed her nothing. But Cody. That was a different story. With Cody he had to ask himself too many what-ifs. What if he'd attended that party? Would he have been able to keep Cody safe? What if he'd gone to his parents and told them Cody was using drugs? Would they have been able to change the situation before it was too late? Would they have restricted him? Kept him home that night? And what if he hadn't pointed out the Jepson mine to Cody in the first place?

"Should we ask Gail if she'll let us use the cabin Saturday night?" he asked.

Baxter hesitated but allowed Noah to return to their former subject without complaint. "You mean the *mansion*?"

One of their best friends, Gail DeMarco, had married box-office-hit Simon O'Neal, who'd recently had a cabin built back in the hills. It must've cost eight million dollars, but that was mere pocket change to them, and the O'Neals often let friends or family use it.

"We could grill steaks, watch a movie, lounge on the deck," Noah suggested.

"Drink a few bottles of wine?"

"If you want," he replied, but this suggestion surprised him. From what he could tell, Baxter had quit drinking. At least, he never drank around Noah. He'd started taking life more seriously, had become all about making money, for himself and his clients, and renovating his house. And then there was that scare, when they thought they'd lose Callie, another friend, to liver disease. Baxter had been singularly devoted to her for most of the summer, even after the transplant that saved her life. He'd probably be at her farm this weekend, helping improve the place, if Callie wasn't on her honeymoon. "But . . . you don't drink anymore."

"I haven't quit entirely," Baxter responded. "I might as well enjoy myself. It's not like I have anything to lose."

As far as Noah was concerned, that was as strange as any of his other comments, because there was an element of anger, maybe even hurt, to it. "What's that supposed to mean?"

Baxter smiled. "It means I'm looking forward to it."

If what he said was true, why did Noah get the impression he meant just the opposite?

7

Gran did a great job of keeping the locals at bay, at least until dinnertime. By then she'd fielded so many calls, she was getting too tired to deal with the on-slaught and took her old-fashioned phone — the kind with no voice mail or answering machine — off the hook. Everyone in Whiskey Creek wanted to show their concern. Several neighbors had brought casseroles, flowers, cards or a combination of the three. Chief Stacy had checked in to tell Adelaide he'd be working late, that if she remembered anything, anything at all, to contact him right away. And Ed Hamilton, from the *Gold Country Gazette,* had pleaded with Gran to have Addy call him before the day was through. He wasn't about to miss the deadline for this week's paper. He wanted to take advantage of having something bigger to report than the completion of movie star Simon O'Neal's cabin not far from town.

That wasn't how he'd described it, of course. He'd told Gran he wanted to use the power of the press to alert the community to possible danger and enlist their cooperation in apprehending the man who'd hurt Adelaide.

With a sigh at the effort moving required, Addy forced herself to come out of her bedroom in time for dinner. She was sore but somewhat rested, not that her long nap had changed her outlook. If she had her preference, she'd return to Davis until the firestorm ended. But she couldn't leave Gran so worried and upset. It was better to stay and act as if she was as desperate for the police to find her attacker as everyone else. That meant she had to at least *pretend* to be cooperating.

"So . . . are you going to call Ed?" Gran had fully embraced the idea that appealing to the public might break the case. She'd shuffled into Addy's room three times to talk about it, hoping, no doubt, that Addy would jump up and give Ed his interview.

"Sure." Addy managed a reassuring smile.

"When, honey? When will you call? He's under a deadline."

That might be true, but what could she safely reveal? She had no idea what Kevin,

119

Tom, Stephen or Derek might think of Ed's article, and their perceptions were as important as reality — no, *more* important. If they thought she was revealing too much, or that she might expose them, she could be in danger again.

It was so hard to guess which of her former rapists had attacked her, exactly how much damage he'd hoped to do, how far he might go in the future and what his expectations might be now that she'd been warned. Other than that gruff threat, he hadn't been particularly clear on what statements or actions would constitute a breach.

She needed to use her laptop to check the website she'd seen on her attacker's sweatshirt. Maybe it would give some clue to his identity. Whether or not she decided to share that information, she was certainly curious.

But there was no internet here at Gran's. Once she was back on her feet, she'd have to go to Black Gold Coffee, the only place in town that offered free Wi-Fi.

Or maybe she wouldn't bother. What good would knowing do? She couldn't turn him in. And one man could be as dangerous as the others. They all had the same thing to lose if she came forward, didn't they? It was even possible that they'd gotten together and agreed on the approach that was taken.

"Addy?"

She glanced over at Gran, who had set about dishing up some meat loaf and potatoes. Gran still made breakfast and a few other simple meals. Her kitchen was her kitchen, and she liked being in charge of it. But these days Darlene used Gran's recipes and did most of the cooking at the restaurant. The meat loaf was something Darlene had brought over the day Addy arrived. Gran was just warming it up so it wouldn't go to waste. Addy had no idea when they'd eat all the food brought by others, because she hadn't had much of an appetite since her return.

"I'll call him as soon as I finish my dinner."

Satisfied with that commitment, Gran seemed happy to relax and do what she did best — put on a meal.

The comfort of being in Gran's kitchen, of smelling her wonderful food, eased some of Addy's apprehension, too. She'd get through this. She'd play it smart, mind her own business and convince Kevin, Derek, Tom and Stephen that she planned to maintain her silence. That way she could stay and do right by Gran. Maybe her mother wouldn't shoulder any responsibility, but Addy wasn't like that, and she was bound and determined to prove it.

Gran's orthopedic shoes squished as she navigated the kitchen without her walker. After watching her struggle to get a plate down, Addy was tempted to take over. She could've assembled the leftovers much more quickly and efficiently. But she knew Gran liked feeling productive, liked bringing her pleasure through food.

"Noelle came by while you were sleeping."

Addy had been twirling a glass of orange juice. At this, she stopped. *"Noelle?"*

"Arnold. Don't you remember her?"

"You mean Olivia's sister?"

"That's right. She wasn't in your grade, was she?"

"Olivia was, but not Noelle. Noelle's two years younger. So why did she drop in?"

There was a shrug in Gran's voice when she answered. "Said she heard about what happened and felt terrible. She brought a gift from that shop where she works."

This was completely unexpected. Addy knew her, but they'd never been friends. "Which shop is that?"

Gran had given her a lot of information over the years. Addy knew that Noelle had married the handsome Kyle Houseman even though Olivia, her sister, had been dating him only a few months before. She knew that Kyle's proposal had a lot to do with Noelle's pregnancy, and that Noelle had aborted the baby after they were married without telling Kyle, which pretty much destroyed any obligation he'd felt toward her and resulted in their divorce. But she didn't know where Noelle had gone to work. She probably would've learned if she'd returned when Olivia married Kyle's stepbrother, Brandon Lucero. She'd wanted to attend the ceremony. She and Olivia had called and exchanged emails for several months after she left town, but Addy had eventually stopped responding. She'd done what she could to break ties with everyone except Gran and those who helped Gran, like Darlene. She couldn't have too many people drawing her back to Whiskey Creek. . . .

"A Damsel's Delights." Gran smiled when she managed to remember the name of the store. Her mind was mostly sound, despite her age. "They have dresses, handmade jewelry, hats and other accessories."

Addy pictured a quaint-looking shop done up in pink and brown with striped awnings and cute tea tables out front. "Oh, it's a couple of blocks down Sutter Street. I saw it when I drove through on Saturday." Once she'd arrived, she'd wanted to see what had changed while she'd been gone and was relieved to find that there wasn't much she didn't recognize. Set in the foothills of the Sierra Nevada mountains, Whiskey Creek had been founded during the gold rush and, like so many other towns with a similar history, had covered boardwalks, old-fashioned light poles and a bevy of restored Victorians and shops that maintained the nineteenth-century feel.

"She's been running the place since her divorce."

"Why's she working? You told me she stuck Kyle for quite a bit of spousal maintenance."

Gran's voice turned sour. "She took him for everything she could. She wanted him for his money — and to hurt her sister."

"I'm guessing it worked on both counts."

"Sure did. Can't say why she went back to retail. Maybe she doesn't have anything better to do." She clicked her tongue. "I feel sorry for her parents. She's always been such a . . . *difficult* girl."

Which Gran understood, thanks to her own daughter.

"Why is she reaching out to me?" Addy asked.

"She probably needs a friend. Everyone who lives here is on to her."

It wasn't like Gran to dislike anyone, but she clearly disliked Olivia's younger sister. "Olivia lives in town these days, doesn't she?" Addy asked.

"Not far. Brandon owns a cabin up in the mountains. But he won't have anything to do with Noelle, so they don't spend much time together. Her parents aren't pleased that he's drawn such a hard line. They blame him for 'breaking up the family,' but . . . if you ask me, he's doing the right thing." Her hand shook with the usual tremors as she carried Addy's plate to the table. "And I think Olivia's secretly happy about the break."

"After what Noelle did to her, Olivia has every right not to spend much time with her sister. Has Kyle remarried?"

"Not yet."

"Is he seeing anyone?"

"Haven't heard, but somehow I doubt it. He wasn't given any choice when his wife aborted his child. And he lost his true love to his stepbrother. Life has been hard on him."

Addy shifted to relieve the pressure on her sore backside. "He got Olivia's sister pregnant, Gran."

125

"He and Olivia were on a break."

"They hadn't been split up very long. Some people would say he deserved what he got."

"Those people don't know Noelle. She's a life-wrecker, just plain wicked. You should see how shamelessly she flirts with Brandon if she ever runs into him. I've witnessed it at the restaurant, and I'm guessing that's why he won't have anything to do with her. He's not about to let her ruin *his* marriage."

Adelaide took a bite of meat loaf. "It takes two to make a baby." After being married to an adulterer, she wasn't letting Kyle off the hook too easily.

"That's true, but Kyle's paid the price for his mistake. He's a good man." She touched Grandpa Davies's war picture hanging near the stove as if to say he wasn't the last good man, after all. "He stood up and married her even though he knew what he was in for, didn't he? Did it for the baby. That's called taking responsibility for your actions, and it's something I don't see too often these days. Everyone wants to make excuses. Anyway, I like him. I hope he can find a woman who'll treat him right."

"Don't look at me." She lifted her hands in mock protest.

Gran didn't laugh; she scowled. "Why

126

not? Don't you think he's handsome?"

He *was* handsome. But so were his friends. Especially Noah. She had to admit that, despite everything, she still felt a sizzle when he was around. She'd have to be dead *not* to feel *something.* He had that much sex appeal. But she'd gone to great pains to extricate herself from this town. She wasn't about to build any relationships while she was here — not with Noah or Kyle or anyone else.

"He's not bad." She pretended to be intent on stirring gravy into her mashed potatoes when she added, "Do you see him with Noah very often?"

"Oh, yes. They come into the restaurant all the time. To this day, that whole group is the best of friends."

Adelaide had always envied them their closeness. Her class had nothing to rival the clique that had included Cody and Noah, Eve, Cheyenne, Gail, Callie, Ted, Kyle and others. Maybe that was why she'd acquiesced so easily when she was invited to that fateful party. She'd known a lot of popular people would be there. She'd accepted in the hope that Noah and his friends might go, too.

And Cody *had* gone. . . .

"Speaking of Noah, I think we should

invite him over for dinner, to thank him for his help last night, don't you?" Gran said.

Adelaide nearly choked on her food. "I'm sure that's not necessary. He doesn't expect anything."

"Maybe he doesn't *expect* it, but he might enjoy it."

Addy had offered him *something.* She'd been loopy when she'd asked what he wanted as his reward, but she could remember the way he'd looked at her when he'd said, "After the past half hour, that's not a fair question to ask me."

She was glad he hadn't taken her up on anything specific. This way, they could both just . . . let it go.

"Don't you agree?"

When Gran turned to face her, Adelaide set down her fork. "To be honest, I'd rather not see him again. It was awkward when he had to take over for you yesterday. We — we don't really know each other that well."

"Oh, don't be silly." She waved Adelaide's words away. "What are a few slivers? A pretty woman like you . . . I'm sure he didn't mind one bit. But we do owe him. What would've happened to you if not for him?"

She hated to imagine. But . . . he wouldn't have had to save her if not for his twin brother. "Maybe when my scrapes and bruises have healed," she mumbled, hoping that small concession would encourage Gran to leave the matter in her hands.

"Noah's a lot like Kyle."

"He's a cheater?" she teased.

"He's a good man!"

Adelaide wasn't so sure. Cody had seemed just as promising — just as smart, handsome, athletic and even more popular. He'd had such innate ability, could do anything and do it well. She'd experienced the effect he had on others firsthand.

But she didn't want to continue discussing Kyle or Noah. "So what did Noelle bring me?" She didn't see any gifts in the kitchen.

Gran motioned with the spoon she'd just rinsed off. "See for yourself. I put it on the table by the front door."

Eager for a reprieve from the conversation, Addy got up to find that Noelle had left a pretty pink-and-brown sack with tissue paper. Inside was a necklace with a pendant on it that read Courage.

"What is it?" Gran called.

Addy brought the necklace into the kitchen to show her. She liked what Noelle had given her. It buoyed her spirits.

But the gift did nothing to soften Gran's

heart, which was a testament to Noelle's past deeds because Gran's heart wasn't normally hard. She took one look at it and frowned. "Whatever you do, don't trust her."

8

Noah couldn't wait to close up for the night. Once Baxter left, he'd gone to his store, conveniently located about ten yards from his front door, and tried to focus on work. Crank It Up had received a large shipment of mountain bikes, and he'd been training a new tech how to build them in the back while Amy handled the register. He loved tinkering with bikes almost as much as he loved riding them. He also loved to shoot the breeze with the fellow enthusiasts who were his employees and customers. Discussing the summer races and guessing what might happen when he hit the circuit next spring was pretty much the highlight of his off-season.

But today, quitting time couldn't come soon enough. Nearly everyone who came into the store wanted to know more about how he'd found Milly's granddaughter and his theories about why she'd been kidnapped, which kept his own curiosity front and center. He'd heard that Chief Stacy had discovered a knife in the bushes by her bedroom door and was looking for its owner. A weapon showed serious intent. Surely, now she'd stop protecting whoever had hurt her.

Noah wanted to talk to her, make certain. But after locking up for the night, he hesitated about going over to Milly's. He wasn't confident Adelaide would be glad to see him. She hadn't acted as if she liked him very much — until he'd carried her to bed. Then she'd given him that sleepy, "I've got to have *something* you want."

That *could've* been interpreted as flirting, couldn't it?

Even if it wasn't, he chose to take it as evidence that he could, with effort, win her over. After all, she'd found him attractive in high school, and he hadn't changed that much.

Actually, that he hadn't changed *more* sort of bothered him. He knew part of it was his profession. Riding bikes was almost too much fun to take seriously. But it wasn't just that. So many of his friends seemed to be growing up ahead of him. In the past couple of years, Cheyenne, Gail and Callie had all married and settled down. Gail had a stepson and a baby, with another baby on the way. Sometimes he felt his friends were leaving him in the dust. Baxter wasn't married, but he seemed older now, more like the others.

Isn't that what you usually want to talk about? How hot your latest conquest was?

God, was he really that immature?

He didn't want to answer that question, not honestly. He hadn't shared what he'd shared with Baxter just to brag. He'd been trying to fend off the sneaking suspicion that his best friend had a thing for him. That justified his behavior, didn't it? It wasn't as if he talked about the women he dated with anyone else.

Just in case it would make a difference, he drove over to Nature's Way, the closest grocery store, and bought Addy several magazines, along with some candy, crossword puzzles and a couple of five-dollar movies. She probably had all the sweets she could eat. She was living with Milly, after all, who made those decadent desserts for Just Like Mom's. But if he showed up bearing gifts he might be able to convince Addy that he hadn't meant to disappoint her fifteen years ago when he failed to notice she was even alive.

He'd certainly noticed her last night, in

more ways than one. Maybe she'd been unremarkable in high school — shy and awkward — but he could tell, despite her injuries, that she'd improved a great deal since.

Fortunately, her grandmother answered his knock, so he knew he'd at least get inside the door. Milly loved him.

"Noah! How nice of you to come by!"

He cast a surreptitious glance over her gray head but couldn't see Adelaide. "How is she?"

"Holding up. Slept most of the day. But her poor eye." She adjusted her walker to allow the door to open wider. "The swelling's going down but it's all black-and-blue."

"She in bed now?" The thought of being unable to see her disappointed him but Milly shook her head.

"No, she's in my office, on the phone with Ed."

"Ed?" he repeated.

"Hamilton. Over at the paper."

"Of course."

"He's going to print her story. Maybe it'll prompt anyone who saw anything to come forward."

"I hope it does."

"Me, too." She stepped back even farther.

"Come in. She'll be off in a minute."

"I wouldn't want to bother her if she's too tired. . . ."

She scowled at his words. "Don't be silly. You're her knight in shining armor. I'm sure she'd love to say hello."

He doubted he could take Milly's word for it, but he'd come this far. . . .

"Would you like a cup of coffee?"

"No, that's okay."

"Why not? It won't take me long to whip up a fresh pot."

"Well, if you don't mind . . ."

"Of course not." The walker thunked and dragged, thunked and dragged as she left him sitting in the living room and made her way to the kitchen.

After she was gone, if he listened carefully, he could hear Adelaide's voice, drifting out of a room down the hall. She told Ed she had no idea who her assailant was, that he'd been wearing a mask and gloves and, again, she insisted she hadn't been raped. She even downplayed the threats she'd received and the beating. But she couldn't come up with any good reason a man would break into her bedroom just to hit her a few times and drag her off to the Jepson mine. She admitted nothing had been stolen. That led Noah to believe the culprit had to be someone who hated her and was hoping to punish her for something.

His mind returned, once again, to her ex. She'd said it wasn't him, but on those true-crime shows, it was always the husband.

Noah decided to see if he could get the name of the restaurant where she'd worked. Davis was an hour and a half away, but it would be worth the drive if he could meet her ex. Maybe the guy had scraped knuckles or showed some other evidence of having been in a scuffle. That wouldn't be conclusive, but it would give Noah *some* indication whether Chief Stacy and his officers were wasting their time looking for the culprit in Whiskey Creek. And it would solve the mystery of her behavior, which had him baffled.

"Okay, Gran. I talked to Ed," Addy called out after she hung up.

"Good." Milly answered from the kitchen. "Did you mention the knife?"

"Didn't have to. He'd already heard about it."

"From who?"

"Who knows? I guess I'm the talk of the town."

"Probably from Chief Stacy. He's excited to have found it, says it shouldn't be hard to figure out who such a special knife belongs to."

Addy didn't respond, but the floor creaked in the hall, suggesting she was on her way to the living room. Noah wished Milly would hurry and announce his presence.

She did — but it was about two seconds after Addy had seen him.

"Oh! Um, hello!" Eyes wide — even the one that was still swollen — she came to an abrupt stop. "I didn't realize we had company."

Noah couldn't help noticing how much more obvious her bruises had become, especially those on her face. "How are you today?"

"Better. Fine." She smoothed the T-shirt she wore with a pair of cutoff sweats. "Really, there's no need for all the fuss. You shouldn't have troubled yourself to come by. Everyone's making too big a deal out of what happened."

Too big a deal? She could've been killed! "From what I've heard, the guy who assaulted you had a knife."

"A knife was found in the bushes, but . . . that doesn't mean he would've used it. I'm not even sure it belonged to him."

"Putting you in the mine was bad enough, Addy. You know my brother died in there."

The color drained from her face, creating

a starker contrast between those bruises and her regular coloring. "I — I know. I'm sorry. Truly. I wish . . ."

He waited for her to finish.

"I wish that had never happened," she said softly.

She seemed so sincere it was difficult to be annoyed with her, although he didn't understand her obstinate refusal to deal with the man who'd attacked her. He bent his head to catch her eye, since she was no longer looking at him, and held out what he'd bought for her. "I thought some of this might come in handy while you recuperate."

Her eyebrows shot up. "What is it?"

He shrugged. "Just a few things to pass the time."

She seemed reluctant to accept his offering but eventually took the bag and peeked inside. "This is . . . nice of you, really, but . . . completely unnecessary."

He fended her off when she tried to give it back. "Consider it my apology."

"For . . ."

"Being too self-absorbed in high school, I guess." He grinned. "That's what you hold against me, isn't it? That I didn't befriend you or — or remember you or something like that?"

"No! I don't hold anything against you. I'm sorry if I gave the impression that I do."

He clapped. "Great. Then we're friends?"

She toyed with a pendant bearing the word *Courage* hanging from her neck. "Um, sure. Of course. But . . . I won't be staying in Whiskey Creek for long, so . . . I'm not someone you'd want to invest any time in."

This surprised him. "Milly's agreed to sell?"

She glanced over her shoulder to make sure her grandmother was still in the kitchen and lowered her voice. "Not yet, but . . . I can't imagine she'll refuse."

He scratched his head. "So you haven't asked her yet?"

"I will. Soon."

"Even if she says yes, it could take months to accomplish!" he said with an incredulous laugh.

She shifted uncomfortably. "Noah, I . . . I guess what I'm trying to tell you is that I appreciate what you did for me, and I don't want to be rude, but . . . I'm not anyone you'd . . . *like.*"

What? He hadn't even decided he was interested in her, not in that way. "Aren't you assuming too much?"

She flushed. "Maybe. I'm just saying . . . in case."

"In case I planned to ask you out."

"That's right. I wanted to . . . to let you know up-front."

"Wow. You don't even want me to *ask*. That's shutting me down pretty hard."

"We wouldn't be compatible."

"How can you tell? I'm cutting my hair shorter than it was in high school or . . . I don't have my baby face anymore?"

"This isn't about looks."

"It's about personality, then? I've already flunked the personality test?"

"Don't worry. There are a lot of other women in Whiskey Creek who'd be thrilled to —" she smoothed her shirt "— to gain your attention."

Other women. This was another first. Never had he had one woman refer him to others. "Just not you."

She blanched when he stated it so baldly but didn't correct him. "Surely that can't disappoint you. You didn't know who I was until yesterday."

It shouldn't have disappointed him, but somehow it did. He'd given her a sack of junk. How could that be considered coming on too strong? He'd been shooting for "thoughtful." "Can you at least tell me what I've done wrong?"

"Nothing." Her lips curved into a sympathetic smile, but that only made it worse. "You're just . . . not my type."

"Really? Because you don't even know what type I am." Suddenly suspicious, he shoved his hands in the pockets of his jeans. "Wait a second . . ."

"What?"

"Is this your idea of revenge? Are you trying to get back at me for . . . for how I made you feel in high school? Because I haven't met many seniors who'd bother with a sophomore, no matter how smart or pretty she is."

Her mouth dropped open. "I'm not after revenge!"

"You were once interested in me."

She hesitated as if she couldn't decide whether to admit it. "Maybe I had a slight crush —"

"So *slight* that you came to every one of my baseball games and looked like you were about to hyperventilate the one time you dared to approach me?"

"*You remember* — ? Never mind." She raised a hand. "Don't answer. It was embarrassing enough the first time. So I had a *big* crush on you. Okay. I'll give you that. But it's irrelevant. I'm over it, er, *you*. That's ancient history, a stupid schoolgirl fantasy."

"Maybe you think it was stupid now, but

it tells me that you used to find me attractive."

She seemed to be getting flustered. "*Everyone* finds you attractive, Noah. They'd have to be blind not to! But I didn't *know* you, so it's not as if . . . as if . . . it was *real.*"

"You still don't know me. That's my point. Is it that you're embarrassed?"

Her forehead rumpled in confusion. "That I was attacked?"

"That I've seen your ass!"

"Excuse me?"

"I thought it was a nice ass, if that's what you're worried about."

She almost smiled in spite of herself. "Quit trying to charm me."

Apparently oblivious to their argument, Milly called out from the kitchen. "Coffee's ready. But save me the trouble of bringing it out and come in here, will you?"

"I'm sorry," Addy whispered. "I know you're used to getting what you want, but . . . I — I'd appreciate it if you'd leave me alone from now on."

He felt himself gape at her. He'd only stopped by to see if she was okay! "You don't even want to be friends."

"I'm afraid not."

"No one rejects *friendship,*" he said. "It makes you look bad."

She squared her shoulders. "Well, I just did so I'll live with however it makes me look."

"Addy, Noah, are you coming?"

Noah wanted to beg off and get the hell out of there. But he'd put Milly to the effort of making coffee and felt he had to drink it.

"Fine. If that's how you're going to act, I don't want to be friends with you, either." He realized how juvenile that sounded, but he felt younger than he had in a while, and certainly more vulnerable. Circumventing Addy, he strode to the kitchen. "Smells delicious."

If his voice was too curt, Milly didn't seem to notice. Fortunately, she was hard of hearing. Smiling brightly, she handed him a cup and all but shouted, "It's nothing fancy like those fresh-roasted blends, but . . ."

"Thank you."

"Addy?" she called. "You coming?"

Adelaide appeared in the doorway, looking miserable. "I'm here but . . . none for me, Gran."

Milly made shooing motions. "You two have a seat and relax. The night is young. Let's enjoy it. Before Noah leaves, I want him to get out his phone and check his calendar — that's how you young people do it these days, isn't it? — so we can pick a date to have him over for dinner."

Noah glanced up to catch Addy's reaction, and saw her stiffen.

"Noah was just telling me that . . . that he's swamped, Gran," she said. "We wouldn't want him to feel obligated to take time out of his busy schedule."

"Oh, phooey! A man's got to eat, doesn't he?" Milly handed him cream and sugar. "You can make time for us, can't you, Noah?"

Obviously expecting him to follow her lead, Addy tilted her head.

Any sane man would decline Milly's invitation, to protect his ego, if for no other reason. He'd already been flatly rejected — in advance. Even his offer of friendship had been thrown back in his face.

But her reaction to him didn't make any sense, especially considering how she'd once felt. She couldn't even tell him *why* she didn't want to see him again.

"I'll make time," he said. Then he saluted Adelaide with his cup. "When would you like to do it?"

9

A week from Saturday. That was the date they'd settled on. November 2. Then Noah would come to the house again, this time for dinner.

Adelaide couldn't believe he'd had the nerve to accept Gran's invitation, knowing she didn't want him there. For once in her life, she'd tried to be firm, even if it came across as harsh. But her rejection shocked him more than anything else — shocked him enough that he became determined to win her over.

She shouldn't have created a challenge. A man like Noah couldn't resist a challenge. He was a professional athlete, after all, someone conditioned to attack the difficult, to prevail. She should've been all dewy-eyed and swooned over him, as if she hoped to drag him to the altar. Then he would've run away as fast as his muscular legs could carry him.

It was a stupid miscalculation on her part. And now she had to face the prospect of spending an entire evening with him and acting polite because Gran would be there.

She couldn't sit across the dinner table looking at him all evening. Her emotions were too scrambled. She'd spent two whole years fantasizing about him. She'd all but *stalked* him at school, loitering at strategic places in the halls simply because he had to go by there to get to class. And not only did she have the residual pangs of that to deal with, she had to cope with the fact that he reminded her so much of the man who'd changed her life forever.

She wished he'd leave her alone. She needed space. After that graduation party fifteen years ago, she'd spent the summer on pins and needles, trying to appear "normal" while everyone else mourned the loss of Cody and she pretended to do the same. No one had ever confronted her with questions about that night, not even to ask if he was alive when she'd last seen him. Maybe it was too unbelievable that the most popular boy in school would waste his time on a lowly sophomore, because even the people who'd seen her in his company hadn't mentioned her. That included Kevin, Tom, Derek and Stephen, who'd dragged her into a different part of the mine before raping her. They were gone when Cody came back — everyone else was gone — but must have guessed she was the reason he'd returned.

If so, they probably assumed she wouldn't be powerful enough to overcome him. Or they'd decided to keep their mouths shut to preserve their own secret. That was all she could figure.

Regardless, as that summer wore on, people stopped talking about the tragedy and, finally, most of those who'd been present at the party went off to college. Then Addy's life got a little easier. She ran into Cody and Noah's parents occasionally. But she didn't have to live, on a daily basis, with the constant reminder that Noah posed.

She'd been so grateful for the reprieve, so relieved when he left, that she hadn't really missed him. She'd scarcely thought of the girlish desires he'd evoked, even though they'd once consumed her. She'd felt only anxiety, fear and regret when he came to mind.

But now that he'd walked back into her life — or, rather, she'd walked back into his — everything seemed to have reversed itself *again*. Cody wasn't Noah and, despite the family connection and their similarities, she was quite clear on that. Noah hadn't attended the graduation party that had ended so tragically. He'd been with his best friend, Baxter North, at a different party, one that included midnight street hockey instead of alcohol.

"Where are you going?" Gran asked, obviously surprised when Addy scooped up her keys.

"For a drive."

Gran lowered the volume on the TV, which had been blaring to compensate for her lack of hearing. "You feel well enough to do that?"

Addy zipped up the sweatshirt she'd pulled on with a pair of jeans. "I've been cooped up all day and I need to get out of the house."

"But I'm not sure it's safe, not until Chief Stacy catches the person who abducted you," she argued.

"No one will bother me while I'm in my car, Gran. If the man who cut my screen door thinks I'm anywhere, he's going to assume it's here."

Her grandmother didn't like her leaving. Addy could tell by the disapproval on her face. But Gran didn't try to stop her. She was probably afraid to push too hard for fear she'd get the kind of backlash she'd always gotten from Adelaide's high-strung mother. "Don't be gone long, okay? It's almost ten-thirty."

Addy welcomed the late hour. It brought darkness and solitude and a chance to enjoy the crisp fall air. Halloween, one of her favorite holidays, was only a week away. She had so many fond memories of the hayrides and trick-or-treating in this town. She wanted to savor all the good things she associated with Whiskey Creek. She also needed a respite, needed to feel inconspicuous and anonymous and in control of her life, even though her love for Gran was forcing her to give up everything that had insulated her from the past. She'd thought that when she returned, she and Noah would have little or no interaction.

Her Toyota 4-Runner started immediately, but it wasn't running smoothly. Over the past several months, she'd had it in and out of the shop. It was getting old and should be replaced — but she couldn't afford another vehicle right now.

Feeling the engine's rough idle, she wondered if she should venture out. But she couldn't make herself go back inside. She had her heart set on seeing if she could find what they'd hit when she grabbed the steering wheel of her abductor's truck. Whatever it was, they'd smashed into it hard enough to do some damage.

That meant there should also have been an exchange of paint.

Although she'd been pretty disoriented at the time, she knew which way he'd turned out of Gran's drive because she knew where he'd been planning to take her. Anyone heading to the mine from Gran's would go left. Only one road went in that direction — the main road that snaked through town — and they hadn't been in the vehicle long before she caused the accident.

From what she could remember, it was something like . . . an eighth of a mile.

Addy crept along, studying every obstacle on the right-hand side. When she'd grabbed the wheel, she'd jerked it toward her, simply because that was the only way she could use her body weight, and they'd veered into a slight gully before slamming against —

There it was. The cinder-block retaining wall separating the lawn mower shop from Lovett's Bridal.

After a brief check in her rearview mirror, she put on her brakes, but someone was coming up behind her, so she turned into Lovett's and waited for that car to pass before walking over to take a closer look. This had to be the place. She could see the damage. The wall had a big crack in it and streaks of paint — white paint.

Standing back, she took a picture of it with her cell phone. She wasn't sure why. She just wanted some kind of proof that the vehicle Kevin, Tom, Derek or Stephen had used had been white.

Feeling uneasy about being out alone, she hurried back to her 4-Runner. But once she was inside, with her doors locked, she wasn't quite ready to go home. She needed more time to regroup. So she drove through the center of town, past A Room with a View, a B and B that had taken over one of the prettiest Victorians; A Damsel's Delights, which reminded her that she still had to thank Noelle for the necklace she was wearing; 49er Sweets, with its barrels of saltwater taffy; a photography studio called Reflections by Callie, owned by one of Noah's closest friends; Harvey's Hardware; Whiskey Creek Five & Dime and several other stores, most of which hadn't changed since she'd left.

Just Like Mom's was coming up on her right. Other than a few updated Halloween decorations, it hadn't changed, either. Painted a tacky purple, it had a forest of fake flowers stuffed into window boxes that desperately needed to be emptied and cleaned. In order to sell it, she knew she should throw out the contents of those boxes, plant real flowers and give the place a facelift. But she'd come to *help* Gran, not upset her. She had to ease her grandmother into the idea of cutting ties with Whiskey Creek.

The restaurant stayed open until eleven every night except Fridays and Saturdays, when it closed at midnight. Since it was nearly eleven, there weren't many people inside. When she passed she could see Darlene, with her brassy yellow hair, through one of the wide front windows holding a pot of coffee as she made the rounds.

Addy needed to determine how things were going at the restaurant, whether it was even viable to sell, and only Darlene could tell her. But before she dove into the management of the restaurant, she wanted to wait until she wasn't sporting so much evidence of her ordeal.

Maybe she'd go in after the weekend, on Monday.

Beyond the restaurant was Crank It Up, Noah's bike shop. It was as dark as the rest of the businesses, but she parked at the curb and gazed in at the posters she could see, thanks to the streetlights, near the register.

Noah was featured in one of them, wearing a silver, sleek-looking helmet, a Crank It Up bike shirt and black spandex shorts that showed the muscles in his legs as he balanced, at a complete standstill, on a big red boulder. She didn't recognize the cyclists in the other posters, except the autographed one of the disgraced Lance Armstrong.

She leaned forward, studying the Halloween Specials of bike tune-ups and other gear advertised on the windows, the green awning that hung over the walkway and the horse hitch that had been turned into a bike rack out front. Noah seemed to have done well for himself.

Would Cody be a partner in Noah's business if . . . if she hadn't caused that cave-in?

The thought of what she'd cost Noah made her sick. She hadn't meant to kill Cody. She'd been acting out of desperation, pain and humiliation, had merely been trying to get away.

But that didn't change the harsh reality.

With a sigh, she twisted around to look down the street. Normally, she loved the Halloween decorations shop owners put up at this time of year. But tonight the glowing jack-o'-lanterns and gauzy ghosts that adorned so many windows, doors and trees seemed to be jeering at her. The fake cemeteries were even worse, since she knew Cody had been buried just around the bend, in the real cemetery located next to the only "haunted" B and B in the Sierra Nevada foothills.

She wondered if the newly dubbed Little Mary's really had a ghost — because if the girl who'd been killed in 1871, possibly by her own father, could come back, maybe Cody could, too.

Feeling a chill, she rubbed her arms. She didn't need Cody's ghost to frighten her. His four live friends posed enough of a risk.

She imagined Kevin, Stephen, Tom and Derek sitting at home, watching TV with wives or girlfriends who had no idea that they'd raped a girl when they were younger. What would *she* do if she were one of those women? If she learned that the man she loved, the man who slept with her at night, had done something so heinous?

You tell anyone about graduation and I'll kill you. I'll stab the old lady, too.

One of those men was frightened that word would get out. They should all be frightened by the possible consequences. In California, there was no statute of limitations on aggravated rape, and aggravated rape included rape by more than one person. It'd been fifteen years, but they could still go to prison.

The only problem was . . . if she came forward, *she'd* have to face the consequences of her actions, too. And, even though part of her felt terribly guilty about Cody's death, the psychologist who'd helped her recover, once she got out of school and had the money for therapy, insisted that none of it had been her fault. Dr. Rosenbaum said she'd been naive not to be more careful about the company she kept. But sixteen-year-olds were often too innocent for their own good. She'd said that Addy had done nothing to deserve what had happened, nothing to provoke them. Dr. R. also said she was required to report the assailants, but since Addy refused to give their names, that hadn't gone very far.

Anyway, Addy knew she'd never speak up as long as Gran was alive, even if she decided to do so later. Dr. Rosenbaum had agreed that dragging it all to the forefront would probably do her more harm than good, since there was no guarantee that justice would be done, so she didn't press her for the information.

After starting her truck, she drove two blocks over, to the high school. She was sitting there, staring at the stone face of the main hall and the words *Eureka High* when

155

she noticed headlights coming up behind her.

A moment of panic made her heart skip a beat. She was afraid she should've listened to Gran once again, until she saw the police decal on the side of the door.

Sagging in relief, she rolled down her window as Chief Stacy pulled alongside her.

"There you are," he said. "Your grandmother told me you were out, but damned if I could find you."

"You've been looking for *me*?"

He smiled. "I have great news."

Addy tightened her grip on the steering wheel. Given that he was searching for a man she didn't want caught, she wasn't sure his idea of good news would match hers.

His next words confirmed it. "I've found the owner of that knife."

She imagined, as she so often had, what it would be like if the whole nasty truth came out. Some of the citizens of Whiskey Creek would take sides, probably a lot of them. She'd have her champions, but she'd also have her detractors, people who remained stubbornly loyal to the men who'd raped her. Noah and his family would likely go into denial and refuse to believe Cody could do such a thing. They'd be furious that she'd dare besmirch his memory. And if the case went to trial, the defense attorneys would do all they could to portray her as asking for what she got by dressing too scantily, or coming on to Cody, or . . . something.

Maybe it wouldn't even go to trial. She could *claim* they'd raped her, but how would she prove it at this late date?

Nothing was ever cut-and-dried, especially in a small town like this, where the Rackhams and their friends held so much sway. Only one thing was certain: no one would come out of it unscathed.

"Who —" she cleared her throat "— who is it?"

"Officer Jones went to pick him up. They'll meet us at the station." He jerked a thumb over his shoulder. "I'd like you to come see for yourself, see if anything about him is familiar from that night."

Aaron Amos?

Addy almost sank to the ground in relief when she saw who was sitting in the hard, plastic chair at the police station. There was no way Aaron could be the man who'd attacked her. He had no connection to what had happened in the mine, hadn't even been invited to the party.

"You have the wrong man," she said

before Chief Stacy could ask.

"What?" He signaled for Officer Jones, who'd been sitting with Aaron, to step aside.

"It can't be him," she insisted. He'd have no way of knowing about the night Cody died, much less have a reason for dragging her back to where it had occurred. Besides, she hardly knew Aaron. Although they'd been in the same grade, they'd been on opposite ends of the social spectrum. She'd been a straight-A student, at the top of her class; he'd gotten himself kicked out of school several times for fighting or ditching, and barely managed to graduate. They'd had no real interaction. She couldn't think of a less likely culprit.

"Told you I didn't do it." Aaron stood as if to walk out, but Stacy blocked the exit.

"Hold on a sec. You sit down. We're not through here."

"Of course we aren't," Aaron responded. "Any time you can think of an excuse to harass me, you do it."

"You're going to get yourself into even more trouble if you don't shut your damn mouth," Stacy warned.

Aaron plopped back in his seat. He was bigger than Addy remembered, and still handsome in a rebel sort of way — but edgier, more hard-bitten and angry. He was, after all, one of the Fearsome Five, as the Amos boys had come to be called. Ever since their father went to prison for knifing a man during a bar fight, they'd been left to shift for themselves. Dylan, the oldest, had dropped out of school at eighteen and taken over his father's auto body shop. He'd managed to turn the business around and keep his brothers together — and now that they were older, he kept them employed — but he hadn't managed to steer them out of trouble. There was some question as to whether he'd tried very hard; before his marriage to Cheyenne, he'd often been a participant. Addy had been living in Davis an hour and a half away and yet she knew Aaron and his brothers had been arrested from time to time. Ed *loved* to report on the hell-raising Amoses.

Chief Stacy turned to her. "How do you know it's not him? This son of a bitch has always been a troublemaker."

"That doesn't make him guilty of abducting me."

"He owns the knife I found in your plants." He lifted the knife from the center of the table, as if seeing it might remind her of how damning this evidence was. "Who else could it be?"

Addy could understand why Stacy would

159

like Aaron to be responsible. That made for a quick, easy answer. Stacy was dying to teach the Amoses a lesson, to show them who was boss in this town. But Aaron wasn't a kidnapper or a would-be rapist. Other than a minor bar fight, he'd never been arrested for anything violent, which was how he'd always escaped with fines or community service. Stacy thought he finally had him dead to rights and could really see him punished.

"I — I can just tell." For a second, she wondered if Kevin, Tom, Stephen or Derek had put him up to it for money or whatever. But he wasn't the type to be anyone's pawn. Whoever had awakened her wasn't that tough or embittered. Her kidnapper had been too frightened of his own actions. *Stop it! I — that's not who I am,"* he'd said in a tortured, pleading whine.

Aaron would not have behaved that way.

"The man who took me didn't have a distinctive voice, but he didn't have Aaron's voice, either," she said.

The police chief pulled out the chair he'd commandeered from Officer Jones, essentially telling her the same thing he'd just told Aaron — *have a seat because we're not finished yet.*

"You need to take your time and think

this through," he cautioned. "Memories can be tricky. And, like I said, we've got hard evidence linking him to the crime scene. This knife belongs to him. I've had several people tell me so." He angled his head in Aaron's direction. "He even admits it, says it was a Christmas gift from his older brother."

Aaron's eyes narrowed into slits whenever they focused on the chief of police, but he didn't seem to feel strongly about her. Thank goodness. That gaze, and the tension in his body, reminded her of a snake, tightly coiled and ready to strike.

"Someone must've taken it out of my jockey box," he told her. "I didn't even know it was gone until this bozo —" he indicated Jones, who stood behind them "— showed up at Sexy Sadie's and used finding that knife as an excuse to pull me out of the bar. I certainly didn't threaten you with murder, and I'd *never* threaten an old lady. I might be an asshole, but I'm not that kind of asshole."

She believed him, but the same couldn't be said for the police. Stacy seemed convinced he'd already solved the case.

"How do you know Milly was threatened if you weren't there?" he asked.

Aaron made a sound of incredulity.

"You're kidding, right? *Everyone* knows. We live in a small town, which is why you get to run around pretending to be so damn important."

"I told you to watch your mouth —"

Addy broke in, before the situation could escalate. "What color is his vehicle?"

They blinked at each other. "He drives a black truck. Why?" Stacy asked.

"I thought it might be a car," she lied. "Anyway, this isn't going anywhere, Chief. He's not the one. He — he would have no reason to do what the real culprit did to me."

The police chief scowled at her. "He intended to rape you. That's the reason."

Aaron kicked the table. "I didn't even know Adelaide was back in town! Anyway, why would I need to rape anyone? The night she was abducted I was in bed with Shania Carpenter."

Addy felt her jaw drop. "Cody Rackham's girlfriend?"

"Cody's been gone a long time." He shrugged and gave her a half grin. "She's still crying over him, and she'd rather have his brother if she can't have him, but I don't mind. Makes me feel safe, I guess," he added with a chuckle. "Anyway —" sobering, he addressed Stacy again "— she was at my place the whole night. She'll vouch for me."

"So how'd your knife end up in Milly's flower bed?" Stacy demanded.

"I told you. Someone must've taken it out of my truck."

"Who?"

"How the hell should I know? Anyone could've done it. I never lock my truck. Never felt the need. Most people don't want to run the risk of what I'll do to them if I catch them stealing from me. And I park all over town — at Sexy Sadie's, the body shop, my place. . . ."

"Where is he?"

A determined, quietly menacing voice intruded, coming from the entrance of the building. Addy looked through the inside window to see Dylan Amos stalking through the reception area like a bull charging at a red flag.

His hair was mussed on one side, and she guessed he'd been in bed when he received the call that his brother had been taken to the police station. Under different circumstances, showing up so rumpled might've made him look boyish, even harmless, but the rock-hard set of his jaw and the flintiness of his eyes convinced her that if he chose to unleash his anger, he'd be anything but harmless.

Someone who'd seen Aaron get arrested at Sexy Sadie's must've alerted him, she thought. Addy didn't get the impression Aaron had been afforded his one call. That might be part of what had Dylan so furious.

"In here, Dyl!" Aaron shouted, but he seemed more upset, rather than less, that his brother was now involved.

Dylan strode past Officer Willis, who made a half-hearted attempt to stop him but didn't succeed. Once beyond that first line of defense, Dylan came into the small interrogation room as if he had every right, even shouldered Officer Jones to one side. "What the hell's going on this time?" he asked Stacy.

The police chief raised his hands in a placating manner but his voice took on a warning note. "Settle down, Dylan. This has nothing to do with you."

"It does if it involves my brother." Dylan's gaze settled on Aaron. "What'd you do?"

Aaron sighed as he raked his fingers through his hair. "Nothing. But they're calling it a lot of things. Kidnap. Assault. Attempted rape. They're coming up with anything they can."

Dylan's hands curled into fists. *"Rape?"*

Aaron's eyes flicked to those closed fists,

but he didn't flinch. He sat taller. "I didn't do it."

"That's serious shit, Aaron," his brother said. "I won't stand by you if you've fallen that low."

"What are you talking about?" Aaron jumped to his feet. "If you want to hit me, then hit me, damn it! We'll go at it right here. But I swear to God, Dyl. You know me. I'd *never* hurt a woman."

Dylan studied him as if he was weighing what he heard with what he knew of his brother. Then, apparently coming to the conclusion that Aaron was telling the truth, he relaxed and turned to Stacy. "He didn't do it."

"We don't know that."

"*I* do. So the way I see it, you have two choices, Chief. Either charge him, at which point he'll lawyer up, make bail and be released. Or let him go."

Stacy hated Dylan even more than Aaron. Addy could feel the animosity in the room. So could Officer Jones, as well as Officer Willis, who'd followed him as far as the doorway. They both fidgeted nervously. It was a cardinal sin to make Chief Stacy appear foolish. But Addy believed Dylan understood enough about the criminal justice system to know he was correct. If

Stacy was going to charge Aaron, Aaron had the right to an attorney. If he wasn't going to charge him, and Aaron refused to talk, Stacy needed to let him go.

She held her breath while she waited, hoping Stacy would back off. All he had as evidence was a pocket-knife that'd been discovered in the wrong place. That knife didn't have any fingerprints on it. Unless they found forensic proof that Aaron had been in her room, or an eyewitness who saw him with her that night, the prosecutor wouldn't have enough to make a case, especially if Shania backed up Aaron's alibi.

"You've got the wrong man," she said again. "I think . . . I think you should let him go, Chief."

A bead of sweat ran from Stacy's hair. It wasn't hot in the room, but he was overweight and in a rage.

"Fine," he snapped. "Go. For now. But this isn't over. I plan to talk to Shania immediately, and she sure as hell better tell me the truth."

"You know where she lives." Aaron tossed them all a taunting grin and swaggered out.

Dylan remained a few seconds longer, shaking his head at the police chief. "Really?" he said. "This has to get personal?"

Stacy hooked his thumbs in his belt. "That boy's a bad seed."

A muscle flexed in Dylan's cheek. "He'll get his life figured out."

The police chief toyed with Aaron's knife, which Aaron hadn't even tried to take. He probably knew he couldn't. It was tagged as evidence. "If not, someday he'll wish he had."

"I'll tell him that. Your approval means a lot — to all of us."

If Addy had been in a laughing mood, she might've chuckled at Dylan's sarcasm.

Stacy said something under his breath, but Dylan ignored him and looked at her. "I'm sorry about what happened to you."

She'd never known the oldest Amos. He was four years her senior, had been out of high school by the time she was a freshman. She only knew what she'd heard. Not much of it had been good, but she liked him in spite of that. "I'm going to be okay."

He gave her an approving nod. "Way to fight," he said and, with that, he joined Aaron, who was waiting in the anteroom.

Once they left, Stacy shoved a chair into the wall. "You'll be sorry if you just caused me to release the guilty party," he railed.

Addy stood. "He *isn't* the guilty party."

"Even if Shania claims they were together,

I'm not sure I can rely on that, not if she cares about him."

"It wasn't just his alibi that convinced me. I knew it wasn't him from the beginning, remember?"

He scowled at her. "How?"

She had to look away. She was afraid he'd guess that she wasn't entirely supportive of his efforts. "Not only did he sound wrong, he smelled wrong, too."

"Smell. We're going by smell?"

"The kidnapper's cologne. It was distinctive."

"In what way?"

"I can't explain it. But I'll know if I ever smell it again."

"Maybe he wasn't wearing it tonight."

"It would still linger. . . ."

He hesitated, then cursed under his breath. "Okay, for now we'll see how your instincts and memories work out. But one way or another, I'll catch the bastard who kidnapped you. And if it's one of the Amos boys, then all the better."

Addy left after that. She didn't want to be around Chief Stacy anymore. He was *too* zealous, *too* determined. And he obviously had an agenda of his own.

She'd been worried that he'd charge the *right* person. But what if he charged the *wrong* person? For her, the effect would be the same, wouldn't it? If he tried to build a case against Aaron Amos she'd have to come forward. She couldn't sit idly by and let him destroy an innocent man's life.

10

It wasn't easy to see her from where he stood, deep in the shadow of the snack bar, but he couldn't walk out into the open because he didn't want to be noticed. The fact that Adelaide Davies was already out of the house, jogging around the high school track as if nothing had happened, troubled him. He'd hoped to make more of an impression on her.

Had he not scared her sufficiently?

He wasn't even sure how much damage he'd done. Although he'd tried, he hadn't been able to get a good glimpse of her face — not since that night. He'd heard she was pretty beat-up. He hadn't intended to hurt her, but when she'd nearly torn off her blindfold, he'd panicked. Then she'd made things worse by grabbing the steering wheel and causing him to hit that retaining wall. His truck was at a body shop right now, getting fixed. He'd had to take it all the way to

Sacramento. They were backed up, but the sooner they finished it, the better. The wall he'd hit was very close to Milly Davies's house. If he'd left some paint on that retaining wall, and someone decided to check it against his vehicle, he could be in trouble. But he had no idea how to get the paint off, not from such a porous substance, and he didn't dare try for fear someone would see him doing it.

With a sigh, he took a sip of the coffee he'd purchased just before noticing Adelaide's 4-Runner at the intersection. It'd been fifteen years. Why'd she have to come back?

What had happened at that graduation party might not have been pleasant, but she'd obviously recovered. She was beautiful, maybe even stunning, bruises or no. And look at her run.

She was fine — no worse for wear.

Cody, on the other hand . . .

"Hey, what's up? What are you doing here?"

Startled, he glanced over to see Joyce Weatherby, one of the teachers at Eureka High, out with her dog.

"Just enjoying the weather," he said, and walked back to his car before he could bump into anyone else.

"So what's Addy like these days?"

This question came from Ted Dixon, one of the ten or so friends Noah met at Black Gold Coffee on Friday mornings. Most of them had known one another since grade school. But the dynamic was slowly changing as people got married and had kids. Today's was a small gathering. Only five, including himself. Gail, Simon and their two children were on location in northern Alberta, where Simon was working on his latest movie. Callie and her new husband had just left for their slightly belated honeymoon. Sophia DeBussi rarely came out since Ted had offended her during the summer. Even Cheyenne and Dylan, who'd married last February, weren't here today.

That left Riley, a single father; Eve, whose family owned Little Mary's "haunted" B and B, where she and Cheyenne both worked; Kyle, the only divorced member; and Baxter, the only gay member.

If he *was* gay . . . Noah wasn't going to ask. Why would he? That would just make him feel weird about all the times they'd gone skinny-dipping together, crashed in his bedroom after a party or showered at the gym.

"She's . . . filled out," he admitted with a wry grin.

The others laughed as Eve elbowed him. "Leave it to you to notice *that.*"

"It's obvious!"

"So she's pretty?" Kyle asked.

Noah wasn't thrilled by that question. He didn't want to incite the interest of his single friends. Although he couldn't figure out why, he was already at a deficit when it came to Addy. "Maybe." He added a non-committal tone to his voice. "Hard to tell with all the swelling and bruising."

"I can't remember her," Ted said. "What does she look like?"

"Tall and thin," Noah told him. "Has blond, wavy hair. Comes just below her shoulder blades." She had a nice ass, too, but he didn't say that. While he hadn't thought much about seeing her bare bottom while extracting those slivers, he was beginning to feel differently about it now.

"She should've become a model," Eve said. "What is she? Five eleven? Six feet?"

"She's at least six feet," Noah replied. "And she's a chef."

The barista called Baxter's name and he went to get his chai tea.

"How long is she planning to stay?" Riley asked.

Noah shrugged. "She told me she's here to help her grandmother. I guess she'll stay until she feels she's . . . done enough."

Baxter returned with his tea and fell back into the conversation as if he'd never been gone. "Will she take over the restaurant?"

"She didn't act like she was going to fire Darlene, if that's what you mean." He dared not say more in case Addy hadn't made her wishes clear to Milly yet.

Ted sipped his cappuccino, ruining the perfect heart the barista had created in the foam. "She's not married?"

Noah wasn't sure Addy wanted everyone to know about her divorce. Regardless, he didn't want news of it to come from him, so he opted for a simple *no.*

Eve stuck a straw in her orange juice. "Some guys are intimidated by tall women, won't even ask them out."

Noah wasn't intimidated. He *loved* tall women, especially if they were confident in their height. But he'd always been tall himself, so maybe that was why. "How well do you remember her from high school?" he asked Eve.

"We had calculus together." She took a bite of her bran muffin. "She's smart. I can tell you that. She often tutored kids who were struggling. The teacher recommended her to me and happened to mention that she'd been invited to move two years ahead when she was in eighth grade."

"She would've graduated with us!" Riley said.

"Why didn't she do it?" Ted asked.

Eve brushed the crumbs from her muffin into a small pile. "There were too many other things going on in her life."

"Like . . ." Noah was more curious than he wanted to be.

"Her mother was . . . flighty and self-indulgent. Addy was embarrassed by her behavior. She also hated feeling she wasn't as important as all the other things her mother pursued. She just wanted to live a conventional life and go through school the way most people did."

Riley rested his elbows on the table. "What kind of 'things' did her mother pursue?"

"Men, mostly." Eve lowered her voice so the other patrons couldn't overhear. "She kept leaving Adelaide with Milly for longer and longer periods of time. It got to the point that she'd only come back to town when she was going through another split or was down on her luck."

"Hi, everyone!"

They glanced up as Olivia and Brandon approached the table, then shifted to make room for them. Olivia and Brandon hadn't been part of the original group, but they'd recently started coming on Fridays. Noah doubted their presence was particularly enjoyable for Kyle. Although he'd screwed up his relationship with Olivia and deserved to lose her, he'd been in love with her since Noah could remember, and now she was with his stepbrother.

In spite of that, Kyle didn't seem to hate Brandon as much as he had when they were growing up. Noah was pretty sure Kyle was the one who'd initially invited them to this weekly ritual.

"How's Adelaide, Noah?" Olivia took a seat while Brandon went to place their order. "I've tried calling Milly's twice, and got a busy signal both times."

Noah slid his coffee to the left to give her more space for whatever she was having. "We were just talking about her. I think she'll be okay."

"I was telling them about her mother," Eve volunteered.

Olivia made a face. "Mrs. Simpson — I think that was her name two or three marriages ago — wasn't much to be proud of.

Addy always preferred Milly."

Brandon returned with a receipt and sat on the edge of his chair, since he'd have to get up again when their order was ready. "We're talking about Adelaide?"

"Isn't everyone, after what happened?" Eve said.

"What's up with her?" he asked.

"That's what we're trying to figure out," Riley replied.

"If she loved being with Milly so much, why'd she stay away so long?" Baxter asked. "I don't think she's been back even once in all the years since she left."

"If she has, *I* haven't seen her," Eve said.

Noah stretched out his legs. "You two didn't stay in touch?"

"Us? Not really. We didn't know each other all that well." She tossed the paper from her straw at him. "I spent most of my time with you guys."

Olivia used a napkin to wipe a few drops of cream from the table. "Addy and I were probably better friends, since we were in the same class. At one point we were pretty close but then she sort of . . . changed."

Bringing his feet in, Noah sat up. "In what way?"

"She became quiet, reflective, hard to reach. I don't know, she just . . . closed up.

Then we both graduated and left for college, and I hardly ever heard from her after that."

"Do you know where she was working before coming here?"

Olivia blinked at him. "Are you about to tell me?"

"No, I'd like to find out."

"I have no clue," she said. "Why do you care?"

Noah wanted to learn why she'd been attacked, and why she was so determined to downplay it. And since she was new in town, he thought those answers might lie in where she'd been before. "Just curious."

"I guess you'll have to ask her," Eve said. "It doesn't sound like she kept in touch with anyone."

Noah nodded as if that was a possibility, and the conversation moved on to Riley. Riley had received another letter from his son, Jacob's, mother. Phoenix had spent Jacob's entire life in prison. She'd even delivered him as a convict, at which point Riley and his family took custody.

"I wish she'd leave me alone," he said with a grimace.

Ted raised an eyebrow at him. "Have you asked her to?"

"I have. She claims she's only staying in

touch because of Jacob. She swears she's a changed person, that she'll be a good mom, that she just wants to know her son."

Noah was sort of glad Dylan wasn't here today. He fell silent whenever the subject of Phoenix came up because he could identify with the dread Riley was feeling. Dylan's father had been in prison even longer than Phoenix and, if J. T. Amos made parole, he'd be out next summer, too.

"You don't believe her?" Baxter asked.

Riley took a second to answer. "To a point I do. I mean . . . I'd feel the same if I were her."

"You can't judge the situation according to how *you'd* feel," Ted said. "She could be using Jacob as an excuse to get close to you again."

"No." Riley shook his head. "What we had was way back in high school and it was brief even then. I'm sure she's over it, especially after all this time. How long were we together? A few weeks?"

Ted threw aside an empty sugar packet. "Long enough for her to become so infatuated and obsessed that she ran down the next girl you dated."

Riley raked a hand through his hair. "She wasn't thinking straight. She was pregnant, and she hadn't told me or anyone else."

"That's no excuse," Ted pointed out. "She was different back then, and she might still be different. You have to remember that prison isn't a cure-all for someone who's not right in the head."

"True," Brandon said. "Most people get more screwed up when they go inside."

"I realize that," Riley conceded. "But . . . she regrets what she did. She's apologized a million times. In every letter."

They called Brandon's name and he headed to the counter.

"How does that change anything?" Ted asked Riley.

Riley jammed his plastic spoon into his yogurt. "I'm not sure it does. That's the problem. I don't want to be hard-hearted or unfair, but . . . I wish she'd go somewhere else when she gets out. I can't believe it'll be good for Jacob to have someone with her history suddenly enter his life, even if she is his mother. *Especially* if she is his mother."

Olivia seemed the most compassionate, but she hadn't been as close to Riley when this was happening as the rest of them, so she wasn't as firmly on his side. "Does Jacob *want* to get to know her? Has he been writing to her?"

"Maybe he would if I gave him her letters. But . . . I'm afraid to pass them along." He rocked back on his chair, balancing against the back wall. "I mean . . . Ted's right. What if she's as unbalanced as she was fifteen years ago?"

"What if she's *worse*?" Kyle said.

Kyle knew a little about unbalanced females. He'd been married to Noelle, after all. But no one was going to say that in front of her sister. Maybe Olivia didn't get along with Noelle, but they were family.

Brandon slid a bagel over to his wife, and she gave him a dazzling smile, one that said she was as much in love as the day they got married.

Kyle flinched, but then he looked away, cleared his throat and asked Riley what his parents had to say about the situation.

"They don't want us to have anything to do with her." Riley dropped his chair back on all fours. "And I feel they have the right to weigh in, since they cared for Jacob during his first year. I was too young, didn't know what to do with a baby. I couldn't have gotten by without them."

Olivia slipped an arm around her husband. "And Phoenix is going to be released *this* summer?"

"If she doesn't get into another fight and have to serve *more* time."

Brandon had just taken a bite of his wife's

181

bagel but he spoke around it. "She *fights*?"

"She claims she was jumped the last time, but . . . who knows?" Riley grumbled.

"I guess the moral is . . . be careful who you sleep with," Ted said dryly.

Riley didn't appreciate his remark. "Thanks for your advice, fifteen years after the fact, Ted. But I was seventeen when I made that mistake. That's only three years older than Jacob is now. Anyway, I honestly can't regret bringing him into my life."

Eve smiled at him. "Of course not. We all love Jacob."

"Jacob was about the *only* good thing to come out of that year," Baxter said.

They'd lost Cody not long after Phoenix hit and killed Lori Mansfield with her mother's car. Noah knew Baxter was referring to his brother's death, but he didn't like the reminder. Neither did he like the way everyone turned to him, wearing sympathetic expressions. He was tempted to pretend he hadn't even heard Baxter, but they were all expecting him to make *some* comment.

"Hard to believe it's been fifteen years," he mumbled. "Seems like yesterday."

"I know. Jacob grew up almost overnight," Riley said. "Or maybe it just feels that way because I'm still not married," he added with a weak laugh.

Eve twirled a lock of her silky dark hair. "I've been feeling my biological clock ticking away, too. As a group, we're pretty late to the marriage party."

"Maybe I'm glad I haven't always been part of the group," Olivia teased.

Noah would've pointed out that she'd only been married a short time, but Eve distracted him by clutching his arm. "That's *her,* isn't it?"

He twisted around to see who'd walked into the coffee shop and spotted Adelaide. She was wearing a pair of sunglasses, probably to hide her black eye because it wasn't that bright outside, and a jogging outfit. Both her clothes and her hair were damp, suggesting she'd been working out, but she was carrying a laptop.

"That *is* her," Olivia confirmed. "I wouldn't have expected her out and about so soon."

Riley whistled under his breath. "Looks like she's back on her feet to me."

Noah didn't respond. Addy froze when she saw him. For a second, he thought she might turn around and head right back out the door. She hadn't been happy when he'd more or less cornered her into having him over for dinner next week. He felt bad about that, but not bad enough to cancel.

Instead of leaving, as she seemed tempted to do, she raised one hand in a quick, obligatory wave. Then she averted her gaze and approached the counter.

Ted leaned to one side, obviously hoping to get a better look at her. "She's pretty, all right."

Noah shot him and Riley a scowl. "Don't get any ideas."

"*You're* interested?" Ted said.

"Of course he's interested," Baxter grumbled. "He hasn't slept with her yet."

Noah shot *him* a look, too, but for an entirely different reason. That had sounded so . . . *jealous.*

"Come on, Noah." Riley winked at him. "Why not let me save her the heartbreak of getting involved with you?"

"I'm not going to break her heart!" he said. But he had a terrible feeling that this might be the girl who could break his.

Ugh! How could she have forgotten?

Addy wanted to kick herself. Noah had mentioned that he met up with his friends on Fridays at the coffee shop. She'd had no idea what time, of course, or how long they stayed, but had she realized there'd be a chance of running into him, she wouldn't

184

have stopped at Black Gold.

Maybe she would've remembered if he'd been the only thing on her mind. Needless to say, he wasn't. She'd gone to the high school track to run, where there were plenty of other people. She'd thought that might make her feel safe, but she'd been looking over her shoulder the entire time, fearing that the man who'd confronted her in her bed might accost her again. She wouldn't have come out of the house at all — part of her wanted to hole up and hide away, at least during the day when she felt so exposed — except she refused to let the men who'd raped her limit her life to such a degree. She needed to establish a normal routine, especially if she was going to be here for a while. The longer she put it off, the more resistant she'd feel about circulating in public.

It wasn't easy to move on as if nothing had happened. She had to deal with questions, expressions of alarm and surprise from almost everyone she encountered. And seeing Noah only made a tense morning worse. He looked so good sitting there. Far more handsome than he had any right to look — to her, anyway. She didn't want to admire him. What did it matter if he was handsome? Or nice? He couldn't be part of

185

her life. If she accepted him, even as a friend, he'd be a constant reminder of everything she was struggling to forget.

And just think how betrayed *he'd* feel if he ever found out how his brother had really died.

Careful to avoid his gaze, she ignored him as well as those who were with him, and tapped her fingers on the counter while waiting for her latte. She'd brought her laptop, hoping to take a peek at www.Skin tightEntertainment.com. But now she wasn't even going to sit down, let alone log on. She just wanted to grab her latte and go, get out of there before she had to engage Noah or anyone else in conversation.

Come on, come on, come on, she chanted silently, but the barista didn't fill her order fast enough. The next thing she knew, Olivia Lucero and Eve Harmon were at her side.

"Addy, it's so great to have you back," Olivia said.

Pretending to be pleased to see them, Addy turned and suffered through two embraces — awkward, given that she was holding her laptop and purse. "Thank you. It — it's good to be home," she lied.

Eve gave her a sympathetic smile. "I'm sorry about what happened."

Addy checked to see if the barista had her

drink ready. Not yet. How long could it take to make a latte? "Crazy, isn't it?"

"Beyond crazy!" Eve exclaimed. "Especially here. That kind of thing doesn't happen in Whiskey Creek."

She wished that was truly the case. "At least . . . at least I wasn't seriously hurt." She'd already spoken the same platitudes several times. It was the only way to satisfy everyone and, she hoped, get life back to normal.

"I bet you're glad Noah was there when you needed someone," Eve said.

Addy told herself not to look over, but her eyes shifted in Noah's direction in spite of herself. He hadn't gotten up. He was watching her from across the room, but that was enough to put the old flutter in her stomach. She'd been so sure she was over him, that the melting sensation she'd always experienced when he was around couldn't survive what Cody had done.

That wasn't true at all.

"Yes, it was . . . kind of him."

Olivia softened her voice. "I hope they catch the guy who . . . who hurt you. He deserves to be put away. It's scary to think there's a would-be rapist in town."

"He *didn't* rape me!"

She realized she'd stated it too emphatically when Olivia hurried to reassure her. "I know. But that was his intent, wasn't it?"

"Hard to say *what* he wanted." Wishing she could go, Addy reached into her purse for her keys and accidentally dropped the wallet she'd taken out.

Eve picked it up and handed it back. "The knife Chief Stacy found should help — if they can figure out who it belongs to."

Addy refastened the snap that had come open on her wallet and slid it into her purse. "They already know who it belongs to."

Olivia's eyes went wide. "They do?"

"That didn't take long," Eve said. "Whose is it?"

Addy decided she might as well share the news. It'd circulate through town whether she spoke up or not. "Aaron Amos's."

"It's *Aaron's*?" Eve covered her mouth.

"Does Dylan know?" Olivia looked over at their friends before nudging Eve. "Maybe that's why he and Cheyenne didn't come this morning."

"I know Aaron's been . . . troubled and Dylan's been worried about him," Eve said. "But surely he wouldn't —"

"No," Addy assured them. "It wasn't Aaron. I mean . . . it *was* his knife. He admits that much. But he's not the one who attacked me."

"You're *sure*?"

She was hugging her laptop so tightly it was cutting into her biceps. "Positive. He kept it in his truck. Someone must've stolen it."

Olivia seemed even more shocked. "Wow, I was sort of hoping it was a . . . a spur-of-the-moment attack. Somehow that's less frightening than thinking someone, someone we probably know, plotted it all out."

"Stealing a knife to commit a crime — basically setting someone up — that takes a lot of forethought," Eve agreed.

Addy rearranged all the stuff in her arms. "It wouldn't be hard to set Aaron up. His reputation makes him an easy target."

"Especially if it was possible to get hold of his knife," Olivia said. "How do you know it wasn't him?"

"He was with Shania Carpenter."

Eve stepped back. "*Shania?* Has she finally given up on Noah?"

"She was after *Noah*?" Addy asked.

"If she couldn't have Cody," Eve told her.

Olivia looked perplexed. "So are Aaron and Shania together now?"

Addy shook her head. "I don't get that impression."

"I'm just glad he has an alibi," Eve said. "And I'm sure Dylan and Cheyenne will be happy about it, too. But . . . if it wasn't Aaron who attacked you . . . who was it?"

"The police are still trying to figure that out."

At last, the barista turned and set her latte on the counter. "Here you go," he said with a smile.

"Thank you." She took it and began to leave, but Olivia blocked her path.

"Hey, why don't you join us? We'd all love to talk to you. Noah was just saying he'd like to know where you worked before coming here. Maybe you can tell us what you've been up to for the past decade or so."

Her eyes darted back to the group at the table. "Noah wanted to know *what*?"

Olivia seemed to realize she'd said something she shouldn't. "We're all curious about where you've been and what you've been doing. We've missed you."

Addy cleared her throat. "That's so nice of you to say. And I — I'd love to join you, but . . . another time?" She lifted the only arm that had any range of movement to gesture at her clothes. "Look at me. I've been jogging and . . . I need a shower."

"Oh, right." Olivia nodded and apparently chose not to mention that she was holding her laptop, which would've led anyone to believe she'd planned to stay, at least long enough to check her email. "No problem."

"How about next week?" Eve pressed. "We come every Friday."

Addy braced her cup against her body with one arm as she inched closer to the door. "Sure, except . . . I'll be helping out at the restaurant by then. That's why I'm in town. But . . . I'll certainly come if I can."

Pushing the door open with her back, she raised the same arm in what would've been a wave if she'd had a free hand and pivoted toward her car. But in her rush to get out, she nearly ran into someone who was coming in from outside.

And when her eyes lifted to the man's face, she recognized him.

11

Adelaide would've known Kevin Colbert anywhere, because he didn't look that different. He had the same straight black hair, dark eyes and Roman nose. Pockmarks and a heavier shadow of beard growth had replaced the acne he'd struggled with as a teen, but he wasn't *bad*-looking. The girls had liked him well enough. According to Noah, Kevin had married petite and curvy Audrey Calhoun, who'd been popular and pretty.

The man she'd long envisioned as a monster was just an older version of the boy she once knew. Although he was thicker — he'd put on at least thirty pounds — he wasn't any taller. She still had him by two or three inches. She noticed because that night in the mine he'd been so intimidated by her height. She could distinctly remember him saying it didn't matter that she was taller when he had her on her back.

Cody had thought that the best joke in the world. . . .

She told herself to walk past Kevin without any acknowledgement. She'd prepared herself for this moment. When she decided to return to Whiskey Creek, she'd known she'd have to face him — the others, too — and probably sooner rather than later.

But her feet wouldn't carry her to her car. They wouldn't carry her anywhere. Her vision narrowed, and she could hear the blood rushing through her ears.

"Hi." He blinked at her, startled when he recognized her. Then he reached out to hold the door as any polite person would. In the process his hand grazed her arm, and she jumped back as if he'd burned her, causing her latte to splatter on the ground.

"I'm sorry!" He glanced past her, at everyone who'd just seen her drop her drink. "I — I didn't mean to knock that out of your hand."

He hadn't touched it, and he had to be aware of that, but Adelaide couldn't draw enough breath to speak.

"Here, let me . . . I — I'll buy you a new one." He bent to pick up her cup, continuing to hold the door as if he expected her to turn around so he could make good on that promise. But she wasn't about to go anywhere with him.

Without a single word, she circled wide and hurried to her 4-Runner. She could feel him watching her as, hands shaking, she struggled to unlock her SUV. She could feel everyone in Black Gold staring through the windows. But she couldn't help the flight instinct that had kicked in. All it had taken was one look into Kevin's eyes and memories of the attack had overwhelmed her.

Noah cut Kevin off before he could reach the counter. "What'd you do to her?"

Kevin looked out of it, as though she'd just hit him with a strong right hook. "What?"

"What'd you do to her?"

"Nothing."

Together, they watched Addy peel out of her parking space. She didn't even take the time to wait for a safe opening in traffic before charging into the street. The driver of a red Honda honked as she cut him off but that didn't slow her down.

"You scared her," Noah said when she was gone.

"No, I didn't do anything, I swear."

"Why else would she run away like that?"

"How should I know? I said I'd buy her another drink. That was all. I think . . . I think it was just that I came upon her so suddenly."

Noah had a hard time believing that could be it. "Maybe she got burned by the coffee. . . ."

Kevin smoothed his Eureka High football T-shirt over the "happy fat" he'd been piling on since getting married. "Could be. But you of all people know she's had a rough week. I can't imagine she was in the best frame of mind to begin with."

Noah couldn't argue with that and yet the encounter he'd just witnessed bothered him. Addy had seemed absolutely . . . stricken.

"What's up with you acting so defensive, anyway?" Kevin put an arm around his shoulders and gave him a playful squeeze. "You pull her from the mine and now you're her designated savior?"

Noah wasn't anything to Addy. She didn't want him involved in her life. She'd made that clear. And yet . . . he felt oddly protective. She was so sensitive and serious. Hearing about her selfish mother, and knowing she planned to help her aging grandmother despite the attack, made him sympathetic. Adelaide put on a tough-girl front. She wanted him and others to believe she could take care of herself. But he had the feeling that she was attempting to protect a very fragile heart.

"She's been through enough. That's all," he said curtly.

Eve and Olivia hadn't had a chance to return to their seats before Addy dropped her drink. They'd stood and watched the scene unfold, just as surprised as he'd been. Now they hurried over to join him. "What happened?" they asked, almost in unison.

"Says he doesn't know," Noah replied.

"I don't." Kevin spread his hands to show his innocence. "If she wasn't burned, maybe it has to do with the attack. She's got to be rattled. Someone threatened her with a *knife.*" He fished his wallet out of his back pocket and checked the menu, written in chalk on a blackboard overhead, even though it seemed unlikely that, after coming here so often, he needed to consult it. "She'll feel better once they catch the guy who did it. And that should happen soon."

Taken aback by his confident tone, Noah stopped him before he could move away. "What are you talking about?"

"Haven't you heard? Chief Stacy identified the owner of that knife he found in the bushes by her door."

Eve spoke before Noah could. "Doesn't mean anything."

" 'Course it does!" Kevin argued. "That

knife belongs to Aaron Amos."

Noah thought he must've heard wrong. *"What?"*

"It's true!" he insisted. "That bastard has never been up to any good. And now they have something on him that might stick. Once they throw his ass in prison, like his daddy, this whole community will sleep better at night." He shook his head. "That boy needs to learn his lesson."

Olivia gave Kevin a disapproving look. "Maybe Aaron's got issues, but he's not the one who attacked Addy."

Noah was relieved to hear this. He'd never spent much time with Aaron, but he knew how Dylan would feel about his brother going to prison. Dylan loved his siblings almost as if they were his own children and had every right to, since he'd sacrificed so much of his time, effort and energy to raise them.

"It was *his* knife," Kevin said. "Who else could it be?"

"Anyone who might've taken it from him," Eve replied. "I'm telling you, Addy just said it wasn't him."

Skepticism drew deep lines in Kevin's forehead. "Come on . . . can she really make that call? The guy who broke into her room was wearing a mask, so it's not like she saw his face. I spoke to Officer Willis this morning — he helped me groom the football field for the Homecoming celebration tonight — and he's sure Aaron's the one. Who else in town would do such a thing?"

Eve came to Aaron's defense. "He has an alibi."

"No, he doesn't," Kevin said. "He claims he was with Shania, but Shania can't remember exactly what night they were together or for how long. She was too drunk. She thinks it was Monday, not Tuesday. And if he says he was with his brothers? What will *that* prove? The Amoses would swear to anything to protect him."

Kevin was getting on Noah's nerves. "Be careful talking crap about Dylan," he warned. "Just let the police do their jobs."

"Hey, I know Aaron's big brother is your friend these days, but . . . the truth is the truth," he said. "And I, for one, hope the truth comes out."

"Everybody does." Noah started back to the table. "But there's no need to lynch Aaron without proof."

"You all set for tonight?" Kevin called after him.

He wished there was some way he could beg off. But how did he tell his father, and everyone else, that he didn't want to be part of the big half-time memorial honoring his dead brother?

"I'll be there," he grumbled.

"How was your run?"

Gran's voice came from the back bedroom as Addy closed and locked the door. But she couldn't answer. Not yet. She was too out of breath. It was almost as if, now that she'd encountered Kevin, she thought Stephen, Tom and Derek would suddenly appear, too — as if they'd been watching her since she came home, maybe even following her. She knew that was highly unlikely. But fear wasn't always rational.

She was also kicking herself for not getting a look at Kevin's vehicle. Was it white? Did it show damage on the front right side?

She couldn't say. She'd left in such a rush, she'd nearly provoked a full-blown panic attack. Only being back with Gran, where she felt safe, softened the sharper edges of what she was experiencing, helped bring it under control.

"Addy?" her grandmother called when she didn't respond.

With a final deep breath, she managed to find her voice. "The run was . . . great. It — it's a beautiful fall morning."

"Good. So —" she made her way into the

hall "— will you feel well enough to go with me tonight?"

Telling herself to relax, that there'd been no reason to overreact, Addy moved away from the door. "Go where?"

"To the big game!"

Of course. It was Homecoming at the high school.

Addy had seen the announcement on the marquee outside Eureka High this morning when she went running but had thought nothing of it. "Don't tell me you still go."

Gran inched closer. "I certainly do. I always sell my baked goods at a booth next to the snack bar and donate the proceeds to the athletic program. You know that."

Addy put her laptop and other belongings on the closest chair so she could steady Gran when she let go of her walker to sit down. The last thing either one of them needed was for Gran to fall. Addy feared the day something like that happened. She'd heard a broken hip could be the beginning of the end for the elderly and, as much as she wanted to leave Whiskey Creek, she didn't want it to be because she'd had to say a permanent goodbye to Gran. "You mean . . . Darlene isn't doing it for you?"

"Heavens, no! She's short-staffed at the restaurant. Anyway, I like doing this myself."

She winked. "It's good advertising for the restaurant."

The restaurant didn't need to advertise. Everyone in town knew it was there, and most frequented it. Addy guessed this was about Gran. She'd had to give up working on a daily basis, but she wasn't about to sacrifice the other things she'd always done for the community.

"You must've had help the past few years. . . ."

"I pay some of the young girls from church — they're, oh, ten or twelve — to carry things in and out and help me wait on customers. I've got two sisters whose parents will be bringing them to the game — Misty and Savannah Busath. But I could use you, too, if you're ready to be out."

Oh, boy. Addy could bump into just about anybody at the game, including the four men she most wanted to avoid. Kevin was the coach, so he'd definitely be there. At least he'd be on the field, away from her. And she'd face the same possibility when she started at Just Like Mom's on Monday. She had to get past her fear, make herself comfortable in Whiskey Creek, or she wouldn't be any good to Gran during the next few months.

That had been her thinking before she'd

headed to the track this morning, and that was her thinking now, even after coming face-to-face with Kevin. Seeing him shouldn't have been as traumatic as it was, she told herself.

"Why haven't you mentioned the game before?" she asked Gran.

"What with all the excitement, I forgot. And then I didn't want to make you feel pressured to go out if you weren't ready. But you're bouncing back quicker than I thought you would. I certainly never expected you to go running."

Addy worked out almost every day. That was how she dealt with stress. But Gran wouldn't understand. Gran was from a different generation, had never been to a gym or a track. "Of course I'll help. What time do you need to be there?"

"Game starts at six, so we should leave here no later than five. We've got to go by the restaurant to get the food. Darlene said she'd have the van loaded."

"Do we already have a sign or a list of the items we'll be selling with the prices?"

"Of course. That'll be in the van, too. I had Darlene add lemon bars this year. They can be messy, but they're delicious."

"*All* your recipes are delicious."

She smiled but that smile soon faded and

a hint of sadness entered her eyes. "Have you heard from your mother since you've been here, honey?"

Addy hadn't heard a word. But she was used to Helen's long silences. She'd learned years ago not to count on her mother for any emotional support. Helen only called when she got into a fight with her current husband and wanted a place to stay, or needed to borrow money. Under those circumstances, Addy almost preferred no communication. It was less upsetting. "Not yet. But I'm sure she's fine. She always manages to get by."

"What did I do to make her turn out the way she did?" Gran asked. "I *tried* to be a good mother."

Addy knelt in front of her and took hold of her gnarled hands. "You were a good mother to both of us, Gran. I don't know what I would've done without you. But we all have our choices to make."

Tilting her head to one side, she gazed into Addy's face. "I can't believe you're back. I'm *so* happy."

The guilt Addy had carried since she left felt like an anvil on her chest. She should've visited before, should've returned again and again, instead of making Gran come all the way to Davis. If only Gran knew the emotional turmoil and fear she had to cope with in order to be here. But Addy couldn't tell her and hoped she would never have to know.

Standing, she gently encouraged Gran to do the same. "Let's go into the bathroom and curl your hair. You want to look your best for tonight, don't you?"

"Oh, I'm too old to look very good," she said with a self-deprecating chuckle, but Addy could tell she was excited by the prospect. She loved having her hair done.

"What are you talking about?" she said. "You're the most beautiful woman I know."

12

The game was packed. Friday-night football was a big deal in Whiskey Creek, especially *this* year. After a decade of losing seasons, they finally had another good team.

Addy had done what she could to conceal her black eye and bruises with makeup, but they still elicited comments from almost every customer. She told herself that would end once the whole town had a chance to express their surprise and dismay, but repeating the details of her abduction, and insisting she didn't know who was responsible, grew old quickly — mainly because everyone told her that Shania couldn't provide an alibi for Aaron. Shania wasn't saying she *hadn't* been with him, but she wasn't committing to any particular hours on any particular night.

Addy wondered if Chief Stacy was going to arrest him. She hoped not. There was no forensic proof.

After the first hour, Gran told her she should take a break and go watch the game for a bit, but Addy wasn't about to leave the booth. Savannah and Misty Busath were smart girls, plenty capable of handling any business that came their way while she was gone, but circulating would only make her more vulnerable to the curious.

"I'm fine," she told her. "No problem."

"I don't want you on your feet too long," Gran said. "I just thought it would be fun for you to get out of the house."

"It *is* fun." Addy sent another surreptitious glance through the crowd of people passing by. She was so busy studying every male face that Noelle Arnold was standing right in front of her before she realized who it was.

Of course, she might not have recognized Noelle even if she *had* been paying more attention to women. She guessed Noelle had had a nose job, at the very least. Somehow, her whole face looked different.

"So you like the necklace?"

Addy's hand went to the Courage pendant hanging from around her neck. "I do. Thank you. I've been meaning to call. But my life's been crazy the past couple of days, what with —"

"Oh, don't worry," she broke in. "You

don't have to explain. I understand what it's like when you're dealing with personal problems." She lowered her voice for emphasis. "*Believe* me, I've been there."

Everyone blamed *her* for her own problems. They blamed her for Kyle's problems, too. But Addy was trying hard not to judge. Whatever had happened between Kyle, Olivia and Noelle was none of her business. "It was nice of you. Truly."

She smiled. "Actually, I can't take all the credit. Derek bought it. I just picked it out."

Addy's breath caught in her throat. "Derek?"

"Rodriguez. You remember him, don't you?"

Addy's nails cut into her palms. "Not really. We weren't friends." And they never would be. . . .

"He says he knows *you.*" She leaned over the counter as if she had a juicy secret to share. "He's hoping you'll go out with him sometime."

"Why would he want that?"

Noelle blinked at Addy's deadpan tone. "Because he thinks you're hot!"

No one had found her particularly attractive in high school. She'd been so shy that she'd hidden behind her hair, her schoolbooks and plain, unremarkable clothing. He couldn't have been referring to the Adelaide he'd known back then. So when would he have seen her since?

Kevin was the only one she'd run into since coming home.

Unless . . .

Noelle was still talking. "He asked me to tell you about the calendar we're doing. I'm on the cover. But he said you could be Miss June, if you want."

Sudden nausea made Addy long to sit down. "What calendar are you talking about?"

"You know . . . one of those sexy swimsuit issues."

"And why would he want *me* to be Miss June?"

"He said it'd be cool to have you pose in a guy's baseball jersey — and nothing else," she whispered with a wink. "He says all the guys who used to play for Eureka High will want one."

Addy grabbed the support beam to steady herself.

"Noelle, we have customers here," Gran said. "Can't you see we're trying to work?"

The interruption saved Addy from having to come up with a response.

"Sorry." Noelle passed Addy a card. "Here's the URL where you can see the calendar so far."

Addy glanced at it, expecting to see the URL from her attacker's sweatshirt. It wasn't there.

Gran frowned at the fact that Noelle had passed her something but she didn't comment. She was trying to help the man behind Noelle, since Noelle didn't seem to care that she was holding up the line. Thanks to a sudden flurry of traffic, the Busath girls were also busy.

"Derek's number's on the back," Noelle called as she moved away. "Feel free to contact him. He's not paying for talent this time around. But . . . it's a start. And it'll give you something for your portfolio, in case you'd like to do some modeling."

Noelle blended into the crowd milling about the snack bar and Addy, too shaken up to bother with the clasp, yanked on the necklace she was wearing in an effort to get it off as soon as possible.

"I'd like a chocolate chip cookie, please."

Addy had Derek's gift in her palm, the chain now broken, before it registered that she had a little boy staring up at her. "What did you say?"

He looked at her as if she had to be crazy to break her own necklace and picked up a chocolate chip cookie wrapped in plastic with a Just Like Mom's logo on top. "I want one of *these.*"

Unable to bear the idea of touching anything that had come from Derek, she tossed the Courage necklace in the garbage.

"You don't want that?" the boy asked.

She didn't answer. "That'll be two dollars," she told him, and accepted his crumpled bills.

She was glad when he was gone, but there were others behind him. She served several people, moving mechanically while asking herself if Derek was the one who'd broken into her bedroom.

"Hi, Addy!" A familiar voice interrupted her thoughts. It was Eve Harmon, whom she'd spoken to earlier at Black Gold Coffee.

"Hi, Eve. What can I get for you?"

Eve seemed slightly disappointed that Addy was all business. Addy had been so eager to become friends when they were teenagers that Eve probably wondered why she was so distant now. But Addy wasn't about to form any more ties to this place, especially with someone so tightly connected to Noah.

"I'll have a couple of lemon bars, three cookies and a popcorn ball." She glanced wistfully at the long line curving around the snack bar. "Ted wanted me to get a hot dog, too, but . . . it's almost half time and I don't want to miss the show."

"They have quite a celebration planned," Gran said. The crowd, which ebbed and flowed, had dwindled enough that Savannah and Misty could handle the line.

"What are they doing this year?" Addy asked.

Eve paid Gran for the treats she'd ordered. "You didn't see the paper?"

"Not the last one. I was too busy moving."

"It's a special tribute to the team that took state fifteen years ago. Coach Nobis is leaving for Arizona. They want to recognize him before he goes." Her voice softened. "And they're retiring Cody Rackham's number. That's why I came."

"Is Mayor Rackham here, too?" Addy asked, but not because she wanted to see Noah's father. She'd been dreading the moment she'd have to face him and his wife almost as much as the moment when she might be confronted by Kevin, Derek or her other rapists.

"He'll be saying a few words. So will Noah."

"I must've read the paper too quickly,"

Gran said. "I didn't know he'd be speaking."

"Cody and Noah completed more passes than any other quarterback/receiver duo in the history of the school," Eve explained.

"They could play almost any sport," Addy said, remembering.

Gran gave her a nudge. "*You* were here when that team did so well. Why don't you go sit with Eve so you can watch the show?"

Addy shook her head. She remembered the excitement the entire student body had felt when their football team won so many games. There were other good players, but Cody and Noah, *the twins,* were the highlight of the team. They'd been standouts on the baseball diamond, as well. "There'll be more people wanting to buy from us during half than at any other time. You need me here."

"Our mother's already planning to help," Misty volunteered.

"She's got my aunt with her. So they'll both be here," Savannah chipped in.

"See?" Gran pushed her toward the exit. "We'll be fine. Go get reacquainted with your old friends, take a rest. I don't want you to overdo it, anyway, not after the past week."

"I'm fine," Addy argued, but Gran insisted

212

and the next thing she knew she was walking to the stands with Eve.

"Those bruises are looking better," Ted said as he slid over to make room for her.

Addy smiled. Of all Noah's friends, she knew Ted the least. He hadn't played sports. He'd been president of the student body, captain of the debate team and was voted most likely to become a politician. That she didn't know him actually made it more comfortable to be around him because, to her, he felt neutral. "They'll go away eventually."

He shifted his attention to Eve, who was handing out the baked goods. "Where's my dinner?" he asked.

Riley didn't seem happy, either. "Oh, man! You didn't bring any dogs?"

"I didn't want to miss half time," Eve said. "Have Jacob go get some."

"He's messing around with his friends." Riley stood and peered over the crowd, searching for his son. "I can't get him to answer his phone. I doubt he can even hear it."

"There's still three minutes, and three minutes in a football game can last ten," Ted said. "You wouldn't have missed half."

"Feel free to risk it, if you want," she told

him. "But seeing them retire Cody's number is the whole reason I came. I'm not going to be standing in line for junk food when that happens."

Cheyenne and Dylan Amos were sitting in front of them. Cheyenne twisted around to say hello, and Dylan gave Addy a nod. Neither she nor he mentioned that they'd seen each other at the police station last night. Aaron wasn't with them. But Baxter was. Addy got the impression that almost everyone was eager for the ceremony, except Baxter. He was too nervous.

"Noah doesn't like this sort of thing, doesn't like talking about Cody," he confided to Eve.

She placed a reassuring hand on his leg. "He'll get through it, Bax."

"He doesn't like it," he said again.

Addy watched him fidget, wondering about the intensity of his empathy. But then the clock ran down and she let it go. She didn't want to be a spectator at this ceremony any more than Noah wanted to be part of it. And yet, once the Homecoming winners had been announced, and the cheerleaders, dance team and band had performed, she couldn't look away. Mayor Rackham had stepped up to the podium, every bit as handsome and poised as she anticipated Noah would look in his fifties. His wife stood behind him, forever the supportive spouse, as he awarded a plaque to Coach Nobis, who waved proudly to the crowd.

From there the principal took over and announced that he wanted to honor a very special young man who had made a world of difference at Eureka High. He talked about Cody's many athletic accomplishments, how he'd lettered in two different varsity sports and set a new weightlifting record. He said Cody was a gifted leader and a popular student and closed by saying he'd never met a boy with more promise. Then he held up Cody's football jersey, now framed, and indicated that it would hang on the wall at the school from here on. He said Cody's number would never be used again, that he'd never be forgotten, and he gave a plaque signifying the retirement of his number to Mayor Rackham, who choked up when he accepted it.

That was hard to watch. But it got even harder when the mayor stepped aside so Noah could speak.

"Oh, my God, here he goes," Baxter whispered.

Eve took Baxter's hand. "He'll be fine. Calm down."

It was one thing to see Cody's parents after so long. To know how much they'd suffered because of the loss of their son. But Addy had never heard Noah talk about his brother's death, not beyond the one statement he'd made to her: *you know my brother died in there.*

That had been stated in irritation and as a cautionary remark. This was different. Noah stood at the podium, staring up into the stands, at a complete loss. For the first few seconds, he wasn't even able to speak. When he did manage a few words, his voice cracked, and he fell silent again.

Tears streamed down Baxter's cheeks. Some of Noah's other friends were crying, too. Addy heard a full-blown sob and glanced around to see that it was Shania Carpenter. She was sitting not far away, absolutely inconsolable, while those around her did their best to provide comfort.

That was when Addy realized there was a whole other dimension to Cody's death than she'd considered before: letting his loved ones go on believing he'd died in an accident was actually the kindest thing she could do. Then they didn't have to face the truth, didn't have to know he wasn't nearly as admirable as they wanted to believe.

She tried to imagine how the mayor would

react if he learned that the son he'd just praised — the boy everyone so admired — had instigated a gang rape. And Noah. What would it do to him?

13

It was late, but Addy couldn't sleep. Chief Stacy had stopped by as soon as they'd returned from the game. He'd wanted to bring them the news about Shania's lack of clarity concerning the night Addy was kidnapped. He acted as if that should confirm Aaron was responsible, but Addy continued to insist he wasn't the one. By the time Stacy had left, she could tell Aaron's lack of a solid alibi wasn't enough for Stacy to arrest him. But the police chief hadn't given up. He was looking for evidence, and he was focusing on Dylan's brother.

His determination made her uneasy.

On top of that, she kept thinking about seeing Noah up on that podium, his soul bared for all to see. Like Baxter, she'd hung on every word, feeling far more empathy than she wanted to feel as he'd finally managed to say how much he loved and missed his brother.

After walking offstage, he'd headed for an exit as though he couldn't get out of there fast enough. His father had tried to stop him, but he'd pushed past both his parents and kept going, which was when she knew he was embarrassed and maybe even a little angry that he'd been asked to speak about a loss that affected him so deeply.

In the end, after the angst of watching him had dissipated, she just felt sorry. Seeing him that vulnerable had torn down her defenses, made her want to protect him, if she could. Oddly, perhaps, it also made her want to comfort him.

But that was her old crush talking. She needed to stay away from Noah. Given the complex nature of the situation, they were *both* better off with no contact.

And yet he'd be coming to dinner next weekend.

Unless he canceled.

Maybe he'd cancel. . . .

Tired of tossing and turning, she got up and went over to the window. Gran had the house so hot she could hardly breathe. Again. But she wasn't about to open the door. She'd decided to crack the window as an alternative, but she didn't even dare do that. Instead, she simply stared out at the yard, feeling caged and claustrophobic and —

She saw movement on the flagstone steps leading up to her door, and a surge of adrenaline nearly dropped her to her knees. That murky shadow had to belong to a human.

Someone was in the yard. But who? The man who'd abducted her? Had he returned with more threats? Or was he hoping to finish her off?

She hadn't been able to keep the abduction a secret. She'd done her best to downplay it, but the entire town had talked of little else despite the details she'd held back.

Surely, he couldn't be pleased about that. . . .

It *was* a man. She could tell that much by his size and the way he walked. But she couldn't identify him in the darkness. She couldn't even make out his features.

He stepped onto the porch, and she covered her mouth to stifle a scream when he tried to peer in her window. He seemed to be staring right at her — which chilled her to the bone — but he couldn't see anything, could he? It was even darker in her room than it was in the yard.

She inched back, seeking her phone. She didn't want to call the police, didn't want the problems to continue. She only wanted to get Gran's affairs in order so they could move to Davis. But she wouldn't be victimized again. Not if she could help it.

Before she reached the nightstand where her phone was charging, she heard a soft knock.

She hesitated, wondering what to do. She doubted anyone bent on causing her harm would *knock*. But . . . how stupid would she feel if she opened the door only to find out she was wrong?

"Adelaide?"

The voice was barely loud enough to hear. Obviously, whoever it was didn't want to wake Gran. But with Gran's hearing loss, that was unlikely. Depending on how deeply she was asleep, even screaming might not disturb her.

Addy grabbed her phone and punched in 9-1-1 but didn't hit the send button. She planned to be ready, just in case. Then she crept to the door. "Who is it?"

"If I tell you, I'm afraid you won't open up, but . . . I don't mean any harm. I swear it. I . . . I've wanted to talk to you for a long time. Can you — can you trust me enough to give me two minutes?"

"No. I'm not opening the door."

"Please?"

"Tell me who you are and say what you've got to say. I can hear you fine."

"It's Tom, Addy. I . . . I saw you at the game earlier, but . . . didn't dare approach you."

"Good choice."

"I know. But . . . I've spent a lot of time over the years, thinking about what happened at that graduation party. I can't believe my own actions. I keep asking myself . . . what if something like that happened to one of *my* girls?"

He seemed genuinely distraught.

Addy stared at the floor. "What would you hope for her attackers?"

"I'd want the boys castrated. I'd want them in prison. I'd be so angry . . . I can't even tell you how angry I'd be. That's what we deserved. Instead, Cody was the only one who lost, and he lost big. I've always attributed his death to . . . to God's justice. But we got away without punishment. Why didn't you go to the police?"

How did she explain? Her feelings after that night were so complex she wasn't sure *she* understood them. Part of her refusal to act resulted from shame, and part stemmed from feeling somewhat responsible for her own fate. Her grandmother had told her she couldn't attend the party, yet she'd snuck out of the house. Had she listened, she wouldn't have been there, wouldn't have been susceptible to Cody's advances. He'd seemed so infatuated with her. It wasn't until he tried to stick his tongue in her mouth that she stopped him. She admired his appearance but was quickly learning that looking like Noah didn't make him Noah.

If she'd kept her distance from Cody, if she'd left after realizing he was stoned, would the night have ended differently?

Probably. That was a difficult thing to come to terms with. She couldn't begin to describe the self-blame and loathing it inspired. Maybe that wasn't entirely rational. In no way had she given her consent for what he and his friends did. But that didn't lift the burden of her guilt.

And her self-blame was only part of it. What if no one believed her? What if the parents of all those boys formed a unified front and the community turned on *her* instead of them? They could easily claim she had emotional problems or been rejected by one or more of the boys she was accusing. She hadn't wanted to be dissected in public. Neither had she wanted Gran to be embarrassed or put in a situation where she had to defend her beloved granddaughter. Taking a stand against so many prominent families would have damaged her business, too.

Bottom line, Gran didn't deserve the pain and trouble Addy's tale would have caused. She'd been through enough with her own daughter. And there was always the possibility that if Addy had told, Kevin and the others would've hurt her even more in retaliation.

She'd just wanted it all to go away. She wanted the same thing now. She especially hated the thought that someone might find out *she* was the reason Cody couldn't come home that night. What would Noah think of her then?

"I was so hurt and humiliated I didn't know what to do," she said.

"I'm sorry. I'd like you to understand that. Even if . . . if you decide to come forward, I'll still be sorry. I wouldn't want what happened to you to happen to anyone. I can't believe I had a hand in it. I got caught up in the fever of the moment. I'm really not that sort of person."

She rested her head against the door. "Is that true?"

"Absolutely."

"So why didn't *you* tell?"

He laughed bitterly. "Isn't it obvious? I'm a coward. I've been terrified for years that someone would find out, that my wife . . ." His voice broke. "God, what would she say? She tells me all the time that I'm a good man, and it makes me feel like such a fraud. I mean, I don't want other people to know — and yet there are times I hate myself so much I'm *dying* to tell. Does that make sense?"

She didn't answer, but he continued, anyway.

"Sometimes I wonder if it isn't harder to live with a lie than to be punished for the truth. Sometimes I consider clearing my conscience. Maybe I should. Maybe that's the only way I can truly get past what I've done." He shook his head. "But then I think about the people it'll hurt besides me. People like Noah. It would destroy him to learn what his brother did that night. It would hurt the whole family. Some actions have so many repercussions."

Addy cracked open the door. On the other side she saw a man about her height and one hundred and eighty pounds, give or take ten, who'd already started losing his hair. With his glasses, she might not have recognized him if she'd seen him in the street. He hung his head, looking miserable and ashamed.

"Noah, he . . . he has no idea?" Addy asked.

"None. As far as I can tell, no one does. It would be such a surprise. The whole community would be shocked."

"You think Noah would take it hard, though?"

"I know he would."

So did she. And she didn't want him to be hurt. "Why hasn't he married?"

"Married! He's never even had a steady girlfriend. He's got a commitment problem or something. Goes from one girl to the next. We tease him about it all the time. He doesn't like hearing he's a player, but . . . the truth is the truth."

A commitment problem. She'd sensed that, too.

"How long after you raped me did you meet your wife?"

"Raped you," he whispered, as if hearing those words nearly knocked the wind out of him.

She didn't soften them. "How long?"

"Five years."

"And you're happy?"

"You really want to know this stuff?" Shifting awkwardly, he scratched his head. "I can't imagine . . . I can't imagine it feels very good to . . . to hear that I've got a great wife, when I don't deserve her."

She wasn't sure how that made her feel. The old anger welled up occasionally, but mostly she'd let it go. She couldn't move forward in life, couldn't heal if she was smoldering with resentment. "Who dragged me to the mine the other night?"

Straightening, he looked up. "It wasn't Aaron?"

"Of course not. It had to be one of you."

"I admit I've wondered about that. But I have no clue. Kevin, Derek, Stephen and I, we see one another once in a while. But we don't talk about that night. *Ever.*"

"Could it have been Kevin?"

Tom seemed genuinely uncertain. "Kevin's got a family, too. And he loves his job. Like me, he probably wishes that night never happened and tries to pretend it didn't."

"And the other two?"

He lifted his hands to show that he had no idea. "Maybe it was Stephen."

"Why him?"

"He's divorced, angry. His life hasn't turned out the way he hoped. He played in the minors — I'm not sure if you knew that."

"I certainly didn't follow him."

"Right, well, he got called up to the majors

after a couple of years. Had a bright future ahead of him. Then he tore his rotator cuff and was never the same. His professional baseball aspirations ended before he ever played in a game." He rubbed his neck. "I don't think he's ever gotten over the disappointment. It's still all he talks about."

Addy felt no sympathy for Stephen. He'd been her least favorite of the five. The rape had originally been his idea. But nothing would've happened if Cody hadn't acted on it. Stephen hadn't had the same amount of pull among his teammates.

"What does he do for a living?" she asked.

"Works for Kyle Houseman, making solar panels."

"Does Stephen have kids?"

"A couple, but they live with his ex-wife somewhere else."

Addy kept her finger on the send button of her phone, even though she doubted she was in danger. "And Derek?"

"Derek's not up to much, but . . . I don't think he'd ever hurt you."

"He already did," she stated flatly.

He winced. "I mean . . . as an adult. Now. These days."

"Do you know anything about a website with the URL www.SkintightEntertainment .com?"

"No. Why?"

"I thought Derek might be involved with it."

"It's possible. He works from home, building websites, optimizing, that sort of thing, but . . . he struggles to get by."

"Noelle Arnold says he's making a calendar."

Tom stretched his neck. "I heard about that. He must be trying to earn a little on the side by becoming a photographer."

"Where does he live?" If she could get his address, she could drive by, see if he had a truck that showed damage — if and when she gathered the nerve.

"God, I'm a mess." He smoothed down what hair he had left. "I hate what I did, wish I hadn't even been there that night. But . . . it feels disloyal standing here answering these questions. I know *they'd* think I'm . . . I don't know . . . trying to shift the blame."

"You're worried about what *they* might think?"

"Fine," he said with a sigh. "Have you seen that fourplex behind the trees as you head south out of town?"

"Where the Powers family used to live?" They'd been among the poorest in Whiskey

Creek. They'd had something like eleven kids.

He nodded. "Derek lives in one of those."

Of the five who'd raped her, Tom had been the only one to show any reluctance. She remembered the others coaxing him. She also remembered that he'd apologized and tried to cover her with his jacket when he was done. "What do you drive, Tom?"

He seemed surprised by the question, but he answered it. "A red Kia."

"SUV?"

"Sedan."

She definitely would've been able to tell if her abductor had shoved her into an economy car. "Do you own a truck?"

"No. My wife has an old VW Bug but she can't drive it far. It's not trustworthy."

Addy nibbled on her bottom lip. "And you work at the post office."

She could see the fear in his eyes when he answered. "I do. We're not rich, but I have a good life, one I'm terrified of losing."

"Is that why you came here?"

"I came because I wanted to apologize, to — to tell you how sorry I am, how much I wish I could take back what I did."

Rubbing a hand over her face, she tossed her phone on the dresser. *"What made you do it?"*

"I wish I knew. Group mentality? Peer pressure? Cody could be so persuasive. If he'd told me to jump off the mountain, into the river, I probably would've done that, too." His chest rose as he drew a deep breath. "Do you . . . do you want me to go to Chief Stacy and confess? Is that why you're back — to speak up? For retribution?"

Retribution? Not after this long. "No. Let it go," she said, and closed the door.

Gail had lent them the cabin. And Lisa had brought a friend, as promised. Yvonne whatever-her-last-name-was — Noah couldn't remember — was even prettier than Lisa. She seemed to like Baxter, too, which was why Noah couldn't understand why Baxter remained so impassive. He'd barely spoken during dinner, had drunk much more than he'd eaten and seemed remote as they were sitting on the elaborate deck, making s'mores over a fire pit.

"The view here is *amazing.*" Yvonne smiled at Baxter; she'd been attempting to win him over all night. Not that it had done her any good. "What river is that?"

When she pointed at the gorge below, Noah felt obliged to answer, since Baxter didn't. "It's the North Fork of the Stanis-

231

laus. It eventually empties into New Melones Lake down by Angels Camp."

"I love that area." She leaned forward to check the marshmallow on the end of her roasting fork, giving him and Baxter a generous view of cleavage. Noah felt his body react, but Baxter grimaced as if he *resented* her attempts to interest him.

What the heck, Bax? Noah thought when Baxter made no attempt to keep the conversation going. They'd brought these girls up here hoping to have a good time. But Baxter didn't seem to be enjoying himself, and that was ruining everyone else's fun.

"It's nice," Noah said.

"Is this really Simon O'Neal's cabin?" Lisa stood and gazed up at the giant home, which was cut into the side of the mountain. She'd already removed her shoes and had been brushing up against Noah at every opportunity. Now she came over and climbed into his lap.

"Hey, I was making you a marshmallow," he complained when he could no longer see what he was doing.

She claimed the roasting fork — apparently rich people didn't use hangers — and took over. "I'd rather have *you* than a marshmallow."

"Chocolate was going to be involved,"

he teased.

She twisted around and started kissing him. "This is better than chocolate, isn't it?"

Noah might've let himself get swept away. He had no strong feelings for Lisa. Until this very second, she hadn't even particularly excited him. But he thought he could get excited. Lord knew he didn't want to think about the things that had been on his mind since he'd stood on that platform last night, crying in front of the whole town. Sex had been the perfect antidote to his pain in college. He didn't see why it wouldn't work for him tonight. He hadn't been with a woman since he'd ended his racing tour.

"You're on fire," Baxter said.

"I am," she admitted, and kissed Noah more deeply.

Baxter cleared his throat. "No, I mean you're *really* on fire."

With a curse, Lisa broke off the kiss so Noah could extinguish her flaming marshmallow. "That's how hot I am," she said to Bax with a laugh.

Noah expected Bax to make some sort of witty comeback. He had the personality for it. But while his best friend responded, he sounded petulant, *not* funny. "That's a matter of opinion."

Before things could get any worse, Noah decided to pull him aside.

"Uh, could you excuse us?" He handed the roasting fork to Lisa. "Make one for me, okay? I like it warm and gooey." He winked to soften Baxter's reaction. "I'll be back."

"Baxter, would you like one, too?" Yvonne called after them.

"Hell, no," he grumbled before Noah could drag him into the kitchen.

"What's wrong with you?" Noah whispered as soon as the French doors were closed. Lisa and Yvonne could see them through the glass but wouldn't be able to hear.

Baxter motioned to the women sitting out on the deck. "This is what you want? Some . . . cheap piece of ass?"

"I haven't had sex in ages. What's wrong with getting some tonight? Everyone understands the rules. We're just having fun."

"Maybe *you're* having fun, but I'm not."

"*Why?* That's the question. Yvonne's beautiful. What's not to like about her? *Or is it that you don't like women at all?*"

Noah knew he'd had too much to drink when that question popped out.

Baxter looked startled, but he quickly rallied. "It's about time you had the balls to ask me. Maybe I should finally tell you the truth."

"Stop it." They were going too far. Noah wanted to reel that question back in before Baxter could answer, before it was too late to retract it. "If you aren't having fun, we'll leave. Not that big a deal. I'm not invested either way."

"No. I'm tired of hiding, Noah. Don't you see? I can't do it anymore. It's killing me to sit back and watch you, to keep pretending I don't ache every time you touch someone else."

A strange desperation took hold of Noah. He squeezed Baxter's arm. "*Think* about what you're saying —"

"I have thought about it! *Every* damn day! Every time I close my eyes you're there. Every time I open them, too."

"Bax, we're best buddies. We grew up together. I'll always be there for you and you'll always be there for me. Don't . . . make it awkward."

"It's already awkward for me, and you know it. At least see me for who I am instead of who you want me to be. Half the time I feel fucking invisible around you!"

Not only was he cursing, he was screaming. Something had just . . . snapped inside him.

Noah turned to see if the girls had heard. They were watching them as if they didn't know what to do. But Noah couldn't care too much about them. He could tell that his whole world was about to shift. He needed to make sure it didn't, needed to put a lid on this.

"Bax, look . . ." He paused, trying to calm down. "You've had too much to drink. We both have. That's all. Don't do this to me —"

He jerked away. "To *you*? Do you know what it's been like watching you sleep with one girl after another? To see you look at them the way I want you to look at *me*?"

Oh, God! Did he really say that? Noah knew it was too late, but he couldn't help trying to control the damage. "Bax, you know me. You *know* I'm not gay. Don't put me in this position. If you . . . if you like men, that's your deal, I guess. I'll accept it. Of course I will. I would never want to live my life without you. But I can't . . . I mean, I don't feel . . ."

Baxter filled in as he struggled to find the right words. "The longing I've felt? No, I'm sure you don't. You have no idea what it's like to be me."

Noah had lost his buzz. He felt light-headed, but sick. "What can I do?"

236

"I don't want you to do anything. I'm leaving."

"You're drunk. You can't drive." Noah started after him but stopped when Baxter swung back.

"On second thought, since this is good-bye, you might as well give me what you gave her so easily. At least it'll be something to remember you by."

"What are you *talking* about?" The girls, watching in such stunned amazement, distracted Noah enough that he wasn't prepared for what came next. He was too busy trying to think of some way to stop the destruction that was taking place, some way to save their friendship. Baxter meant much more to him than this date or those girls. But he didn't feel anything sexually for him. He couldn't even understand how Baxter could be attracted to men.

He opened his mouth to say he was sorry for dragging him up here, to admit that he'd suspected for a while and should've been more honest with himself. But the next thing he knew, Baxter was pushing him up against the wall and kissing him with as much passion as Lisa had.

Noah's first impulse was to throw Baxter off him at all costs. Rage charged through his veins like acid. He didn't want this kind of contact, found the sexual aspect of it stomach-churning. But pushing Baxter away would hurt and humiliate him. And he cared enough about his best friend not to show how deep his repugnance went. He stiffened, but he neither welcomed nor rejected the kiss.

When Baxter pulled back, he seemed surprised. "Well, you didn't break my jaw like I expected. That was decent of you," he said and, head bowed, shoulders slumped, he walked out.

Noah slid down the wall to the floor. What had just happened? Had he really been kissed by a *guy*? By his own *best friend*?

"Holy shit," he whispered, but as his shock faded, his regret escalated. This was his fault. He shouldn't have brought Baxter up here. He'd pushed him into declaring himself by trying to force him to behave like a regular dude, all in an effort to perpetuate the illusion he'd been clinging to for so long. But he knew, had known for some time, that Baxter's sexual orientation wasn't the same as his. No matter how hard he'd tried to ignore the signs, or talk himself out of what he was sensing, it was always there, wasn't it?

The door from the deck opened and closed as the girls came in. "Did . . . did your friend really just stick his tongue down your throat?" Lisa asked, obviously horrified. "I mean . . . he did, right? I saw him. I saw him with my own eyes."

Noah covered his face as he struggled to hold down his dinner. He didn't know what made her think her tongue was any better than anyone else's, and yet, if he was being honest with himself, he was every bit as grossed out as she was. He prided himself on being open-minded. He respected an individual's right to live as he saw fit. But . . . *shit,* he felt as if he'd been sexually assaulted!

"Please go," he said. "And don't . . . don't ever call me again."

"I won't now that I know you're gay," she snapped. "Why didn't you *tell* me you have a boyfriend?"

He raked his fingers through his hair. "I *don't* have a boyfriend." He'd had a *best* friend, one he'd known since he could talk, but he was ninety-nine percent sure he didn't have that friend anymore.

"As if we can believe *you.*" Yvonne rolled her eyes. "What's wrong with guys these days?" she muttered in exasperation. "*All* the hot ones are gay."

He didn't get the chance to defend his masculinity. But he didn't care to even try.

Lisa and Yvonne had no idea how much his friendship with Baxter had meant to him over the years and how much he'd miss it in the future. As far as Noah was concerned, Baxter had become a brother to him. In some aspects, he'd replaced Cody.

Why couldn't Bax feel the same? Why did they have to turn out so different?

Since this is goodbye. . . .

Baxter never would've kissed him, certainly not like a lover, if he'd planned on maintaining the friendship. That he'd take it so far, that he'd let his feelings tempt him into crossing that line, upset Noah more than anything else.

Lisa had been getting her keys out of her purse. When she lifted her head, she said, "I need gas money."

He blinked up at her. "What?"

"You're the one who had us drive all the way up here for nothing. I think you owe me a few bucks."

He'd fed her a nice dinner. That wasn't *nothing.* "You can't be serious."

"I'm completely serious!"

Could he have drunk more than he thought? Because this night just kept getting crazier.

He managed to dig a twenty out of his pocket, which he threw in her general direction. Then he got up and scooped his keys off the counter. He had to go after Baxter, get him off the road before he hurt himself or someone else. They could sort everything else out later. Once they'd both had a chance to . . . to calm down and sober up.

But then he realized if *he* had his keys, Baxter didn't. He'd driven. So Baxter must've left on foot. He had a long walk ahead of him if he decided to hike back to town on his own, but he had a cell phone. He could call someone. At least he wasn't going to get into a drunk-driving accident.

"Thank God," Noah muttered, and sank back down to the floor.

"Grab that bottle of wine, too." Lisa motioned toward the counter, talking to Yvonne. "I'm going to need it after seeing *that.*"

Her friend seemed a little hesitant. "That hasn't been opened. We can't just —"

"Take it," Noah snapped.

Yvonne hugged the bottle to her chest as she walked past him, but even gas money and a good bottle of wine wasn't enough to get rid of Lisa without further comment. Her lip curled in disgust as she turned back for a parting salvo. *"Fag!"* she spat, and slammed the door behind her.

14

Kevin Colbert stood behind the bar he'd had Riley Stinson build in his basement. This part of the house was *his* domain, a place his wife rarely visited, except to clean. His kids liked to come down here. So did his football players, because he had a pool table, a big-screen TV with the most extensive sports package available on satellite and the latest gaming system, along with plenty of comfortable seating. It was the perfect man cave. But it was late, even for a Saturday night. His kids were in bed. His wife knew he had friends over; she was upstairs reading yet another book — she went through four or five a week. And his football players hadn't been invited. Tonight he'd asked only Stephen Selby, Tom Gibby and Derek Rodriguez to stop over for a few minutes — and they'd each reluctantly agreed.

"Have you seen this?" He pushed Adelaide's front-page story in the *Gold Country Gazette* across the wooden bar.

Folding the paper in half, Derek set it aside. "Look, we all know why you asked us here. So let's just cut to the chase and get this over with so we can go home. I don't like meeting with the rest of you, especially after midnight. Someone could see our cars out front and put two and two together — figure out that we're in a panic and scrambling to cover our asses."

"And how would anyone do that?" Kevin challenged. "We've been friends for years. We have the right to socialize."

Stephen gave him a look that said he was out of touch with reality. "We haven't hung out in ages, Kevin. Not since you started thinking you were too good for the rest of us."

He was the most successful of the four of them, wasn't he? Although Tom had a family and a reliable job, he didn't have the public image Kevin had. Besides, Tom was weak, run by his wife. Kevin no longer had any interest in these people but, thanks to the past, he was tied to them whether he liked it or not.

"What are you talking about?" he asked. "I've just been living my life. And so have you. It's not like you've extended *me* any invitations in the past decade."

"No one's extended any invitations." Tom shook the ice in his glass. "Why would we? Seeing one another reminds us of what we did, and what we stand to lose if it gets out. At least, that's what it does to me."

Stephen laughed as if he didn't care. "Yeah, well, some of us stand to lose more than others."

"You think it's funny?" Kevin kept his voice down. He definitely didn't want to attract his wife's attention. She could be oblivious, but that didn't mean she was outright deaf. "Maybe you don't understand that we could *all* lose our freedom."

"That's unlikely," Stephen scoffed. "Maybe it'll cost you your job and your marriage. Tom, too. But I doubt we'd go to prison. They've got to prove we did it first."

"It's better if we don't go down that road." Kevin had been so on edge ever since he'd heard Addy was back he'd scarcely been able to function, and this was only making his anxiety worse. "I've looked into it. There's no statute of limitations on gang rape in California."

Stephen sucked the foam off his beer. "Is that why you panicked and kidnapped her? Because we all know Aaron didn't take her to the mine."

Kevin shook his head. "It wasn't me. That's why I called this meeting, to make sure we all understand that kind of shit can't happen again."

"Why not?" Derek wanted to know. "I, for one, am grateful. Maybe now the bitch will keep her mouth shut." He chuckled softly. "I had Noelle deliver a message making the same point. I wish I could've seen her face when she found out the necklace she was wearing came from me. *Courage.* I knew she'd eat it up. You gotta love that."

"You don't get it," Kevin said. "If one of us gets caught doing something stupid, it puts the rest of us in jeopardy. Hurting her will only make things worse."

"You mean hurting her *again*," Tom said.

"Fine. Again." He didn't hide his impatience. "But even you will like this next part," he told Tom. "From here on out, we leave her alone. If she says anything about what happened at the mine, we deny it. It's that simple. There are four of us and only one of her. Together we have a lot more friends than she does. Her accusations won't go anywhere."

"I don't want to make what we did worse by calling her a liar," Tom said.

A flash of anger, and desperation, nearly made Kevin lash out. "Would you rather go

245

to prison?" he responded in a harsh whisper.

"Of course not. I just — I feel so bad."

"You'll feel a lot worse if your wife has to live with the shame and embarrassment of what you did, if she has to raise your kids without you. *She* hasn't done anything wrong, any more than my wife has."

When Tom kneaded his forehead but didn't answer, Derek shot Kevin a glance that confirmed he was concerned about Tom's state of mind, too. They all had to stand together. If Tom cracked . . .

"We might be able to avoid criminal charges by denying it," Derek said. "But even being accused of rape will create doubt and suspicion, and that could follow us around for years."

"There's no help for that," Kevin said. "The people who really count will believe us." At least, he prayed that was true. He'd never done anything to his wife that would lead her to think he was capable of rape. But if Addy spoke up, he was afraid Tom would finally cave. Or maybe others who'd been present at the party would start remembering certain details — snippets of conversation or having seen them drag Addy into the other part of the mine. So far, no one had come forward but then, the specter hadn't been raised. Who knew what would happen if it was?

Stephen finished his drink in several quick swallows. "You're certain that's our best course?"

A creak sounded overhead. Kevin waited to be sure it wasn't his wife, crossing the floor to come to the top of the stairs. When he was satisfied that she wasn't about to yell down at him, he continued. "As far as I can tell. Think about it. No one's going to want this to come out, not even the damn mayor."

Derek nodded. "Mayor Rackham thinks his son could walk on water," he said. "You saw the tribute Cody received last night. No way would Mr. Mayor want anyone to learn that his son instigated a gang rape. He wouldn't believe it even if he was told."

"Exactly." Picking up the paper Derek had shoved aside, Kevin slapped it in front of them again. "We can't have any more of this. We have to agree not to touch her."

"I'm finding it hard to believe you didn't take her back to the mine," Tom muttered, staring at Kevin.

It came as no surprise to him that Tom would be the one to say this. His guilty conscience was driving Kevin crazy. Tom was as dangerous to them as Addy. "I'm telling you I didn't."

He frowned. "Someone did."

They all looked at one another, but no one confessed.

"Fine." Kevin made a dismissive motion. "I can see why no one would want to take responsibility. That's not necessary, anyway. It's over and done with. We just have to hope Stacy remains focused on Aaron Amos. But even if he doesn't, we stay calm. We don't react. Otherwise, we could really get ourselves in trouble."

"Kevin, honey?"

Kevin held his breath. His wife was at the top of the stairs. "What?"

"Are you almost done?"

"I'll be right up," he called back.

"My wife will be wondering where I am, too." Tom slid off his stool. "I've got to go."

"So what do you think?" Kevin intercepted him before he could reach the stairs. "Are we on the same page? You're not going to confess, are you? You don't want your girls to live the rest of their lives knowing their father was a rapist. You don't want your wife to leave you."

"Of course I don't want that." Tom looked tired as he rubbed his face. "But you know what hurts the worst? Besides the fact that what we did will never, ever go away?"

Kevin feigned interest, but he didn't want to hear it. Why agonize over something he wouldn't bother regretting if there wasn't any danger of getting caught? It was something stupid they did at a high school party. So what? "I'm listening."

"I don't remember enjoying the sex. It was brutal and degrading — to her and to us."

"You can thank Stephen for getting us into that one," Derek piped up. "As I recall, it was his idea."

Stephen slammed down his glass. "Don't you dare blame me!"

"It *was* your idea," Tom said sullenly.

He slid off his stool, too. "Cody's the one who wanted her, but she wouldn't let him touch her."

"So you told him to rape her," Tom said. "Told him she deserved it. Said she'd been leading him on all night."

"Shut up!" Kevin didn't like where this was going. "I don't want to discuss it anymore."

There were a few seconds of strained silence. They were all laboring under a certain amount of fear. But they had no choice; they *had* to control it.

Finally, Derek picked up his keys. "Why the hell didn't she tell anyone back when it happened?"

"Because she doesn't want anyone to know, either," Kevin said. "See what I'm saying? We lie low and everything will be okay."

"Sometimes I wish I'd been crushed in that mine instead of Cody," Tom said.

Shocked by the vehemence behind those words, Kevin seized his arm. "Look, you have to forgive yourself and put it behind you."

"You have a daughter," Tom responded. "Don't you ever think about what you'd do if something like that happened to her?"

"No."

"Because . . ."

Kevin refused to even entertain the possibility. "Because my daughter won't turn out to be a stuck-up bitch, okay?"

Noah wasn't sure why he eventually made his way to Milly's. He had plenty of friends to turn to — except they were Baxter's friends, too, and he didn't feel he could go to any of them. Whether Baxter decided to come out of the closet was up to Baxter. Noah couldn't out him; a guy deserved more from a lifelong friendship. Besides, he didn't want anyone to know what had happened at the cabin. He was humiliated by it — and yet he felt the need to talk to someone. He sure as hell didn't want to be alone right now.

Fag . . .

He'd never been called that before in his life. He shuddered to think what Baxter would endure if he openly admitted that he was sexually attracted to other men. Imagining the repercussions made Noah angry — angry with those who'd feel superior enough to put him down and, perhaps illogically, angry with Baxter for being vulnerable in the first place. And how was it that Baxter had fallen in love with *him*?

He certainly hadn't done anything to solicit that type of interest.

Taking another pull on his bottle, he stared at Adelaide's house. She didn't want anything to do with him. So . . . why had he come here?

Because he was just drunk enough to ignore his better judgment. He'd sobered up so he could make the drive from the cabin, but as soon as he arrived home, and started thinking about Baxter kissing him *like a lover,* he'd decided he couldn't handle being clear-headed quite yet. He'd gone directly to the liquor store down the street and had been walking around town ever since, trying to ease the upset that had both his mind and his stomach churning.

When he swayed and almost fell, he knew he needed to go home and call it a night. It was twelve-thirty, too late to pay Addy a visit. He'd scare her by banging on her door in the middle of the night.

But home was beginning to feel like a very lonely place. He already dreaded morning. No matter how much he drank, the reality of what Baxter had done, what he'd revealed, would hit him hard.

"Shit." He walked away. He only lived a few blocks down. But when he reached the corner, he pivoted and headed back. He might as well *knock.* Addy had her own door. She didn't have to open up if she didn't want to.

He tripped as he climbed the porch steps, grabbed for the railing and dropped his bottle. Fortunately, it fell into the bushes and didn't break, but he cursed as he caught himself.

The noise must have awakened her because the light went on.

"It's just me," he said when he saw her peeking out the window.

The door opened, which gave him hope, but she stood in the narrow opening, watching him with uncertainty. "What are you doing here, Noah?"

The porch seemed to be spinning. He put a hand on the door frame to steady himself. "I . . ." He searched for something he could say to make this moment seem natural, but couldn't come up with a single reason he should be on her porch.

He'd dragged her out of bed for no apparent reason. They didn't even know each other that well.

Somehow this had seemed like a much smarter idea a few seconds ago. "I don't know. Coming here was a mistake. I'm sorry."

He started to go, but she came out after him.

"You've been drinking."

"Yes."

She gave him a funny look that he would admit it so readily. "Do you get wasted very often?"

He couldn't remember the last time. "Hardly ever." He loved biking too much to even be tempted. "But tonight —" he whistled "— tonight there just didn't seem to be a better answer."

She tucked her hair behind her ears. "For what?"

Instinctively, he wiped his mouth as if he could erase the memory of Baxter's kiss. But it was no use. There would be no forgetting. "I — I can't talk about it."

"Why not?"

"Loyalty, I guess." He probably wouldn't

have told her, anyway. He felt too exposed — a lot like he'd felt standing on that podium last night. There was the same telltale tightness in his chest and throat. If his Homecoming debacle had taught him anything, it was that he wanted to avoid so much emotion.

"To whom?" she prompted.

"Never mind. I shouldn't have bothered you."

"Tell me what's wrong." She seemed truly concerned.

"Nothing." He'd screwed up the whole night, first by taking Baxter out with those girls and then by coming here inebriated, making Addy think he had a problem with booze.

Intent on getting as far from her as possible, he turned away. What the hell was wrong with him? He needed to cope on his own. But when she jogged after him and grabbed his hand, he wanted to stay much more than he wanted to leave.

"Hey." She tugged him to a stop. "Are you okay?"

The sharp edge of panic cut deep when he felt his eyes begin to water — so he purposely avoided the shrewd perception he saw in her face and dropped his gaze. "I like your pajamas."

"I'm wearing a shirt and some sweats."

"Okay, so they're not very revealing. But, because of the other night, I know what I can find under them." He hoped the sexual nature of that comment would divert her, suggest a reason he'd knocked on her door, since he didn't really have one. It was easier to come on to her than it was to tell her he'd just lost his best friend.

He thought that would put a decisive end to his visit, but she didn't push him away, didn't tell him he was a shallow jerk, like he deserved. She caught his face, forcing him to meet her eyes. "Why did you *really* come?"

Part of him wanted to level with her. To tell her he was confused, torn, even angry. But he couldn't think of how to say it without including Baxter, and when tears of frustration came more readily than words, he did what he had to in order to distract her before she could realize he was standing on an emotional precipice.

"Because I want you," he whispered, and he knew she'd have to believe it because, in spite of everything else, that was most definitely true.

Addy couldn't figure out what was going on with Noah, but this wasn't about sex. At least, not entirely. If she had her guess, alcohol hadn't worked to numb the pain of whatever was bothering him — could it be Cody's death, after all these years? — so he was trying something else.

She told herself to back away. She couldn't get involved. But he seemed so vulnerable. And she'd dreamed of kissing him so many times over the years — in high school and even since she'd been back — that she couldn't bring herself to move an inch. When he lowered his head, she stood in the chill autumn air, her bare feet seemingly frozen to the concrete. Then their lips touched and she experienced such a visceral reaction she could only lean in.

This was the boy she'd always wanted. And he kissed even better than she'd imagined. . . .

"I'm happier already," he murmured, sliding his arms around her and bringing her up against his chest.

Since he'd lifted his head to speak it was the perfect moment to break off the embrace. Instead, Addy clenched her hands in his hair and brought his lips back to hers, kissing him with all the passion she'd held at bay for a decade and a half. Soon they were both gasping for air and pressing into each other as if they were tempted to climb inside each other's clothes.

"Wow," he said. "See? You *do* like me. I don't know why you had to make me feel like you didn't. That wasn't very nice."

She almost smiled at his petulance. *Liking* him had never been the problem. Right now, surrounded by darkness and quiet, with all of Whiskey Creek asleep and unaware, it was easy to forget there *was* a problem. All that had come before, and all that might come after, didn't seem important. Especially since she knew this brief interlude wouldn't change anything — except maybe for the better. If she wanted Noah to forget about her all she had to do was give him what he wanted, become another of the many women who passed through his life. Once he conquered the challenge she'd stupidly provided, he'd move on. Tom had told her as much.

"It's cold out here," he said. "Let's go to my house so I can get you warm."

She was shivering, but cold had nothing to do with it. On the contrary, she was burning up inside, feeling more desire than she'd ever thought possible for someone who'd gone through what she had. How could it be that she still wanted Noah? That what she'd felt in high school had never really changed?

257

Her therapist would say she was a testament to the power of the human spirit to overcome and disassociate. Dr. Rosenbaum had said it before, but the fact that she could feel so normal, so much like she imagined other women felt when they encountered such a desirable man, surprised Addy.

"Gran can't wake up to find me gone," she said, struggling to hold on to the reality of her situation. "Not after —"

"Don't think about what happened the other night," he broke in. "I'll get you back before she wakes up."

She shook her head. "I'm sorry. I can't . . . I can't sleep with you."

His breath fanned her skin as he kissed her neck. "Why not? I can tell you want to."

He was right. He'd caught her at a weak moment. All these years she'd denied herself the kind of abandon she was experiencing now. She desperately wanted to forget, to let go at last. But she couldn't have a relationship with him even if he decided he was interested.

"Why?" he asked when she didn't answer.

That old attraction had come out of hibernation stronger than ever, making her ask herself: *What about one night?*

It wouldn't mean anything to him, so she

didn't have to worry that he might be misled or get hurt. And *she* already understood their limitations.

There was just one problem.

"You're drunk," she said.

His tongue outlined the rim of her ear. "I'm not so drunk that I can't make love."

Oh, boy . . . Scarcely able to breathe, she dropped her head back as his hands moved up, under her T-shirt. "I mean, you're not capable of giving consent."

At this, he lifted his head. "Are you serious?"

"Absolutely."

"You don't have to protect me."

She stiffened. "Because . . ."

"I'm a guy. We want sex whether we're drunk or not. And we don't complain about getting it afterward."

She could tell he was partly joking, but she wanted to be sure he knew what he was doing. "You should have a clear head when you're making that choice."

"Trust me." He rested his forehead against hers. "I know what I'm asking for. And I'd choose you no matter what."

He meant he'd choose having sex as opposed to not having sex. Tonight she just happened to be his potential partner. She had to keep the details straight, but it wasn't

259

easy, considering that his palms were lightly passing over the tips of her breasts.

Catching his wrists, she stopped him long enough to make him pull his hands out from under her shirt. "Sleeping with me won't solve whatever has you so upset, Noah."

He grinned as he gazed down at the response he'd drawn from her body, which was obvious despite her T-shirt. "But it'll sure as hell make for a better night than *not* sleeping with you." His smile faded as he looked up again. "I can deal with the rest in the morning. I'll have to, anyway."

"The rest of *what*?" she asked. What was wrong with him? Was this about last night? Or about something else?

"Don't ask. It'll just ruin . . . *this.*" He kissed her again, soft and lingering and wet enough to make her think she'd lose her mind if she continued to resist.

She thought of Gran. She thought of Cody, Kevin, Derek, Tom and Stephen. And she thought of the therapist who'd helped her recover. Dr. Rosenbaum would, no doubt, warn her against this. She'd come so far since the attack, didn't want to backslide.

But couldn't this be called progress? She felt so *alive,* so eager to be physical. With the men who'd come before him, she'd just wanted to pull away.

"Don't start thinking," he said.

"Why not?"

"Because I don't want you to say no."

She chuckled at how straightforward he was. "Let me get some shoes. I'll walk you home, make sure you don't fall in a ditch or stumble into the road."

He gave her a searching look. "You won't stay the night?"

"I can't," she replied.

But once they reached his house, he seemed so disappointed by the idea of being rejected, she couldn't maintain her refusal.

"I don't have a breathalyzer," he said as he urged her inside, "so what am I going to have to do? Walk a straight line? Recite the alphabet backward?"

It didn't say much for her resolve that he didn't have to do either of those things. All he had to do was kiss her and keep kissing her until they were in his bedroom.

15

Adelaide knew this wasn't the way to come out of the nose dive that had been her first week in Whiskey Creek. She was supposed to be keeping her distance from Noah, not cutting anchor and sailing straight into the storm.

But she couldn't imagine this would be the start of anything long-term. He'd never had a serious girlfriend, so there was that consolation. By morning, he'd say he wasn't looking for a committed relationship but he hoped they could remain friends. And she'd say she understood completely and hoped the same thing. Then they'd go their separate ways, and if she was lucky, he'd feel so self-conscious about not calling her afterward, he wouldn't even come into Just Like Mom's.

Having him step out of her life would be so much easier than trying to force him out. Then she wouldn't have to battle her natural inclinations. She could mind her own business, like she'd planned from the beginning, and try to forget this potent high school crush that kept reasserting itself, despite that nightmare of a graduation party *and* the passage of fifteen years.

"You're thinking again. . . ."

She couldn't help it. She was looking for pitfalls. She didn't want to regret this later. But she was pretty sure she'd regret stopping even more. It wasn't as if she'd feel this way about just any guy. Not counting the rape, she'd slept with two men, including Clyde, who'd become her husband, but there'd been very few fireworks involved.

One big hurrah and then . . . Noah would exit stage left.

Refusing to be hampered by any more doubt, she tugged on his shirt, and he lifted his arms so she could peel it off. "You look . . ." She didn't want to reveal how much she admired what she saw — since she knew she felt more than she should. "Just like I thought you would," she finished.

"Let's see if I can say the same." He fingered the hem of her T-shirt to indicate that he wanted to take it off.

Despite a nervous flutter in her stomach, she raised her arms.

"Beautiful." He tossed her shirt away but he certainly wasn't looking in that direction when he said this. He seemed mesmerized by the sight of her, and Addy could honestly say she'd never felt anything more exciting.

When he didn't make any move to touch her, however, she covered herself with her arms. She wasn't bold enough to continue standing there with her shirt off and the lights on. "I've always been kind of skinny."

Sometimes she still felt like that awkward girl he'd so casually ignored.

"Don't be nervous." He removed her hands. "You might've been skinny before but you're perfect now."

"So —" she swallowed hard "— why are you just . . . *staring* at me?"

He pinned her arms at her sides as he kissed one breast. "The anticipation is half the fun."

That sent another ripple of pleasure through her. Obviously, he was better at this than she was. But she'd expected to be a novice in comparison. "Okay, maybe . . ." She cleared her throat. "Maybe we could turn off the lights."

He chuckled. "Are you *still* that shy?"

"No." She shook her head, adamant. "Not anymore." She'd worked so hard to over-come that. "It's just . . . I haven't been with very many men. I'm not as used to this as you are."

He stepped closer, until his bare chest brushed against hers. "You were married."

It was becoming increasingly difficult to keep track of the conversation. "For a few months. And I'm pretty sure he slept with one of the waitresses at the restaurant more than he slept with me." She laughed as if she'd been making a joke, but she'd always feared that Clyde had preferred the waitress because she wasn't any fun in bed.

"Was he your first?"

"My second. There was one other guy . . . before."

"They always turned off the lights?"

"I guess." She couldn't remember. But she hadn't been as self-conscious with them, hadn't cared as much what they thought of her. That was why she'd chosen them. They were safe, nothing like Noah. At that point in her recovery, she hadn't been ready for a man who affected her as deeply as Noah.

"I'll turn them off if you want, but . . . this is a sight worth seeing. Just looking at you makes me hard as a rock."

When her face heated, he chuckled again. "Wow, it's been a long time since I've seen a woman get embarrassed so easily."

Suddenly afraid she was making a mistake,

she pulled away. "I'm not very good at this. I should go."

She tried to circumvent him so she could get to her shirt.

"Addy." His hands rested on her shoulders as he turned her around. "Don't go."

"I don't have the experience you want."

"I don't care about experience. All I care about is being with you. The lights can go off. You can have anything you want."

When she glanced at her shirt as if she was still tempted to pick it up, he grasped her chin. "It's okay," he murmured. "I wasn't making fun of you. To be honest, it's been a long time since I've wanted a woman so badly."

The sincerity in those words almost had her believing them. But she told herself comments like that had to be common when it came to casual sex.

She hesitated, but before she could decide what to do, he backed her up against the wall, where he could reach the light switch.

"You have nothing to worry about," he insisted, and plunged them into darkness.

"What about birth control?" she asked.

"I've got birth control."

She had other things to worry about. But once he lowered his head to her breast she couldn't remember a single one.

■ ■ ■ ■

Sex had become so mechanical lately, so
meaningless. But it wasn't that way with
Addy. Making her gasp or moan made it all
feel new. The first time they made love,
Noah was too caught up, couldn't worry
much about anything. He just went with
the demands of his body. But the second
time, he was determined to bring *her* to
climax — and became frustrated when he
couldn't. She wouldn't relax, wouldn't let
go. It was only when he refused to give up
that she finally admitted she'd *never* had an
orgasm while making love.

He could hardly believe it. She'd been
married. What had been happening in that
bed if she hadn't been getting any sexual
gratification from her husband?

"It's okay. I've had fun," she said when he
slumped over to rest.

It was almost four in the morning. After
what had occurred at the cabin, this night
felt as if it had lasted a week. But Noah
couldn't leave her unsatisfied. He wanted to
be the one to make it happen, and not just
because of male pride. He hated that the
two guys she'd been with before hadn't, for
whatever reason, helped her have that

experience.

"There must be something wrong with me," she said with a self-deprecating laugh.

She was offering him an excuse to finish without her. She'd probably offered the same excuse to the other two men she'd been with, and they must've accepted it or she wouldn't be in this situation. But he highly doubted she had a physical problem. It was her shyness that stood in the way. She was so quick to withdraw, to assume a protective stance, physically and emotionally. He could *feel* her holding back. . . .

"You can't be defensive or self-conscious or it won't work," he said.

"I'm not defensive." She didn't argue about being self-conscious. "I told you in the beginning . . . I'm not good at this."

"That's bullshit," he said. "That belief is part of the problem. You're not being graded, you know. I've loved every minute of it, but I want you to love it, too." He'd been aroused and so intent on keeping *her* aroused, on exploring her body, that he suddenly realized he might not have given her what she really needed — and that was a little more gentleness, a little more reassurance. She had to be able to trust him enough to quit shutting down as soon as she felt she might lose control.

"There's no reason it should be difficult," he added. "You're safe with me."

Her hands gripped his arms. "Noah, I . . . I really don't think I can."

"I know you've been through some shit in the past. Your ex must be to blame for that. What a bastard. But I'm not your ex. Let go of whatever happened before, okay? Abandon all resistance."

"You think I'm resisting?"

"I know you are." He kissed her again, this time soft and slow. "I want you to come," he coaxed. "Let me make you come."

"I've been trying!"

"Here . . ." He rolled onto his back, which brought her on top of him. "You take charge and do anything that feels good."

There was a heartbeat of silence. Then she said, "*You're* what feels good to me."

The way she made that statement led him to believe it encompassed more than the physical. It was usually the kind of declaration that frightened him, that made him believe he was getting into a sticky situation. But somehow, tonight, he responded to that deeper element, *wanted* it to be there.

He liked this woman. He liked her a lot.

"You're what feels good to me, too," he

admitted.

She stared down at him. He could see the shine in her eyes, even though she was barely visible in the moonlight cutting through the blinds. It felt as if he'd finally reached her on a profound level. And that made a difference. When she started to move, it wasn't all about the gasps and groans and physical pleasure he'd experienced so many times before. This was a more intimate connection. He didn't care if the sex was perfect; he only cared that she felt safe to enjoy it. And, oddly enough, he wasn't thinking about how he could slip out of the relationship without hurting her when it was over. He was letting himself go, too, in a way he'd never let go before, and that made this very different.

How ironic that he would feel what he was feeling on the night Baxter had tried to kiss him. It was as if the pendulum of his emotions had swung all the way back to the other side. He was excited, turned on, attracted enough to pursue this woman.

"See?" he whispered. "Feel the rhythm. You can start out nice and easy. . . ."

She did move nice and easy, but not for long. He smiled as the tension began to escalate, because he could tell she was experiencing the same growing pleasure he was. Too carried away to respond to his instructions, she arched her back and rocked faster and faster, and he helped her keep the rhythm with his hands on her thighs.

Considering how hard he'd tried the first time around, he'd expected this to take a while. But it didn't. After just a few minutes, he sensed that she was close, and that got him so excited he almost ruined it for her.

"Addy!" He could only say her name, but he was trying to warn her that he couldn't hang on much longer.

"Not yet," she gasped.

Clenching his hands in the bedding, he scrambled to concentrate on other things in an attempt to last. But then he heard her groan and felt that distinctive shudder and nothing could've stopped him from joining her.

Addy woke from a deep and dreamless sleep to the feel of a warm body curved protectively around hers. It took a moment to remember where she was, to realize this wasn't Clyde, who was the only man she'd ever woken up with before.

Then panic set in. What time was it? Had Gran gotten up and found her gone?

Lifting her head, she searched the darkness for Noah's alarm clock — and sagged in relief. It was only five-twenty. Gran didn't get up until six or six-thirty. If she hurried, she could make it back to her room before Gran even knew she'd been gone.

Careful not to wake Noah, she slid out of bed and began searching for her clothes. Her shirt and shoes were in the living room. She remembered that. But her panties and sweat bottoms had to be here . . . somewhere.

"Hey, you okay?"

Noah's sleepy words made her freeze. "Fine. I'm . . . everything's okay. Go back to sleep."

"I'm not going back to sleep. I don't want you out alone." He started to get up. "I'll walk you home."

"No. You can't. Someone could see us together."

She heard the rasp of his beard growth as he rubbed his face. "Oh, right. And the way we look, there'd be no question as to what we've been doing." He laughed as if imagining the sight they'd make. "What time is it?"

"Early, but there could be a few cars out and, in Whiskey Creek, that's all it would take."

He raised himself into a sitting position. "Will you be okay on your own?"

She used her feet to feel across the carpet. "Of course. It's only a couple of blocks."

"But after what happened on Wednesday, I'm afraid —"

"That won't happen again."

The tone of his voice changed. "How do you know?"

He was asking her to be honest with him about the night he'd rescued her from the mine, but she couldn't. What he knew from having found her was all he could ever know. Even that was too much. "I just do."

"Will you tell me something?"

She found her panties. "What?"

"Your ex-husband's name?"

She said nothing.

"That's a no?"

"Why does it matter?" she asked.

"I'd like to talk to him."

"About what?" She located her sweatpants hanging over the arm of a chair. "You don't even know him, and he's no longer part of my life."

"He's the one who hurt you, right?"

"No!"

"You're protecting *someone*."

"Forget it, okay?" she said as she slipped on her sweats. She started for the living room, then realized she should say something in parting. "Um, thanks for . . ."

"For?" he prompted when she couldn't come up with the appropriate words.

"A good time." She blanched at how clichéd that sounded but tried to rally. "I had fun."

There was a slight pause. "So did I."

She'd been covering her bare chest even though it was probably too dark for him to see her. "Bye."

"Wait a sec. Will you turn on the light?"

"I'm not dressed."

"You don't want me to *see* you? After last night?"

"There's no need for you to wake up all the way," she said, and dashed out to get her shirt.

She could hear him getting up. The light went on a second later. He was naked when he carried out a slip of paper. "Here's my cell phone. Give me a call after you've had a chance to get some sleep. I'll take you to dinner."

What was he talking about? They'd already had sex. This was supposed to be when he said he wasn't interested in a romantic relationship and he just wanted to be friends.

She stared at his outstretched hand. "That's okay."

His eyebrows slid up. "You don't want it?"

274

"It's not that I don't *want* it. It's that . . . we live in the same small town. If we're seen in public, people might make a big deal out of it. They might think we're . . . you know . . . dating when we're not. So . . . it'd be better to . . ."

"What?" He scowled. "*Not* see each other?"

He seemed to be getting upset, so she took the paper. She didn't *have* to call him. He'd probably forget he'd even given her his number. "Never mind. I, um, I have a busy day, but I'll see how things go."

He caught her at the door and turned her around. "You're not upset . . ."

"Of course not."

"Good. Because last night was one of the best nights I've ever had. Once we got here," he clarified.

She had a hard time believing last night had been very special for him, but it was a nice thing to say. "Given my lack of experience, that's shocking."

"It shouldn't be, because it wasn't about performing like a porn star."

And this wasn't ending with the brush-off she'd been expecting. "I'd better go."

He bent his head as if he'd kiss her good-bye, but she pretended like she didn't realize that was his intention and slipped out.

275

"Thanks again."

After walking a couple of miles down the narrow mountain road leading away from the cabin, Baxter had called Eve on his cell phone and had her pick him up. She'd been worried when she saw him, of course, had wanted to know what was wrong, but he'd managed to minimize the situation. Telling her that he and Noah had had an argument because they'd both been drinking and had hit on the same girl was easier than revealing what he'd been hiding since the fifth grade. It wasn't that he didn't trust Eve. It was just that the fewer people who knew, the better. If his parents ever found out, they'd never speak to him again.

They had a greater chance of finding out today than they did yesterday. He was aware of that. Since he'd lost control and acted so recklessly, he didn't know what to expect. The image of Noah standing there, too shocked to react, too shocked to even push him away, made Baxter want to weep. Noah probably hated him. The crazy thing was that he couldn't understand why, after keeping himself in check for so long, he'd done what he'd done. The part of him that was dying to come out had simply tried to bury, once and for all, the front he'd been showing the world. And now he had to deal with the fear of losing his friends *and* his family.

He'd been so upset he hadn't even gone to bed.

If only Noah hadn't acted as if it was so much fun to have those girls around.

If only Baxter hadn't had to watch Lisa climb into Noah's lap and kiss him so sexually when Baxter knew damn well that Noah felt nothing for her.

If only they hadn't been drinking.

Over the past few years, he'd been so careful to avoid alcohol when he was in Noah's presence.

"Shit." He couldn't take stewing alone any longer, so he grabbed his cell phone off the side table and called the hotel where Callie and Levi were staying in Hawaii. He hated to bother them on their honeymoon, but he had to talk to someone, and because Callie was the only friend he'd ever confided in, she was his best option. The gay men he socialized with in San Francisco didn't understand his situation and certainly didn't agree with his choices.

"Hey," he said when he heard her sleepy hello. "Did I wake you?"

"Who is this?"

"You've forgotten me already?"

"Bax!" There was a pause, and then she

chuckled. "I'm out of it. It's four-thirty here. What's going on?"

He hadn't even checked the time. "I'm sorry to wake you. I held off as long as I could, but . . ."

"Is something wrong?" She sounded worried.

"No. Never mind." He shouldn't have disturbed her. She was doing better now, but she'd nearly died over the summer. He needed to let her get all the rest she could. There was still a possibility that her body could reject the new liver. That was partly why she and Levi had had to wait a couple of weeks after the wedding to leave. They'd needed a doctor's clearance to go so far from home. "I'll call you later."

"No, wait! Don't go!"

He didn't hang up but the lump in his throat made it almost impossible to speak.

"Are you there?" she asked.

He swallowed hard. "Yeah."

"You're scaring me."

"I told him," he said.

"You told . . ." After a brief pause, she seemed more awake. "What are you saying? You told who what?"

"I told Noah the truth."

Her voice took on a tentative tone. "About . . ."

He laughed but it was a bitter sound even to his own ears. "Actually, I didn't *tell* him. I showed him."

"Baxter, what are you talking about?"

"I kissed him, Callie. I —" unable to believe it, he shoved a hand through his hair "— *kissed* Noah."

This revelation met with stunned silence. Then she said, "Bax, are you drunk?"

"Not anymore."

"You were? Oh, God."

"Yeah. Shit. What am I going to do now?"

"That depends. Hang on." There was some rustling. He guessed she was getting out of bed and going into the bathroom so she could talk without disturbing her husband. "How did he react?"

"It was . . . sort of anticlimactic."

"You didn't enjoy it as much as you thought you would?"

"He didn't exactly pull me into his arms."

"You *knew* he wouldn't."

"True, but get this, he didn't shove me away, either."

"What does that leave?"

"He stood there, Callie. He just stood there, which makes me feel like even more of an idiot."

"He must have said *something* eventually."

The way her words echoed told him she

was indeed in the bathroom.

"I didn't wait to hear it. I took off."

"Where were you when you . . . when this happened?"

"Gail's cabin."

"And now?"

"Home."

"Have you heard from him since?"

"Of course not. What can he say? 'I hate you for loving me? I'm completely grossed out by the fact that you want to get naked with me? Stay the hell away?' He doesn't *have* to say those things. I know he feels them."

She sighed into the phone. "Was anyone else around?"

He went to stand at the window. It was getting light outside. He was glad of that, glad the long night was finally over. Not that daybreak made his situation any easier. Now he'd have to face the results of his actions. "No one I need to worry about."

"Wow," she breathed. "So . . . what's next?"

He glanced around his house. Built in 1894, it was listed on the historic registry, along with a handful of other buildings in Whiskey Creek, and it was spectacular, everything he'd hoped it would be. He'd spent three years restoring it, but now he felt he'd been foolish to remain in such a conservative community, to perpetuate the illusion he'd maintained since he first began to suspect he was gay. His love for Noah and his other friends had held him here, but there suddenly didn't seem to be any reason to hang on. He needed to sell his place. He could find a condo or other accommodation in San Francisco, where he worked. "I guess I'll move to the city."

"Bax, I want you to be happy. You know I do. So if San Francisco will make you happier, I'm all for it. I'll drive over often. But . . . don't go because you feel we won't accept you for who you are. Give us a chance."

"Callie, if word gets out, I'll *have* to leave. My father's the biggest homophobe in Northern California. I don't want to be an embarrassment to him."

"He loves you."

That was about all she could say. It was true. But that love held him hostage. He couldn't bear the thought of losing it. "I'm his only son. Every time I see him, we have to go hunting, as much as I hate that, or watch a football game. You know, scratch our balls, beat our chests, talk about how much we love big tits. A few months ago he took me to a strip club, for crying out loud."

"Your mother didn't mind?"

"He said there are a few things we don't tell her."

"He's not cheating . . ."

"No, he's just trying to make a man out of me."

"Imagine setting all that aside."

He recognized the sarcasm in her voice but didn't react to it. "I can't imagine it, because I'd be setting my father aside at the same time. That's who he is."

"He has to suspect, Bax. The way you look at Noah. I hate to tell you this, but sometimes it's obvious."

"Not to my dad. He doesn't notice how I look at other guys because he doesn't want to see it. I can hunt. I can fish. I can play sports. I've had girlfriends. I pass the 'not gay' litmus test. He doesn't care if I have to pretend."

"I'm *so* sorry, Bax. I wish . . . I wish there was something I could do to change that."

"So do I." A gunmetal-gray Dodge Ram pulled out of the stream of traffic traveling down Sutter Street and stopped in front of his house, and his heart leaped into his throat. "Holy hell."

"What?" she cried.

"Noah's here."

16

Noah had never felt more awkward in his life. He wasn't even sure why, after Addy left, he'd gotten up, showered and driven over to Baxter's Victorian. His relationship with Bax could never be what it was. As far as Noah was concerned, the very nature of who Baxter was had changed. So what did he have to gain by coming here?

Maybe nothing. But Baxter had been part of his life for so long, he couldn't remain angry.

He hoped they could find some middle ground, some way to continue as friends, even if things were a bit uncomfortable for a while. And he figured it was better to get this first painful confrontation over with as soon as possible. If he put it off, or they weren't able to work through the strong emotions the incident at the cabin had provoked, the rest of their friends would pick up on the strain and it would become a big issue, possibly dividing the whole group.

Learning that Baxter had a crush on him was hard enough to deal with; Noah didn't want to challenge his other relationships at the same time.

"I'm surprised to see you." Baxter didn't open the door very wide, didn't invite Noah in.

Noah shifted from one foot to the other. He'd never seen his friend's eyes so red. He'd never seen him this unkempt, either. Somehow Baxter managed to look his typical stylish self even when he had a hangover. But not today. Today he had on the clothes he'd worn last night, sleeves rolled up and shirttails hanging out. And his skin was unusually pale beneath the dark shadow of beard that covered the lower half of his face.

Noah guessed he hadn't been to bed. "I'm surprised to be here," he admitted.

"Why'd you come?"

He shrugged. "We've been friends all our lives. I guess that's why."

Baxter said nothing.

"Does anyone else know?" Noah asked.

He winced. "About last night?"

"That you're *gay,* Bax. Let's start with that."

"Are you kidding?"

"No, I'm not kidding! I mean . . ." Noah gazed off into the neighbor's yard before looking back. "Am I the only one who *didn't* know?"

Somehow the thought of that bothered him as much as all the rest of it.

"No. I haven't said a word to anyone. Except Callie." He leaned into the door. "And only because she kept badgering me about it."

Baxter had spent a lot of time with Callie this summer, while she was sick. Noah could see why he might confide in her, but that made him feel betrayed by both of them, as if they were keeping this great secret from him. Callie was his friend, too. She could've warned him. Instead, she'd allowed him to be blindsided.

"You should've told me."

"You didn't want to know."

Noah couldn't refute that, which made it hard to blame Callie, too, so he continued listing his grievances. "*You pretended to be straight!* You talked about girls. You . . . you played football. You took showers with us. You went skinny-dipping at the water hole whenever we went. Hell, we got laid for the first time on a double date the week we moved into our dorm at San Diego State. We slept with so many girls that year it wasn't even funny."

Baxter's jaw tightened. "Because that's what *you* wanted. And I was still fighting the truth. Don't you get it? I wanted to be like you. I *tried* to be like you. I just . . . wasn't!"

Noah didn't know whether to be mad at himself for ignoring all the signs, or mad at Baxter for taking advantage of his determined loyalty. "And you didn't feel you could level with me?"

"You think I should've blown up our friendship years ago?"

Noah wanted to deny that Baxter's sexual orientation would affect the friendship, but there was little doubt that this would change the whole dynamic. For starters, what they talked about would change. So would *how* they talked about it. "*Is* this a friendship, Bax? Or is it something else? In your view, anyway. I mean . . . what you did at the cabin . . ." He couldn't finish, couldn't get any closer to The Kiss than that. Thank goodness for Addy. It was being with her afterward that'd given him a chance to put it in perspective. He couldn't help that he was attracted to her. Maybe Baxter couldn't help his attractions, either.

They stared at each other for several seconds. Then Baxter said, "Are we really going to talk about *that*?"

"You're saying we shouldn't?"

"I'm shocked that you're willing."

"I'm here because I'm trying to under-stand!"

"So you're going to look under the bed even though you know what you're going to find will scare you? Don't bother. It won't change anything. I've got to go." He began to shut the door but Noah blocked it.

"What do you mean you have to go?"

"I mean I can't see you anymore. I have a lot of changes to make. They'll be painful enough without . . . without trying to fake a friendship with you."

Noah felt as if he'd just been slugged. "Why would it be fake?"

"Because it can't be anything else!" he said, and closed the door.

Shocked, Noah stood there for probably fifteen minutes. He expected Baxter to re-alize that he'd just cut off his best friend. He thought Baxter would eventually calm down and come back and they'd be able to work out . . . something. But he didn't, and when Noah knocked again he just yelled, "Go away!"

Black Gold Coffee was crowded. When the weather was good, Sundays saw an influx of

tourists. Like other gold-country towns —
Grass Valley, Placerville, Cool, Coloma,
Plymouth, Angels Camp — it was a popular
stop along Highway 49.

All these towns were a throwback to the
1800s and had a surfeit of old-fashioned,
quaint charm, but none more so than
Whiskey Creek. Some of the locals complained about the occasional crowds and
the lack of street parking, but the gift shops
and other businesses thrived on their pa-
tronage, including Just Like Mom's. Today
Addy *liked* having so many unfamiliar faces
around. Being in the presence of strangers
made her feel less conspicuous as she sat in
the corner, booting up her laptop.

"Mocha frappuccino!" the barista called
out.

She glanced around before going to collect her drink. She was hoping she wouldn't
see Kevin or anyone else this time, and that
included Noah. It wasn't easy, but she
hadn't let herself dwell on being with him
last night. There were moments she caught
her mind drifting back to what it had felt
like to touch him, to kiss him, and she had
to reel her thoughts back in. She supposed
that was only natural. But she couldn't see
him again. She'd spent half her high school
years craving him; that was enough. Noah

had commitment issues. That meant she couldn't have a relationship with him, even if they didn't have Cody's death standing between them. Whenever she began to feel wistful, to remember how satisfied and complete she'd felt in his arms, she reminded herself that there was no use crying about something she couldn't change. Her life was what it was. She had to accept that and do what she could for Gran.

She connected to the free internet while sipping her frappuccino. She didn't want to stay out in public for long. She just wanted to take a peek at www.SkintightEntertainment.com. For her own peace of mind, she hoped to figure out who'd broken into her bedroom. It could be useless information, or it could help her defend herself later, if she was ever forced into that position again. At least she'd know which of her four attackers had the nerve to threaten her with a knife.

But the website that came up made her regret checking it. It was a porn site — with bondage and rape as a major theme.

The thud of her heart seemed to reverberate in her chest. Had her attacker worn that sweatshirt on purpose? As a way to intimidate her further? Or . . .

She remembered Noelle standing at her

289

grandmother's booth during the Homecoming game, inviting her to model for a calendar.

Noelle had given her a URL where she could see what Derek had created so far. She'd put that card in her purse.

She took a few seconds to dig it out so she could visit that site, too.

Sure enough, Derek had some pictures posted. The site said the calendar wasn't finished, that it wouldn't go on sale until December 1, but there was a preorder campaign in place, and Noelle's picture was used as the enticement.

Olivia's sister wasn't naked. She was wearing a string bikini, but she was posed on a beach with her knees falling open, her hands on her breasts and her head thrown back as if she was inviting the viewer closer. *A lot* closer.

Could Derek Rodriguez be involved with that calendar *and* the porn site?

Absently fingering her cheekbone, where the worst bruise from her ordeal had yet to fade, she surfed through all the links. There was a contact number for Derek, but no address. Tom had told her he worked from home doing websites but wasn't very successful.

He certainly seemed more likely to be

connected to www.SkintightEntertainment
.com than Kevin or Tom. But what about
Stephen? According to Tom, Stephen was
probably behind what had been done to her.
She already knew he had a rape fantasy.
Without the spark he'd provided at that
graduation party, she doubted Cody would
ever have violated her in that way. He
certainly hadn't needed to use her for sex.
He'd been sleeping with girls since the
eighth grade. Rumors went around the high
school all the time that Shania was pregnant,
or that she'd had an abortion.

Addy knew it was her innocence they'd
been after, and Stephen had taken more
pride in destroying that than all the rest of
them put together. She'd actually been
surprised that it was Cody who'd come back
for more. . . .

"Addy, is that you?"

She glanced up to see one of the waitresses
who worked at her grandmother's restaurant, probably the only one who'd been at
Just Like Mom's since before she left.

"Hi, Luanne."

"It's been a long time."

They'd talked on the phone now and then
when Addy had called Darlene or Gran at
the restaurant, but Addy hadn't seen her
since returning to Whiskey Creek. "It has.

It's great to see you. Are you off today?"

"I usually spend Sundays with my kids, but . . . my mom took them to Disneyland for a few days."

"That's nice of her."

She winced as she indicated Addy's eye. "Whoever attacked you did a fine job of it, didn't they?"

She smiled. "They could've done worse."

"I guess so. You must be healing well to have such a good attitude."

"I'll be fine."

"Will you be coming into the restaurant soon?"

She closed her laptop. "Tomorrow, as a matter of fact."

"Oh." She hesitated as if she had more to say, but seemed to reconsider. "I work tomorrow, too. I guess I'll see you then."

"Luanne?"

She turned back. "Yes?"

Addy studied her. "Was there something else you wanted to say to me?"

Her gaze slid to the floor before rebounding. "I just . . . I felt like maybe I should warn you that Darlene might not be happy to have you . . . get involved."

"In running the restaurant?"

"She's been doing it pretty much on her own lately."

"I'm not planning to take her job, not if I can help it." Even if Gran agreed to sell the restaurant, the new owners might need Darlene to remain as manager. "I tried to make that clear when I called to tell her I'll be returning."

"I know. But . . ." She smiled. "Never mind. I'm sure everything will be fine. See you then."

Adelaide watched her go. Was Darlene going to give her trouble?

Maybe she had more problems than she'd realized.

Was it just yesterday that he'd thought he'd been enjoying himself a little too much? That he needed to get serious and grow up?

What had happened with Baxter showed Noah how quickly life could change. Gone was the feeling that he had things too good. As darkness fell on Sunday evening he felt slightly bereft, unsettled, even torn. He wanted Baxter to stay in Whiskey Creek, but he could see that wouldn't improve the situation. Baxter would still crave something he couldn't find here, and he deserved the right to pursue what would fulfill him, like everyone else.

It didn't make Noah feel any better that Addy hadn't called. He'd never dreamed that, after last night, she wouldn't be eager to get back in touch with him. They'd had such a great time. He'd never had to worry about being blown off like that.

"What are you doing here?"

He blinked as his mother confronted him. He'd been reaching for the door when she opened it. "Don't my parents live here?"

"The parents you rarely visit?"

"What are you talking about? I see you all the time."

"You wouldn't even talk to us at the game the other night."

"I wasn't in a particularly good mood."

"You don't seem to be in a great mood now. What's wrong?"

"Nothing's wrong." He scowled as he moved past her. "What's for dinner?"

"You came to eat?"

"Sure. Where's Dad?"

"It's Sunday."

"I know."

"So he's playing golf, like always. You went with him a couple of weeks ago, remember? But he should be home any minute."

Noah lingered as he passed several pictures of him and Cody that were hanging on the wall. Baxter was in some of those photos, almost as if he'd been raised a member of the Rackham family.

"Is this about Friday night, honey?" she asked, her voice softening as she came up behind him.

"I don't want to talk about Friday night."

"It's okay to mourn your brother, Noah. If you'd let yourself grieve, maybe the pain would go away."

He put his arm around her. "Use your psychology degree on someone else, Mom," he said. "It's been years. I'm fine."

"Losing a twin is harder than losing a regular sibling. They've done studies."

"I've been through it, remember?"

"So that's all I'm going to get out of you?"

He wanted to say more, but he couldn't tell her or anyone else about Baxter. He'd come here for the distraction. Sitting at home, obsessing over the Big Revelation wasn't helping. It was only making him feel worse. And then there was Addy. He wasn't any more comfortable with rejection than he was with grief. He'd been tempted to stop by her place instead. She'd been a hell of a distraction last night. One he could go for again. But he hadn't gotten her number, although he'd given her his. He'd never imagined he wouldn't hear from her. He'd given Addy her first orgasm, for heaven's sake.

"Food sounds good." Maybe afterward he

could have a word with his father about the investigation into Addy's abduction. No matter what happened, he wanted to know who'd kidnapped her and see the bastard punished.

Once he sat down, his mother massaged his shoulders for a few seconds before kissing his cheek and moving over to the stove. "So what's been going on with you?"

He toyed with the salt and pepper shakers she'd put on the table. "I've just been working at the store."

"When you're not rescuing damsels in distress." She turned to grin at him.

"Finding Addy in the mine was definitely . . . out of the ordinary."

"Word has it Aaron Amos kidnapped her. Have you heard?"

"It wasn't Aaron."

She dropped her spoon in what he thought was gravy and had to fish it out. "Who was it, then?"

"I don't know. And she's not saying."

"*She* knows?"

He wanted to admit that he suspected she did, but bit his tongue. "The guy was wearing a mask. I guess that makes it pretty difficult."

"I would think so," she said. "But it *is* a little weird that he'd take her to the mine."

"What do you mean?"

She seemed reluctant to answer, but when he cocked an eyebrow as if demanding she explain, she continued. "We got a note once, not too long after we buried Cody."

He sat up straighter. He'd never heard this before. "From who?"

"No idea. It was anonymous."

"What'd it say?"

She seemed to *want* to tell him. The words, whatever they were going to be, almost came out. But his father walked through the front door at that moment.

"Hey," he called out, "don't tell me my son has actually deigned to visit his old man."

"Mom?" Noah whispered, prompting her before Brent could reach the kitchen.

She sent a furtive glance over his head. They had a minute or two while his father put away his clubs, but that didn't seem to matter. "It was nothing," she said. "Just . . . one of those things like a . . . a crank call where someone tries to torment a bereaved family."

"Someone tried to torment us? With *what*? And who would do such a thing?" No one had ever mistreated him or Cody. His parents, either, as far as he knew. His father didn't have any political enemies. He was probably the most popular mayor the town had ever had. He hadn't been mayor back then, anyway.

"It was nothing," she said again. "I don't want to upset your father by bringing up the past. So don't tell him I mentioned it, okay?"

He didn't get the chance to answer. She turned back to her cooking, as if they hadn't been discussing anything important, the second Brent walked into the room.

17

The next few days weren't easy, despite the fact that Addy didn't have to face any of the men she wanted to avoid. She got up and went to the restaurant Monday morning, as planned. She did the same on Tuesday, Wednesday and Thursday, and worked late each night. There were a lot of things she saw there that she wanted to change. At odd moments, when she looked at the surroundings she'd loved growing up, she even felt a sense of creative excitement. After everything she'd learned in culinary school and working for the Kingsdales, she could do so much to update and improve the restaurant.

But Luanne had known what she was talking about when she tried to warn Addy that there might be trouble with Darlene. Gran's manager wasn't *overtly* unfriendly, but she couldn't quite hide her resentment. She liked having free rein over the restaurant, didn't want Addy to question any of her policies or curtail her authority, especially since Addy had been little more than a child when she'd worked here before. Maybe Darlene had guessed that Addy wanted to get the restaurant ready to sell, because she was acting so proprietary, and that only made things harder.

Addy couldn't stop thinking about Noah, even though she hadn't seen or heard from him since their night together. She still felt anxious leaving the house for fear of running into Kevin, Tom, Derek or Stephen. And, on Thursday, Gran came down with such a bad cold that she couldn't get out of bed. Addy was worried that the infection would turn into pneumonia. On top of that, Darlene had chosen Thursday — just called at the last minute — to take a personal day, which made Addy angry. Gran's manager had implied that her absence was a direct result of feeling as if she had someone looking over her shoulder all the time. No doubt she hoped Addy wouldn't like bearing a hundred percent of the responsibility for the restaurant — that she'd give up and leave.

But Addy wasn't about to let Darlene win the power struggle between them. Whether Darlene wanted to acknowledge it or not, she didn't own the place. She wasn't even doing such a great job of managing it. Since she'd taken over, the restaurant was making less money than before. For one thing, they needed to raise their prices to keep up with the cost of food. It'd been a decade or more since Gran had overhauled the menu. . . .

Addy was pondering that change, and musing over her idea of adding some organic options, when a voice — far more familiar than she would've expected after so many years — sent chills down her spine.

"We'll sit over here in the corner, if that's okay. And if you can tell her we'd like a word, that would be great."

Leaving her post at the back desk, Addy went to peek over the saloon-type doors leading into the dining area. Derek Rodriguez was strolling across the restaurant. Noelle Arnold, who'd gone back to her maiden name, was with him. When Addy noticed Luanne coming toward the kitchen, she knew without having to be told that she was the person they'd asked for.

"He has some nerve," she mumbled. Addy had been thinking a lot about what Derek had asked Noelle to pass on. What was that business about having her pose almost-naked in a *baseball* uniform? A cruel joke? A veiled threat? Maybe he was taunting her about the fact that he'd gotten away with what he'd done. It was even possible he thought she'd welcome the reminder. She'd learned in her counseling sessions that some rapists justified their actions by convincing themselves that their victims asked for what they got, or at least enjoyed it.

The crazy thing was that Derek hadn't seemed like a bad kid when he was a teenager. None of them had seemed like bad kids. They were the popular crowd, the boys most likely to succeed — not be brought up on sexual assault charges.

Luanne touched her arm. "Did you hear me?"

Addy stared at her, drawing herself out of the past. "You said Derek and Noelle want to say hello."

Pausing as she slipped her order pad into the pocket of her apron, Luanne gave her a funny look. "That's right."

Suddenly, she was grateful Darlene wasn't around. One battle at a time, she told herself, and proceeded into the dining room. She regretted giving Kevin the pleasure of seeing how deeply he affected her and didn't plan to make the same mistake with Derek. The only way to maintain some power in this situation was to pretend she'd gotten over the incident completely.

She needed to take charge and stop being

a victim — as much as that was possible.

"Hi, Noelle." She forced a smile for Olivia's sister as she came up to the table. Then she turned to Derek. "And you are . . ."

His eyebrows shot up. "Don't you remember me?"

She adopted a baffled expression as Luanne brought some water. "I'm afraid not."

"Derek. Derek Rodriguez. I used to play on the baseball team."

"He's the one who bought you the necklace I dropped off after that terrible experience you had in the mine," Noelle volunteered.

The necklace she'd thrown away as soon as she'd learned. Sensing that he might bring up the party in order to jog her memory, she pretended to have figured out who he was. "Oh! Right. I remember you now. Vaguely." She wrinkled her nose. "Have you put on weight or —"

"I've put on at least twenty pounds — all of it muscle." He flexed his arms to prove it, obviously proud of the work he'd put in at the gym.

"If you say so." She turned her attention back to Noelle. "Luanne said you wanted to see me?"

"Derek would like to recruit you for that

modeling job I told you about. Isn't that cool?"

Could he really be that obtuse? Or was he trying to torment her?

It had to be the latter.

"I'm afraid I don't have any time for modeling."

"That's too bad." He gave her a taunting smile. "Even at night?"

Especially at night. She wasn't going anywhere near him, and certainly not in private. "Sorry."

He clicked his tongue. "I'm looking for just one more, and you'd be perfect. You're much prettier than you were in high school."

"Am I supposed to thank you for that comment?" she asked dryly.

"I'm just being honest," he said with a laugh.

"He has to be objective," Noelle explained. "Like the judges on *The X Factor* when they tell those singers not to quit their day jobs. Anyway, it's not like he said you look *worse.* I'd be pissed if he said *that* to me."

"You're a real stunner these days," he said, winking at Addy. "And I'd love to have you in the calendar. I think maybe it's time we were friends."

"Friends?" she repeated.

Although Addy couldn't see any reason she should, Noelle seemed to adore him. "He's a *great* photographer," she gushed. "Without him I wouldn't even be in modeling. Didn't you go to that link I gave you?"

Addy swallowed hard. "I did."

"And? What'd you think?"

Anger, maybe even hatred, seemed to be getting the best of Addy. Taking care of Gran didn't mean she had to socialize with one of her attackers, or even Noelle. She resented that Derek had used Noelle to trick her with that necklace, knew he probably found it funny that she'd been wearing it. "Posing naked is not my thing. But I wish you well with it."

She started to walk off, but Derek's next words made her freeze.

"This isn't about what happened at graduation, is it?"

A jolt of panic sent Adelaide's pulse racing. Had he just referred to the rape in the middle of the restaurant as if it was no big deal?

Acutely conscious of Noelle's presence, Addy scrambled to defuse the situation. "As far as I'm concerned, *nothing* happened at graduation, so I'm not sure what you're referring to."

"Glad to hear it. I was hoping you didn't

have any hard feelings, because that was all in fun, you know? Kevin just mentioned it to me last night. We were so shitfaced we didn't know what the hell we were doing."

"*That's* how you both remember it?" Addy asked. With Noelle looking curiously between the two of them, she was crazy to make the situation any more remarkable than it already was, but she was so shocked she couldn't help it.

He waved a hand. "It's mostly a blur to us. But I remember how excited you were to be there, how badly you wanted our attention."

Addy's ears were ringing so loudly she almost couldn't hear. He'd held her down. He'd taken his turn. He couldn't simply excuse that by laughing it off and saying he was "shitfaced."

Frowning in confusion, Noelle took a sip of her water. "I don't think I was at that party."

"Naw, you were too young," he told her. "But you would've liked it."

"So what happened?"

"What *didn't* happen?" He looked to Addy for confirmation, then whistled and shook his head.

A drop of sweat rolled down Addy's back even though she wasn't remotely warm. She was holding herself too rigidly, but she couldn't relax. "Cody Rackham lost his life as a *direct* consequence of that party. I guess I don't remember it as fondly as you do," she said, and walked away.

Her emphasis on "direct" was probably the closest she'd ever come to admitting she'd had a hand, however inadvertently, in Cody's death. But she desperately wanted Derek to know that the consequences of their actions hadn't been minimal, as he pretended to believe. That rape had cost them their beloved leader, their most admired friend. It had cost Noah his twin brother. They couldn't shrug *that* off, even if they could shrug off how badly they'd hurt and traumatized her.

"Let me know if you change your mind about the calendar," he called after her.

Because Gran was sick, Addy didn't feel she could stay late, but with Darlene gone, she couldn't leave early, either. Carla, the assistant manager, had opened at eight and gone home at five. She was a single mom with two kids. It wasn't fair to ask her to pay for extra child care when Darlene had done the scheduling and had slotted herself to close — and then decided to take the day off.

At five-thirty Addy called home and couldn't get an answer, so she tried Darlene's number. She was hoping to get her to come in for a few hours, so she could check on Gran and see that she had some dinner.

"It's Adelaide," she said when she had Darlene on the phone. "I was wondering if you'd taken care of whatever you needed to do today. Gran's sick, so I'd like a couple of hours tonight."

"I'm afraid I can't help you, Addy. I never dreamed you wouldn't be able to cover the whole day. I thought it would be the perfect time for me to take care of a few things here."

The "perfect time" would be on her regular days off. She had two a week. But Addy didn't say so. Darlene had been around a long time. Addy was still hoping they'd work out their differences. She hadn't even approached Gran about selling yet. "I was more than happy to fill in and give you a break, but that was yesterday, before Gran got sick. She was fine a little while ago, but now she's not answering. I really need to get over there and make sure she's okay."

"The waitresses know what they're doing. Just put Luanne in charge while you're gone."

Was that what she did? Did she come and

go at her leisure, leaving the restaurant without a manager on duty? Addy could see doing that midafternoon, maybe — but this time of day? They were always busy at dinner. "What if Gran needs me to stay with her? Who'll close and take the receipts to the bank?"

"Whoever you trust enough to do that, I guess. I'm afraid I can't help."

Besides referring to some nebulous "things" she had to do, she had yet to say why. Addy didn't want to assume the worst, but she got the feeling that Darlene was taking pleasure in her predicament, as if she saw it as payback because Addy had involved herself in the restaurant. Darlene clearly felt she had no right — even though she had *every* right.

"Okay, I'll have to do what I have to do, but . . . I wonder what you would've done if I wasn't here."

"Fortunately, you are here, and you *love* being at the restaurant."

Addy stiffened at her flippant tone. "Actually, I do."

The ensuing pause was fraught with resentment.

"Is something wrong?" Addy asked.

"Does Milly know she's not in charge anymore?" Darlene replied.

"She *is* in charge, as much as she's capable of being in charge. I would never take that from her. I'm just here to do what she can't."

"We've been getting along fine. You realize that."

Addy sat up taller. "You mean without me?"

Darlene quickly improved her tone. "You don't have to disrupt your whole life on our account. We have our routine, and we're good at it."

In other words, *butt out*. Addy heard that loud and clear.

"Milly still trusts me, doesn't she?" Darlene was saying. "I've given that restaurant twenty years of my life."

"Of course. We both trust you. But that doesn't mean there won't be some changes."

"What kind of changes are we talking about?"

"I haven't completely decided. I'd like to discuss my ideas with Gran first."

"You've been gone for thirteen years, Addy."

"So?"

She could tell Darlene knew better than to say more, but was too frustrated to stop. "If you cared so much about Milly, why didn't you come back before now?"

Addy stood up so fast she hit the desk drawer with her thighs, but she ignored the brief flash of pain. Apparently, everything she'd sensed in Darlene, everything Luanne had warned her about, was accurate. Darlene had been good to her when she was a child, but she wasn't willing to accept that now Addy was doing a little more than "helping out."

"Darlene, I'd like us to get along," she said. "I have fond memories of you. But if you can't cope with having me back, we'll need to make other arrangements."

"Meaning . . ."

Addy heard the shock in her voice. She hadn't talked to Gran, wasn't sure she should even make this statement. But she couldn't tolerate insubordination, not if she planned to work at Just Like Mom's — and she had to, since Gran no longer could. Darlene had obviously grown far too comfortable with being in charge. "I think you know what that means."

"Everything's *fine* at the restaurant, Addy. I don't see why you have to come in and take over."

"You don't have to see."

The resulting silence was openly hostile.

"Are you going to be able to adjust?" Addy continued, pressing her sudden and very slight advantage. "Or do I have to let you go?"

"I've worked at that restaurant for two decades! Milly would *never* let you fire me!" she cried, and hung up.

"Is everything okay?"

Addy had dropped the phone and was resting her forehead on one fist. At the sound of Luanne's voice, she glanced up, then stood. "Fine. But . . . could you keep an eye on things for a while? I have to go home and check on Gran."

"Of course."

She wrote her cell phone number on a Post-it and stuck it to the wall above the desk. "Call me if you need anything."

"Addy?"

Adelaide had already started for the door. She was fighting tears. She didn't want any of the employees to see her like this, but she wasn't willing to be rude to someone who'd always been so nice to her.

She was glad she'd turned back when Luanne took one look at her and hugged her tight. "Was that Darlene on the phone?"

She nodded against the other woman's temple, since she was so much taller.

"She's just feeling threatened, honey. Don't let her upset you. *I,* for one, am glad you're here." She tightened her squeeze for emphasis. "Now . . . are you gonna be okay?"

Addy nodded. "Of course. I've been through worse," she said with a wobbly smile.

Gran was a lot better. That came as a relief. Addy kept in touch with Luanne at the restaurant but stayed home for a few hours, even after seeing that Gran had supper. She needed to go back to close, but Gran stopped her every time she got up to leave by asking for another game of cards. She was bored now that she couldn't move around like she used to. She'd always been so strong, so dominant and energetic. But she was getting old. Addy wondered how her own mother could be so indifferent to the passing time. Didn't she realize that Gran wouldn't be around forever? Would she someday regret ignoring her greatest blessing?

Addy had long since stopped asking herself these kinds of questions, but tonight seemed to be the night for facing harsh realities. She hadn't yet decided what to do about Darlene. She'd planned to discuss the situation with Gran, but Gran seemed so happy, Addy didn't want to ruin the evening by dumping work woes in her lap.

"You get some rest," she told her. "I have to go back to the restaurant."

Gran seemed surprised by this. "Why can't Darlene close?"

Addy had already explained that Darlene had taken a personal day. "She's off, remember?"

"Oh, that's right. But you've been working too hard this week. I'm sorry so much is falling on you."

She bent to kiss Gran's wrinkled cheek. "I don't mind."

"At least those nasty bruises are almost gone. Have you heard from Chief Stacy?"

Not since he'd come by to inform her that Shania wasn't providing Aaron with an alibi. "No. But I'm sure he'll call if there's anything new."

"I'm disappointed he hasn't apprehended the culprit. I expected more."

"He'll get him eventually," she murmured, and turned on a TV show Gran liked before leaving the house. She was just getting into her truck when she realized there was a note under her windshield wipers.

She glanced around but saw no one, except the people driving on the street that passed Gran's and went on to wind through town.

After throwing her purse inside and putting the key in the ignition, she climbed back out to retrieve the note.

It was half a sheet of copy paper and contained three typed words with no signature. *I'm watching you.*

18

Noah punched the end button and dropped his cell phone on the couch beside him. That was the third time he'd tried talking to his mother about the strange comment she'd made last weekend. He wanted to know what she meant by saying someone had tried to "torment" their family. That couldn't be interpreted as the throwaway statement she'd been trying to suggest it was ever since. But she wouldn't go near the subject again. Whenever he pressed her, even if he knew his father was gone, she'd say it was nothing.

"It sure seemed like something when you didn't want Dad to hear," he grumbled to his empty living room, and slid down so he could rest his head on the back of the couch.

It had been one hell of a week. Normally he sailed through autumn. Unlike the energy and effort required when he was racing, in the off-season he had nothing particularly demanding to cope with. Sure, he'd been feeling a little empty and dissatisfied recently, as various friends married and moved on with their lives. But, other than Cody's death, he'd faced no monumental problems in all of his thirty-three years. Until last Saturday, when everything had gone haywire.

Leaning over, he retrieved his phone and checked the call log. Nothing from Addy or Baxter. Again.

Shit! He understood why Baxter hadn't been in touch. He wasn't quite sure what to do about that, or if he *could* do anything. Maybe Baxter would be better off on his own. But he missed his best friend. And it didn't make the situation any easier that Addy hadn't tried to reach him, either. It'd been five days since they'd slept together and he hadn't heard a single word from her. Not "I had a nice time." Not "Are you still coming to dinner on Saturday?" Not even "I just want to be friends."

Silence. That was all. As if he didn't matter enough for her to give him a second thought.

He should've gotten her number — if she'd been willing to give it to him. But he'd had no reason to think that would be any more successful. They'd been so compatible, enjoyed themselves so much. He'd thought the great sex, if nothing else, would bring her back. He was certainly dying to see her. . . .

Trading his phone for the football lying on the carpet near his feet, he passed it from hand to hand. He'd heard she was working at Just Like Mom's. He'd been tempted to go in there, see what her reaction might be. Maybe it would remind her that he'd asked to see her again, or at least elicit an excuse as to why she hadn't responded to his dinner invitation.

But he hadn't wanted to make her feel cornered, hadn't wanted to push too hard.

"Damn," he breathed. How could she kiss him as hungrily as she had, as if she'd been craving the taste of him her whole life, and then . . . walk away without a backward glance?

The contradiction made no sense, but the irony of his thoughts didn't escape him. He was getting his just deserts. He'd put many women through what *he* was going through now — not because he'd wanted to but because he hadn't felt strongly enough to develop a deeper relationship. Acknowledging the disappointment he'd caused didn't make his own disappointment any easier, though.

He tossed the football higher in the air. What was his night with Addy really about? Had she come home with him for old times' sake? To prove to herself that she wasn't missing out on anything, after all? To see if she could finally get his attention and leave *him* wanting more?

If so, she was definitely having her revenge. He was obsessed with her, and he couldn't even confide in Baxter, like he would've if life had been normal. He hadn't spoken to Bax for as long as he hadn't spoken to Addy. But Noah had noticed a for-sale sign in his yard. The sight of it had made him sick, still made him sad.

He wanted that sign to come down and for everything to go back to the way it used to be. But if Baxter couldn't get the kind of love he needed here in Whiskey Creek — and that was impossible if it included romantic love with *him* — he should be free to find happiness elsewhere.

Squinting, Noah tried to read the clock on the opposite wall, but it'd gotten dark since he'd come home and he hadn't bothered to turn on a light. He checked the time on his phone instead.

It was only nine. What was he going to do with the rest of his evening? Sitting home alone sucked. Every other night this week he'd stayed late at the shop, fixing bikes his tech could have fixed during the day. He wasn't interested in going out with Riley or Ted to meet girls. He was too intrigued by the one he'd found. He didn't want to see his other friends, anyway. They'd just want to discuss what was going on with Baxter. Since Baxter had put his house up for sale, Noah had received numerous calls from almost everyone — Ted, Eve, Cheyenne, Riley, even Gail from Simon's film location in Canada. They all asked why Baxter was moving, but Noah couldn't tell them any other reason than the one Baxter had given himself — that he was doing it to be closer to work. After insisting that something else *must* be going on, they hung up more frustrated and curious than when they'd called. Before long, they'd call back and try again by asking how *he* felt about Baxter's leaving and how he was going to handle it.

He evaded those questions, too, because he didn't know the answers. He'd never been without Bax for any extended period.

Hoping to distract himself from his recent misery, he grabbed the remote and turned on Sports Center. But his interest waned after an hour or so. How many times could a guy watch a clip of a bad call in a football game and hear the analysts discuss it?

Finally, too restless and bored to hold out any longer, he went in search of Addy.

Noah was glad when he found Addy's 4-Runner parked at the restaurant. It would be far more comfortable to go in and get a meal, he decided — it didn't matter that he'd had a burger earlier — than to knock on Addy's grandmother's door at ten-fifteen.

Because it was a school night, there weren't many patrons inside. The hostess, Tilly Bowman, led him toward a booth on the far side of the restaurant, but he didn't see Addy. He supposed she was in the back.

Carl Inera sat in the corner with several guys Noah had never seen before. He got the impression they were transacting a business deal, but given Carl's reputation for selling drugs, Noah didn't want to know any more.

Gail's brother, Joe, sat at a different table with his two daughters. Other than that, the restaurant was empty.

"Hey, what's up?" Joe said when Noah stopped to say hello.

"Not a lot. What's up with you?"

He motioned to his kids. "They don't have school tomorrow so they're spending Halloween out here with me."

Noah eyed their ice cream sundaes. "Looks like they're getting an early start."

"They have to come here every visit."

"We *love* it!" Josephine, the youngest at eight or nine, grinned up at him. She was cute because she had a lot of personality, but she wasn't as pretty as her older sister, who was the spitting image of her father.

"I heard from Gail this week," Noah said.

"So did I," Joe responded. "I guess everyone's pretty worked up about Baxter moving, huh? What's going on with that?"

Ah, shit. Here, too? "Wish I knew," Noah said. "He won't tell me — other than to say it's time for a change. My guess? He's tired of the long commute."

"I can understand that. But I'm sorry to see him go. I'm sure you will be, too."

"We'll remain friends, no matter where he lives." At least, Noah hoped that was the case. If he gave Baxter a chance to sort out who he was and what he wanted, would they someday be able to redefine their relationship? He'd always assumed he'd be godfather to Baxter's children and Baxter would be godfather to his. Now he wasn't sure if Baxter's plans even included children. Maybe talk of that had simply been part of the facade.

"Gail moved away." Noah flashed him a

smile. "But we've managed to forgive her."

"Maybe *you* have," Joe teased.

"Do you know Uncle Simon?" Josephine had chocolate around her mouth, but she had a bow in her hair and was sitting in a very mature fashion with one leg crossed over the other.

"You mean the big movie star?"

When she blushed, as if she was as much in love with Simon as the rest of the female population, Noah chuckled. "Rich and famous. That's a tough combination to resist, isn't it?"

"I just think he's cute," she mumbled.

Joe laughed and changed the subject. "How's Cheyenne?"

"She's good."

"She's happy? I mean . . . with Dylan?"

The gravity behind this question took Noah by surprise. Joe could have asked Gail about Cheyenne. Or maybe not. His sister didn't live here anymore and had gotten so busy she didn't socialize with Cheyenne quite as often as Noah did. "I think so, yeah."

He nodded. "Glad to hear it."

Was he really? Or was there more to that query than Joe wanted him to believe. "You and Cheyenne never . . ."

"No." He shrugged. "Dylan got there

before I could, but I can't help feeling I shouldn't have let her get away."

Joe had once been interested? That came as news to Noah.

"You seeing anyone?" Joe asked.

Noah refused to glance over his shoulder in search of Addy, but that was where his mind went. "No."

"Dad needs a wife," Summer announced in a loud and dramatic whisper.

Joe rocked back. *"I do?"*

"What does it take to find one?" Noah asked, playing along.

Summer couldn't tell him, but Josephine seemed perfectly serious when she piped up with the answer. "You have to fall in love with someone and prove you won't *ever* stop loving them."

Noah suddenly felt a bit awkward. It sounded as though Summer blamed her father for breaking up their family. The way Noah had heard the story, Suzie had been cheating on Joe, but the girls probably didn't know that. Gail had once said that Joe didn't want *anyone* to know because he didn't want his children to feel as betrayed as he did.

"That's how you get to happily ever after," she stated in no uncertain terms.

"I need a wife, too, so I'll keep that in

mind," Noah said. "Enjoy the rest of your ice cream." Seeing that Luanne was coming over to take his order, he gave Joe a sympathetic smile and moved to his own table.

"Hey, good-lookin'." Somewhere in her late forties, Luanne had been working at Just Like Mom's forever. Noah liked her. With dark hair and eyes, and a ready smile, she was attractive — and her personality made her even more so. "You all alone tonight, honey?" she asked.

"Are you making me an offer?" he teased.

She grinned as she shook her head. "If only I were twenty years younger. You wouldn't be able to keep up with me." She raised a finger. "But I'd be careful to guard my heart. That's for sure."

Noah couldn't help bristling. He wasn't as much of a womanizer as everyone said he was. For one thing, he'd never led anyone on, never given anyone false hope. He'd always been careful. "What's that supposed to mean?"

She didn't soften at his wounded expression. "I'd know not to expect a commitment."

"Because . . ."

"Because you can't make one!" she said with a cackle.

"That's not true!"

She smiled as if she didn't believe him, and that irritated him even more. "What can I get for you?" she asked.

"A better reputation, apparently."

Sobering, she gave him a searching look. "You're sensitive tonight."

"Tired of being characterized as a heart-breaker, that's all."

"Honey, you can't help it. You break hearts just walking by in those jeans."

This comment made him feel a bit better. "You want a big tip." He winked at her. "I'll have the salmon and rice."

"I'm not sure if we have any more salmon."

"Fine." He handed her the menu the hostess had left on the table, even though he'd never opened it. "Then bring me the meat loaf and mashed potatoes."

"Comfort food. Good choice, considering your mood," she added, and hurried away as if he might come after her.

He considered calling her back to the table so he could ask if Addy was around but decided to wait and see if he spotted her without actually having to summon her. He didn't want to put up with Luanne's reaction, for starters.

You've met your match with her. If she said that, she'd be right.

"Good night," Joe called when he left with his kids.

Carl and his group finished and left soon after. Then he was the only patron still there.

Tilly and Luanne spent most of their time in the back. From the sounds of it, they were cleaning up and getting ready to close. When Luanne brought out his food, she was wearing her coat and had her purse hanging off one shoulder. "I'm heading home, but Addy'll be here. She'll act as cashier and see you out."

Perfect. He seemed to be regaining some of his former luck. Feeling a surge of anticipation, he said goodnight. He'd wanted to see Addy ever since she left his house so abruptly on Sunday morning.

But the moment she came out to check on him, he could tell that she hadn't realized it was him. When Luanne went home she must've said she still had one table or something like that.

"Hi." She smiled, but it looked pained, as if she wasn't happy to see him. He actually felt that his presence was upsetting to her. And then he understood why she hadn't called. For whatever reason, she was no longer interested.

The rejection stung. The night they'd been so intimate had made him expect more.

What he'd read into her actions then was so different from what he saw on her face now.

But he wasn't going to force his attention on any woman. He wanted to ask her to explain. He couldn't understand why she'd come home with him. He was the one who'd had to talk *her* into climaxing, so it wasn't as if she'd been using him. But he was afraid he'd sound as disappointed as he felt. So he threw a twenty on the table to cover the bill and slid out of the booth.

"I'm sorry I showed up," he said, and walked out.

19

It was all Addy could do not to go after Noah. The bell over the door echoed in her head as she stood in the center of the dining room, telling herself to buck up and move on with her night. She doubted Noah would be coming to dinner on Saturday. This created the decisive end she'd been looking for, right?

But she couldn't return to work. She couldn't even make herself go over and lock the door for fear she'd run out and chase him down. She'd thought of him so many times this week, wanting to see him.

She pulled her phone out of her pocket and stared at it. Couldn't she call him, at least? Tell him that what was happening had nothing to do with him?

No, because what was happening *did* have something to do with him, something very personal. Revealing how torn she was or telling him she cared about him but couldn't see him would only raise questions in his mind, and those were questions she couldn't afford to answer.

Dropping her cell on the table, she sank into the booth he'd just vacated and looked glumly at his food, which he'd barely touched. She'd never dreamed that he'd remain interested. Not only had she acted hot and cold, what she'd been through had stunted her sexual development. Contributing to that was the fact that she still saw herself as the smart but geeky girl who hadn't been able to turn his head fifteen years ago. Maybe that was why it was so tempting to respond to any advances he made; his attention was something she'd never had and always craved.

"Stop! I'm not losing anything!" She spoke out loud in an effort to stem the disappointment. Even if she felt free to date Noah, what was the most she could expect? That they'd have a great time for a few months? He'd forget her once he left for Europe in the spring. He'd never hung on to any other woman. So why did she feel as if she was denying herself some fabulous opportunity?

When the bell over the door jingled again, she turned, halfway hoping, despite everything, that it was Noah. But Kevin Colbert stood there, wearing an "at last" smirk as he jammed his hands in the pockets of his Eureka High football windbreaker.

Addy shoved the table as she scrambled out of the booth, making Noah's silverware rattle against his plate. "What do you want?" She reached for her phone but he crossed the restaurant and snatched it out of her hands before she could call for help.

"It's time you and I had a talk." He slipped her cell into his pocket. "Now that we have a few minutes of privacy."

They certainly had that. She'd let all the employees go home; there would be no one to intervene — or save her, if necessary.

"Didn't we already have a talk when you dragged me up to the mine last week?" She eyed the fork Noah had used at dinner, trying to gauge whether or not she could grab it should she need to.

"You think that was *me*?"

"Why wouldn't I?"

"Because it wasn't."

Did he have a white truck? She'd been so busy with the restaurant, and so fearful of approaching his house, she hadn't checked. But she'd been meaning to. "I'm supposed to take your word for it?"

"One mistake doesn't define an individual, Addy. Just because I got involved in something I shouldn't have fifteen years ago doesn't mean I'd hurt you again."

"Is that how you sleep at night? By using euphemisms like 'involved' instead of more honest terms? And believing that one mistake doesn't prove you're a bad person?"

He scowled. "Stop being so dramatic. You're making such a big deal out of what happened."

"You mean out of what you *did*? Don't talk about it as if it was beyond your control."

Rubbing his neck, he sighed. "Look, I'm just trying to tell you that you don't have to be scared of me, of any of us. I've talked to the guys. We don't intend you any harm. I'd prefer it if we could all be friends. At least you and I."

"You've got to be insane!"

"Fine. If that's the way you want it. But I'm not going to let you come back here and ruin my life. Maybe what I did was wrong. But it's in the past. It's over, and I can't change it. You understand?"

She laughed without mirth. "Yeah, I understand. You're shrugging it off like it was nothing. You want to go about your business as if you never raped me."

"What are my other choices?" He was getting upset, starting to shout. "What would *you* rather I do? Hate myself forever because you've decided to feel sorry for yourself indefinitely?"

She shook her head in disgust. "You're a real prick. You know that?"

"There was no damage done."

No damage? She wasn't sure he could've said anything that would make her angrier. "You and your buddies held me down while you took turns climbing on top of me! *Raping* me! You think that didn't *hurt*?"

He grimaced as if she'd just presented him with a mental picture he didn't want to see. "It wasn't really like that. And if you say it was, I'll claim you came on to me, that we had sex because *you* wanted it."

"You'd say I wanted all five of you — even though I was a virgin and only sixteen? You really think you can sell that?"

"I have more friends in this town than you do."

"Congratulations. You've just set a new standard for despicable."

With a curse, he pivoted to go but then turned back. "Come on, I was hoping we could end this in a . . . a truce, at least. Agree to be polite to each other, if not friends."

"You're delusional if you think I'll ever spare you a kind thought. Get out of here and quit leaving notes on my car."

"I'm not leaving you any notes. And you *did* want us," he said. "You followed us around like a whipped puppy our entire senior year."

She lowered her voice. "Because I thought you were something special. Imagine my surprise when I realized you weren't."

He reared back, looking stung. She got the impression he was egotistical enough to want her to think well of him despite what he'd done. As the football coach, he was a notable figure in Whiskey Creek. He liked the attention and esteem his job gave him, and had obviously bought into the illusion that he was an important individual.

"It was fifteen years ago! We had sex. So what? Look at you. You're fine. Beautiful."

"No, don't look at me. Don't speak to me. Don't speak *of* me and don't victimize anyone else or —"

"Victimize anyone else?" He stared up at the ceiling as if he couldn't believe his ears. "God, you make it sound like I'm some sort of predator. I'm a husband and a father. I'm a *coach,* for crying out loud. Cody was the one."

She raised her chin for emphasis. "Don't shift the blame to Cody. You gang-raped a girl the night you graduated from high school, and that girl happened to be me. Maybe it's time you owned it."

With another curse, he pressed three fingers to his forehead. "So what does that mean? That you're going to tell? That you're just waiting for the right moment to bring out your old panties stained with our semen?"

She wished she'd kept that kind of evidence. But she'd gotten rid of her clothes — at the first opportunity — by throwing them into the Dumpster behind Just Like Mom's. She'd been too afraid that what was on them would tie her to Cody. "Just keep your distance," she said, "and don't come back in here."

"I can't eat at Just Like Mom's?" He acted appalled, as though he had just as much right to Gran's restaurant as she did.

"If you do, I'll . . . I'll put something bad in your food." She knew she sounded juvenile, but she didn't care.

"It's football season. And that's nasty!"

She doubted she could ever go through with that threat, but it felt great to have a *little* power. "Your assistant coach can come in with the team on Mondays. Not you. And don't come anywhere near my house, either."

He threw up his hands. "Fine! What the

hell am I worried about? It won't do you any good even if you do talk. Consensual sex produces semen, too."

"You're such a selfish liar!"

"I should let you destroy my life instead? Cost me my wife and kids? My job? A man has a right to defend those things!"

"If what you've built in the past fifteen years is at risk, it's because of *your* actions, not mine. Just leave me alone, like I said, and you can continue living your lie, as long as the people around you think you're worth it."

His face bloomed red. "I came in here to make amends. It didn't have to go this way," he began, but the bell over the door rang yet again, signaling the entrance of someone else, and that silenced him.

Startled that anyone would come in after hours, Addy angled her head to see around Kevin. Thriller writer Ted Dixon stood next to the row of high chairs near the entrance.

"Am I interrupting?"

Addy drew a deep, calming breath. "No. Come sit down. We're technically closed, but, um, I can make you a bite to eat if you'd like." The kitchen had been cleaned, but if it meant that Kevin would leave, she'd clean it again.

Kevin glanced between them. "Right, uh

—" he waved at the dishes Noah had left "— thanks for dinner. It was great."

She said nothing. She knew she should do what she could to help him pretend. No doubt Ted could feel the negative energy in the room. But she didn't have the necessary reserves.

Ted waited until Kevin had put her phone on the table and walked out before addressing her again. "Are you okay?"

"Of course." She started clearing Noah's table so she wouldn't have to look at him. "Why wouldn't I be?"

"I heard some shouting when I was coming in."

"Coach Colbert wasn't happy with his meat loaf."

"Didn't he just say it was great?"

She motioned to one of the other tables. "Would over there be okay? I'll get you a menu."

As he watched her slide her phone into her own pocket, she wondered what he'd made of Kevin's having had it.

"I didn't come to eat, Addy. I saw your car, so I stopped in. Kevin's wasn't in the lot, which is why I was surprised to find him here."

Of course Kevin wouldn't park in the lot, not after hours when she was the only one here. That didn't come as a revelation, but the part where Ted said he'd stopped in because he saw her car did.

"Do you need some catering for a book signing or . . ."

He smiled at her guess. "Not this time. I wanted to invite you to a Halloween party tomorrow night. It won't be anything big. I decided, last minute, to have a few friends over and thought you might like to join us."

She assumed Noah would be there, which meant she had to decline. "I'm having a little trouble keeping the restaurant staffed right now. Darlene needed to take today off, and I'm not sure she'll be back tomorrow." Or ever, if they couldn't come to some accord. "You'd better not plan on me."

"It'll be going until one or so. Maybe you can drop by for a few minutes on your way home."

"I'll try," she promised. "Are you sure I can't get you a cup of coffee or something?"

He slid into the booth she'd indicated earlier. "Will you come talk to me while I drink it?"

Although Addy knew there were people who'd argue with her, she didn't find Ted nearly as handsome as Noah. He didn't seem as good-natured, either. Addy could tell it in the stiffness of his bearing. While Noah was open and trusting and eager to sample all the world had to offer — as if he believed he could never get hurt — Ted showed more restraint. He knew life had some sharp corners. And although he kept himself on a tight leash, she sensed that he had a temper.

Still, she liked him. And she admired his many talents. While he'd been student body president, Eureka High had done more to help local charities than the Rotary Club and Sisters for a Better Whiskey Creek combined. Ted was a natural leader. After he'd been voted Most Likely to Become a Politician in high school, Addy had always imagined he'd be mayor someday. Maybe he'd run when Noah's father retired. . . .

He laughed when she told him what she saw in his future. "I doubt I'll ever get into politics," he said.

"But it's not really politics. Not here. It's more like a popularity contest. And you're one of the most popular people I know."

"It'd be a lot of work. I'd have to save the rest of the historic buildings, figure out a way to clean up the leftover tailings from the mines, expand the park downtown, create a new source of revenue for the museum. The list goes on."

She grinned. "In other words, you'd *make* it a lot of work." Just like he'd done with the position of student body president. What high school senior expected to accomplish the goals he'd set for himself? "You're a chronic high-achiever."

From there the conversation segued into what had been going on in Whiskey Creek while she was away. He caught her up on everything Gran might've missed, especially among his friends. There were more details on the renovation and name change of the B and B owned by Eve Harmon and her family. The discovery of Cheyenne's true identity. The scare Callie Vanetta had given them when her liver stopped working last summer. They even discussed Kyle and Noelle's brief marriage and the rumor that she'd aborted Kyle's baby without asking him. Then Ted wanted to know all about her and what she'd been doing for the past thirteen years.

Pretty soon Addy was enjoying herself so much she almost forgot there were certain things she couldn't mention — like the name of her ex-husband or the restaurant where she used to work. Noah had shown interest in acquiring both pieces of information, and while she didn't think he'd go to any great amount of work to ferret out the details of her past, she didn't want to drop them in his lap. She couldn't allow her life here and the life she'd known in Davis to overlap. She hadn't told many people about the rape. But she *had* told the man she'd eventually married. She'd visited the therapist who'd helped her get past the rape for a "refresher" before saying "I do" and Clyde had joined her for a few sessions.

Even if someone confronted him, Addy doubted he'd give her away. But their relationship hadn't ended particularly well. She wasn't convinced she could count on his discretion, especially if he were to encounter Noah. When she'd found out about Clyde and his waitress girlfriend, she'd told him she'd never really loved him, anyway, that Noah was the only man she'd ever wanted with her whole heart. Considering how hard he'd taken that, she wasn't completely sure Clyde would forgo the opportunity to exact revenge.

"Have you ever been married?" she asked.

Steam rose from his cup as he poured himself more coffee. "No."

"Engaged?"

"Not yet."

"Would you like to get married?"

"Isn't it a bit soon for you to propose?"

She laughed. "That did sound like a proposal."

"I'd like a family, with the right person," he said. "You?"

"I've always wanted two or three kids. But . . . I can't see that happening."

"Because . . ."

"I don't plan on marrying again." She'd never felt more helpless and cornered — more vulnerable — than when she'd been Mrs. Clyde Kingsdale. Why put herself in a similar position?

"Considering how your ex behaved, I can understand why," he said.

She'd told him about the cheating. But tonight she realized that wasn't all that had split them up. With Clyde, she'd never felt the kind of excitement she'd experienced last Sunday with Noah. But accepting her lack of emotional commitment meant she also had to accept partial responsibility for the failed marriage. "It might have been different, better, if I'd been in love."

His cup clicked on its saucer. "Why'd you marry him if you didn't love him?"

"I guess if you don't really love someone, you sort of . . . limit your liability."

"You were protecting yourself?"

"To a point. I didn't realize it at the time,

342

but I wasn't willing to go all in, if that makes sense."

"Sometimes that's not something you can control."

"It sounds like you're speaking from experience."

"I am."

"What happened?"

"She got away."

Did he mean Sophia? The girl he'd dated in high school? Or someone else? She doubted he'd tell her, so she didn't ask.

He took a sip of coffee. "Didn't you used to have a thing for Noah?"

She rolled her eyes. "How'd you guess? Was it that I drooled whenever he walked by? That I went red as a tomato and began to stammer if he deigned to talk to me? Or was it that I just 'happened' to be wherever I might run into him?"

Chuckling, Ted slid lower in his seat. "I wouldn't be too embarrassed if I were you. You weren't the only one."

"No. A lot of girls liked Noah. And he probably slept with every one of them." *Except me.*

"Actually, Noah didn't lose his virginity until college. All he cared about was sports. But Cody made up for it."

She did what she could to read his expression, but Ted wasn't nearly as transparent as most people. "Because he had a steady girlfriend, you mean?"

"Whether he had a girlfriend or not didn't matter. Shania still mourns his death, still talks about how different her life would be if he hadn't died. But . . ." He gave a little shrug as if he shouldn't say it but was going to, anyway. "I highly doubt he would've made a good husband. Noah tried and tried to get him to settle down. He just wouldn't. You don't hear that now that he's been canonized. You only hear how wonderful he was. He did have a lot of potential, but . . . whether or not he would've achieved it is another story."

"He wasn't a very nice person," she said.

Her agreement seemed to surprise him. "How well did you know Cody?"

"I danced with him once or twice. That's all. But . . . there was something sort of . . . superficial about him."

"You were there at the party on graduation, right?"

A tremor of foreboding swept through Addy; she'd said too much. But she couldn't deny having attended the party. Too many people had seen her there.

She nodded.

"There were *so* many kids at the mine,"

Ted murmured. "It's strange that he was the only one to get hurt, don't you think? I mean, why would he be the last to leave? And why would he be by himself? Cody was never by himself. Even if Noah wasn't around, he *always* had a posse."

The vinyl upholstery squeaked as she shifted. "I heard he forgot his coat and went back for it."

"I heard that, too, but . . . it doesn't make a lot of sense to me. He wasn't fastidious. He could've retrieved it the next day, when he was sober. Why go all the way back to the mine if you've already been out all night?"

Cody hadn't appeared *too* late. Even after their encounter, she'd had time to walk the five miles or so to the road, thumb a ride and arrive home before dawn. A cement contractor from Jackson had stopped on his way to a six o'clock job in Angels Camp. When she portrayed herself as having partied too much and gotten separated from her friends, he bought into the whole thing. She didn't say a word about the mine or Cody or having been raped. He'd attributed her disheveled state and her presence on the side of the road to alcohol, had even mentioned some of the crazy stuff he'd done the night he graduated from high school.

"Maybe Cody wasn't thinking straight," she said. "When I saw him earlier in the evening, he was completely wasted."

Ted shrugged. "That could account for it, I guess."

Suddenly uncomfortable, she stepped out of the booth. "I'd better clear this up. It's getting late."

He stood, too, and dug a five-dollar bill from his pocket. "Thanks for the coffee."

She refused his money. "My treat."

"You sure?"

"It was a cup of coffee. Don't worry about it."

"Thanks. I enjoyed getting to know you," he said. "I hope you'll make it to the party tomorrow. And, if you come, bring your swimsuit. I have a Jacuzzi. Might feel nice to get in if it's as cold as tonight."

She tucked her hair behind her ears. "Will Noah be there?"

A smile curved his lips. "Would you like him to be?"

Absolutely. But she didn't want Ted to catch on. "I know better than to get involved with him."

"What does that mean?"

"From what I've heard, he's left a string of broken hearts in his wake," she said because she couldn't say anything more.

"Don't worry about the gossip. Noah's a good guy. He just hasn't met the right girl, never really fallen in love."

She held Ted's cup and coffee spoon in her hands. "Maybe he's incapable of it."

"Maybe, but . . ." He winked. "Maybe not."

20

Addy wasn't really expecting it, but Darlene showed up for work the next morning. Even more surprising, they got through breakfast without a conflict — but only because they pretended they'd never had that conversation on the phone. Like the other employees at Just Like Mom's, they were both dressed up for Halloween and smiling. Darlene was an angel — ironic from Addy's perspective. Addy was a flapper, since that was the only costume Gran had that she could alter quickly enough.

At ten, after politely dancing around each other, serving breakfast and passing out free orange-frosted donuts and balloons for the kids, Addy decided to leave. Darlene had managed the restaurant for this long. She could get through another day, even a busy one, on her own. Addy needed a nap. She'd been up for several hours after Ted left, looking up Kevin's, Derek's, Tom's and

Stephen's addresses in the Whiskey Creek phone book and trying to talk herself into going by each house to see who owned a white truck with damage on the front. She held off until two before deciding to wait one more night. Halloween would provide a much better opportunity. People would already be out. And she'd have the perfect excuse to wear a costume.

When she got home, she didn't get to nap, however. Gran needed her help preparing for Halloween. She wanted to be ready when the trick-or-treaters came by.

Addy made the caramel apples everyone expected her to give out. She also applied Gran's green face paint and fake warts for her witch's costume.

"Are you leaving?" Gran asked when, finally finished, Addy got her purse.

"I have a few errands to run." She adjusted the black hat she'd fastened, purposely askew, on Gran's long black wig.

"Like what?" Gran reached up to help but couldn't do much wearing her fake purple fingernails.

Addy searched her mind for a plausible excuse but could think of only one thing Gran would accept without hesitation — a social outing. "Ted Dixon invited me to a party tonight."

"He has? And it starts this early?"

"No, it doesn't start until later, but I'd like to get a costume that fits properly."

Gran's scowl turned into something far more pleasant. "How nice! You run along and do that, dear. I'll be fine here. You've got my rocking chair out on the porch and that green flashlight I use?"

"Of course. And the apples are in the plastic container right next to the rocker."

"It wouldn't be Halloween if I wasn't out on the porch. The kids count on it."

"Yes, they do. Don't forget to turn on the organ music when you go out. And cover up with the blanket. You've had a cold. I don't want you outside very long."

"The little ones are done by eight or eight-thirty. I won't go in late. And it's not raining on Halloween for a change."

Addy gave her a hug and hurried out.

The costume section at the mercantile was picked over. If she planned on snooping around Addy needed a costume that would mask her identity. But the biggest one they had left was a purple goblin sized for a ten-year-old.

"So much for that idea," she grumbled, and waved to Harvey Hooper, the owner, as she dodged a little princess and Batman who, together with their parents, were coming down the aisle.

"Excuse me." She'd just decided to put a sheet over her head and be a ghost — that would cover her completely — when her gaze strayed to Crank It Up down the street. The open sign was still lit.

Was Noah there?

She got in her 4-Runner and drove past at a slow creep, craning her head to catch a glimpse of the people inside. But all she could see was a young woman with long hair, straightening bike helmets near the front window. After checking her rearview mirror to make sure no one was behind her, she slowed to a stop in the middle of the street so she could look at the portion of his house visible behind the shop.

She'd only been there for a second when she realized that someone was watching her. Even before her eyes darted back to the store, she knew instinctively that it was Noah.

Sure enough, he stood in the doorway, wearing a pair of jeans that fit him perfectly, a Crank It Up T-shirt and a bemused expression. He started to walk out as if he intended to talk to her. But she had no idea how she'd explain what she was doing so she drove off, leaving him staring after her.

"You're an idiot," she muttered to herself.

He had to be so confused by her actions. *She* was confused.

She needed to stay away from him.

So why couldn't she?

"Who was *that*?"

Noah watched as Addy's taillights disappeared around the corner.

"Noah?"

He blinked and turned his attention to Amy, who'd come out to stand next to him. "What?"

She gazed in the same direction. "In that 4-Runner."

"No one."

"*No one?* You just about knocked down all the helmets I stacked trying to get outside before she could drive off, and it's no one?"

He pivoted and went back inside. "It wasn't who I thought it was."

She rolled her eyes. He didn't see her do it, but he could hear it in her voice. "You've been acting a little nuts lately. Have I told you that?"

How else was he supposed to act? He usually didn't have any trouble getting people to love him, but in the past week his best friend had written him off and the first girl he'd gotten excited about in ages had slept with him and then tossed him aside.

So why had she come by the store?

His cell phone went off. Motioning for Amy to finish closing the register, he headed into the back to clean up his tools. " 'Lo?"

"You coming tonight?"

Ted. Noah smothered a sigh. His friends had been bugging him to join them for their annual party, but he didn't want to make Baxter feel uncomfortable. "Not sure. Things here at the shop are busy."

"On Halloween? You're selling a lot of bikes, huh?"

There wasn't a soul in the store. He couldn't go quite that far. "I'm *fixing* a lot of bikes."

"Which can wait."

He glanced around. He was actually more caught up on his work than usual. "Do I have to wear a costume?"

"Yes, but you can throw on those spandex shorts you wear to impress the girls and be a biker."

He would've laughed. They teased him about his shorts all the time. But he wasn't in a very good mood. "I *am* a biker."

"So it'll be even more convincing."

"Will Baxter be there?"

Silence. Then he said, "Would you mind?"

"Of course not." God, he hated the rift

that had changed *everything.*

"There's *something* going on between you two. What is it?"

With a grimace, Noah remembered, once again, that wet kiss. He wanted to tell Ted how terrible it had been, how sick he'd felt afterward and how lonely he felt now, despite his repugnance. But Baxter wasn't talking, wasn't giving the others a reason for the fact that they were no longer speaking, so neither could he. "We had an argument at the cabin last weekend."

"You've never had a fight that's lasted this long. What kind of argument was it?"

"Just an argument."

"Over . . ."

"Women."

"You mean the fact that he's not attracted to them?"

Noah's free hand automatically curled into a fist. But he wasn't sure whom he wanted to hit. Baxter, for being gay? Ted, for figuring it out without such a rude awakening? Or himself for struggling with the fallout?

"You still there?" Ted asked.

"Yeah," he breathed.

"Did he finally tell you?"

"When did he tell *you*?"

"He didn't. But he's had a thing for you

since I can remember. It's been obvious."

"You could see it?"

"I think most of us could."

"So . . . have you all been sitting around, talking about what an idiot I am for missing it?"

"No. We haven't discussed it. But even if we did, we'd be more concerned with how it would affect your relationship than making fun of the situation."

"I don't believe you. You guys have talked about it. It's too scandalous *not* to talk about."

"Believe me. We care too much about both of you. We've been afraid to address it, at least openly."

That was pretty nice, but Noah wasn't sure he could appreciate such generosity, not fully. "Shit . . ."

"Is something wrong?" Amy had come back to ask him a question. He told Ted to hang on while he dealt with it.

"No."

She scowled at his curt tone. "Fine. I'm done. Can I take off early? I have plans tonight."

He nodded. "Have fun," he said absently.

"Who was that?" Ted asked when she was gone.

"Amy."

"See? Even she's going out tonight."

"Why didn't someone tell me?" he growled. He didn't have to explain that he'd already gone back to the "other" subject.

"Wasn't our place. But I'm glad the news is out. That volcano's been about to erupt for ages."

"The news *isn't* out. He's not telling his parents, doesn't feel he can. That means we can't tell anyone, either."

"I'm not going to say anything, Noah. I love Bax, too."

"I don't love him in *that* way. I never could."

He laughed softly. "You don't have to explain to me."

But if the others knew, he felt he had to explain it to them. He didn't want them secretly wondering if Baxter could turn him. Or thinking that maybe they'd been fooling around, just to see. "Not everyone will take that on faith."

"Everyone we know will. That's all that matters."

"So . . . is he coming tonight?" he asked again. "Because if he is, I'm not."

"You can't be around him?"

"It's not me. It's him. He doesn't want anything to do with me. Says he needs some space. But he needs friends, too, and . . .

and if he won't let me fill that role any longer, I'm hoping he can still hang on to you guys."

"That's generous of you, Noah, but he told me he's going to San Francisco tonight."

Where he probably had gay friends — friends Noah was now seeing in a whole new light. What kind of life did Baxter lead when he went there? It had to be a hundred and eighty degrees different from the one he led here.

As much as Noah had been hoping that what had happened would simply blow over, it wasn't going to. He'd known that in his heart, but there'd been moments, *were* moments, when he still wished. "Is he really selling his house?"

"From the looks of that sign out front, yes."

"I don't want him to go."

"No one does. But I do have a bit of good news."

Noah climbed onto his work stool. "What could that possibly be?"

"I invited Adelaide to the party tonight."

He jumped to his feet again. "Did she say she'd be there?"

"She didn't make any promises but . . . she might come. Just leave your car at home. I'll pick you up."

"You're going to trick her into thinking I'm not there? Why doesn't she want to see me?"

"Because she wants to see you too much."

Could that be it? When she looked at him, she seemed to feel what he felt — an attraction. But her actions were so inconsistent with that. She had him confused as hell. "How can you tell?"

"You can't?"

Adelaide felt ridiculous walking around wearing a sheet, but being able to hide her identity without drawing attention to herself was simply too good an opportunity to pass up.

She'd left the house as a flapper and created her alternate costume in her 4-Runner, purposely doing a sloppy job to make her look like a teenage boy. She'd cut the eyes out unevenly and surrounded them with black marker. She'd cut a jagged hole for her mouth, nothing for her nose and added an old straw hat that had belonged to Grandpa Davies. She'd even gone back to the mercantile once it got dark and bought a red pair of canvas high-tops so her shoes would be juvenile *and* unrecognizable.

So far she'd passed numerous children

wearing costumes ranging from cowboys to firemen to Catwoman to the Little Mermaid. The older ones ran in packs, while the younger ones walked with their parents. She turned a few heads; it was impossible not to stand out when she was six feet tall and out alone. She'd tried to think of a way around that, but she couldn't exactly ask someone to lend her a kid. She joined up with various groups but floated away before they could ask any questions.

Kevin's house had been easy to canvass. Tom's, too. They both lived in well-lit areas that saw a lot of traffic. She managed to time her approach for when trick-or-treaters were at the door. She stood at the periphery and checked the driveway and the street before moving on. Kevin owned a black truck with a lift kit. In her opinion, his truck matched his inflated ego. But it was higher than the truck she'd been forced into the night of the abduction, it wasn't the right color and there wasn't a scratch on it. Maybe he had another vehicle in the garage, which she couldn't see because the door was down, but chances were slim it would be another truck.

Tom had been telling the truth about his vehicles. He didn't own a truck or an SUV. He had a compact car and that old Bug he said belonged to his wife. She could tell that he wasn't as well-off as Kevin. His house was smaller, more modest. The handmade welcome sign on the door, and the home-made curtains suggested that his wife was a stay-at-home mom — which meant they were living exclusively off his postal employee's wages.

Stephen's place was in the country, on Kyle Houseman's property. From what she could surmise, Kyle had built a couple of simple homes for his workers on some land behind the factory. According to the phone book, Stephen lived in one. Addy wasn't sure who lived in the other. There were no trick-or-treaters out here. The place looked deserted. She wasn't even sure Stephen still lived at this address. Unlike the house next door, his had no Halloween decorations, no porch light burning and no car sitting out front.

She was just leaving when she passed him on the road. She didn't immediately recognize him or his vehicle — an old white Chevy with a camper shell — but she saw him turn into the driveway when she glanced into her rearview mirror.

"There you are." After giving him a few minutes to park and go inside, she flipped her 4-Runner around and went back, but she was too nervous to get out. She hadn't seen any damage on his truck, but by the time she realized it was him, it was too late to really check.

Deciding she'd come back later, when he was asleep, she moved on to Derek's fourplex, where she hoped to have better luck.

A lot of vehicles crowded the lot. Some even spilled out into the road. She could hear scary music and laughter, which grew louder every time a certain door opened and closed. Pot and cigarette smoke hung in the air, telling her this Halloween party had nothing to do with children.

Was Derek in there? His unit's lights were on, but that didn't mean he was home.

After parking down the street, out of sight, Addy walked back and slipped through the motorcycles, cars and trucks. She had no idea which of the many vehicles might be Derek's, but it didn't matter. A few were damaged, but none of the white ones showed evidence of a recent scrape on the front right panel.

Through the process of elimination, that left Stephen. He was the only one with a white truck. But her approach had hardly been scientific. She didn't know what was in Kevin's garage. She wasn't sure whatever Derek drove was even in the lot. And there was always the possibility that her abductor had borrowed a vehicle that night.

Her cell phone rang. After hurrying back to her 4-Runner, where she felt safe, she got in and answered Gran's call.

"Everything okay?" Addy asked.

"Oh, yes. I'm in and locking up now," Gran replied. "The kids loved my apples."

"Of course they did."

"When are you going to Ted's?"

She wasn't. Not really. "I don't know. Why?"

"He just called, looking for you. It scared me that you left so long ago and hadn't shown up yet."

"Sorry about that. I was out —" she made an effort to fill in the blank "— enjoying the Halloween decorations."

"Well, I told them you're on your way. They have a movie and they want to start it, so you'd better get over there."

Great. Gran had committed her?

She frowned, wondering if she could get out of it. But she didn't see how she could. She was afraid someone would mention her absence to Gran if she didn't show up. She could easily see Ted bumping into Milly at the grocery store or Just Like Mom's. *Hey, where was Addy the other night?*

Besides, now that Gran expected her to

be gone for several hours, how would she pass the rest of the evening if she didn't go?

She figured she could hang out near Stephen's and wait for him to go to bed so she could check the front of his truck. But those minutes would pass *very* slowly. Why sit there for so long when she could simply come by later?

Going to Ted's had to beat waiting in the dark for an indeterminate length of time. If Noah arrived, she could always leave. "Okay. I'll head over there now."

21

Adelaide wore her flapper costume and left her ghost creation wadded in a ball under her backseat. She wasn't thrilled with what putting a sheet over her head had done to her hair, but the headband with its big feather helped camouflage that.

Ted's house was impressive. Located about five minutes outside town on a fairly large piece of property near the river, it was several levels high and loftlike. He'd apparently renovated an old mill.

She didn't see Noah's truck on her way in, but he was there, dressed as a caveman. He looked over as she entered, his tan perfect for pulling off a costume that required a loincloth, and she immediately regretted that she hadn't chosen to stake out Stephen's place instead. She was embarrassed that he'd seen her driving by the store earlier. She didn't have a good reason for that, except the obvious — her crush was far from over. But the obvious once again contradicted the rest of her behavior, and she could tell he wasn't happy about the inconsistencies.

When she glanced away instead of returning his smile, he didn't get up from his place on the couch, where he was holding a beer. He didn't say anything to her, either. He just watched as the others greeted her — Ted (a pirate), Kyle (a fireman), Riley (a doctor), Eve (an old-fashioned barmaid), Dylan (a bad-boy biker), Cheyenne (a bad-boy biker's chick), Brandon (Frankenstein's monster) and Olivia (a vampire). But a few minutes later, when she caught his eye again, his expression itself was a question: *What's going on with you? Didn't we have fun together? What'd I do?*

Noah's anger made it easy to avoid him, because once she'd set the tone he avoided her. Addy tried not to think about him, but she couldn't deny that regret tore at her restraint. Fortunately, she liked his friends, found them pleasant to talk to. After two glasses of wine, she began to relax and have a good time.

She didn't go home after an hour, as she'd initially planned. They played liar's dice and a couple of card games. They laughed, talked, ate snacks, including meatballs in a bloodred sauce on ceramic skeleton plates, and watched *Psycho,* in honor of Halloween.

The movie was over and Noah was in the middle of a game of pool with Dylan when Ted suggested they get into the Jacuzzi.

Addy knew this was the perfect time to head home. She told them she'd forgotten her swimsuit, even though she hadn't brought it because she hadn't planned on attending the party in the first place. But Eve spoke up to say she had an extra one. And Addy felt she couldn't leave without apologizing to Noah. She kept thinking she'd feel better if she did. Then maybe she could go on her way without the sinking sensation that made it so difficult to leave things as they stood.

She'd blame her hot and cold reactions on her divorce, she decided. If she admitted she was attracted to him, but claimed she'd been too burned to get involved with anyone else, at least she'd be giving him a *reason* why she wouldn't follow up on their night together.

Now that she was hoping for a chance to talk, she agreed to get in the hot tub. Ted tried to convince Noah to join them, too, but he stayed at the pool table until Cheyenne persuaded her husband to finish the game later. Then Dylan dragged Noah out, but he was the last to join them and — purposely, it seemed — he walked around to the other side of the Jacuzzi to sit as far from her as possible.

The warm water felt good but Noah's cold shoulder didn't. Addy tried making up for her initial unfriendliness by smiling at him a few times. But he ignored her, got out a few minutes later and went to dress.

Ted, who was sitting next to her, nudged her and lowered his voice. "I'm sorry about Noah. I've never seen him like this."

"It's okay." She could hardly hold Noah's reaction against him when she was to blame.

"He's had a bad week," Cheyenne concurred.

Eve swished the steam and bubbles away from her face. "I wish Baxter had come. I know that would've made Noah feel better."

"It would've made us *all* feel better," Kyle said.

Cheyenne motioned for them to be quieter. "Noah will get angry if he thinks we're talking about him."

"Why *didn't* Baxter come?" Addy whispered.

Riley shrugged. "He and Noah had some sort of falling out last weekend. Neither of them will talk about it, so we're not sure what happened. But . . . Bax is moving now. You've probably seen the real estate sign."

Addy hadn't noticed. She'd been too consumed by her own problems. But she remembered Noah coming to her door stumbling drunk last weekend. He'd been upset about something but wouldn't say what.

Had it been an argument with his best friend?

"Does this type of thing happen often?" she asked. It certainly hadn't when they were in high school. Baxter was *always* with Noah.

Eve, in an attractive white bikini, sat on the edge of the hot tub to cool off. "Never. That's why we don't know what to do. We're hoping —"

Noah emerged from the house, wearing his caveman costume beneath a jacket, and Eve shut up before he could hear her. "I'm taking off," he called to Ted. "Thanks for tonight."

Riley pulled a skeptical face. "Yeah, we can tell you enjoyed it."

"I did," he said, but his tone was flat and unconvincing.

Ted started to get out. "You do realize you don't have a car."

Noah waved him back. "Stay. I'll walk."

"It's too far," Eve argued.

"It's not *that* far."

Adelaide got out of the water. "I'm leaving, too. I'll give you a ride."

She thought Noah might refuse. She braced herself for the embarrassment of having him do that in front of his friends, but he didn't.

"Thanks, Addy." Ted sank back into the hot water, his smile just smug enough to indicate that, with this latest development, he'd accomplished what he'd set out to do when he invited her.

"It'll take me a second to change," she told Noah, and toweled off before hurrying inside.

Noah was silent on the drive home. Addy kept trying to think of a way to start a conversation, but what would've been a long walk wasn't that long a drive. They were at his house before she could decide how to bring up what she wanted to say.

"Thanks for the ride," he said, and started to get out, but she stopped him.

"Noah."

He twisted around. *"What?"*

"I thought maybe we could . . . talk."

"Fine," he snapped. "Talk."

369

Her heart sank as she stared at him. She couldn't win here, no matter how much she wished otherwise. "Never mind," she said quietly. "I — I'm sorry. I really am."

Although he stepped out, he turned back. "Damn it, Addy. I want you. I think I've made that clear. But I don't know how to reach you. For whatever reason, you're determined to . . . to punish me for high school or something. How many times am I supposed to let you push me away? Will it make any difference if I keep trying?"

She couldn't believe she was sitting here, facing that question from *him.* This was the last thing she'd expected when she'd decided to come home. "I'm not punishing you. How you behaved in high school — you were fine. That isn't the problem."

"Then what is?"

Her divorce was the answer she'd devised. But she was no longer sure she could sell it. She'd never felt as passionate about Clyde as she should have. She'd just been determined to take the opportunity to start a family, since she doubted she'd ever find another man who'd marry someone with her particular "issues." It wasn't until they were actually living together that she knew something crucial was missing. Even then, she wasn't aware of what that meant until he was out of her life and she was relieved instead of regretful.

Noah propped his hands on his hips. "I'm waiting."

She made a stab at using the excuse she'd planned. "Divorced people can be . . . hesitant to get involved a second time."

"I understand that. But when you talked about your marriage before, it didn't sound as if your ex was much more than a mistake you quickly fixed. So now you're saying he scarred you?"

He hadn't scarred her; Cody had. Clyde had just been incapable of helping her heal, of making her whole. "Like I said at the beginning, I'm not a good candidate for you."

"*Why?* That's what I want to know. Why does your mouth say no but your body say yes? Your eyes strayed to me a million times tonight. It was almost as if there was no one else in the room. And making love to you last Sunday . . . it was so damn *good.*"

She couldn't deny her preoccupation with him. But she did have something to say about last Sunday. "How could it have been that good . . . for you?" she clarified. "You had to take a lot of time and trouble, and it wasn't easy to convince me to cooperate. I know you've been with other women who are . . . less complicated."

"I'm not looking for easy, Addy! Making love is about discovery. I liked discovering you, being with you. Was I the only one who enjoyed that?"

He was being so open and honest that she couldn't help responding. "I enjoyed it," she admitted. "If you think I've been able to forget what it felt like to have your hands on me, to feel you inside me, you're crazy."

Those words had come out in a rush, before she could hold them back long enough to edit them. She knew, even as she heard herself speak, that she was only making matters worse, but she couldn't seem to stop.

Somewhat mollified, he hooked his fingers above the window of her vehicle and leaned down. "Then why didn't you call me this week?"

"I don't . . . I'm not ready for a relationship, Noah."

He stared at the ground for a few seconds. He wasn't as pleased as when she'd admitted how she felt about last Sunday, but his expression remained tentative. "What *are* you ready for?"

Oh, God. Just looking at him made her want to be with him again. She was succumbing to her desire for him. . . . "Friends,

I guess."

His big shoulders lifted in a shrug. "Well, that's progress, I guess. You didn't even want to be my friend at first." Chuckling without any enjoyment, he closed her door.

She rolled down the window. "That's it?" she called after him. "That's all you've got to say?"

"I'm sorry. I was hoping for a little more," he replied, and went inside.

Addy sat in her truck, resting her forehead against the steering wheel. *Go home. You'll ruin your life here,* she told herself. But the danger didn't matter. *Nothing* seemed to matter as much as Noah.

Turning off her 4-Runner, she took a deep breath, slid her keys inside her purse and walked to his door.

She had to remember who she was dealing with. Whatever sprang up between her and Noah wouldn't last. So why fight the attraction? Either she'd be leaving town, or he would. He went to Europe every spring.

She supposed she could get over him as easily then as she could now.

"Would friends with benefits work?" she asked when he answered her knock.

Noah was almost afraid to trust Addy's change of heart. "There are other things

I'm not happy with," he said.

She slanted him a suspicious look. "Like . . ."

"What happened the night you were kidnapped? Who did that to you? Chief Stacy has that knife of Aaron's. Yet you say it's not Aaron."

"It's not."

"Then who was it?"

"Now you're asking for too much." She smoothed the fringe on her costume. "Maybe I should've been clearer. This is a take-it-or-leave-it offer."

He tossed his club and the wig he'd been wearing earlier onto the couch, along with his coat. "I wish I had the ability to 'leave it,' " he said, but he couldn't. The fact that she'd refused to see him had been driving him crazy all week. He wasn't going to quibble over stuff that didn't directly involve him. At least she was here. Maybe she'd open up later.

He pulled her into his arms as he closed the door.

"You're going to bend my feather," she teased.

His grin slanted up on one side. "I'm planning to do a lot more than that."

"And I'll probably let you, since your costume is so damn appealing." She'd been admiring it all night — what it did and didn't expose. "It's that cheetah print. You were right when you said I couldn't look anywhere else."

"All part of my mind-control techniques."

She watched as he untied his sandals and kicked them to one side. "Will I ever be the same?" She wasn't really joking, but she was glad he didn't seem to realize that.

"Not if I can help it," he told her, and slipped the straps of her dress off her shoulders.

"I can't believe you were so mad at me," she said when they were lying, spent, on his bed.

She could hear the lazy satisfaction in his voice when he answered. "I'm not mad at you anymore."

"Of course you aren't. You got exactly what you wanted."

He rolled over, pinning her beneath him as he nipped at her neck. "Don't pretend it was just me."

"I'm blaming that darn costume," she teased. "It showed way too much of you."

"I guess I'll have to wear it every time we make love."

"No more costumes." She frowned down at her bare chest. "Your fake whiskers have gotten black paint all over me."

"We could shower and then get into my hot tub."

"You have a Jacuzzi, too?"

"It's a bit old-fashioned — made out of wooden slats because I like the smell of cedar — but it's every bit as effective as Ted's fancy plastic one. A good hot tub is actually a requirement in my profession."

"Where is it?" She hadn't seen it when she was here before.

He pulled her out of bed. "In back. Come on. Let's clean up and go out."

"I don't have a swimsuit."

"You won't need one."

"What if someone sees us?"

"It's fenced." They took a quick shower before he guided her onto a wooden deck. There was so much foliage in his backyard she doubted anyone would be able to peer in at them even in broad daylight and without a fence.

"You have quite a gardener."

"I do it myself. I like it a little untamed."

"That suits you." She glanced at the starry sky. "What time is it?"

"Does it matter?"

"I don't want to worry Gran."

"Can't be past two."

"That's late!" she said with a laugh.

"Stay awhile longer."

She waited until he took off the tub's cover and tested the water.

"Perfect. Come on."

The air was chilly and smelled of rain, but the water was so hot she had to climb in slowly. She hadn't even submerged herself all the way when Noah came up behind her.

One hand cupped her breast and the other moved lower as he brought her against him. "You smell good," he said, suddenly holding her tighter, more possessively. "You feel good, too."

Guilt threatened to ruin her enjoyment, but she willed it away. She'd never wanted anyone like she wanted Noah. She wasn't going to let what had happened in the past take this moment away from her.

Closing her eyes, she let her head fall back on his shoulder as his mouth moved down her neck.

"I was stupid not to notice you in high school," he said. "I must've been blind. But . . . why'd you have to stay gone so long, pretty Adelaide?"

Addy didn't want to talk, not about that. Turning, she put her hands on his chest and kissed his mouth, gently encouraging him to stand before she started kissing other things. She circled one of his nipples with her tongue, then paused to smile up at him. "I'm here now."

The motor and all the bubbles sounded loud in Addy's ears as she moved lower, but the noise couldn't mask Noah's gasp when she took him in her mouth.

Twenty minutes later, Noah held Addy on his lap as he played with the silky strands of hair that floated on the water.

"So . . . when you say you won't be staying in Whiskey Creek, are you thinking . . . three months? Six? More?"

He could tell she didn't like to talk about the future, but he wanted to have *some* idea of what to expect.

"I'm not sure yet."

"But even after you leave, you're only going to Davis. That's not like saying you'll be moving across the country."

She didn't respond.

"And Milly hasn't agreed to sell the restaurant. Maybe she won't."

"You'll be leaving in the spring for another racing season."

She said that as if it would be the end — if the end didn't happen sooner. But tonight had been so incredibly fulfilling he didn't want to call her on the finality in her voice. Maybe she had problems with trust from her divorce, like she'd indicated. Or maybe something else had occurred when she was abducted, something she didn't want to admit. There was no need to push, no need to spook her. Noah believed in letting things develop naturally. They were seeing each other; for the moment, that was enough.

"What happened between you and Baxter North?" she asked.

He cupped her breast and lowered his head to kiss it. "He's moving."

"That makes you mad at him?"

"No. He's got the right to do whatever he wants."

"So why are all your friends worried about him?"

"He's going through some . . . personal issues."

"That's polite talk for 'I'm not going to tell you,' " she said with a laugh.

He nuzzled her neck. "Sorry."

"Will you be sad to see him go?"

"Absolutely." But Noah felt it might be more complicated if he stayed. He changed his mind on that day by day, almost minute by minute.

Once they'd both established what they wanted out of life, he hoped they could be friends again. "We're at a crossroads."

"What does that mean for him?"

"A future in San Francisco, where he works."

"And for you?"

"I'm thinking of retiring."

She sat up straight. *"From biking?"*

"If not this year, next."

"But . . . you love it, don't you?"

"I can't compete forever. I'll be thirty-four soon. It's sad when fifteen-, sixteen- and seventeen-year-olds are starting to give you competition." He wiped the water from his face. "Some of them are amazing."

"What would you do if you retired?"

"Run my store. What else?"

"You wouldn't sell out? Leave Whiskey Creek?"

"And go where? This is my home. I like it here." He saw a wife and kids in his future, but he didn't add that. He didn't want her to think he was being presumptuous.

He let the silence linger for a few minutes. Then he said, "Do you really have to sell Just Like Mom's? I mean . . . why not stay and run it? What's in Davis that's drawing you back?"

"I have friends there."

He pressed his forehead to hers. "You could always visit them."

"I've just never seen myself settling here."

"Why not?"

She got up. "I have to go."

He watched her, gilded in moonlight, as she climbed the steps. "Will you still be talking to me in the morning?" he asked.

She must've heard the teasing note in his voice because she cast a smile over one shoulder. "Yes."

"I'll take that on faith. But, if it's all the same to you, this time I'll get *your* number."

"That's fine." She laughed, then sobered. "Just . . . I'd rather no one else knew . . . if we see each other again."

He got out, too, and handed her one of the towels he stored in a cupboard. *"If?"*

"What we do is no one's business."

He didn't like the sound of that. "Things don't really work that way in Whiskey Creek. We wouldn't be able to go *anywhere* if we want to keep this private. Why the big secret?"

"I'd feel more comfortable. At least at first."

"You're a mystery to me." He kissed her forehead as he said it. He decided they'd just take what they felt for each other one day at a time. He had no idea what might or might not develop.

But he soon figured out one possible reason she was so hesitant to let others know about their relationship. He went out to start her car while she dried her hair, so the heater would be on since it had begun to rain, and found a piece of paper stuck under her windshield wiper.

There was only one line of typed text. It was smeared because of the rain. But he could read it.

Stay away from Noah or that mine will be your *burial place, too!*

22

Noah didn't mention the note to Addy. He folded it up and shoved it in the pocket of his zippered sweatshirt before she could come out. Only after he'd kissed her goodnight, warned her to be careful and followed her home in his own vehicle to make sure she got in safely did he take it out and read it again. Then he drove slowly up and down her street as well as his to see if someone was around — following her, watching her.

What was going on? Who would leave such a note? *And why?*

The tone sounded like that of a jealous woman. But he hadn't been with anyone else in months, except Lisa, and he doubted she'd bother driving out to Whiskey Creek from the Bay Area, where she lived, just to torment whatever woman he was dating — not now that she thought he was gay. She didn't even know about Cody, would have no reason to refer to the mine.

No, considering that and the fact that Addy had been abducted, he didn't think it was Lisa or any other woman. Something else was going on. He couldn't guess what, exactly, but he knew one thing for sure. Whoever had put that note on her windshield had to be keeping a close eye on her. They hadn't left the party until midnight, so there wasn't a lot of traffic when they drove home. And his house was tucked back behind the store. Her SUV couldn't easily be seen from the street.

Someone knew where she was and what she was doing, and that worried him, because if she was being intimidated, her abduction and beating wasn't an isolated incident. She said if she kept her mouth shut, it would be over. But it seemed to him that someone was harassing her in an ongoing, well-orchestrated and targeted campaign.

When Noah parked in his driveway, he sat there for a few minutes, waiting to see if he'd notice anyone lurking about. He'd been so caught up in the fallout of Baxter's revelation and decision to move, and coping with Addy's initial rejection, that he'd simply pushed on with his own life, treating her abduction with curiosity but no commitment, as if it were none of his business.

That was how *she* treated it. She'd let him know in no uncertain terms that she didn't want him getting involved.

But whatever was going on felt very much a part of his business now. How dare anyone tell her she couldn't see him? And, if she was still having trouble, why hadn't she gone to the police?

He should've tried harder to find out the name of her ex. Whatever was happening, it had to stem from her life in Davis. She hadn't been in Whiskey Creek for thirteen years, so there was no way it could've started here.

Or . . . this was a long shot, but maybe Kevin Colbert had something to do with what was going on. He seemed to have a strange effect on her. There was that moment outside the coffee shop, when she dropped her drink and ran to her car. And before she arrived at the party last night, Ted had mentioned that he'd seen Kevin at Just Like Mom's. He said Kevin and Addy had been in the middle of an argument, after which Kevin had given back *her* cell phone.

What would they have to argue about? As far as he could tell, she barely knew Kevin. She'd asked about him that first night, when they were driving home from the mine. But she'd also asked about Tom Gibby and other people.

Taking a deep breath, he pulled out his cell phone and called her.

"Hello?"

He smiled at the husky sound of her voice. Even the way she talked was sexy. "You okay?"

There was a slight pause. "Of course. Why?"

He just needed to be sure. He'd watched her walk into Milly's and close the door behind her, and yet . . . he was unsettled and a little angry that he didn't know, couldn't guess, what she was up against.

"I had a nice time tonight," he said.

"So did I."

"When can I see you again?"

She laughed. "I've only been home for fifteen minutes."

But the way she'd acted before, and what he'd read in that note, made him nervous. "See what you do to me?"

"You're coming to dinner tomorrow night, right?"

He'd forgotten about that. "Right."

"So I'll see you then."

She was about to hang up, but he stopped her. "Have you heard from Chief Stacy lately?"

"About the mine incident? No. I don't think he's too pleased with me." She chuckled. "He so desperately wanted it to be Aaron. Case closed."

Noah tapped his fingers on the steering wheel. "You're not scared, are you?"

"That . . ."

"Whoever kidnapped you will hurt you again?"

There was a brief silence before she said, "It should be okay."

He combed his fingers through his hair, which was stiff with chlorine from the hot tub. "Kevin Colbert hasn't been giving you any trouble . . . ?"

"No, why would you think that?"

"Ted said he was with you at Just Like Mom's the other night, that the two of you were having an argument."

"He was complaining about his meal. That's all. I comped his dinner and that was the end of it."

"You're sure?"

"Positive."

"So why would he have your phone?"

"I'd left it sitting on a nearby table. He thought someone had lost it."

"I . . . see."

Silence fell. Then he said, "Are you ever going to trust me enough to tell me what's going on, Addy?"

Another long pause. "Let's just enjoy the time we've got, okay?" she said.

As soon as he started getting close, she backed away. "Until . . ."

"I leave or you do."

That would be a while, so he didn't see any reason not to agree. But he stared at the note he'd found on her car long after they'd hung up. Why would anyone care if they got together? Especially Kevin Colbert? He was married and had three kids. . . .

Raised voices dragged Addy from a deep sleep.

"I didn't call because I wanted to surprise you! What's wrong with that?"

"I needed to talk to you. I told you it was important. I left at least three messages."

"I've been busy. But I'm here now. So talk."

Their voices dimmed briefly. Then Addy heard, "If she got through it, if she's fine, what's the big deal?"

With a groan, Addy rolled out of bed. This could be none other than her dear mother. She missed the next part of the conversation, but then she heard Gran say, "So where's your latest husband? You didn't bring him?"

"*Latest?* You had to add that?"

"What else am I supposed to say? You switch so often I've lost track. I don't even bother learning their names anymore."

"And you wonder why I don't call as often as you think I should."

"As often as I think you should? I don't *ever* hear from you — unless you need something. And I was trying to reach you about your daughter!"

"Who hasn't called me, either — not in ages. So you might as well get off your high horse."

"How dare you blame her!"

"Who else am I supposed to blame? She has a phone. She knows my number."

"Isn't it obvious, Mom?" Addy whispered. "You. We both blame *you.*"

"She checks in with *me* regularly." Gran, forever her defender. "Always has."

"Don't rub my nose in that, Mother. She checks in with you because you spoil her."

"Lower your voice. She got into bed late last night, needs her sleep."

"Oh, for God's sake, she's not a child anymore! I think she can handle a short night here and there. What about *me*? I drove for ten hours straight to get here."

"*Why?* That's the question."

Addy had the same question — together

with one other. How long was her mother planning to stay? If she'd split up with her husband, which usually precipitated these unexpected visits, she could be staying for a few weeks. Until she met someone else or came up with another way to escape the town she grew up in without actually having to support herself.

With so much going on in her life, Addy didn't think she could handle a prolonged visit from Helen. She'd slept with Noah last night. That was the stupidest thing she could've done, but she couldn't pretend she regretted it, or that she wouldn't do it again.

"I wanted to see you, to come home!" her mother cried.

"Because . . ." Gran was skeptical and had every right to be.

"You just can't take it at face value, can you?"

"I've learned from past experience to be wary. Did you get in a fight with your husband? Are you filing for divorce? I'm too old for surprises, Helen. If there's bad news, I'd prefer to hear it up front."

"There's no bad news! Neal had to go out of town on business and I didn't see any reason why I should sit home, twiddling my thumbs."

A short pause ensued, during which Addy

put on her slippers. When Helen spoke again, her voice sounded petulant.

"I don't have to stay if you don't want me here. I could go back."

"Don't talk like that. Of course we want you here." Gran had already given up the fight. She'd never understood Helen, never been able to completely overlook her self-absorption, but she loved her. That meant Helen won every time.

Love makes you weak, Addy thought. She'd always believed it. The person who loved was the person who suffered. Helen had taught her and Gran all about that. But Addy mustered a smile as she smoothed her hair down and shuffled into the living room. "Mom, I thought that was you."

"Hi, baby! How are you?"

"Great."

"Is it good to be home?"

Addy loved Whiskey Creek as much as anyone, but her homecoming was getting more complicated every day. "Of course."

Helen grasped her chin and studied her face, like she might do to a child. "This is what some bastard did to you?"

Although most of her injuries had healed, the bruise on her cheek lingered as a subtle greenish discoloration about the size of a quarter. Addy could cover it with makeup when she went out. She hardly noticed it anymore. But she wasn't wearing any makeup at the moment and the morning sun shone brightly through the windows.

She shot an exasperated look at Gran. He'd done a lot more than give her a small bruise. But what was the point of telling her mother everything that had happened? Or even some of it . . . Addy had heard her careless response of a few seconds ago: *If she got through it, if she's fine, what's the big deal?* "It's almost gone, nothing to worry about. So . . . how long can you stay?"

Her mother dropped her hand. "For a few days, at least."

That was more than the weekend her husband was supposed to be out of town. Addy suspected there was trouble in paradise *again.*

"How's the restaurant?" Helen asked. "In good shape?"

Addy thought of Darlene but glossed over her problems with Gran's manager, too. "Fine. As always."

"And your love life? Did you leave anyone special in Davis?"

"No."

"You should never have let Clyde get away. That man was hot, wasn't he?"

Adelaide ground her teeth. "He cheated

on me, Mom."

She shrugged. "Most men cheat. That doesn't mean they don't love you."

With such low expectations, her mother could settle for just about anyone, as long as he had money. To her, that was more of a prerequisite than fidelity.

Eager to change the subject, Addy gave Helen an appraising once-over. "You look beautiful."

She flipped her hair, dyed jet-black, over one shoulder. "How do you like my nails? I just got them done." She flashed long, acrylic zebra stripes at them. "These are real diamonds," she said, indicating the gems embedded in her pinky nails.

It was a good thing her mother was beautiful, because Addy couldn't find many other redeeming qualities. "Aren't you afraid they might fall out?"

"They're not going anywhere. And if they did, it wouldn't be a huge loss. They came out of a pair of hundred-dollar studs. No biggie."

"They're nice." So were her expensive bag and shoes. And the obvious Botox treatments. Her mother hated aging. It impeded her ability to attract the men she wanted. "They expect us to look seventeen forever," she often complained.

Helen cocked her head. "Have you had a boob job?"

Addy blinked in surprise. "Me? No! Trust me, I'm not one to volunteer for pain."

"But you're bigger than you used to be."

"I'm the same as I was the last time you saw me."

"I don't believe you. Let me feel them."

Fortunately, the doorbell rang, giving her a good excuse to swat her mother's hands away. "I'll get it."

Addy wasn't prepared for company. She'd just rolled out of bed but anything was a welcome distraction when her mother started acting like this. She loved to embarrass Addy. She always had, probably because *nothing* embarrassed her.

A deliveryman stood at the door with a giant bouquet of flowers. "Delivery for Adelaide Davies," he said.

Addy felt her eyebrows go up. "*I'm* Adelaide Davies."

He hefted the vase to one side, resting it against one hip so he could have her sign his clipboard. "Enjoy your flowers."

"Wow! Where did you get those?" her mother demanded as she closed the door.

Addy shook her head, allowing Helen to take the flowers while she removed the card herself.

" 'I can't stop thinking about you,' " she read.

Gran pressed close. "*Who* can't stop thinking about you?"

Noah had signed his name, so it wasn't as though she could lie. "They're from Noah. He was —" she cleared her throat "— he was at the party last night." So much for being discreet. She'd told him she didn't want anyone to know they were dating.

"Noah who?" her mother asked.

"Rackham!" Gran supplied as if she'd really caught a big one this time.

Helen stepped back. "You're already seeing someone *here*?"

"Not really," Addy mumbled, but she doubted her mother heard because Gran spoke over her.

"Not just anyone, Helen. The mayor's son! And he's a lot cuter than that Clyde she was with before. I personally never cared for Clyde. He had beady eyes."

"He had *wandering* eyes," Addy said. "Anyway, Noah and I are not officially seeing each other."

Her mother's laugh sounded more like a cackle. "Honey, who cares whether it's official? A man doesn't send a woman roses unless he's *seriously* interested. Those must've cost him a hundred bucks."

Addy scrambled to rein in their excitement. Noah wasn't the type to be *seriously* interested in anyone, not the way her mother and grandmother seemed to believe. They were enjoying each other, and they felt an *attraction.* That was all. "He's just being nice, Mom, probably because he's coming to dinner tonight. This is . . . his contribution to the meal."

" 'I can't stop thinking about you'? Ha! Don't kid yourself." Eyes alight with prurient interest, Helen clapped her hands. "Well! We can't let him down."

Addy narrowed her eyes in suspicion. "What do you mean?"

"If we're going to have a special guest for dinner, we've work to do in order to be ready. I'm taking you to a day spa in Sacramento."

"No, that's okay." She'd been hoping to go by Stephen's, to finally get a good look at that white Chevy.

"Come on! You'll get a full Brazilian, maybe do a little tanning and splurge on one of those chemical peels that don't actually peel."

"Anything else?"

Helen didn't seem to hear her sarcasm. "No, that should do it. At least you already got a boob job."

Addy didn't bother to continue the argument over whether or not she'd had certain enhancements. "But I was going to the restaurant this morning and then making dinner." She hadn't been looking forward to facing Darlene again, but she *had* been looking forward to preparing tonight's meal. She hadn't cooked since she'd come home.

"Darlene can handle the restaurant. And I'll take care of dinner." For once, Gran was siding with Helen. "You go with your mother and have a great time."

Addy couldn't complain about being whisked off. She had the wax first, which was painful, but everything got better from there. She'd never been so pampered in her life, or felt more attractive once her spa experience was over. She'd had her hair and nails done, too. And, afterward, her mother — with her husband's money, no doubt — insisted on buying her a new dress: a clingy number that would've been *way* beyond her own budget. She liked the vibrant color and stretchy fabric; Helen couldn't get over how "flattering" it was to her figure.

"You should've been a model," she said.

Addy smiled as they returned to the house. She'd actually enjoyed her mother and couldn't wait to see Noah. Although a big lump of guilt sat in her stomach and didn't seem likely to go away, a rebellious streak had her shaking her fist at all her reservations and telling herself she'd do as she damn well pleased for a change. Except for that one graduation party, when she'd disobeyed Gran to sneak out of the house, she'd always lived her life by carefully observing the rules. That one night had burned her badly. She'd also seen where bad behavior had gotten her mother. But she'd never wanted anything the way she wanted Noah. That forced her to risk a relationship, even though she knew they could only be together for a few months — *if* his interest lasted that long.

"Look at you!" Gran made a big fuss over her when she walked in. "You're gorgeous!"

"Thanks." The kitchen smelled of several delectable flavors. "What's for dinner? Sweet potato casserole?"

"In addition to steak, salad and asparagus. Apple pie for dessert."

"He'll love it."

Gran glanced at the clock. "He should be here any minute."

Addy wasn't too happy that Noah would be meeting her mother. She had no idea what Helen might say. Helen could make some sexual innuendo that would be embarrassing, or simply be too bold in her praise — of his body, for instance. Helen loved being irreverent, loved shocking the opposite sex. Guaranteed, she'd flirt with him shamelessly. But Addy couldn't ask her mother to leave. What kind of daughter did *that*?

Helen made a sound of excitement and Addy turned.

"Oh, my God! Is that *him*?" She stood at the window, gazing outside. Noah had just driven up.

"Yes, but —"

Her mother cut her off. "Tell me he has an older brother who's single!"

"For . . . for *you*?" Addy sputtered.

Her mother used her long nails to fluff her hair. "Doesn't hurt to assess my options."

Addy looked at Gran, who was too busy getting the casserole out of the oven to be paying attention. "You're married!"

"Things change. You've pointed that out yourself."

"And you got mad at me for it. You kept saying you're happy."

"Sometimes I'm happier than at other times. Do the Rackhams have money?"

The doorbell rang, but Addy made no move to answer it. "Mom, I know you're joking. At least, I hope you are. But *please* don't talk like that in front of Noah. And whatever you do, don't mention a brother. I guess you don't remember, or you weren't in town long enough to learn, but he had a twin and that twin was —" she struggled with the memories and her sense of responsibility "— killed at the mine the night they graduated from high school. I don't want Noah reminded of it. It's been . . . hard on him."

"Oh, right. I heard about the cave-in. It really tore you up," her mother said, but she didn't seem particularly sensitive to his loss or to Addy's reaction. There was a shrug in her voice when she added, "So maybe his father's ready for a change."

Adelaide guessed her mother was joking again, but grabbed her arm, anyway. "Mom, I'm serious. Don't —"

"What? *Tease* him?" she interrupted, obviously exasperated. "He can't take a *joke*?"

"I'm just saying that . . . I *care* about this one, okay?"

Her mother sobered. "Whoa! Mom, did you hear that?"

Gran didn't say anything, but she turned to stare. A little over a week ago, she'd told Gran she didn't want Noah over for dinner.

"Addy's finally met someone capable of

stealing her heart," Helen was saying. "And so soon. She just got back here. Before you know it, she'll be settling down next to you, right where she grew up."

"I would love that," Gran said.

Living next to Gran had once been Addy's dream. But she knew it was impossible. "I'll get the door."

23

Noah had spent much of the day calling restaurants in Davis. Although very close to the Sacramento metropolitan area, it was a small town — a college town — and the list of restaurants wasn't so daunting that he couldn't get through them in a reasonable amount of time. He wasn't sure why he hadn't thought of doing the research this way before. He'd been relying on Chief Stacy to do his job while he dealt with his own problems. But after finding that note on Addy's car, he was determined to get to the bottom of what was happening to her, because it certainly didn't seem as if anyone else was.

He'd started with the high-end restaurants, the type that might hire a true "chef," and began working his way down. It wasn't long before he found someone who recognized Adelaide's name. It was at a restaurant called Tsunami, "famous" for its "California cuisine." The person who answered said that Adelaide Davies no longer worked there. So Noah had asked for the manager of the restaurant — from what he'd heard the night he pulled her from the mine, that should be her ex-husband — and was told that Clyde Kingsdale wasn't in.

Noah left his name and number but no message. He figured if he didn't hear from Clyde he'd try later. Or maybe it would be smarter to go to the restaurant and speak to him in person. . . .

The more he thought about it, the more Noah believed that was the case. He just needed to find out when the guy would be working, and another call to Tsunami should tell him that.

"Hey," he said as Addy opened the door.

She glanced over her shoulder into the room behind her, seemingly distracted. "Hey." She stepped aside. "Come on in."

From what he could see, her bruises were finally gone, and she'd had her hair layered. Noah felt his heart beat a little faster at the sight of her. She did something to him no one else ever had; he wasn't sure why. He'd met a lot of pretty girls over the years. "You look great."

She gave him a shy smile. "Thanks. I'd like to introduce you to my mother, Helen

Simpson."

A woman almost as tall as Addy, and attractive in a well-preserved way, reached out to shake his hand. "That's Helen *Kim,*" she corrected.

Addy blushed to have gotten her mother's name wrong but didn't apologize. She waved to a chair. "Dinner's just about ready. Can I get you a glass of wine to start?"

"That'd be great. Thanks."

She went into the kitchen as Helen sat down across from him and made small talk. She asked what he did for a living and how his family was doing. He asked where her home was now and how long she'd be visiting. She told him she lived in Salt Lake City with her husband, adult stepson and two Chihuahuas. The stepson — who, according to her, was a little "off" and had never married — was caring for the dogs while she and her husband were out of town.

He wondered how Addy had managed to mess up her mother's last name, but from what Eve and Olivia had told him about Helen, he thought he could probably guess.

"Addy mentioned that you've done a lot of traveling over the years," he said. "And that you once lived in Germany?"

"When I was married to Frank. That was quite the time."

He could hear Addy talking to Gran in the kitchen. "Sounds like it was a great opportunity to see the world."

"It was. And I never miss an opportunity." She winked at him. Then she leaned forward. "How long have you known Addy?"

"Since high school," he said. "We didn't socialize, but . . . we knew each other."

"And then you rescued her from the mine."

"I was lucky to be in the right place at the right time," he said.

"She's a great girl, but she doesn't really know how to go after what she wants." She said that like, *More's the pity,* as she laughed. "You can probably tell she doesn't take after me. Still . . . she's special."

He wondered if Addy understood how her mother felt about her. "I can tell that."

Addy returned with his wine. "Here you go."

"You two make such a handsome couple," Helen said.

"That's enough, Mom."

"What? I'm just stating a fact. He's got to know he's gorgeous."

Addy shot Helen another warning glance. "Mom, please. If you can't refrain, we'll go out and leave you here with Gran."

Noah couldn't help smiling. Taking Addy's hand, he pulled her into his lap. "Addy's pretty gorgeous herself. I like this dress."

Noah handled her mother like a pro. No matter what she said, he deflected it, softened it with humor or changed the subject. Addy was grateful that he didn't seem put off. She'd been so uptight at first, angry at herself for not postponing this dinner the second she learned Helen was in town. But as the meal progressed, she slowly relaxed. Her mother was her mother. She couldn't change or control her. And Noah seemed to understand, despite having grown up in an ideal environment, with parents who were community icons and knew the difference between having people laugh with you and having them laugh *at* you.

When dinner was over, Gran started cleaning up. Addy wished her mother would step up and do it. She hated that Gran had so much difficulty getting around. But her mother never troubled herself to help with any of the household chores. Helen was already making excuses, saying she was tired and needed to lie down.

Addy asked Gran to leave the dishes for her. She said she'd take care of them later, but Gran wouldn't hear of it.

"I've got this." She motioned toward the living room and, apparently, the front door beyond. "You two go out on the porch and enjoy the autumn air."

Helen followed them outside instead of lying down. When she began talking about some man who'd hit on her at a gas station while she was driving over — *Can you believe it? He thought I was only thirty-five!* — Addy knew they needed to go farther than the porch.

She tolerated Helen's intrusion for a few minutes, but when Noah took her hand, she squeezed his, hoping he'd understand her desperation. Not long after that, he mentioned wanting to show Addy his bike shop. He extricated them from the house so well, so seamlessly, that Addy couldn't be sure he hadn't been planning to squire her away from the beginning. Regardless, it *felt* like another rescue, and she was grateful to him for that, too.

"I'm sorry about my mother," she said as they walked. His truck was at her place, but the weather was good and she'd told him she preferred to head over on foot.

"You have nothing to apologize for."

Afraid someone in town might see them together and start gossiping about it, she avoided putting her hand within reach of his. She had no idea how Kevin or the others might react to her seeing Noah; they were already afraid she might tell the authorities. "Stop being polite." She sent him a knowing look. "My mother can be . . . a little over the top."

"Um . . . you two are very different. I'll say that."

"Diplomatically stated. But it's no wonder I'm different. She hasn't had much influence on my life."

He smiled as if he was thinking, *Maybe you should be grateful for that,* but he didn't say anything.

"Do you miss living in Davis?" he asked.

She suddenly realized she hadn't missed it at all. She'd scarcely even thought of her former home. She'd been too concerned with navigating the shark-infested waters she had to swim here. "Not too much."

Confusion etched two lines between his eyebrows. "So why do you want to go back so badly?"

She should've said yes, she missed Davis. It would've been simpler. "I don't know. It's . . . all I'm familiar with besides this town."

He gave her an enticing grin as he pulled out a key and unlocked his store. "What's wrong with this town?"

Nothing — except what had happened fifteen years ago. That was the tragedy of it. She loved Whiskey Creek. But she shouldn't be here. If not for Gran, she wouldn't be. "There's too much history."

"You left when you were eighteen. How much history could there be?"

She shrugged as he held the door and she went in. "Sometimes it's best to start over."

She could tell her answers hadn't satisfied him, but now that they were at the store, he was distracted by his eagerness to show her what he'd created with his life so far.

"I'm considering going into business with Brandon Lucero and expanding the shop to include snowboards, skis, that type of thing," he said as he flipped on the lights. "If I retire soon, that's what I'll do."

Brandon had carved out a name for himself in extreme skiing. Addy had been impressed by some of the video footage she'd seen of him — especially when he was dropped off on a mountaintop via helicopter and then raced down the steepest of slopes, none of them groomed. "He's officially retired, then?"

"He never went back to it after that nasty fall where he broke his leg so badly."

Addy had seen the footage of that, too. "The Fall" had been on all the news channels, and the *Gold Country Gazette* had chronicled Brandon's injury and his recovery.

"The paper said he was going back to skiing after he healed."

"He was keeping his cards pretty close to his chest."

"So that injury forced him out of the sport?" She was beginning to understand why Noah considered giving up racing. He was getting older; why wait for a tragic accident to convince him it was time?

"He might've been able to keep going for a few more years. But then he met Olivia, and that changed his focus."

"Right. Women weaken legs. I've seen *Rocky*, you misogynist."

"I'm wounded," he said when she shoved him. "I was merely saying it takes a lot to make a man leave a woman he loves." He pulled a pink tunic off the rack. "Do you bike?"

"I've ridden before. But . . . I'm more of a runner."

"Because you haven't experienced all the possibilities. You should go out with me sometime."

She rolled her eyes. "I'd be going maybe ten miles an hour, especially if we went off-road. And if I came to a pothole or a rock,

I'd get off and walk my bike around it. You'd be bored stiff."

"I doubt that." He lowered his eyes to her new dress. "You'd look *great* in spandex."

"But I can't say the helmet would do much for me," she said with a laugh.

"We'll get you a cool one." He started gathering up items. "You'll also need some shoes and padded shorts. I wouldn't want you to get a sore ass. Then you might not let me touch it."

She slugged his arm halfheartedly. "Stop."

"What about this?" He showed her a tight-fitting windbreaker with pockets for various necessities in back. "This will come in handy when it's cold."

"Noah, I don't even have a bike!"

"We're getting to that."

She glanced at the rows of expensive bikes lining the showroom. "No, we're not."

"Sure we are. I want to take you biking tomorrow."

She caught a glimpse of the price tag on the helmet he'd selected. Biking stuff was *expensive*. "But I can't afford all this. Not right now."

"You have plenty you could trade." He slung what he'd been collecting over a rack and pressed her up against the register. "Want to pay now?" He nipped at her mouth. "Or later?"

She couldn't resist his lascivious smile, especially since he *intended* it to be lascivious. He tempted her to be so carefree, so happy. She felt satisfied when she was with him in a way she'd never felt satisfied before, and that scared her. Because she knew their . . . connection, or whatever it was, couldn't last.

Purposely avoiding any thought of the ending to come, she batted her eyelashes at him. "That depends on what payment includes."

He kissed her, slow and soft. "It'll definitely include the removal of your panties."

She slid her arms around his neck and pulled him in for another kiss, only hers wasn't sweet and coaxing like the one he'd just given her. It was sexy and raw. Demanding. She put everything she had into it because she couldn't share her feelings any other way — and she was desperate to enjoy him while she could. "What if I'm not wearing panties?" she whispered.

All playfulness disappeared from his expression as he slipped one hand up her dress. "Good thing I have a condom in my wallet."

By the time they were ready to leave the

store, Noah felt dazed. He had carpet burns on the backs of his hands where he'd shielded Addy's backside as he drove into her in the break room, but he wouldn't have done anything to change the experience. He'd never felt more possessive of someone, more hesitant to let go. Always before, he could walk away after sex. He'd *preferred* being able to go on with his life without any obligations, which was probably why he'd felt so defensive whenever his friends teased him. What they had to say was, to a large extent, true.

But things were different with Addy, which made every minute of being with her that much better. It made the sex better, too. Actually, it made the sex unbelievable.

He was high on infatuation and hormones. He wanted to kiss her and keep kissing her, whether he was capable of making love again yet or not. But he didn't find that realization upsetting. He was *glad* to know his heart wasn't defective, as he'd feared. He didn't care if she kept reminding him, in subtle ways, that she'd be leaving town. He'd deal with that when the time came. Right now, it seemed like such a far-off possibility. She'd only been home two weeks; it certainly wasn't time to start packing her bags. And he'd found a way to reach her ex-husband. He'd get to the bottom of that mine incident eventually, figure out if Clyde Kingsdale was driving over and harassing her. And when he caught whoever had hurt her, he'd make sure the bastard never touched her again.

"There's a Redbox at the Gas-N-Go," he said. "Let's get a movie and take it to my place."

She was straightening her dress. "Okay, but . . . let's walk."

"It's not too cold for you?"

"It's better than going back home while my mother might still be up," she said with a rueful laugh.

He ran around to his house for a coat, slipped it over her shoulders and took her hand, but she pulled away once they were out on the street. He halfway expected her to give his coat back.

"Why are you so afraid of people finding out that we're seeing each other?" he asked.

"You mean that we're sleeping together?"

He stopped walking. "Aren't we doing both?"

She didn't comment one way or the other. She just tugged on his arm to get him moving again. "I told you. It's none of their business."

Was it really that — or something else?

Something that had to do with that note he'd found on her 4-Runner? "They'll adjust once they get used to the idea."

"I . . . prefer to stay out of the limelight."

"Was your ex a jealous person?"

"I don't really know," she said, as if the answer surprised her as much as him.

He looked over at her. "What do you mean you don't know?"

"I think he was more intent on getting *me* to feel some jealousy."

"Why would he want that?"

"To prove I cared about him, I guess."

"That's why he cheated on you?"

"In his mind, it started there. At least, that was how he tried to explain it. He said if I could just love him more, he'd be satisfied. But . . . who knows? I don't think I ever really knew him."

"Then why did you marry him?"

"I *thought* I loved him, and he was so convinced we'd be happy together. I hoped that would be enough to build on. But . . . I doubt he really knew me, either."

Noah was just admitting to himself that she *was* hard to know when she changed the subject.

"Have you ever been in love?"

He'd asked himself that many times before and, sadly, always came to the same conclusion. "There've been certain women I've liked more than others, but . . . head over heels? No."

She offered him an encouraging smile. "You'll find the right person eventually."

How did she know *she* wasn't the right person? Didn't she want to be?

Sometimes she acted like it. Back at the store, she'd acted as if he was the only man on earth. But she'd already retreated. "Why do you keep pushing me away?" he asked.

"I don't want you to get hurt," she replied.

Noah had expected her to point to his less-than-stellar track record with women, to the gossip floating around town about his "commitment issues," to say she didn't trust him after the way he'd ignored her in high school. He hadn't expected *this*. He'd heard similar things before. But Addy wasn't playing hard to get, wasn't using that statement to gain the upper hand. She was sincere in her concern, which gave him the odd feeling he'd had from the beginning — that he might've met the one woman who could break his heart.

"You don't think you could ever love me?" he asked.

She seemed to struggle for the right answer, but before she could speak, a car swerved and nearly struck them both. Noah

416

shoved Adelaide behind him, assuming it was some kind of attack like when she'd been abducted. But then he recognized the car. It was Eve's.

"Noah!" The way Eve staggered when she got out made him wonder if she was drunk, but the alarm in her voice told him it was emotion and not alcohol that had her acting so unsteady.

"What is it?" he asked.

"I — I've been looking all over for you. Baxter, he —" She broke down, couldn't even speak she was sobbing so hard.

The cold hand of terror ran down Noah's spine. "What is it?" he asked again.

"He's in the hospital."

Noah stepped forward impatiently. "What's wrong? *What happened to him?*"

She glanced at Addy, but Noah got the impression she didn't really see her. "He overdosed."

The strength left his legs. He was glad Eve rushed into his arms, because that gave him something to hang on to.

"On what?" he choked out. "Baxter doesn't do drugs. . . ."

"Sleeping pills. I don't have all the details, but the doctors think he took over two thousand milligrams of Ambien, and he'd been drinking, which of course makes it

417

even worse. The doctors are doing what they can. Meanwhile, we've been trying to find you."

"Why didn't you call me?"

"We tried! Again and again!"

He patted his pockets before remembering that he'd left his cell phone in his truck when he went in for dinner. At that point, nothing had mattered more than spending an enjoyable evening with Adelaide.

"He's not going to die. . . ." He didn't want to ask for fear of the answer. His voice didn't even sound like his own. Suddenly, that kiss at the cabin, Baxter's sexual orientation, the changes his being gay would require of their relationship — it all seemed so small, so manageable, in comparison to a final goodbye. Surely Baxter wouldn't have taken his own life over what happened last weekend. And surely Noah's reaction hadn't added to his despair. . . .

To his relief, Eve shook her head, but he could feel the wetness of her tears through his shirt. "I don't think so. We . . . we're lucky his neighbor went over to his house. He needed a — a bottle opener. Can you believe it?" She laughed but then her chest jerked against his as she tried to stifle a sob. "If his neighbor hadn't needed that damn bottle opener . . . it would've been too late.

As it was, he barely had a heartbeat when the paramedics got to him. They're doing what they can to revive him, but it's not yet clear whether or not he'll pull through."

Noah's throat tightened. "Where'd they take him?"

"Mark Twain St. Joseph's Hospital in San Andreas."

"Let's go." Determined to get to the hospital as fast as possible, he hooked his arm around Addy's neck and started for the car. "We'll drop Adelaide off on our way."

Addy pulled out of his grasp. "No, I'm fine. I'll walk. You two get on the road."

"It'll only take a second," he insisted. "I don't want you walking home in the dark."

She seemed to realize it would take longer to argue. "Fine. But what about your truck?" she asked as they climbed into Eve's Acura. "If you give me the keys, I'll drive it over to your place so it'll be there when you get home."

"There's no need. I'll pick it up when I come back." He thought briefly of the note he'd found on her windshield. Leaving his truck at her place would definitely be making a statement.

But he wasn't about to let anyone tell him he couldn't see her.

24

Noah sat in the waiting room with Eve, Ted, Kyle and Riley. Cheyenne hadn't answered her phone when they tried to reach her. No one had called Sophia. They'd been deliberating whether they should, but Noah was against it, and so was Ted. Ted didn't even like her appearing at coffee, so that came as no surprise. Noah was too protective. He didn't want news of this to spread any farther than it had to. That meant Callie was the only person who should know what was going on but didn't. Other than Noah, she was Baxter's closest friend. But she had a week left in Hawaii, and there was no point in ruining her honeymoon, not until they learned more. So far, they knew next to nothing. The hospital staff wouldn't allow Noah to see Baxter. They wouldn't even let Baxter's parents in the room. All his closest loved ones were stuck together, worrying and waiting.

As Noah watched Mr. North comfort Mrs. North off in one corner, he wondered how well they really knew their son. Did either of them have any clue about what might've caused him to attempt *suicide*?

Noah wanted to tell them, to get the truth out in the open so they could all reassure Baxter. But he wasn't convinced Baxter's parents would be able to accept him for what he was. Samuel North loved his son — Noah had no doubt about that — but he had a specific vision as to the kind of person Baxter should be, and being homosexual didn't fit that vision. He'd be ashamed and embarrassed, not the emotions a child hoped to evoke in a parent. Noah had been hunting and fishing with Baxter and his father, had heard some of the denigrating statements Mr. North had uttered. Noah hadn't thought too much about his remarks at the time, since they didn't affect him personally. But in light of the past week, those memories cut like glass. He was hearing them from Baxter's point of view now. They'd once been on a campout when they'd run into a couple of guys Baxter's father had deemed to be "fags." Mr. North had said that "such scum" deserved to have their penises cut off and shoved down their throats.

Guilt for worrying about how Baxter's sexual orientation would affect *him* weighed so heavily that Noah felt he might sink into the floor. How could he have put even more pressure on Baxter to be something or someone he wasn't? Now it was easy to see how hard Baxter had tried to meet everyone's expectations.

The silence of that room was broken only by their occasional whispering — *How much longer . . . ? If they can't save him I don't know what I'll do. . . . Surely, in this day and age they'll be able to revive him. . . .*

"Shit," Noah muttered.

Riley glanced over at him. "You okay?"

"No." Unable to sit any longer, he got up and headed down the hall to the drinking fountain. Although some of the people in the waiting room, like Ted and probably Eve, knew Baxter was gay, no one, other than Callie and him had had it confirmed. Noah wished Callie was here, so he wouldn't be the only one who understood just how conflicted Baxter was. The odd thing was that Bax had never acted depressed, never talked about ending his life, never complained at all. This had come out of nowhere, which upset Noah as much as everything else. He wished he'd had some warning, so he would've known he needed to do something to stave it off.

If they saved Bax, what would he do next? Would he continue to hide behind the image he'd created so none of the people he loved would think any less of him? That kept the situation status quo — tempting in such a small town. But was it possible to go on like that? How long would Baxter, or anyone else, be able to last if he was unfulfilled in the most important areas of his life?

Noah thought of Adelaide and how much he'd enjoyed being with her since she'd returned to town. She'd been on his mind constantly this past week. And he'd derived so much satisfaction from making love to her. Would it be fair to expect Baxter to live without those same feelings of romantic excitement and contentment?

Noah had no answers. Part of him wanted to tell Baxter to come out, but the reality of what that might do, how it might make matters worse, stopped him. He couldn't set Bax up for a life without the love and support of his family. That was too big a sacrifice to encourage someone to make.

"Noah." Samuel North's voice interrupted his thoughts.

Nerves tingling, Noah turned away from the fountain and faced Baxter's father. "Yes, sir?"

"I just . . . I wanted to see if . . . if you'd noticed anything unusual about Baxter lately." He rubbed his hands together, as if he wished he was putting them to some useful task but couldn't think of one. "I can't wrap my mind around this, can't believe it's true. He came over for dinner earlier. Other than a brief argument over whether he should sell his house and move to San Francisco, which we told him we'd hate to see, everything went like it always does. He never said a word about being upset. His sister called from Portland. They talked on the phone for a few minutes. There's . . . no answer for this. I mean . . . he's a handsome, successful, *good* man. What would lead him to — to try and take his own life?"

Acid churned in Noah's stomach. What could he say?

"Was it a breakup with a woman we didn't know about?" his father pressed, casting about for answers. "Was it a setback at work?" He lowered his voice. "He hasn't lost his job, has he?"

"He would've told you if he'd lost his job," Noah said.

"Maybe not. That job means a lot to him."

Noah suspected it meant even more to *them,* because it confirmed Baxter's success and reflected well on how they'd raised him

— to excel, to achieve, to be somebody. "I wish I could say something that would . . . bring you comfort," he hedged. "I'm not sure exactly what was going on in his mind. But I know your son is everything you say he is — a wonderful human being."

It hadn't surprised anyone in the group that Callie had confided in Baxter when she contracted nonalcoholic fatty liver disease. He'd be the most likely to handle such catastrophic news with the right amount of empathy and support.

"He'll be okay," his father said. "Don't you think?"

The uncertainty in Samuel's eyes terrified Noah. He wasn't convinced Baxter would recover because the problem that had caused this still loomed large. Did Bax even *want* to wake up?

"Of course he will," he said.

Noah's phone rang.

Hearing that, Samuel sighed. "I'll see you back in the waiting room."

Noah answered with a nod.

"Is everything okay?"

It was Addy. Just the sound of her voice was like a buoy. "We're still waiting to find out."

"You haven't heard anything?"

"Not yet."

"I'm sorry, Noah. I can't believe this happened."

"I can't, either."

"Is there anything I can do to make it easier?"

He managed a smile, even though no one was around to see it. "This call helps."

"I didn't want to interrupt, but . . . I've been worried."

He rubbed his temples with his free hand. He felt as if he was about to burst, that he *would* burst if he didn't tell someone what was going through his mind. "Addy?"

"Yes?"

He stepped outside, into the cold, where there was no danger of being overheard. "Baxter tried to kiss me last week — and I mean . . . like a lover."

There was a long silence.

"No comment?" he said.

"I'm searching for the right one."

"You don't seem particularly surprised."

"I'm not. I saw how he reacted to your distress during half time at the football game."

He didn't want to remember that humiliating moment, but this piqued his interest. "What do you mean?"

"He was so upset for you, so worried. He knew you'd hate being up there in front of everyone, and . . . I'm not sure how to say this without upsetting you even more, but . . . it reminded me of how someone's girlfriend might behave, not their best buddy."

Apparently, she'd picked up on what so many people had missed, or discounted in an effort to give Baxter the benefit of the doubt. "I love him — just not in that way. It could never be that way."

"I know."

"So what do I do? I feel like maybe I'm to blame for this."

"How did you react when he tried to kiss you?"

"I was shocked but . . . I didn't hit him." He told her about their conversation the next morning, and how Baxter had said he needed space.

"You're not to blame, Noah. He knows you. He knew you wouldn't respond to his kiss. If I had to guess, I'd say that was more of an act of desperation, of wanting to *finally* be who he is instead of the person he's created for public consumption. This has more to do with his family, and his life here in Whiskey Creek, beyond you. It's *all* of it."

"So how do I help him?" Noah asked.

"You continue to be his friend no matter what."

Noah glanced back at the hospital. He hoped he'd have the chance.

Adelaide thought Noah might call once he learned how Baxter was faring, so when her phone rang an hour after they'd talked, she snapped it up without even looking at caller ID.

"Hello?"

"God, that sounded breathy."

Clyde. Addy hadn't heard from her ex in weeks. She couldn't imagine why he'd be calling her now. "My mother's asleep down the hall. I'm trying not to wake her."

"Your mother's around? What, is she in the middle of another divorce?"

"That hasn't been completely determined." Adelaide hoped not. She didn't relish the idea of having her mother live with her and Gran. It wasn't like she'd be able to leave Whiskey Creek, even if that happened. Helen couldn't be relied on to stay, or to do anything useful while she was here. She'd be more of a burden on Gran than anything else. . . .

"So what's going on?" she asked. "Is everything okay?"

"With me? I didn't think you cared anymore."

She flinched. "Clyde, let's not start in on

the past."

"Fine. We'll talk about the restaurant, then. It hasn't been easy finding a chef who can do what you did, but . . . we're getting by."

Why was he calling? "I'm glad to hear it, but it's late and —"

"I realized it might not be the best time to call. I almost didn't, but . . . then I thought, 'What the hell, maybe she'll want to know.' "

"What?"

"That boy you used to have a crush on? Noah something?"

She didn't bother reminding him of Noah's last name. In fact, she regretted ever mentioning him. "Yes?"

"He called the restaurant, looking for me."

Her heart began to pound. "He did?"

"According to a note I received from Becka."

She remembered Becka, a hostess at the restaurant. Addy missed her and yet not enough to want to go back. She was happier here in Whiskey Creek. Despite the memories, despite the secrets, despite everything, *this* was home.

Noah played a big role in that, but she didn't want to acknowledge his importance. *What we have won't last.*

"What did he want?" she asked, but she

429

could guess. Eve had told her at Black Gold Coffee that Noah was interested in finding out where she'd worked before and who she'd been with. He thought that might solve the mystery of who dropped her into the mine. He'd even asked *her* for her ex's name.

"That's what I'd like to know. Wasn't it his twin brother who raped you?"

She wished she could say no, but that was more of a rhetorical question. "I'd rather you didn't talk about what happened back then, Clyde. With anyone."

"Is that why he's calling me? Does he suspect? Is he digging for answers?"

Fortunately, he didn't even know to ask those questions. . . . "I can't say for sure, but . . . it's important that he never find out. I can . . . I can trust you, can't I?"

"Why don't you finally bring those bastards to justice?" he demanded.

"It's complicated, as you well know."

"That kid died while you were defending yourself, Addy. It's not as if anyone could blame you."

Except for Noah and his parents and everyone else who might view the situation differently. They hadn't been there. They didn't understand how hurt and terrified she'd been. And, after seeing that presentation at the football game, she was positive they could never imagine Cody doing what he did, even less now than before. "I've got it under control."

"We both know that isn't true. Maybe if you'd come forward years ago, our marriage would've had a chance."

Closing her eyes, she searched for a way to diffuse his pain. Now that Noah had Clyde's name and number, she definitely needed to keep this as amiable as possible. "That isn't what destroyed it."

"You're blaming *me*? Saying it was my affairs?"

He'd been drinking. She could hear it in his voice, and that worried her. What if Noah reached him when he was drunk? "I'm not pointing any fingers. I'm not even searching for those kinds of answers."

"Well, I am, damn it! I never had a chance with you. You didn't even give a shit when I cheated on you."

She wished she could say that wasn't true, but she hadn't cared as much as she should have.

"I wouldn't have looked at other women if you'd been capable of loving me like a wife should," he went on.

"It wasn't the rape that stopped me," she said.

"What then?"

She'd already been in love . . . with Noah. He was the only person she'd ever felt strongly about, and she couldn't seem to change that. But she knew better than to reiterate the fact that Noah had overshadowed their relationship. Clyde would reveal her secret for sure. "You and I . . . we weren't meant to be."

"That's bullshit!"

"It doesn't matter anymore, anyway. Listen to yourself. We've been divorced for over a year."

"It wasn't much of a marriage to begin with."

"Then you didn't lose anything."

He didn't respond for a moment. "Maybe you're right. I don't know what I'm talking about. You just . . . drive me crazy. You always have."

"I'm sorry."

He ignored her apology. It wasn't the first one she'd offered. "So what should I tell Noah if he calls back?"

"Tell him you never did anything to harm me. Tell him you don't know anyone who would."

"What the hell is that supposed to mean?"

"Just say it, okay? Please? That's all you need to do."

She heard him sigh.

"Maybe, maybe not," he said, and hung up.

Addy sat on the edge of her bed, nibbling on her bottom lip as she agonized over what would happen if Clyde decided to be spiteful. She had to quit seeing Noah. She was being selfish, reckless, even foolish, to continue sleeping with him.

But no sooner did those thoughts go through her head than she heard a soft knock at her door. "Addy, it's me."

Noah. She told herself she'd find out how Baxter was doing and say goodbye. But Noah looked so emotionally strung out that she couldn't turn him away, even after she learned that Baxter would recover. His best friend had almost died; Noah was still worried about what the future would hold. So when he slipped his arms around her waist and buried his face in her hair as if he'd reached his safe place, her resolve instantly crumbled.

She could tell him tomorrow that she wouldn't see him again. . . .

"I'm sorry if I woke you. I had to touch you," he breathed, and a few seconds later all their clothes were on the floor and they were in her bed.

■ ■ ■ ■

Noah made love to Addy slowly, gently. He didn't want to wake her mother by causing the headboard to bang against the wall. This wasn't about satisfying his physical desires. He just wanted to feel close to Addy, to take comfort in the warmth of her body. That was also the reason he didn't leave immediately afterward. Curling around her, he stared into the blackness that cloaked her room as her breathing evened out.

He hadn't told her that Baxter refused to see him at the hospital. Although he'd been relieved to hear the doctors say Bax was going to be okay, his rejection hit Noah hard. He'd never thought he'd see the day when his best friend wouldn't want anything to do with him.

Baxter's refusal to let Noah come into the room confused Mr. and Mrs. North, too. And it surprised the hell out of the rest of their friends — especially since no one else was banned. Noah had left the hospital feeling as if everyone thought he must be to blame for what Baxter had done.

As Addy shifted, he moved to allow her more room.

"You okay?" she murmured.

He kissed her temple. "Yeah."

"Baxter will eventually come to terms with who he is and what he wants out of life. He's just . . . having an identity crisis."

"I know," he said, but he also knew that whatever happened, he and Baxter would never be the same.

She covered a yawn, but didn't go back to sleep. She roused enough to ask, "How did his father behave?"

"He's stunned, hurt — and oblivious."

"To Baxter's sexuality."

"Yes."

"The pressure we put on people to be what *we* want them to be sometimes isn't fair."

He stroked her side. "Has someone put that kind of pressure on you?"

"Clyde."

He lifted his head. "You're using his name?"

"He called me tonight."

"Do you hear from him very often?"

"Not anymore. He wanted to tell me you've been trying to reach him."

He went silent because he wasn't sure how she was going to react to that.

"He isn't the one who hurt me, Noah. I promise."

"Then why won't you tell me who did?"

"Some things are better left as they are. Trust me on that."

He hated not knowing, couldn't imagine why she wouldn't tell him. But that wasn't what bothered him the most, not at the moment. He was trying to figure out how Clyde had known his call was connected to Adelaide. He hadn't mentioned her — or even Whiskey Creek. He'd provided his name and number, which shouldn't have been enough to give him away. His area code covered a wide section of Northern California.

"Would your ex have any reason to recognize my name?" he asked.

She stiffened. He could feel her reaction.

"Not really. I mean . . . I probably mentioned you once or twice. That's all."

"In connection with what?"

"Because I used to have a crush on you. That's what I'm guessing."

Noah tried to accept her answer. But he couldn't believe that most men would remember the name of an old crush mentioned once or twice over a long period of time, not if they'd never met the guy. It wasn't as if he'd ever dated Adelaide, or remained in touch. As far as he was concerned, Addy would've had *very* little reason to bring him up.

"Why don't you want me to talk to him?" he asked.

"Because he's my ex! Would you want me talking to anyone *you* used to date?"

Possibly not. He could see that side of it. But there was something about Adelaide that made him nervous. He liked her too much. Otherwise, maybe the fact that she was keeping secrets from him wouldn't seem so threatening.

"Where are you going?" she asked as he got up.

"Home."

She said nothing until he was dressed. "Are you upset?"

"A little."

"Why?"

"Because I'm starting to care about you."

Silence.

"The fact that you have nothing to say is not reassuring," he said.

"I — I appreciate that you're open to . . . feeling something."

He frowned. "Again, not quite the reaction I was looking for."

"I don't know what you want me to say. I'm hoping we can remain friends."

He rounded on her. "*Friends,* Addy? We've made love several times in the past week. Is that what you do with your *friends*?"

She spoke even more quietly. "You know I don't."

"So what is it? What's standing between us? You don't trust me? I don't have a good track record? I'm not reliable? I hurt you before without realizing it? *What?*"

"Why are you trying to put this on me?" She was still whispering, but her words were harsher. "You're the one who isn't the type to settle down, to . . . to commit. You've *never* had a steady girlfriend. I'm just saying I understand and accept your limitations."

"*My* limitations? Since when did I tell you I don't want a commitment?"

"You haven't. But you haven't asked for one, either."

"Because it's too soon. That doesn't mean I won't."

"You don't have to. I'm not pressuring you."

"I think that's the problem. I'm the only one who wants more. So what do we have? An open relationship?"

She seemed flustered. "I guess . . . if that's okay."

"And if it's not?" He stopped her before she could respond. "I know what you're going to say. You tried to warn me. You agreed to be friends with benefits. Never mind that

I assumed you were joking."

She crossed the room, touched his arm. "I'm sorry, Noah. I . . . I was wrong to get involved with you. I never dreamed you'd want . . . more than I could give."

This wasn't going the way he'd thought it would. She was about to break off whatever they had. He could hear it in her voice. But that made no sense. They had a *great* time when they were together. He could feel the chemistry, could tell she liked being with him. So what was the problem?

"I'm not one to take things too fast. This is unlike me. I'll give you that. But . . . I sense this odd resistance in you. I could wait, see what happens, except I get this really weird feeling that no matter how well it goes, you'll back out in the end."

She said nothing.

"*Why* have you been sleeping with me?" he asked.

"Because I haven't been able to stop myself!" she admitted.

"But you would if you could."

"Yes!"

He raked his fingers through his hair. "Great. Well, *I* feel something for *you.* That's got to make a difference," he said, and walked out.

He was getting into his truck when he realized someone was sitting across the street, watching the house. He tried to get a good look at the man's face, but whoever it was didn't relish the scrutiny. Snapping on his headlights, the other driver shot into the street.

But Noah knew that vehicle. It belonged to Kevin Colbert.

25

Kevin could see Noah's headlights bearing down on him in the rearview mirror and cursed under his breath. He shouldn't have gone to Addy's. He'd given the others that big speech about lying low and staying away, but he couldn't seem to abide by it himself. He wanted to believe he'd be fine if she spoke up, that he'd just refute any claim that he'd raped her. He doubted she'd be able to prove it, not at this late date. But he couldn't stand the thought of having his reputation ruined. He was respected here in Whiskey Creek. The position he held as head coach of the football team meant more to him than anything, even his rocky marriage.

When he realized that Noah would follow him all the way home, he pulled over and waited for Cody's brother to come to his window.

It was cold out and the wind was picking

up. Noah wasn't wearing a coat, but didn't seem to feel the chill breeze that ruffled his hair and rippled his clothes. "What the hell were you doing at Addy's?" he demanded.

Kevin had never seen him so angry. Noah had *always* been congenial. Of the two Rackham boys, Cody was the one who'd had the temper. "Nothing."

"It's three o'clock in the morning, Kevin. There has to be some reason you're not home in bed with your wife."

The excuse he'd planned to give suddenly seemed lame, but he couldn't come up with a better one. "I was . . . curious about her. I mean . . . we haven't had a scandal in Whiskey Creek for a long time, if you don't count Noelle killing Kyle's baby without telling him." He attempted a laugh at the deliberate way he'd phrased that, but it fell flat. "I thought maybe I'd see if someone was skulking around."

"Someone *was* skulking around," Noah said. *"You!"*

"But not because I mean her any harm. If you're thinking I'm the one who dragged her to the mine, you're wrong. She's a beautiful woman and . . . and . . ."

"You're married," he stated flatly.

"Right, but —" his mind finally latched on to something that might be believable

"— Audrey and I haven't been getting along. We had an argument a few minutes ago —"

"In the middle of the night?"

Determined to convince him, he rushed to explain. "That's right. I couldn't sleep, so I woke her up for a little . . . you know what, and she wasn't too happy about it. That brought up a whole bunch of other complaints. So, after I'd had enough of her bitching, I stormed out. But I didn't have anywhere to go. So . . . I thought I'd drive by and see if anything strange was happening at the Davies' house."

Noah's expression remained skeptical, but he didn't say anything.

"I didn't expect to see your truck," Kevin continued. "You two aren't dating, are you?" He'd known they were seeing each other, of course. He'd been making Addy's business his business. But he'd been telling himself not to worry. Noah never lasted long in a relationship.

With a scowl, Cody's brother shoved his hands in his pockets. "She's scared of you. Why?"

"She's not scared of me! She would have no reason to be."

"I saw how she reacted to you at the coffee shop. And Ted mentioned that you were with her at the restaurant one night. That there was an argument."

"Not really. She didn't want to seat me at closing time, that's all."

Resting his forearms on top of the car, Noah leaned in, all but glaring at him.

"What?" Kevin snapped.

"If anything happens to her — if she gets hurt again — I'm coming to you for answers. Do you understand?"

Kevin sat where he was for several minutes after Noah drove away. What the hell was going on? Obviously, Noah was sleeping with the girl he and his friends had raped. Noah didn't know it, or he would've had very different words at finding Kevin outside her house. But . . . how long before Adelaide came clean?

"Son of a bitch," he muttered, and punched the gas pedal. Things weren't going the way he'd hoped, but if his wife noticed he was gone, they'd get even worse.

I *feel something for* you. *That's got to make a difference.*

Addy wished it could. She'd never wanted anything more. But she was keeping too many secrets. Those secrets would tear them apart eventually — which reminded her that she needed to drive by Stephen's place to get a good look at his truck.

Going out into the dark and cold didn't sound appealing, but this was the first chance she'd had since Friday. It wasn't as if she'd be able to sleep. Not after the way Noah had left.

She pulled on some thick, warm sweats, a beanie to cover her ears and a pair of tennis shoes. Then she slipped out through her bedroom door and put the transmission of her 4-Runner in neutral so she could coast farther away from the house before starting the engine. Gran could sleep through anything, but she had her mother to worry about. She definitely didn't want to explain to Helen why she was sneaking out of the house. Her mother would, no doubt, make a big deal of it: *Aha! See? You're not so different from me.*

Fortunately, her engine started right away. Considering how rough it had been running, she was hesitant to drive it, but she didn't think this errand would take long.

She turned up the radio to distract herself while she drove. When Whitney Houston's "I Will Always Love You" began to play, she quickly changed the station.

Stephen's house came up on her right. Like before, it was dark, but chances were good that Stephen would be home and in bed. It was Sunday night; most people had to work on Monday.

This time the garage door was down. She guessed — hoped — she'd find his truck inside.

Careful not to veer into the ditch that ran parallel to the road, she parked some distance away and shut off her headlights. Then she sat there, staring at herself in the rearview mirror.

You can do this. Just run back, open the side door and take a peek.

But Stephen frightened her more than the rest of them. She'd never forget the expression on his face when they stripped off her jeans.

You're here now. Do it.

Taking a calming breath, she slipped her phone in her pocket, found the flashlight she'd used when she was pretending to trick-or-treat and began to trudge to his place.

There weren't any streetlights this far from town, so she was forced to turn on her flashlight before she really wanted to. She stopped walking as she did and listened.

She heard nothing except a few crickets and the hum of electricity passing through the transmission lines overhead. The house next to Stephen's had the porch light on but was otherwise dark. She seemed to be out here all alone.

Make it fast and get it over with.

She jogged to the edge of Stephen's property, where she stopped again to listen.

Nothing. Thank God. She was grateful that she could see the side door she planned to use. Most homes had fenced backyards, which would have limited her access, but Stephen's had no improvements, no landscaping. He lived on a big piece of raw land.

Was he the one who'd slit open her screen door and threatened her with Aaron's knife?

Maybe she was about to find out. . . .

Since she didn't have to approach the house from the front, she cut across the property at an angle. She was feeling braver now, more confident. There were no windows on this side of the house, or none that had any view of her. And he wouldn't be expecting company.

The main door wasn't shut all the way, but she had trouble getting it open far enough to fit through. There was too much junk behind it.

Stephen's white Chevy was there, all right. She just couldn't see the front of it. So she shoved the door, hoping it would give.

Something scraped and fell against the wall, but it didn't make much sound and the door swung free.

Two more seconds and she'd be gone. . . .

Stepping carefully to avoid tools, boxes and baskets of random articles, she went inside and around his vehicle. Then she crouched near his washer and dryer, raised her flashlight — and blinked in surprise. There was no damage.

"What the . . ." She lifted a hand to feel the smooth metal body. Not so much as a dent or a scratch marred the paint or the bumper. How could that be?

She stood, intending to walk around the rest of it, but tripped over an obstacle she hadn't seen. It hit something, which fell against the door she'd used, and the resulting *thud . . . smack* seemed deafening. Afraid the noise would bring Stephen to the garage, she hurried to get out even though she'd wrenched her ankle. But a set of bedrails had fallen against the door and they were now wedged behind a freestanding cabinet. She was frantically shoving other stuff out of her way so she could hoist those rails straight up when the light snapped on.

"What are you doing here?"

Stephen stood shirtless in the doorway leading to the house, squinting against the brightness. From the marks on his face and the state of his hair, he'd been in bed. He was still attractive, however. Fit, too.

Addy pressed her back to the wall. Unfortunately, the button that raised the main garage door was on the other side, near him. Unless she could clear the path she'd used to get in, she wouldn't be able to leave.

"I — I have my phone," she warned. "You . . . you'd better stay where you are, or I'm calling the police."

He rubbed a hand over his face as if he was half-asleep but trying to focus. "What do you want here?" His expression darkened. "Are you trying to get my DNA so you can take it to the police?"

"I just wanted to see your truck. That's all."

"Why?"

She didn't say anything.

"Why?"

"To find out if you were the one who dragged me to the mine!"

Seeming to relax, he scowled and scratched his chest. "Wasn't me."

She eyed the vehicle in question. "You're the only one with a white truck."

"So? I didn't do it."

"You're saying it was one of the others?"

"Maybe. Tom wouldn't hurt you. Kevin would, if he thought it was in his best interest, but he's asked *us* not to do anything, so

I doubt he would. My guess would be Derek."

"Now you're trying to be helpful?"

He shrugged. "Why not? If you were going to come forward you would've done it by now. That begs the question, Why haven't you?"

She wanted to lift those bedrails so she could escape his garage. But she knew unblocking that door would take both hands, and she wasn't about to put her phone in her pocket. He could be on her in a matter of seconds. "A lot of reasons."

"Is Cody's death one of them?"

Her heart jumped into her throat. "I don't — I don't know what you're talking about."

"Yes, you do." He studied her rather dispassionately. "You know opening your mouth about grad night will ruin your life as well as ours, and I'm betting you're too smart for that. The others are all shitting their pants, wondering what you'll do next, but . . . revealing the past isn't the reason you came back to Whiskey Creek."

She gripped her phone more tightly, even though she knew she'd never make a call, not after what he'd just said. "Then why did I come?"

"To help your grandmother, like you've been telling everyone. Having you back makes for an uncomfortable situation, because it puts us all in close proximity again. But I know Milly means that much to you. And I, for one, am willing to let sleeping dogs lie," he said, and went inside.

Addy wasn't feeling so good when she woke up the next morning. Rehashing various conversations — with Clyde, with Noah, with Stephen — had kept her up the few hours she might've slept. So she was none too pleased when her mother waltzed into her room bright and early and raised the blinds.

"Mom, it isn't even eight o'clock," she complained.

"Rise and shine!" Helen sang out.

"Because you've made breakfast?"

"Don't be sarcastic."

Addy let her fake smile wilt. "I didn't think so."

"It's time to share all the juicy details from last night." She perched on the edge of the bed. "Noah's cute. I mean *really* cute. And he comes from money. So?"

Addy barely resisted pulling a pillow over her head. "So what?"

"How'd it go?"

"He's nice. He showed me his bike shop, which is also . . . nice."

Her mother rolled her eyes. "That's *all* he showed you? I take you to get your hair and nails done and bring you home so gorgeous you could turn *Gandhi's* head, and that's all you've got to say? He's *nice*?"

He was also good in bed. But she didn't have a lot to compare him to, so she didn't consider herself much of an expert. "What did you expect? We're just friends."

Her mother wagged a finger at her. "Oh, no, you don't. You don't get to play it both ways. You said you liked him. *Really* liked him. And I could tell by the way you looked at him last night that it's true."

Adelaide avoided her gaze. "He has commitment issues, Mom. Whatever is going on between us will be short-lived." Even shorter than her mother thought, since she wasn't sure she'd see Noah again.

"You never know where it might lead."

"Actually, I do," she said. That was what frightened her.

"What are your plans for the day?" Helen asked.

"I have to go to the restaurant." And deal with Darlene, although she wasn't looking forward to it.

Clearly not excited by her answer, her mother pursed her lips. "Work, huh?"

"That's what most people do with their

time, Mom."

She clapped her hands. "Okay, I'll go with you."

Adelaide rose up on one elbow. "You'll *what?*"

"I'll go, too, and help out. You're not the only one who ever worked in that two-bit diner, you know."

"But . . . *why?*"

"I've got to have something to do, don't I?" She shrugged as she stood, but the effort required to feign interest in an activity she'd never normally be interested in was a bit too obvious.

Adelaide kicked off the covers. "Oh, boy, you and Neal are splitting up."

Suddenly deflated, her mother grimaced. "He kicked me out."

"Right before you came here."

"Of course. Wouldn't even let me take the dogs."

"What about the money you spent on me?"

At this, she smiled. "He hasn't made it to the bank yet to close our checking account."

Addy put a hand to her head. "I was afraid of that."

"Don't worry. The bastard owes me for putting up with his son for so long. Spending a little on *my* daughter was the least he could do."

"So what are you doing next?"

She took a deep breath. "What I always do. Move on."

"Have you ever really been in love?" Addy asked.

"I'm not sure I know what love is," she said.

Addy was pretty sure *she* did. But she wasn't convinced that made her position any better than Helen's.

"You do realize what's happening?"

Recognizing Derek's voice, Kevin held the door for his wife and kids as they trooped into Any Way You Slice It to order a pizza. He stayed outside so he could talk on his phone without being overheard. "What are you talking about?"

"Adelaide's seeing Noah."

"I know." He checked to make sure he was alone before continuing. "I've been watching her. I've put a couple of notes on her car, too, reminding her to keep her mouth shut and warning her to stay away from him. But . . . the one telling her to stay away hasn't done any good. I found his truck at her house last night."

"Maybe the other one hasn't done any

good, either. If she tells him we raped her —"

"Kevin? Aren't you coming in?"

Kevin glanced up to see his wife poking her head out of the restaurant. "In a sec."

"Who is it?" she asked.

"Just one of my players who can't make practice on Monday. Go ahead and order. I'll be right there."

"*That's* so important you have to take the call outside in the cold?" she grumbled, but disappeared inside.

"Addy won't tell Noah," he said to Derek.

"You can't be sure. If he's getting in her pants —"

"It won't last. You know him. She's just the flavor of the month."

"It doesn't have to last. If they get too close, she might decide to tell him despite your notes *and* the warning you gave her when you threw her back in the mine."

"I told you, *I* didn't throw her in the mine."

"Then who did?"

"How the hell should I know? Maybe *you*. Or one of the others. It wasn't me."

"It wasn't me, either," he insisted.

"Then forget about that and listen." He had no time to wrangle over who'd done what. If he didn't get inside the restaurant

455

soon, and help with the kids, his wife would be irritable for the rest of the evening. "She hasn't said anything yet, so maybe she's not going to."

"That's leaving a lot to chance, buddy. Because if she tells him — and he believes her — we're screwed."

Noah had a lot of credibility. Kevin felt the same fear, but he couldn't go anywhere near Addy again. Not after Noah caught him there last night. And he couldn't trust any of the others not to make the situation worse. "He won't believe Cody was part of a rape any more than his old man believed it."

"What are you talking about?"

Audrey kept craning her head to look out the window at him. He waved to let her know he'd just be another minute. "Someone sent the Rackhams an anonymous letter the summer we graduated, telling them what happened."

"What?"

"You heard me. I'm guessing it was Tom. Had to be. Who else would do it? But no one knows for sure. The note wasn't signed and had no postal markings."

"Mr. Rackham asked you about it?"

"He came to see me, even showed it to me."

"What'd you tell him?"

"That we had sex with her at the mine, but it was voluntary."

"And he believed you?"

"Of course. In his mind, someone was trying to play a cruel trick on him. His son could never be guilty of something like that, which gives the rest of us a pass, too. Anyway, I told him she'd been following us around for a year. That she wanted to do the whole team to celebrate graduation but only some of us participated."

"Why didn't he contact me?"

"I don't think he talked to anyone else. I told him what he wanted to hear, and he accepted it. He was already suffering because his son was dead. It wasn't as if he wanted any doubts about Cody's integrity. Brent Rackham's a proud man. He prefers to believe he and his family are above question."

"But if Noah saw that letter —"

Kevin could see Audrey giving the kids some quarters for the video games in the corner. "He didn't. Brent said Mrs. Rackham found it under the doormat and brought it to him. If Noah knew about it, he would've asked us to confirm or deny. The only other person who knows is Shania."

"You gotta be shitting me. How did *she* find out?"

"I thought whoever wrote that letter might send others. So I told her Addy got drunk and kept coming on to us and things got out of hand."

"But why bring Shania into it?"

"Because she wouldn't believe it of Cody, either. We need to ally ourselves with whoever will work hardest to protect him, because that means they'll protect us, too."

There was a slight pause as he absorbed this logic. "And? Did she buy it?"

"That Addy *wanted* to have sex with us? Hook, line and sinker. What was her alternative? To think Cody didn't really care about *her*? That he'd cheat on her without a second thought? It's always easier to blame the other woman."

"Damn it, man. That was taking a risk. And you did it without even talking to the rest of us."

Kevin ignored the sulky tone that had crept into Derek's voice. "I knew what I was doing. I think strategy for a living. That's what football is, right?"

"This is a little more serious than a game."

"I was protecting myself, protecting all of us, in case the truth ever came out."

"It was brilliant, actually. You've destroyed

Addy's reputation, at least with certain key people. Now they'll never believe a word she says."

"Exactly." It wasn't a lot on which to hang their hope, but it would certainly give them a better chance of avoiding prison. Addy had been gone for thirteen years. He didn't know a soul, besides Milly, who'd be on her side.

Provided Noah stayed out of it, of course.

26

Addy didn't have the heart to tell Gran about the state of her mother's most recent marriage. She figured Gran would learn soon enough, if she hadn't already guessed.

After a quick shower, she took Helen to the restaurant, where she tried to deal with the tension between her and Darlene by ignoring it, as she had before. She planned to pull Gran's manager aside eventually, but she was looking for the right time, and that wasn't easy to find with Helen around. Addy didn't want Darlene to feel they were ganging up on her. She just wanted to have a quiet discussion and agree on some kind of compromise so they could continue working together — at least for the immediate future.

But it wasn't long before Helen approached Addy, visibly upset. "What's wrong with *her*?" Her mother jerked a thumb at an irritable Darlene, who stood at the other end of the breakfast bar, pouring coffee.

Addy had just rung up some customers. She waited until they were out the door before responding. "Maybe she's having a bad day."

"It's more than that," her mother complained. "She gives me a dirty look whenever we pass each other. She *definitely* doesn't want me here."

"It's not just you," Addy said. "She doesn't want me here, either."

"But she's always liked you. You've worked with her before."

"When I was a teenager! There's a big difference between ordering me around and taking orders *from* me."

"She thinks you shouldn't have any say?"

Addy gazed over the tables that had customers. Thankfully, all seemed to be going well. "I guess. Although I've tried to make it clear that I'm stepping in for Gran. I have some ideas for modernizing the place and getting it running more efficiently." She didn't admit why — that it would make the restaurant more enticing to a buyer. "But she doesn't want *anything* to change, and she's let me know it."

"Who does she think she is?"

"Mom —" Addy started, but it was too

late. Helen was already marching over to Darlene.

"What's *your* problem?" Helen's voice seemed to echo through the whole dining area. It was between breakfast and lunch — not their busiest time — but Addy didn't want a scene in the restaurant.

"Save it for later or go out back." She hurried after her mother, but Helen didn't stop, and if Darlene heard Addy, she was upset enough to ignore it. She'd been dying to air her discontent, and Helen had given her the perfect opportunity.

"*My* problem? What's *your* problem?" she responded. "I've been here day in and day out for the better part of two decades. Where have you two been? In all that time, you've hardly stopped in long enough to eat. And Addy hasn't walked through those doors since she graduated from high school. Now that she smells an inheritance, she wants to take charge?"

"You're fired!" Helen snapped. "Do you hear? Grab your coat and get your ass moving!"

Darlene shoved the coffeepot back onto its burner. "You can't fire me. Only Milly can do that. So we'll just have to see what she says."

The bell went off over the door. Addy

glanced up to see Noah's parents come in and felt a fresh burst of alarm. She didn't want them to witness this. . . .

"The mayor's here," she murmured, trying to get them to calm down.

Her words had no impact. Stiff and unyielding, her mother and the manager continued to glare at each other.

"You need to understand something," Helen was saying. "If my mother has to choose between you and Addy, she'll choose Addy."

"I doubt it. She knows she can't count on either one of you to stick around."

Addy forgot about who might or might not overhear. "That's out of line!"

Her mother pointed at the door. "Get out before I throw you out!"

Red-faced, eyes sparking, Darlene ran to collect her coat and left.

Adelaide exchanged a look with her mother, but they couldn't discuss what had happened. The hostess was on break. Addy had to seat the Rackhams.

Pasting a courteous smile on her face, she approached them. "Welcome to Just Like Mom's. Would you like a booth or a table?"

"Is it true?" Noah's dad asked.

Addy was reaching for their menus but paused. She'd thought they might express some surprise about Darlene's getting fired right in front of them, but . . . "Is what true?"

"That you'll be leaving again in the near future?"

She remembered the many times she'd warned Noah that she'd take off at the first opportunity. "I'm not . . . I'm not sure of my plans."

"Does our son know that?" Mrs. Rackham asked.

"Of course, but . . . Noah and I are just friends," she mumbled, and waved at the closest booth. "Is this okay?"

"It's fine." Mayor Rackham took his wife's coat and draped it over a nearby chair as they settled in. Addy handed them their menus and hurried to the kitchen, where she notified the waitress in charge of the corner section that she'd seated another table.

Her mother scooped her keys off the desk and tossed them to her. "You'd better get home. I bet Darlene's gone to Mom's. I'll watch the restaurant."

"I don't want to put Gran in the middle of this," she said.

Helen motioned to the door. "You no longer have a choice."

■ ■ ■ ■

Sure enough, Darlene's Toyota was in front of Gran's house. Parking on the street so she wouldn't block Darlene in the drive, Addy marched inside.

Gran and Darlene were sitting in the living room. Darlene's face was streaked with tears, leaving trails of mascara, but she held a cup of coffee, which suggested Gran had made an attempt to mollify her. Seeing that, Addy was afraid of what Darlene had said. She'd done her best to be kind. It wouldn't be fair if she'd been represented in any other way, but she knew the nature of this type of dispute. Darlene's perspective was probably far different, and in her distress she'd no doubt exaggerated.

"I'm sorry, Gran," Addy said. "I didn't want you to have to deal with this."

"I know." She gestured at a seat. "Why don't you join us?"

"What's been said so far?"

"Darlene claims Helen fired her. Is that true?"

Technically Helen had done the firing, but Darlene deserved it. "She might've said the words, but I've had to threaten Darlene with her job before. I believe Mom had the right of it."

Darlene's eyes jerked to her. "You've been looking for any excuse to get rid of me! You want the restaurant all to yourself."

Addy sat back and crossed her legs. "I appreciate what you've done for Gran. I just don't appreciate how difficult you've been since my return."

Gran didn't comment. She waited for Darlene's response.

"You're the one who's been making things difficult!" Darlene cried.

"How?" Addy countered.

The manager set her coffee aside. She was too wound up to even hold the cup. "You came in and took over as if I haven't done anything right in twenty years."

"And what did I change?" Addy asked.

There was a brief pause as Darlene searched for an answer. Finally, she said, "You haven't changed anything yet, but . . . you've talked about it."

"So that's enough to make you belligerent? Unfriendly?"

"I'm not *unfriendly*!"

"That's exactly what you've been. The hostility I've felt coming from you has made this transition much harder than it had to be."

Darlene turned beseeching eyes on Gran.

"Milly, I've done a good job for *two decades.*"

Gran lifted a hand. "No one's questioning that. But is what Addy says true?"

"No! I haven't done anything wrong!"

"Then why would Helen fire you?"

"Because she . . . she . . . flew off the handle!"

"For no reason? And Addy supports her in that?"

Darlene didn't seem to have an answer.

"Maybe if it was just Helen . . . but I can't believe my granddaughter is different from the person I've known her to be all these years. I trust her opinion."

Darlene came to her feet. "So you're taking her side? You weren't even there. I think you owe me more than that."

"I don't owe you anything," Gran said. "I've employed you for twenty years, as you say. And I've treated you well and paid you as much as I can. I'd continue if only you'd be a bit more flexible. But you're mistreating my granddaughter, and I'm afraid I can't live with that."

A vein popped out in her neck. "So you're letting me go?"

"Unfortunately, I am. Consider this your two weeks' notice."

"I'm not coming in again at all." Darlene

pointed a finger at Addy. "You have no right to get involved after so long and ruin everything!" she said and, after purposely knocking her coffee cup off the table, stormed out.

The china broke as it hit the wooden floor. Addy winced at the clatter but she didn't get up right away to retrieve the pieces and neither did Gran. They sat in silence until Darlene had peeled out of the drive.

"That's . . . too bad," Gran said. "I was hoping for better."

"I'm sorry," Addy murmured. "I wish I could've come back over the years, Gran. I wish —"

"Addy."

She stopped talking.

"I came to you instead because I sometimes get the feeling that . . . something chased you away. And what's happened since you've come home seems to confirm it."

Addy's heart was beating hard and fast. For the first time, she was tempted to tell Gran about that graduation party. She might have done it, might have blurted out the truth right then so her grandmother would understand why she hadn't been able to return.

Except she knew that Gran would insist

on telling Chief Stacy, and she couldn't abide that. Regardless of the statute of limitations, reporting the crime would come too late to do her any good. And she couldn't bear the thought of Noah finding out she was the reason his brother had died.

"I'm here now," she said. "That's all that matters."

It was one of the longest and loneliest Sundays Noah had ever spent. He'd been holed up in his house, going back and forth, trying to figure out what to do. He wanted to visit Baxter in the hospital, but doubted he'd be welcome. Would Baxter recover more quickly without him? Or should he try to fix what was broken between them?

He collected his keys half a dozen times, determined to try. But he always set those keys down again.

Eventually, he allowed himself to call. Eve was at the hospital. Ted, too. They asked Baxter to talk to him, but Baxter refused.

"What's going on with you two?" Eve whispered when she called him back a few seconds later.

From her question, Noah knew Baxter hadn't admitted the truth. Not to anyone. That was when the reality of the situation hit him. Baxter was obviously planning to go on pretending. But he *couldn't* pretend anymore. Noah firmly believed that was what had driven him to attempt suicide.

"Nothing's going on," he told Eve, and hung up before she could put any more pressure on him. No one would understand until Baxter explained. They looked to Noah for answers, but it wasn't his place to give them.

Or was it? What would happen if he did the unthinkable? Maybe keeping his mouth shut only enabled Baxter to continue the behavior that was so damaging to him. What if Baxter got out of the hospital but, later, tried to take his own life again?

The prospect of that made Noah's heart pound, because it was possible that he'd succeed. He'd almost succeeded this time.

Baxter needed help, but he couldn't get the right kind of help as long as he went on lying.

Noah stood immobile in the middle of his living room. He didn't want to ruin Baxter's relationship with his family, but if he kept Baxter's secret and Baxter died, he'd never forgive himself. And how much could a relationship be worth if it was based on a lie to begin with?

That was the question that got him. That was what made him head out into the cold.

He was terrified that he might regret what he was about to do. But he'd kept his mouth shut for Cody. And Cody was dead.

27

Noah's palms were sweating when he showed up at the Norths'. He'd spent a lot of time at their house when he was a kid, but he hadn't been back that often since college. After San Diego State, he and Baxter had rented an apartment above the mercantile in town until Noah had launched his cycling career and earned enough to open the store and buy a house. He'd moved out of the apartment after a couple of years, but Baxter had chosen to stay there until he could afford his own place.

Although the Norths' middle-class rambler was both familiar and comfortable to Noah — his own parents still lived next door — Noah was feeling anything but comfortable right now. What he was about to do went against everything he'd always believed about letting people work out their own problems.

But he'd thought it through carefully, and

he was committed. Maybe Baxter wouldn't thank him, but the truth needed to be told — and if he had to be the one to take the fall, so be it.

The porch light went on before the door opened. "Noah!" Baxter's mother smiled. "What a pleasant surprise."

Noah glanced at his watch. It was 9:45 p.m., a bit late to be visiting, but he'd needed some time to work up the nerve.

"Sorry to bother you. Is Mr. North around?"

"He is. We got back from the hospital an hour ago. He's watching the Niners. He recorded the game on the DVR while we were out."

Noah already knew the Niners had won, but he didn't say anything about that. "I'd like to talk to both of you, if you don't mind."

"Of course not. Come in." She held the door and he stepped past a couple of jack-o'-lanterns that were starting to soften and cave in.

"Sam, it's Noah," she called.

"Noah?"

As Noah entered the room, the TV went silent and Baxter's dad leaned forward, bringing his recliner to a sitting position.

"Don't get up," Noah said.

"What brings you over?" Mr. North asked. "Were you next door visiting your parents?"

"No, I made a special trip."

At Noah's somber tone, his eyes narrowed slightly. "What for?"

"I'd like to talk to you."

Mrs. North smoothed her blouse. "Of course. Have a seat. Can I . . . can I get you a drink or —"

"No, thanks. I'm fine."

"What's this about?" Mr. North asked.

"It's about Baxter."

"I figured as much. But . . . he's going to be okay, Noah. He's through the worst of it. And we're getting him the help he needs. I've been calling around, looking for a reputable psychologist. He's agreed to get some counseling."

"That's a good idea. But . . . I think it's going to take more than that."

After a moment of silence, his father said, "What do you mean?"

"I think it's going to take the truth."

Mr. North frowned at his wife before returning his attention to Noah. "And what is the truth?"

"Your son is gay, Mr. North."

His jaw hardened. "Excuse me?"

"I believe he's struggling with self-esteem issues, and I highly doubt he can overcome them until he feels he's accepted by you, just as he is."

"Baxter's no filthy homosexual! What gives you the right to come here and tell me this, anyway?"

Noah's stomach churned. "He's my best friend. That's what gives me the right. Although, after this, he probably won't be my friend anymore. Regardless of that, I'm hoping the truth will . . . will *finally* let him feel comfortable in his own skin."

Mr. North got to his feet. "Are you his *lover*? Is that what you're saying? You know he's gay because you've been having sex with my son?"

The mental image that evoked made Noah squirm. "No!"

"Then he admitted it?"

No way was Noah going to tell anyone besides Addy about The Kiss. "It wasn't easy for him, but, yes."

"You're lying!" Those two words seemed to thunder through the whole house. "There would've been some sign. He . . . he wouldn't make that choice. He knows I hate homos. *Even God hates homos!*"

"I think it's that sentiment that's at the root of the problem," Noah said.

"I don't believe it!" His hands flexed and unflexed. "Martha, he's saying he knows our son better than we do. He's talking non-sense. He —" Mr. North fell silent when he saw his wife. She was sitting on the couch with her hand over her mouth, tears streaming down her cheeks.

"You agree with me, don't you?" he pressed. "I'm right, aren't I?"

"Sit down, Sam," she said.

"No, I won't sit down. I want this bastard out of my house. Get out, Noah! We don't need you to come around here, telling us what's best for our son. And shame on you for spreading such nasty rumors. Baxter's not even talking to you. There's got to be a reason. You two had a falling out, and this is how you're getting back at him."

Noah had felt like slugging Baxter's father when he'd said God hated homos. But he wanted to hit him even more now. He felt it might knock some sense into his thick, bigoted skull. But he knew he couldn't let his temper get involved. "I care about your son. I want to help him."

"He knows what he's talking about." Martha had spoken so quietly it took a second for what she said to sink in. When it did, Sam turned on her as if he'd tear her to pieces, and Noah got up, just in case.

"I . . . I found something once." Martha gazed up at her husband with tears in her eyes. "Some . . . magazines. I . . . put them back under the bed where he'd hidden them, and I never said a word to him or to you, but . . . they weren't the typical girlie magazines a mother might expect to find under her son's bed."

Sam looked as if he was trying to incinerate her with his eyes. "You don't know they were his! Maybe he was hiding them for someone else, a . . . a friend. Maybe even Noah!"

"No." She dropped her head in her hands. "His sister and I have talked about this before. She . . . she's wondered. I told her not to bring it up. But it . . . explains so much."

"Then you can both get the hell out!" Mr. North shouted.

Mrs. North's eyes widened in obvious hurt, and that seemed to bring him in check. At least a little.

"Ah, shit!" he said, and stalked out of the room.

Noah stared down at Mrs. North's bent head. "I'm sorry I had to be the one to tell you," he said. "It . . . it was his place, not mine. But . . ."

She wiped her cheeks. "I know why you did it."

"I'm sorry," he said again.

"I know that, too. But . . . it's better if you go. I — I'll handle Sam."

"You'll be okay?"

"Of course. He's just upset. This is his son, his only son. I think every man wants a boy who takes after him, and . . . Baxter definitely doesn't."

"Different doesn't make him any less worthy."

She forced a smile. "It's a shock, that's all."

He nodded. It'd been a shock to him, too. "Good night."

As Noah closed the door quietly behind him, he felt sick inside, terrified that he'd made Baxter's life worse. What would the Norths do? How would they respond?

He was so busy cursing himself for trying to help in what was probably the wrong way that he wandered over to his parents' house instead of going to his car. He wasn't planning to tell anyone else about Baxter, even his folks, but he thought it might comfort him to visit his mom and dad, to feel a hint of the security they'd provided when he was a kid. This had to be one of the worst weekends of his life. He'd hoped Addy would call today, but he had to battle that disappointment along with all the rest.

He was just edging past his mother's

Lexus when he noticed that his father's Range Rover had been damaged. When did that happen? He and his father had taken the Range Rover to go golfing just . . . what? Three weeks ago?

"Hello?" he said as he strode into the kitchen through the garage.

"In here!" his mother called.

He found his parents in the office/library situated off the living room, where they each had a desk. They were wearing reading glasses so when they glanced up, they both peered at him over their lenses.

"How'd we get lucky enough to receive another visit from you so soon?" his mother teased. "I thought you might be too wrapped up in the new woman in your life to bother with us."

Noah didn't respond to that comment. He *was* wrapped up in Adelaide. Too wrapped up to feel at ease about it. "What happened to the Rover, Dad?"

His father rested his elbows on the arms of his chair. "What do you mean?"

"It's been in a crash."

"Oh, that." He waved a hand. "Just a little fender bender."

"You never mentioned it."

"Dylan over at Amos Auto Body will fix it up once I have a minute to get it in."

His mother spoke at the same time, her voice full of exasperation. "He hit a tree. Can you believe it?"

Noah lounged on a love seat by a coffee table laden with magazines. "When?"

"Last week." His father closed his laptop. "How's Baxter?"

"Doing better." Noah didn't want to go into any more detail than that, didn't want to tell them he'd been next door.

"Glad to hear it. And —" his mother cleared her throat "— Adelaide?"

His father spoke before he could reply. "I'm not sure she's the right kind of girl for you, Noah."

"The right kind of girl?" he echoed.

"What do you see in her, anyway?"

Noah couldn't help being offended. "Besides the fact that she's beautiful? And smart? And sweet?"

"You told me you weren't going to say anything," his mother murmured, chiding his father. "You said it would blow itself out."

His dad's expression turned contrite. "I know. I should have taken my own advice."

"But now it's too late for that . . . so, what don't you like about her?" Noah asked.

His mother's eyes darted between them. She could've answered this question; she obviously agreed with his father. But she waited for Brent to take the lead.

"In high school, she used to come on to Cody all the time," he said. "She was *so* forward, wouldn't leave him alone."

Noah felt his jaw drop open. "You can't be serious."

"I'm completely serious. Shania will tell you. Ask her."

"If Shania felt threatened by Addy, I would've heard about it long before now," Noah said.

His mother frowned. "Not necessarily. She's a good Christian, doesn't like to gossip."

But if anyone was forward, it was her. How many times had she approached *him* since Cody's death? "There would've been a major fight, at the very least," he insisted. "Anyway, I was with Cody far more than she was. I think I'd know if Addy was coming on to him."

"I'm telling you how it was," his father said.

"Do you have any idea how shy Addy was in high school?"

His mother removed her glasses. "Apparently, she wasn't as shy as you thought."

"Yes, she was." She'd also had a huge crush on *him*. She'd admitted as much. To the best of his memory, she'd never even mentioned Cody. "She's slept with three men in her whole life. She married the second one. *I'm* number three."

His father shook his head as he chuckled. "She's slept with a lot more than that, son. From what I've heard, she even slept with your brother."

Noah felt as if he'd been punched in the face. *"When?"*

"At the graduation party."

"That's a lie!"

"Ask Shania," his father said with a shrug.

"She wasn't even there. She went to Europe right after she got her diploma."

"You weren't at the party, either," he pointed out, but Noah scarcely heard him. He was heading outside, to his car.

Kevin waited in the empty lot behind the liquor store for Shania to join him. She'd texted him earlier, when he was leaving church with his family, saying she needed to speak to him. He'd sent her this location and "six o'clock" so she wouldn't show up at his house, then left "to run an errand" while his wife was making dinner.

It was the first time Shania had contacted him in years. She had to be upset about something.

Kevin had a feeling he knew what it was.

When she pulled in, she didn't waste time on hello. She got out of some boxy little Nissan, slammed the door and led with, "Can you believe that bitch Adelaide is going out with *Noah*?"

"I've heard." And he'd been wondering how to defuse Shania's reaction. He'd been strategic in sharing information with her fifteen years ago, but there were pitfalls to any game plan. Right now, his future hung in a very delicate balance. No one was talking. He needed to keep it that way, couldn't let anyone tip the scales for fear they'd fall in the wrong direction.

"It's not fair," she railed. "If he only knew!"

Kevin moved toward her so she'd lower her voice. "Whatever you do, you can't tell him."

"Why not? She deserves for *everyone* to hear what she's really like, especially Noah!"

"Think about how she might react. What she might do."

She kicked a pebble and sent it skittering across the broken pavement. "What *could* she do?"

"She could claim we raped her! She put that in a letter to Cody's parents the summer Cody died, remember?"

She studied him for a second. "You told me that letter was anonymous."

"Who else would have written it?" Kevin responded. It had to have come from Tom, but he didn't want her to know that. "Who else would lie about grad night?"

"It won't matter. It's her word against yours. And Tom's. And Derek's. And Stephen's. You're all well-known and well-liked. She hasn't even been in town for . . . years."

"We can't rely on being well-liked. For all we know, she's kept DNA evidence. Her panties or something. They can test for semen years after a crime. I've seen it on TV."

"So your semen's on her underpants. What does that mean? Consensual sex isn't rape. Everyone was drunk at that party. How will she prove she wasn't a willing participant?"

This was the tricky part. But Shania *wanted* to believe him, so he had that going for him. "You and I know she had a thing for baseball players. She came to every single game and hung around the team as much as possible. She wanted to do us *all* that night, even though most people would say she was too shy to be so sexually aggressive."

"A lot of people aren't shy once they get some alcohol in them," she pointed out.

"And why would she keep her panties?"

"As a trophy. What else? Or . . ." He hesitated, purposely being dramatic to pique her interest.

"What? Say it."

"In case anyone ever tried to hold her responsible for Cody's death."

There. He'd dropped the bomb. And he saw that she was reacting with the appropriate shock when her face went pale.

"The last thing Cody said to me was that he was going back to make sure she was okay," he added.

"Why wouldn't she be?"

"We were in a different part of the mine when we were . . . you know, fooling around. He wasn't sure she'd be able to find her way out. And she didn't have a ride. She'd come with Sophia, but Sophia went home with someone else."

"It wasn't his coat he went after? You're saying Cody wouldn't have died if he hadn't gone back for *her*?"

Shoving his hands in his pockets, Kevin lowered his voice to give his next remark the proper emphasis. "He was fine when he turned around to go back."

She clutched his arm. "But it was an accident, right?"

"Who knows what it was? She might've

gotten angry, regretted what she'd done and tried to blame him. Or he wanted to do her again, she refused and that caused a fight —"

"Ick! No!" Shania wrinkled her nose. "What would he want with *her* when he could have me?"

Kevin held up his hands. "Maybe it was the other way around. It's just a little strange that she walked out of that mine and he didn't. I've always wondered if . . . if she had something to do with his death. And if she *did,* she might've kept her panties in case she ever faced that accusation. Then she could twist everything, make herself the victim."

Shania leaned against the cinder-block wall of the liquor store. "That's unforgivable . . . ?"

"For all we know, she hit him over the head with a rock and buried him in all the rubble that was lying around. Stranger things have happened."

"Noah should be told what type of person he's getting involved with," she whispered.

The commitment in those words made Kevin fear he'd gone too far. He couldn't have her flapping her mouth. "He won't believe you, even if you tell him. And if you speak up, my wife will know I was with someone else after she left that party. She'll never forgive me."

"That was before you were married."

"Doesn't matter. It'll be a betrayal all the same. You and Cody weren't married, either, but do you really want everyone to know he cheated on you the night he was killed?"

He was banking on the fact that she wouldn't. She'd always been so proud of her status as Cody Rackham's girlfriend. If word got out that he'd been with someone else, it would suggest he didn't care that much about her, after all. She'd lose the image of a perfect love tragically ended, the image she still used to garner sympathy.

"No, I don't want anyone to know," she admitted. "I still can't believe he did it. He wouldn't have if she hadn't initiated it."

"We all took a turn with her. It was just sex. It didn't mean anything."

"*Just sex?*" she snapped. "He wouldn't have liked it if I was spreading my legs for anyone else."

Kevin knew she was struggling with jealousy but this reversal almost made him want to strangle her. He'd been under so much pressure since Addy returned to town. For his sake, Shania couldn't give in to those emotions. "How can you even be worried about *that* now that he's gone?"

She gaped at him. "He was the love of my life! And Noah's his twin brother. I don't want her walking off into the sunset with Noah if it was her fault Cody was killed."

Kevin could believe that. After Cody's death, she'd made play after play for Noah but wound up empty-handed. He'd never been interested. "Noah will move on soon enough. The last thing you want is to force him to choose sides."

Her sullen expression reminded him of a child. "He wouldn't choose her, not if he knew what happened on grad night."

"But he won't know! We could tell him, but he wasn't there, and she'll plead her case, too. Trust me, you've got to keep your mouth shut."

With a grunt of exasperation, she stomped off but pivoted after a few steps. "It's not fair that she gets exactly what she wants when she cost me everything."

"Their relationship won't last," Kevin promised her. "You'll see." He bent his head to catch her eye. "So . . . are you with me?"

She didn't answer.

"Shania?"

"I'm with you," she said, suddenly more glum than angry. "But only because I don't want Addy to tell the world that what she put in that letter to Cody's parents is true. It would hurt them so much."

"There you go," he said, and hurried to his car. He had to get home before his wife finished making dinner. But as he was pulling away, he saw a flash of movement.

Had someone been close by, possibly in the alley, while they were talking? And, if so, had they heard what was said?

Heart thumping, he slammed on his brakes and got out to check. He'd seen something — a woman's coat? But he couldn't find anyone.

"Who's there?" he called, just to be safe.

Satisfied when he received no answer, he got back in his car. He must've been imagining things. He was getting paranoid these days.

28

Addy was at Just Like Mom's, tallying the receipts for the day when someone banged on the door. Because the restaurant was closed and all the employees had left, she'd locked up. She hadn't wanted to risk having someone who frightened her walk in and catch her unawares, like Kevin had on Thursday.

Hoping it was her mother — that Helen had returned even though she'd said she was heading home to bed — Addy peered around the corner and found Noah standing there. She would've been excited to see him. She was *always* excited to see him. But he looked upset.

He banged again before he realized he'd caught her attention.

"I'm coming," she called.

He waited, hands on his hips, as she brought out the keys and turned the lock.

"What's wrong?" she asked as he brushed

past her.

"I need you to be honest with me," he said.

She swallowed hard. She couldn't make any promises about honesty, not with everything she was hiding. "About what?"

"Did you ever sleep with my brother?"

Addy could tell he didn't believe she had. He was expecting her to confirm it. He'd asked as if the very thought was outlandish.

Only . . . she *had* "slept" with Cody. Maybe not in the way Noah meant, but that night at the mine had changed everything and would forever stand between them.

She wanted to tell him. She was tired of the self-recrimination, the resentment, the regret. She didn't feel she could hold back the truth any longer, no matter what the fallout might be. Ever since she'd returned to Whiskey Creek, one thing after another had shoved her back into that damn mine — literally and figuratively — until the rape and Cody's death felt as if they'd happened yesterday.

But she had more than herself to consider. At this point, she was afraid that what she had to say would hurt Noah more than it would hurt her. So she tried to keep carrying the cross she'd picked up at that graduation party fifteen years ago.

Except the words to convince him wouldn't come. Tears streamed down her face instead.

He stepped closer. "Addy, what's wrong?"

Before she could decide how to deflect his concern, Darlene walked in, eyes shining, face flushed. She looked excited, which confused Addy.

"I thought that was your truck, Noah," she said.

Noah didn't want to be distracted. "Addy and I are having a conversation," he said, not taking his eyes off her. "Would you mind giving us some privacy?"

"Not at all. But I think you're going to have a lot more to talk about after you hear what *I* have to say."

Adelaide couldn't imagine where Darlene was going with this, but there was a coldness about her that told Addy something terrible was about to happen.

"You've been looking for *me*?" Noah said.

She smiled. "I have."

He shifted his attention to her, but Adelaide could hear the impatience in his voice when he said, "What is it?"

"I just heard Kevin Colbert and Shania Carpenter talking behind the liquor store."

The mention of Kevin Colbert sent ice through Addy's veins. She lifted her hand in a futile attempt to stop what was coming next, but Darlene merely glared at her.

"So?" Noah said.

"Darlene, no," Addy murmured, but it didn't do any good. Gran's ex-manager didn't even hesitate.

"They said Addy screwed half the baseball team on grad night and that she's the reason your brother didn't make it out of the mine alive."

Noah scowled at her. "What are you talking about? Cody was caught in a cave-in when he went back to get his coat. That could've happened to anyone, anytime. The mine wasn't safe."

"He wasn't getting his coat, Noah. He was cheating with your new girlfriend. But she was the only one who survived. Maybe he tried to tell her he was already in a relationship."

A bewildered expression brought Noah's eyebrows together as he turned to her. "Is that *true*?"

Addy's mind urged her to say no, to insist that she hadn't been there that late. Who'd refute it? Kevin, Tom and the others were as eager as she was to keep the door closed on the past. But something else had already caused Noah to ask her if she'd been with Cody. That lent Darlene's words enough credibility to make him wonder. And Addy had reached a point where she could no longer bring herself to deny it.

"I was with him."

Darlene looked as stunned as Noah did, but Noah ignored her. "What are you saying?" he asked Addy.

Fresh tears rolled down her cheeks. "I'm sorry."

Noah sat up alone the rest of the night. He wanted to shut out the thoughts swirling through his head, but sleep was too far away. He hadn't even bothered to undress or go into his bedroom. After making Darlene leave the restaurant, he'd heard what Addy had to say. He'd heard what his parents had to say when he went back there after. And he'd heard what Kevin, Tom, Derek and Stephen had to say, following that. He'd hauled them out of bed, one after the other, so he could compare stories.

But what Addy told him was so different from what everyone else had said. She claimed she was gang-raped by Cody *and* his friends on graduation night. She said that when Cody came back, she panicked, thinking he might hurt her again. He was so wasted he could hardly stand, and yet he tried to drag her out of the mine. He claimed he was going to take her home, but she couldn't trust him, couldn't be sure. They fought until she managed to shove him into a support beam that gave way. The next thing she knew, the ground was rumbling and she couldn't breathe for the dust, but she ran and kept running and never looked back. Kevin found Cody the next morning.

But could Cody's death really have happened in that way? Kevin, Tom, Stephen and Derek denied the rape. His own parents refused to even entertain the possibility that Cody could have been involved in anything like that. Noah didn't want to believe it, either. No one could've loved Cody more than he did. But he kept going back to the moment when Adelaide had approached him on the baseball field to congratulate him on a good game. He didn't see how it was possible that such a shy girl would want to have sex with the whole team. Maybe some girls were that aggressive at sixteen, but not Addy. The image others painted of her was contrary to everything he knew her to be.

Problem was, so did the crime she accused Cody, Kevin and the others of committing. The people she claimed had raped her were his friends. He'd grown up with them, hung out with them over the years. He'd never known them to hurt anyone.

Still, *someone* had put her back in that damn mine. He'd found her there himself, saw how frightened and hurt she was. He'd also found that threatening note on her car: *Stay away from Noah or that mine will be* your *burial place, too!* And what about the night he caught Kevin outside her house?

He wished he could discuss the situation with Baxter, so he'd have someone he trusted to talk to, someone who'd known Cody almost as well as he did. Baxter's opinion would be helpful. But for all he knew, Baxter's parents had disowned him and Baxter would never speak to him again.

His phone rang just after dawn. Noah didn't feel like rousing himself, but when he saw that it was his father, he answered. "What are you doing up this early?" he asked.

"Checking on you," came the reply. "We might have a rough day ahead. I'm pretty sure Adelaide Davies has called Chief Stacy."

"What makes you think that?"

"He's already tried to reach me twice."

"You haven't called him back?"

"Not yet."

"Why not?"

"I wanted to talk to you first."

Noah massaged his temples. He could feel the beginning of a headache. "About . . ."

"About what's going on, of course. I'd like to know where you stand on this. We have to be united. There's no way I'll let Adelaide Davies ruin Cody's memory."

"How do you know she's lying, Dad?"

"Because Kevin, Tom . . . all of them agree."

Noah stared down at his feet. "They have good reason to agree! Do you think they'd admit to a gang rape? A couple of them are married, have families. They all could go to prison."

"Nothing will happen to them."

"How do you know?"

"She can't prove a thing, Noah."

"Prove." Noah didn't like that word. It didn't say anything about true culpability. As a matter of fact, it smacked of ducking responsibility. "Are you only interested in what she can prove? Or what really happened?"

His father took a second to respond. "Cody was a member of the family. Unless she has some way to convince me, beyond any shadow of a doubt, that he acted so . . . reprehensibly, I'm going to maintain my faith in him. I won't let some . . . *whore* destroy my respect for him."

If it was anyone but Adelaide, Noah knew he'd probably feel the same — family first. Cody was his brother, his *twin* brother. He didn't want to learn that Cody was capable of being so selfish and callous.

But Adelaide wasn't a whore and no one knew that better than he did.

"Wouldn't you want the same level of commitment from me if it was you?" his father asked.

Noah pinched the bridge of his nose. "I've got to go."

"Where? The bike shop doesn't open until ten."

Standing, Noah pulled his keys from his pocket. "To Davis."

"What's in Davis?"

"I'm not quite sure, but I'm going to find out."

"You're not making any sense," his father said, but Noah didn't try to explain. He hit the end button and went to brush his teeth.

Adelaide was actually glad her mother was in town. With Darlene no longer working at Just Like Mom's, someone had to help manage the restaurant. She simply wasn't up to it today. She'd told Noah the truth last night. She'd gone home and told her

498

mother and her grandmother the same, and they'd called Chief Stacy. Gran had put him off when he wanted to come over, but Addy had an appointment with him this morning.

She wasn't all that keen on having him press charges against those who'd attacked her. She knew how ugly it would get if others didn't believe her. And why would they believe *her* when they knew the men she was accusing so much better than they knew her?

Still, she was relieved that the truth was out. She hadn't realized just how difficult it had been to harbor such a terrible secret. No matter what happened to her from here on, at least she didn't have to live with the threat of someone learning about that damn party anymore.

Fifteen years was a long time to fear discovery.

"Addy, would you like a cup of coffee?" Gran stood in her doorway.

"No, thanks."

"Chief Stacy is on his way."

"I guessed as much. The alarm on my phone went off a few minutes ago. I'm about to take a shower."

"Do you think — do you think we should have an attorney present?"

"No."

Gran didn't seem convinced. "It might be smart."

"Maybe we'll need one later, if he decides to press charges against me. But my story won't change, Gran. Not one tiny bit. Because I'm telling the truth." She was reconciled to facing the consequences, whatever they might be. Nothing could be worse than knowing she'd never get to be with Noah again, anyway. She'd understood all along that they didn't have a future, but those few stolen moments were precious, and now there'd be no more of them.

Gran nodded. "I'm so sorry, honey. What they did to you . . . it was a dreadful thing—"

"I shouldn't have disobeyed you and gone out," she said.

"You were sixteen years old! Do you realize how young that is?"

Too young to go through what she had. But she'd survived.

"Which one of them came here with Aaron's knife and threatened you, Addy? Which one took you back to the mine?"

Addy shook her head. "Whoever it was had a white truck."

"How do you know it was white?"

After she explained in detail what had really taken place the night she was abducted, Gran said, "We'll have to remember to tell Chief Stacy about that."

Addy smiled for the first time since Noah walked into the restaurant last evening. "Yes, we will."

Tsunami was an upscale restaurant that served lunch and dinner and didn't open until eleven. Noah had been banking on Clyde Kingsdale having to get to the restaurant early to prepare for the lunch rush. Clyde was the manager, after all. But Addy's ex strolled in right at eleven, looking a little rough around the edges.

Thanks to the hostess, a girl wearing a name tag that said Becka, Noah had been allowed to wait inside. When Clyde walked past the register, she pointed and mouthed, "That's him," but she didn't stop her manager or introduce them. Noah got the feeling she knew Clyde wouldn't want to be interrupted regardless of his reason for coming. Since Clyde's parents owned the restaurant, maybe he didn't have to worry about being fired so he was just putting in time.

Noah followed him halfway across the dining area before Clyde noticed he had company.

"Whoa, who are *you*?" he said, looking over his shoulder when he heard Noah behind him.

"Noah Rackham."

Addy's ex halted in his tracks and they sized each other up. Clyde wasn't quite as tall as Noah, but Noah could see that he was handsome.

"What are *you* doing here?" he asked. "I don't have anything to say to you."

"How do you even know who I am?" Noah replied.

"You're kidding, right?"

"I'm *not* kidding. You told Addy I'd tried to call you, but I have no idea how you realized I was from Whiskey Creek. To my knowledge, we've never met."

Glancing toward the kitchen as if it offered refuge, he sighed. They could hear voices calling out about getting this item or that item ready. The restaurant was open but there were, as yet, no customers. "I'd heard your name before, okay?"

"From where?" Noah asked.

When someone rushed out of the kitchen and nearly collided with them, Clyde pulled him off to one side. "From Addy, of course."

"Because she once had a crush on me? That was years and years ago. We never even dated, so it seems unlikely that she would've talked about me very much."

"Let's just say you left an impression. And

your twin left an even greater one." He checked his watch. "That's all you'll get from me."

Addy's ex knew the whole story; Noah could tell. That made the rape, and what happened afterward, all too real.

"She told you she caused my brother's death."

Clyde's eyes widened. He started to say something, then, smoothing his goatee with a thumb and one finger, changed his mind. "If you already know, why are you here?"

Because he'd needed some kind of confirmation. He didn't want to think his brother could hurt *any* woman in that way, especially an innocent sixteen-year-old. Especially *Addy.* And he certainly didn't want to believe she'd caused the cave-in that took Cody's life.

But Clyde, someone who wasn't remotely connected to Whiskey Creek and all the loyalties and prejudices that existed there, obviously had a clear understanding of Addy's past.

His brother had helped gang-rape a girl on the night of his death. . . . "I guess I'm having a hard time coming to terms with it. She told me quite a story."

"Yeah, well, whatever she told you, you can bet it was that bad and worse, because she probably modified the truth to protect your feelings. What those bastards did to her messed her up for years. It cost thousands of dollars in therapy, and it ruined our marriage."

Noah dropped his head in his hand. "I was hoping you were going to say something else."

"You'd rather believe she's lying?" he challenged.

That was a good question, but there wasn't a good answer. He couldn't win either way. "Cody wasn't just my brother . . ."

"I know. He was your twin. Why do you think she gave him the time of day to begin with?"

"Because he reminded her of me?"

"That's the version I've always heard."

"God." He still wanted to see Adelaide, to touch her. That hadn't changed, even now. She seemed so . . . good, so down to earth. He couldn't really believe she'd lie about something that could destroy so many lives.

But taking her side would pit him against his family, several of his old friends and those in the community who supported them. And he'd only known her, in any significant way, for a couple of weeks.

"Did she tell you someone kidnapped her

from her bed and dragged her back to the mine after she returned home? That he threatened her with a knife?"

Clyde shook his head. "Is that why she finally decided to tell the truth?"

Noah remembered the look on her face when he'd confronted her at Just Like Mom's last night. "I think after everything that's happened since she's been home, she just reached her breaking point."

"I begged her to come forward years ago," he said, "but she wouldn't listen to me."

"Why not?"

"She had a lot of reasons. But part of it was that she didn't want you and your family to have to know what your brother did and what she'd done as a result."

"She was worried about *us*?"

"She once told me you were the only man she ever wanted with her whole heart." He laughed but there was no humor in it. "You asked me a second ago why I remembered your name. Now you know."

29

When Noah returned to town, he told himself to drive right by Milly's. He had no business siding with Addy, a woman he'd known for such a short amount of time. He owed his family more loyalty, especially because Adelaide could've lied to her ex-husband. Kevin, Derek — they were all denying what she said. And his parents were supporting them wholeheartedly. He'd received several calls on his way home, enough to know where everyone stood. He'd even received a call from Shania Carpenter.

But it didn't matter. He couldn't escape the fact that he believed Addy, couldn't add to what she'd been through by calling her a liar. Now he understood why she wouldn't say exactly what had happened the night she was abducted, why she'd told him they couldn't see each other, why she got threatening notes while dating him, even why she'd reacted to Kevin Colbert as she had at Black Gold Coffee.

Maybe his family would hate him for it, but he was going to stand by her.

When Milly answered the door, she didn't seem to know what to say. Instead of being her usual cheerful self, she was somewhat subdued, and he could tell she'd been crying.

"Is Addy okay?" he asked.

"Chief Stacy just left. It was . . . rough on her to . . . to have to recount everything in such detail. Those details weren't easy to hear, either."

He was grateful he hadn't been around for that part. He was afraid of what he'd do to Kevin and the others, despite the fact that his brother seemed to have instigated the attack.

"Can I see her?"

"She doesn't want to put you in the middle, Noah. She told me to tell you, if you came by, to go on about your business. She — she wishes you well and wants you to be happy."

She started to shut the door but he stopped it. "Nice try, but no thanks," he said, and squeezed through the opening despite Milly's walker. "Addy?" he called.

Helen came out of her bedroom. "I just

gave her a sleeping pill," she said. "She'll be fine after she gets some rest."

"I'm glad to hear that, but I'm not leaving." Circumventing Helen, too, he let himself into Addy's room.

She lifted her head when she heard him come in. "Noah, you need to leave before someone sees your truck."

He didn't respond. He scooted her over to make room in the bed. Then, even though it was only mid-afternoon, he got in, wrapped his arms around her and drew her up against him.

"Go to sleep, Addy," he murmured. "We'll figure it all out when you wake up."

"Addy? Chief Stacy needs to talk to you again."

Noah had drifted off. When he heard Milly trying to wake Adelaide, he raised his head. "She's finally resting. Can't she talk to him later?"

"He asked me to wake her. He says word that the coach of the football team and other respected members of the community might've been involved in a gang rape is spreading all over town. Everyone's riled up. He wants to get to the bottom of it as soon as possible, which means he needs her full cooperation."

"*Might've* been involved?" Helen stood in the doorway behind Milly. "Tell him they *were* involved, those sons of bitches. My baby wouldn't lie about that."

The police chief's wording worried Noah, too. Didn't Stacy believe her? And, if not, was it because of the pressure his father was bringing to bear? Brent was, after all, the mayor.

The mere idea that his father might be actively working against Addy made Noah angry.

"Who's at the restaurant?" Addy was coming around but sounded groggy.

"Relax, everything's fine there," Helen replied. "I'm going back now. I just came home to check on you."

"I'm okay," Adelaide insisted, but Noah was worried for her. His father would be a formidable foe.

Milly inched closer, hampered by carrying the phone while trying to use her walker. "Honey, Chief Stacy says that none of the men you've accused of raping you owns a white truck or a white SUV, except Stephen. And his hasn't been in an accident. Stephen is saying you came by and saw that for yourself."

"If they don't own one, it has to belong to a friend or neighbor. Someone here in

Whiskey Creek is driving a white vehicle that's banged up on the front right panel."

Noah stiffened when a vision of his father's Range Rover popped into his mind. It was white, and it was damaged exactly where Addy said it would be.

But none of his old baseball buddies would've had access to his father's car.

"What's this about a white vehicle?" he asked.

Addy curled in on herself. "Don't worry about it."

"I *am* worried. How can you be sure the person who abducted you was driving a white truck or SUV? Weren't you blindfolded?"

"I was, but I could tell it wasn't a car. And we hit the retaining wall down the street between Lovett's Bridal and the lawnmower shop. Stacy can check that wall himself. It has white paint all over it."

Milly relayed this message to Stacy, who was still on the line. A moment later, she covered the phone. "Chief Stacy's wondering if maybe your abductor hit something else and the damage to that wall happened another time, to a different car."

"No." Addy remained adamant. "It was only a minute, if that, after we left the driveway. I remember hearing the scrape.

He freaked out when I grabbed the wheel and he slugged me." She touched the eye that had been so swollen.

Milly repeated this to Chief Stacy, as well. But Noah had stopped listening. His mind was stuck on what he'd seen in his parents' garage. Had his father really hit a tree? Surely, Brent wouldn't do anything to hurt Addy unless . . . unless he truly believed Addy was to blame for what went on at that party.

A sense of foreboding set in as Noah slipped out of bed. "I've got to go take care of a few things," he said.

Adelaide grasped his arm. "Noah?"

He smoothed the hair out of her face. "What?"

"Don't come back."

"What are you talking about?"

"It's not too late. We've been seeing each other for what . . . two weeks? You don't owe me anything."

Helen had left, presumably to return to the restaurant; Milly was talking to Chief Stacy. "You don't think what we've had, what we could have, is worth fighting for?"

She wouldn't meet his eyes. "I think this is the beginning of something that could tear your family apart. I don't want to be responsible for that. And . . . how will we ever get beyond it?" She paused. "You'll meet someone else."

But that was it. He didn't *want* anyone else. He never really had.

He remembered Joe's daughter, Josephine, telling him at Just Like Mom's what it took to find a wife. *You have to fall in love with someone and prove you won't ever stop loving them.*

"You're not just another woman to me," he said.

His father's receptionist seemed relieved when he showed up at city hall. "Noah's here!" she said into the intercom.

His father appeared almost immediately and ushered him into his office. "Why haven't you been answering your phone?" he asked as he closed the heavy wooden door.

"Because I turned it off."

"Chief Stacy said you've been at Adelaide's all day. He saw your truck."

"That wasn't meant to be a secret."

"I don't want you seeing her anymore, Noah. If she'll say what she's saying about Cody, there's no telling what she might accuse you of doing."

Noah found that preposterous, a desperate attempt to influence him. Addy was trying to push him away, to protect him — not hurt him. She was the only one who wasn't pleading her case and demanding his support. "Mom said you got an anonymous note after Cody died. It's time you told me about it."

"I don't know what you're talking about."

"Sure you do."

His father made an imperious gesture, one that revealed his irritation with being questioned. "It said nothing — nothing of the truth, anyway."

"Was it about the party? Was it a message from someone who knew what happened and was trying to alert you?" What else would have "tormented" his parents, except the fear that their dearly departed son might not have been as admirable as they'd always believed?

"What if it was?" his father responded. "There was no signature, so it doesn't matter one way or the other. For all we know, that letter came from Adelaide."

Noah gaped at his father. "Have you thought this through, Dad?"

"I've thought of little else since she returned to town, I'll tell you that."

"Then maybe you can answer this: Why would Adelaide falsely accuse Cody or anyone else? Especially now, after all this time? What does she have to gain? Do you honestly believe she wasn't raped?"

He turned to stare out the window. "Whatever happened, it was fifteen years ago."

Noah stepped toward him. *"So?"*

His father glowered at him over one shoulder. "Cody's dead, Noah! Destroying everything he was won't serve any purpose. It certainly won't help Addy."

"And the others who participated? *They're* not dead."

"No, but they've become decent men, upstanding members of the community. Throwing them in prison for something they did — might have done — a decade and a half ago won't do anybody any good. Two have wives. Three have kids. The people who love them have no culpability in whatever took place. Do you want to see innocents suffer for an act that even she claims was perpetrated when Cody and his friends were barely eighteen and too drunk to know what they were doing?"

"So you believe her?"

"I'm saying *if.*"

His father's logic made Noah afraid to ask his next question, the one he'd come here to ask. "Did you really hit a tree in the Range Rover, Dad?"

He whirled around. "Now you're doubting *me*?"

"The man who kidnapped Addy was driving a white truck."

"You think I don't know that? You think Chief Stacy hasn't been staying in close touch with me? I'm the mayor of this town!"

"So if you didn't kidnap her, who did?"

He scowled. "It doesn't matter."

"You're saying *you* didn't do it, but you know who did?"

"Like I said, it doesn't matter!"

His father was getting impatient, but Noah pressed on. He wasn't going to settle for *It doesn't matter.* "Chief Stacy just called Milly. He said none of the men Addy's accused of raping her owns a white truck or SUV, except Stephen, and his hasn't been in an accident."

"Chief Stacy's going to investigate, come up with nothing and let it all go. We've already talked about it. That's what's best for everyone."

"What?" Noah shoved a chair out of his way as he closed the gap between them. "You and Chief Stacy — you're going to protect those who were responsible? You *do* believe her! *You've* just decided what justice should look like!"

"You'd rather see Coach Colbert and Tom Gibby torn from their families?"

"That isn't what I want at all! But the truth isn't for you to decide. Neither is the punishment. The one person you keep forgetting in all of this is Addy. She's the *victim* here. She deserves our sympathy and our support."

"She's fine. You've been in bed with her yourself. You know she's recovered well enough."

The casual way he addressed their relationship infuriated Noah. His father wanted to think it was all about sex, but it wasn't. "I have been in bed with her, Dad. *I've made love to her.* That's why I know how deeply what they did affected her. They don't have the right to sweep this under the rug — and neither do you. I won't let you."

"What are you going to do to stop me?" his father demanded.

"Anything I have to," he said.

Noah didn't leave Addy's side for the better part of a week. Either he was at Milly's, or he took her to his house. She knew he was afraid she might suffer some sort of backlash if he wasn't there to protect her. That was why she hadn't gone in to work. Too many Whiskey Creek citizens were upset with her for "trying to ruin the reputations of four good men" in addition to the memory of the golden boy they'd lost. They didn't understand how she could accuse Cody of such a terrible crime — which meant, of course, that she had to be lying about Coach Colbert, Tom and the others, too.

Addy thought Tom might speak up and tell the truth. He'd been so contrite when he came over to apologize that night after the football game, so filled with regret. But, according to Chief Stacy, he was keeping his story consistent with that of the others.

Noah didn't work much that week, either. He let his employees handle the bike store while he searched for a connection between Kevin, Stephen, Derek or Tom and a white vehicle that'd been damaged. He was afraid his father had been more involved than he was willing to admit and desperately wanted to prove otherwise. Addy wanted that, too. Although Noah didn't talk about it, she understood how hard it was for him to lose his good opinion of his brother. It felt almost as if he was suffering through Cody's death again, this time the death of his image. He didn't want to think his father would go to such lengths to cover it up. Addy wasn't sure he'd ever be able to forgive his father if that was the case. But they weren't having much luck. He could find no connection between Kevin, Tom or

Derek and a white truck. And Stephen was keeping his Chevy locked in his garage.

On Thursday morning, Noah had to run over to the store to help his tech finish a bike repair he was having trouble with, so Addy decided to get started on revamping the menu for Just Like Mom's. Although she no longer planned to suggest that Gran sell the restaurant — she feared it would be too much for her grandmother on the heels of everything else — she still wanted to improve it. She'd been keeping herself busy bringing the accounting up to date, cooking and cleaning and creating new recipes, but she was going stir-crazy staying in so much. She was afraid she might have to move back to Davis in order to live a normal life. But she didn't know how long her mother would stay with Gran. Helen had been talking to her husband at night on the phone. Addy had heard bits and pieces of their conversations and thought they'd probably reconcile. Not that it would last, even if they did. They fought all the time.

Then there was Noah. She didn't want to leave him. They'd grown so close the past few days. It was all she could do not to tell him how much she loved him. She would have, except she wanted him to feel free to change his mind about her. . . .

She'd just finished the first draft of the menu when the doorbell rang. Wondering whether or not it would be wise to open it, she hurried to the window but couldn't see more than one muscular arm and some denim. "Who is it?" she called out.

"Dylan Amos."

Aaron's brother. She opened the door right away. "Dylan, how are you?"

"I'm fine. I have some good news."

She blinked in surprise. "You do?"

He grinned. "For you and Noah. Is he around?"

"He's at the store."

"I peeked in but didn't see him."

"He must be in the workshop."

"Then I'll stop by and talk to him on my way back. But I wanted to tell you it wasn't Mayor Rackham's car."

She gripped the door frame. "How do you know?"

"Because I finally found what I've been looking for." He handed her a facsimile of a work order from A-1 Auto Repair, which had a Sacramento address.

"What's this?"

"It's where Stephen Selby took his Chevy to have it fixed after hitting that retaining wall as he was driving you to the mine."

"How do you know he took it to this place?"

"They told me." His smile turned devilish. "I've been calling every auto body shop in Northern California. Some of them didn't want to take the time to mess with me, so I pretended to be a P.I. investigating a rape, which made them much more eager to do what they could."

She couldn't help laughing. "I hope you can't get into trouble for impersonating a private investigator."

"Even if I can, as far as I'm concerned it'll be worth it."

She doubted Cheyenne would feel so cavalier about that. She was too much in love with her husband not to want to protect him. But Dylan was definitely his own man and made his own decisions. "So . . . it *was* Stephen," she breathed.

"The little bastard," Dylan muttered. "I *knew* it had to be him."

"Makes sense, since he was the only one with a white vehicle."

"But the others could've gotten access to one. I knew it was him because, out of the four you named, he's the only one who's ever hung out with Aaron."

"*That's* how he got Aaron's knife!"

A muscle flexed in Dylan's jaw, giving her

the impression that he was tempted to punish Stephen himself. He nodded.

"I knew he wasn't a nice guy," she said, "but . . . as far as I'm concerned, none of them are."

"We won't let them discredit you."

We. She liked the sound of that, except she knew she was splitting the town in two. "But if Chief Stacy isn't going to go after him or the others, will anything we do really help?"

"Sure it will. I'm about to call Ed over at the paper. If we put enough pressure on him, Stacy will *have* to investigate."

"He won't be happy you're trying to force his hand."

"I'm going to do more than try. Chief Stacy has been so eager to bust my balls, I'm finding this a pleasure." With a wink, he added, "Give Milly my best."

When he learned that Callie was back, Baxter felt the first sense of relief he'd experienced in several days. She'd called as soon as she landed in San Francisco to let him know she was coming. She must've dropped Levi off at their ranch once she hit town because she stood alone on his porch when he answered the door.

"I leave for eighteen days and all hell

breaks loose," she complained in lieu of hello.

"And I'm not sure you've heard the latest," he said, eager to take the spotlight off himself.

She hugged him before coming inside. "You mean about Cody and his baseball buddies committing a felony at that grad night party? I've heard."

"Do you believe it?"

"Don't you?"

"I don't know what to believe."

"Noah is siding with Adelaide Davies."

"I've heard. But you realize he was seeing Adelaide when the news came out, right?"

"I do. He's still seeing her. He's smack in the middle of the whole thing. Poor guy. But . . ."

"But?" Baxter repeated.

"Goes to show you're not the only one who has problems." She surveyed his living room. "Jeez, would you look at this place?"

He shrugged at the mess. He'd never let his house go before. But it just wasn't in him to care anymore.

"You'll never be able to sell it like this," she said.

"That's all you've got to say? I got drunk and *kissed* my best friend, who doesn't have a homosexual bone in his body. I took a

whole bottle of sleeping pills because I
didn't want to deal with the reality of my
situation anymore. My parents have learned
that I'm gay and my father hasn't spoken to
me since. And you're worried about me selling my house?"

He'd finally said something that surprised
her. He could tell by the way she cocked
her head. "Who told your parents?"

"My mother said Noah paid them a visit
last weekend."

"Wow, he's on a roll."

"Making friends all over."

He expected her to be upset with Noah.
He was. But she pursed her lips, studied
him for a moment and said, "He did the
right thing, Bax."

"What?"

"You heard me."

"That's bullshit!" he said, but he actually
found Callie's approach refreshing and
welcomed the opportunity to react frankly.
Eve, Ted, Cheyenne — the rest of them had
been killing him with kindness since he got
out of the hospital on Monday. They were
obviously afraid the slightest misstep might
push him over the edge again. He hated
that.

"It's not bullshit," she insisted. "I'm sure

that wasn't an easy decision for him to make."

"You think he had my best interests in mind?"

"Knowing him, I do. Embrace who you are. Once you do, everyone else will, too." With that she started straightening up his living room.

"Stop cleaning!" he yelled.

"Nope, sorry. Makes me feel better to be doing something."

He thought of the many times he'd done the same thing to Noah and almost laughed. "Well, it makes me feel like shit."

"You already feel like shit."

She had a point, so he didn't argue. He just sat down.

"You could help," she said when he merely watched.

"Looks like you're doing a pretty good job."

When she stopped working and folded her arms across her chest, he knew he was about to hear the bottom line as she saw it. "You can't go on like this, Bax."

"That's it? That's all you've got for me?"

"That's it."

"What else am I supposed to do, Cal?"

"You only have one choice — pull your shit together."

For the first time, he heard anger in her voice and couldn't help bristling. "Easy for you to say."

"No, it's not easy for me to say. After what I went through last summer, I know how precious every minute should be. I didn't fight for my life so you could throw yours away. Dark times only last if you let them. Pick yourself up and reconnect with the people and things you care about."

"I care about Noah." He missed his best friend, missed knowing they were okay. It had been hard the past few days, hearing what was going on with the Rackhams and wondering how Noah was handling it.

Her lips curved into an understanding smile. "Then call him."

"I can't."

"Of course you can." She brought his phone from where he'd left it on the counter. He had a slew of calls he hadn't returned, from friends and clients. And a whole list of texts.

"He's dying to hear from you," she said. "Just because he doesn't want to have sex with you doesn't mean he doesn't care about you. Rebuild a relationship with him — one you can both live with."

He stared at his "favorites" list on his phone. "And my father?"

"He's got some adjustments to make, some apologies, too. But he'll come around."

30

Baxter was nervous as he dialed Noah's number. He felt so fragile, wasn't sure he could handle the emotions hearing Noah's voice would evoke. But staying away from him wasn't easy, either. Their group of friends had been together since grade school, and the events of the past two weeks had upset them all — like a beehive that'd been struck and was suddenly in chaos.

"Bax, is it really you?"

He couldn't help smiling at Noah's relief. "Yeah, it's me. You okay?"

"I've had a shitty week, but no worse than you."

As Baxter looked around his house, he felt as if he was seeing it for the first time in a long while. "We've both had better."

"I'm sorry," Noah said. "I'm sure you know this by now, but I'm the one who told your parents. I didn't do it because I was trying to hurt you, though. I hope you believe that."

Callie was watching him a little too closely. Baxter waved her off to let her know she could quit worrying. "I do," he said. "Maybe it was time for the truth. And maybe it'll be for the best. I'm not sure I would've been able to summon up the nerve. The look on my father's face when you told him —" he winced, imagining what that had been like "— it must've been pretty bad."

"Your mom seems to be handling it better."

Baxter guessed he'd been right about his father when Noah dodged the question like that. "She's come to see me a couple of times."

"But not your father."

"Not yet."

"I feel bad, Bax. I really do."

Baxter rested his head on the back of the couch. He'd thought this call would be difficult, but the familiarity of talking to someone who'd been such a big part of his life more than compensated for any awkwardness. He just wished he hadn't kissed Noah. He was embarrassed he'd taken it so far. "It's okay. I'll survive."

"You scared the shit out of us. You won't do anything like that again, will you?"

Baxter didn't want to address his suicide

attempt. He couldn't even say why he'd done it. He'd just been so desperate for a way out. "I won't, no." He couldn't promise too much at this point, but he owed his friends *some* reassurance. "I'm going to make some changes that should . . . help," he finished simply.

"Like therapy?"

"And moving away from Whiskey Creek until I can figure out who I am and who I want to be."

"We'll miss you."

"I won't be that far," he said, but he knew what Noah meant. The distance was already there. "And we're getting older. Change happens."

"That doesn't mean it has to be a bad thing."

"True." Eager to drop that topic, Baxter moved on. "I owe you an apology for how I behaved at the cabin —"

"Forget it. There's no need to discuss that. I was an idiot for dragging you up there."

Relieved to be able to put *that* subject behind him, too, Baxter drew a deep breath. "So . . . how are things with your family?"

"I'm getting along with my parents about as well as you're getting along with yours," he said with a rueful laugh.

Baxter smiled at Callie, who sat down next

to him, put her arms around him and leaned her head on his shoulder. "Do you really believe Cody raped Adelaide, Noah?"

There was a long pause. "I don't want to, but . . ."

"You do."

"Yes. You don't?"

"The boy I remember . . . I can't see him doing that. He had Shania, the whole world at his feet."

"Maybe that was the problem. He thought he should be able to have everything."

"I could see that. Do you think your parents will ever believe her?"

"I bet they already do. They just don't want to face it. But I'm not going to let them treat her as if she's lying."

"I'm getting the impression you really care about this woman."

"She's different from the others," he admitted. "Are you coming to coffee tomorrow?"

"I don't know."

"I'd really like to see you."

"I'm not sure I'm ready."

Callie lifted her head to frown at his response, but he arched his eyebrows as if to say it was the truth.

"We're your friends, Bax," Noah was saying. "Your *best* friends. We don't care if you're gay. We only care that you're all right."

"I appreciate that, but . . . it's not going to be easy to get over you." Baxter had intended that to come off as a flippant remark, a joke making light of The Kiss. He thought things might be more comfortable between them if they could laugh at the situation. But it was too close to the truth to be funny.

"You'll find the right person, Bax," Noah said. "It isn't me, but . . . I don't want to lose you as a friend."

Baxter said nothing.

"I mean that," Noah insisted. "Will you be there tomorrow?"

"I doubt Callie will let me stay home even if I want to."

"Damn right," she said, and kissed him on the cheek.

Noah wanted Adelaide to accompany him when he went to coffee the next morning. She was hesitant, because she wasn't sure how his friends felt toward her. They'd been close to Cody, too. Did they believe he was involved in a gang rape? Or did they believe what Kevin, Tom, Derek and Stephen kept telling everyone, with the support of Shania and the Rackhams? Because that was the thing about Whiskey Creek. They were all so connected, all so familiar with one another. It was difficult to find anyone who'd be unbiased.

As she walked in with Noah, Adelaide was thinking that she would've been smarter to give it more time before showing up at Black Gold, but Kyle, Cheyenne, Dylan, Eve, Riley, Brandon, Olivia, Ted, Callie and a man she'd never met — obviously Callie's husband, since she knew they'd been on their honeymoon — were already there. They all got up to greet her with a hug.

"I'm sorry for what you've been through," Eve murmured.

"I wish we'd been closer, that I could've been there for you fifteen years ago," Olivia told her. "I can't even imagine how hard it's been."

Dylan's hug was a little tighter than the others. "You're going to be okay," he whispered in her ear. Then he shared what he'd found out about Stephen's truck with the others, which got everyone mad that Chief Stacy wasn't doing more to bring those responsible to justice.

When Baxter walked in, the entire group seemed relieved to see him, but they also seemed slightly ill at ease. Addy sensed that they weren't used to having problems within the group. Fortunately, because they knew this moment was significant for Noah, they stayed seated and allowed him to be the only one to meet Baxter as he crossed the floor.

"Hey, I'm glad you came," Noah said, and embraced him.

Once Baxter joined them, everyone seemed so happy to put the rift of the past week behind them that Addy forgot her own problems for a while. Then Noah had to go to work. It wasn't until he dropped her off at Gran's that the hope and happiness she'd enjoyed at the coffee shop disappeared.

And it started with the arrival of his mother.

When Noah returned to Milly's a few hours later, he was surprised not to see Adelaide's 4-Runner. It had sat in the drive all week because she hadn't really gone anywhere, other than his place.

"Where is she?" Noah asked Milly, who answered the door.

She frowned as she shook her head. "I'm sorry, Noah. She packed up and left."

"Why?"

"Because she thought it was the best thing — for you, for your family, for everyone here in Whiskey Creek."

"But . . . that's not true."

"Isn't it?" she asked sadly.

He didn't know what to say. He wasn't pleased with what his parents were doing, but he'd never been more convinced that Addy was telling the truth. "What about the restaurant? She — she's been creating new menus and —"

"That was when she thought her mother would be heading back to Salt Lake. Now Helen's getting a divorce. She'll be here, at least for a while. Addy seems to think it might be healthy for her mother to have some responsibility and . . . something to care about each day."

But would Helen be reliable? From what he could tell, she seemed to have calmed down a bit since her younger years, but . . . who could say what she'd do if she suddenly decided to reunite with her husband, since it seemed to go back and forth from one day to the next, or if she met someone else?

"What caused this?" he demanded. "Everything was fine when I dropped her off."

Milly pursed her lips as if she wasn't going to say. She didn't soften until he put his hand over hers. "I'm in love with her, Milly. I think we're meant to be together. You have to help me. What made her go?"

"Your mother came by," she admitted.

"My *mother*? What'd she say?"

"She said, 'I only have two sons. You've already taken one from me. Can you really be hardhearted enough to take the other?' "

With a sigh, Noah shoved a hand through his hair. "Oh, God."

"I don't think Addy can live with the constant hate and anger she'd face here, Noah. That's why I didn't have the heart to try and stop her," Milly said as she closed the door.

Addy wasn't sure where she was going. She didn't care as long as it was away from Whiskey Creek. Kevin, Tom, Derek and Stephen had achieved what they wanted, with a little help from their friends. She wished it could be otherwise. Noah meant everything to her. But his mother had made her see the truth — that even if Chief Stacy aggressively pursued the investigation and eventually put all four men behind bars, there'd be long-lasting resentment. She'd run into Kevin's wife or parents at the grocery store or Just Like Mom's. She'd see his kids around town. The same went for the others. There was no reason for her to make life so difficult for people who were as innocent as she claimed to be, Mrs. Rackham said. If Noah loved her, he'd make arrangements to see her wherever she lived.

But Addy knew Mrs. Rackham didn't believe that was the case. Noah had never had a long-lasting love interest. His home *and* business were in Whiskey Creek. So were all his friends. Mrs. Rackham thought if she could get Addy to leave, she'd be able to bring her family together again.

And maybe she could. Addy hadn't been with Noah long enough to expect him to make any great sacrifices. She'd begin looking for an apartment and a job. Only this time she'd head to Los Angeles or somewhere even farther. She needed a fresh start in a place where she wouldn't have to be reminded of the past.

Her phone rang. It was Noah. But she turned it off. She wasn't in any kind of shape to talk to him right now.

When Noah arrived at his parents', he found his mother's car in the drive. She was home, apparently. Good. Because he had a few choice things to say to her — to both of his parents.

They were eating dinner when he stormed into the house.

"How dare you!" he burst out.

His mother rocked back at the interruption, but she wiped her mouth, set her napkin aside and tried to explain herself. "Noah, you need to understand that I was only being honest with Addy. I didn't say anything that wasn't true. It was all stuff she should consider."

"You were wrong to take matters into your own hands, to get involved. You've been wrong from the start. Cody was on coke on graduation night. Did you know that? He'd been doing drugs for months. I didn't tell you. I couldn't. I felt it was too big a betrayal. But, in a roundabout way, that makes me as guilty for what he did to Addy as he was, because the rape probably wouldn't have happened if he'd been able to control himself. That doesn't excuse his behavior, but it makes me damn sorry I didn't speak up."

"Sorry enough to protect a woman who may or may not be telling the truth?"

"Stop pretending you don't believe it's true," he said. "Cody and his friends raped the woman I now love. That's a terrible thing for us all to have to live with. But . . . I'll tell you this — nothing would be more terrible for me than living without her."

His father bumped the table as he stood, nearly toppling the wine goblets. "Noah, let's face it. Women come and go in your life. Addy's only been home for a few weeks.

Give this some time. Let the intensity of the emotions die down. And then see how you feel."

He whirled on his father. "Maybe I don't have the most stellar track record when it comes to commitment, Dad. But how do you know this girl isn't the one who can change all of that? I've never felt like I have since I got with her. Are you really willing to ruin my happiness in order to preserve an inaccurate image of my dead brother? To protect some men who feel so little remorse for what they did, and so little compassion for their victim, that they're trying to make a pariah out of her? Wouldn't you rather stand on the side of truth and justice?"

He threw his napkin down. "I would if I knew what the truth is!"

"You *know* what the truth is. You just don't think telling it should require a sacrifice."

Noah was halfway to his truck when his father came after him. "Noah!"

Because he refused to turn back, he was inside his car, starting the engine, when his father knocked on the window.

"Will you give me a minute? I think you're going to want to hear this."

Something about his father's expression

made Noah roll down his window. "What is it?"

"You win," he said.

"What does that mean?"

"I know who sent us that note fifteen years ago. Come over to my office. I want to show it to you."

Of all the times for her 4-Runner to break down, Addy couldn't believe it would be today. She was stranded on the side of the road and it was getting dark. She had to call for a tow. But Joe DeMarco owned the only towing service she knew of, and that was in Whiskey Creek. She was afraid if she went back there, she'd never scrape up the determination to leave again. She already missed Noah so much she could hardly stand it.

"I'm leaving *because* I love him," she reminded herself, and clicked on a phone application that would search for the closest towing service. She was just about to call one in Jackson, even though it was farther away, when she got a text.

Come back to me.

It was from Noah. She'd been avoiding his calls. She'd also been ignoring his texts, but this one was more poignant than the others, which were mostly questions. Where are you going? Why are you leaving? What happened?

You're better off without me, she wrote.

I don't want to be without you. I love you.

She stared down at her phone. She was pretty sure he'd never told another woman that.

How do you know?

Because I'll sell my house and my store if that's what it'll take for us to be together.

She smiled through the tears filling her eyes. I'd feel too guilty taking you away from Whiskey Creek.

I don't want to be here if you can't be happy here with me.

I can't separate you from your family. You know that.

Things have changed since you left.

How could they? I've only been gone a few hours.

Tom confessed.

Her heart began to race as she stared at those two words. She'd given up on Tom. She'd decided his apology and all the other things he'd had to say that night hadn't been sincere.

To you?

To Chief Stacy two days ago. Stacy was keeping it quiet, but my father has agreed to get out of the way and let Stacy pursue this case as aggressively as he would any other.

What changed your father's mind?

Two things. A note Tom left for him right after it happened.

And?

I told him I don't want to live without you.

A smile stretched across her face as she read those words. Then her phone rang.

"So are you coming home?" Noah asked when she answered.

"I'm afraid you're going to have to come and get me." She wiped her wet cheeks. "And bring Joe with his tow truck."

"You're broken down?"

"I am."

She gave him her location.

"Can you be happy here, living in Whiskey Creek? Or should I put my house up for sale?" he asked.

Even though Helen was around now, Addy hated to leave Gran. She wanted to spend as much time with her own family as possible. Gran didn't have long, and Addy had never had a good relationship with her mother. Maybe that could change if they worked together to make Just Like Mom's an even better restaurant. And Noah was happy in Whiskey Creek. He'd already told her that. "We can try to make it work, Noah."

"I can't imagine anyone would give you any trouble. Not now that Tom's admitted the truth. What happens to him and the others is out of your hands. Chief Stacy will investigate, put together a case and the D.A. will try them. At that point, their fate will be in the hands of a jury."

"I'd be fine with an apology and probation."

"Seriously? You're too forgiving."

"I'm not out for vengeance," she said. "As long as I have you, that's all I care about."

She could hear the tenderness in his voice when he answered. "You definitely have me."

She remembered thinking that love made one weak. Somehow she didn't feel that way anymore.

EPILOGUE

Stephen's case was the last to come to trial. By the time that occurred, it was nearly September and Addy was married to Noah and pregnant with her first child. She didn't want to relive what she'd gone through at sixteen for a fourth time. Giving testimony about that night was never easy. But she'd been so happy the past eleven months that she'd put some emotional distance between the woman she was now and the girl she'd been then. So she made herself testify but afterward told the judge what she'd said at the other trials: somehow she'd managed to forgive her attackers and wasn't holding out hope for a stiff penalty. She felt they'd be judged by a higher power some day and was content to let God take care of it, since only God knew whether they were truly as penitent as they professed to be when they apologized to her in court.

But her forgiveness didn't make as much

difference in Stephen's case as it had the others. If he hadn't kidnapped and dragged her to the mine when she'd returned to Whiskey Creek, he, too, might've gotten off with four hundred hours of community service. Instead, he was sentenced to two years in prison.

When it was all said and done, Kevin Colbert lost his job and Audrey left him. He was trying to sell his house so he could move out of town and start over somewhere else. Tom lost his job, too. But he took Stephen's job at Kyle's solar plant and his wife stood by him — maybe because he was the only one who'd had a conscience. Derek continued to make do as he'd been making do, but his life had never been all that great. Addy figured he now had his chance to improve it, but doubted he would. During the investigation it came out that www .SkintightEntertainment.com, which was on the sweatshirt Stephen had worn when he abducted her, didn't have any connection to Derek. It was just something Stephen had picked up somewhere, knowing that if she looked up the website, it would frighten her, considering the ordeal she'd suffered fifteen years ago. But probably the best part of going through the whole process was seeing how much those trials affected Noah's parents, how much more understanding they'd become. Sometimes Addy wondered if they'd finally embraced her because of the baby. But then she'd catch his mother smiling at the way Noah protected her from anything that might upset her, or kissed her, or simply watched her cross the room.

"He really loves you," she said to Addy the day they sentenced Stephen.

"I really love him," Addy responded.

"I can tell. I'm sorry, you know. I was wrong to react the way I did last year."

Addy squeezed her hand. "It's okay."

"I'm glad I've been around to see how kind you were to Kevin, Tom and the others."

"Kind?" Addy wasn't sure she'd go quite that far.

"Because you were capable of forgiving them, I can believe that you really *have* forgiven me."

She had tears in her eyes when she said that, which convinced Addy she was sincere. "We're going to be able to put the past behind us."

"You're sure?"

She touched her belly, which was just beginning to swell. "Why hang on to hard feelings when we have so much to look forward to?"

The employees of Thorndike Press hope you have enjoyed this Large Print book. All our Thorndike, Wheeler, and Kennebec Large Print titles are designed for easy reading, and all our books are made to last. Other Thorndike Press Large Print books are available at your library, through selected bookstores, or directly from us.

For information about titles, please call:
  (800) 223-1244

or visit our Web site at:
  http://gale.cengage.com/thorndike

To share your comments, please write:
  Publisher
  Thorndike Press
  10 Water St., Suite 310
  Waterville, ME 04901